Lesley spun a suddenly as open and saw ___ ___ her in shock.

'What are you doing here?' She felt naked as his eyes slowly raked over her, from the top of her head, along her body, and then all the way back again.

Alessio couldn't stop looking at her. Any other woman would have been overjoyed to be the centre of his attention, as she now was, but instead she was staring straight ahead, unblinking, doing her utmost to shut him out of her line of vision.

He had never wanted a woman as much as he wanted this one right now. Mind and body fused. This wasn't just another of his glamorous sex-kitten women. This thinking, questioning, irreverent creature was in a different league.

Cathy Williams is originally from Trinidad, but has lived in England for a number of years. She currently has a house in Warwickshire, which she shares with her husband, Richard, her three daughters, Charlotte, Olivia and Emma, and their pet cat, Salem. She adores writing romantic fiction, and would love one of her girls to become a writer—although at the moment she is happy enough if they do their homework and agree not to bicker with one another!

Recent titles by the same author:

THE ARGENTINIAN'S DEMAND
SECRETS OF A RUTHLESS TYCOON
ENTHRALLED BY MORETTI
HIS TEMPORARY MISTRESS

**Did you know these are also available as eBooks?
Visit www.millsandboon.co.uk**

THE UNCOMPROMISING ITALIAN

BY
CATHY WILLIAMS

Published in Great Britain 2014
by Mills & Boon, an imprint of Harlequin (UK) Limited,
Eton House, 18-24 Paradise Road, Richmond, Surrey, TW9 1SR

© 2014 Cathy Williams

ISBN: 978-0-263-24999-6

Printed and bound in Spain
by Blackprint CPI, Barcelona

THE UNCOMPROMISING ITALIAN

To my wonderful daughters.

CHAPTER ONE

LESLEY FOX SLOWLY drew to a stop in front of the most imposing house she had ever seen.

The journey out of London had taken barely any time at all. It was Monday, it was the middle of August and she had been heading against the traffic. In all it had taken her under an hour to leave her flat in crowded Ladbroke Grove and arrive at a place that looked as though it should be plastered on the cover of a *House Beautiful* magazine.

The wrought-iron gates announced its splendour, as had the tree-lined avenue and acres of manicured lawns through which she had driven.

The guy was beyond wealthy. Of course, she had known that. The first thing she had done when she had been asked to do this job had been to look him up online.

Alessio Baldini—Italian, but resident in the UK for a long time. The list of his various companies was vast and she had skipped over all of that. What he did for a living was none of her business. She had just wanted to make sure that the man existed and was who Stan said he was.

Commissions via friends of friends were not always to be recommended, least of all in her niche sideline business. A girl couldn't be too careful, as her father liked to say.

She stepped out of her little Mini, which was dwarfed in the vast courtyard, and took a few minutes to look around her.

The brilliance of a perfect summer's day made the sprawling green lawns, the dense copse to one side lush with lavender and the clambering roses against the stone of the mansion facing her seem almost too breathtakingly beautiful to be entirely real.

This country estate was in a league of its own.

There had been a bit of information on the Internet about where the man lived, but no pictures, and she had been ill-prepared for this concrete display of wealth.

A gentle breeze ruffled her short brown hair and for once she felt a little awkward in her routine garb of lightweight combat trousers, espadrilles and one of her less faded tee-shirts advertising the rock band she had gone to see five years ago.

This didn't seem the sort of place where dressing down would be tolerated.

For the first time, she wished she had paid a little more attention to the details of the guy she was going to see.

There had been long articles about him but few pictures and she had skimmed over those, barely noting which one he was amidst the groups of boring men in business suits who'd all seemed to wear the identical smug smiles of people who had made far too much money for their own good.

She grabbed her laptop from the passenger seat and slammed the door shut.

If it weren't for Stan, she wouldn't be here now. She didn't need the money. She could afford the mortgage on her one-bedroom flat, had little interest in buying pointless girly clothes for a figure she didn't possess to attract men in whom she had scant interest—or who, she amended with scrupulous honesty to herself, had scant interest in *her*—and she wasn't into expensive, long-haul holidays.

With that in mind, she had more than enough to be going on with. Her full-time job as a website designer paid well and, as far as she was concerned, she lacked for nothing.

But Stan was her dad's long-time friend from Ireland. They had grown up together. He had taken her under his wing when she had moved down to London after university and she owed him.

With any luck, she would be in and out of the man's place in no time at all.

She breathed in deeply and stared at the mansion in front of her.

It seemed a never-ending edifice of elegant cream stone, a dream of a house, with ivy climbing in all the right places and windows that looked as though they dated back to the turn of the century.

This was just the sort of ostentatious wealth that should have held little appeal, but in fact she was reluctantly charmed by its beauty.

Of course, the man would be a lot less charming than his house. It was always the way. Rich guys always thought they were God's gift to women even when they obviously weren't. She had met one or two in her line of work and it had been a struggle to keep a smile pinned to her face.

There was no doorbell but an impressive knocker. She could hear it reverberating through the bowels of the house as she banged it hard on the front door and then stood back to wait for however long it would take for the man's butler or servant, or whoever he employed to answer doors for him, to arrive on the scene and let her in.

She wondered what he would look like. Rich and Italian, so probably dark-haired with a heavy accent. Possibly short, which would be a bit embarrassing, because she was five-eleven and a half and likely to tower over him—never a good thing. She knew from experience that men hated women who towered over them. He would probably be quite dapper, kitted out in expensive Italian gear and wearing expensive Italian footwear. She had no idea what either might look like but it was safe to say that trainers and old clothes would not feature on the sartorial menu.

She was fully occupied amusing herself with a variety of mental pictures when the door was pulled open without warning.

For a few seconds, Lesley Fox lost the ability to speak. Her lips parted and she stared. Stared in a way she had never stared at any man in her life before.

The guy standing in front of her was, quite simply, beautiful. Taller than her by a few inches, and wearing faded jeans and a navy-blue polo shirt, he was barefoot. Raven-black hair was combed back from a sinfully sexy face. His eyes were as black as his hair and lazily returned her stare, until she felt the blood rush to her face and she returned to Planet Earth with a feeling of sickening embarrassment.

'Who are you?'

His cool, rich, velvety voice galvanised her senses back into working order and she cleared her throat and reminded herself that she wasn't the type of girl who had ever been daunted by a guy, however good-looking he was. She came from a family of six and she was the only girl. She had been brought up going to rugby matches, watching the football on television, climbing trees and exploring the glorious countryside of wild Ireland with brothers who hadn't always appreciated their younger sister tagging along.

She had always been able to handle the opposite sex. She had lived her life being one of the lads, for God's sake!

'I'm here about your… Er…my name's Lesley Fox.' As an afterthought, she stuck out her hand and then dropped it when he failed to respond with a return gesture.

'I wasn't expecting a girl.' Alessio looked at her narrowly. That, he thought, had to be the understatement of the year. He had been expecting a Les Fox—Les, as in a man. Les, as in a man who was a contemporary of Rob Dawson, his IT guy. Rob Dawson was in his forties and resembled a beach ball. He had been expecting a forty-something-year-old man of similar build.

Instead, he was looking at a girl with cropped dark hair, eyes the colour of milk chocolate and a lanky, boyish physique, wearing…

Alessio took in the baggy sludge-green trousers with awkward pockets and the faded tee-shirt.

He couldn't quite recall the last time he had seen a woman dressed with such obvious, scathing disregard for fashion.

Women always tried their very hardest when around him to show their best side. Their hair was always perfect, make-up always flawless, clothes always the height of fashion and shoes always high and sexy.

His eyes drifted down to her feet. She was wearing cloth shoes.

'I'm so sorry to have disappointed you, Mr Baldini. I

take it you *are* Mr Baldini and not his manservant, sent to chase away callers by being rude to them?'

'I didn't think anyone used that term any more...'

'What term?'

'*Manservant*. When I asked Dawson to provide me with the name of someone who could help me with my current little...problem, I assumed he would have recommended someone a bit older. More experienced.'

'I happen to be very good at what I do.'

'As this isn't a job interview, I can't very well ask for references.' He stood aside, inviting her to enter. 'But, considering you look as though you're barely out of school, I'll want to know a little bit about you before I explain the situation.'

Lesley held on to her temper. She didn't need the money. Even though the hourly rate that she had been told about was staggering, she really didn't have to stand here and listen to this perfect stranger quiz her about her experience for a job she hadn't applied for. But then she thought of Stan and all he had done for her and she gritted back the temptation to turn on her heel, climb back into her car and head down to London without a backward glance.

'Come on in,' Alessio threw over his shoulder as she remained hovering on the doorstep and, after a few seconds, Lesley took a step into the house.

She was surrounded by pale marble only broken by the richness of a Persian rug. The walls were adorned with the sort of modern masterpieces that should have looked out of place in a house of this age but somehow didn't. The vast hall was dominated by a staircase that swept upwards before branching out in opposite directions, and doors indicated that there was a multitude of rooms winging on either side, not that she wouldn't have guessed.

More than ever, she felt inappropriately dressed. He might be casual, but he was casual in the sort of elegant, expensive way of the very wealthy.

'Big place for one person,' she said, staring around her, openly impressed.

'How do you know I haven't got a sprawling family lurking somewhere out of sight?'

'Because I looked you up,' Lesley answered truthfully. Her eyes finally returned to him and once again she was struck by his dark, saturnine good looks. And once again she had to drag her eyes away reluctantly, desperate to return her gaze to him, to drink him in. 'I don't usually travel into unknown territory when I do my freelance jobs. Usually the computer comes to me, I don't go to the computer.'

'Always illuminating to get out of one's comfort zone,' Alessio drawled. He watched as she ran her fingers through her short hair, spiking it up. She had very dark eyebrows, as dark as her hair, which emphasised the peculiar shade of brown of her eyes. And she was pale, with satiny skin that should have been freckled but wasn't. 'Follow me. We can sit out in the garden and I'll get Violet to bring us something to drink... Have you had lunch?'

Lesley frowned. Had she? She was careless with her eating habits, something she daily promised herself to rectify. If she ate more, she knew she'd stand a fighting chance of not looking like a gawky runner bean. 'A sandwich before I left,' she returned politely. 'But a cup of tea would be wonderful.'

'It never fails to amuse me that on a hot summer's

day you English will still opt for a cup of tea instead of something cold.'

'I'm not English. I'm Irish.'

Alessio cocked his head to one side and looked at her, consideringly. 'Now that you mention it, I do detect a certain twang...'

'But I'm still partial to a cup of tea.'

He smiled and she was knocked sideways. The man oozed sex appeal. He'd had it when he'd been unsmiling, but now...it was enough to throw her into a state of confusion and she blinked, driving away the unaccustomed sensation.

'This isn't my preferred place of residence,' he took up easily as he led the way out of the magnificent hall and towards sprawling doors that led towards the back of the house. 'I come here to give it an airing every so often but most of my time is spent either in London or abroad on business.'

'And who looks after this place when you're not in it?'

'I have people who do that for me.'

'Bit of a waste, isn't it?'

Alessio spun round and looked at her with a mixture of irritation and amusement. 'From whose point of view?' he asked politely and Lesley shrugged and folded her arms.

'There are such extreme housing problems in this country that it seems crazy for one person to have a place of this size.'

'You mean, when I could subdivide the whole house and turn it into a million rabbit hutches to cater for down and outs?' He laughed drily. 'Did my guy explain to you what the situation was?'

Lesley frowned. She had thought he might have been

offended by her remark, but she was here on business of sorts, and her opinions were of little consequence.

'Your guy got in touch with Stan who's a friend of my dad and he... Well, he just said that you had a sensitive situation that needed sorting. No details.'

'None were given. I was just curious to find out whether idle speculation had entered the equation.' He pushed open some doors and they emerged into a magnificent back garden.

Tall trees bordered pristine, sprawling lawns. To one side was a tennis court and beyond that she could see a swimming pool with a low, modern outbuilding which she assumed was changing rooms. The patio on which they were standing was as broad as the entire little communal garden she shared with the other residents in her block of flats and stretched the length of the house. If a hundred people were to stand side by side, they wouldn't be jostling for space.

Low wooden chairs were arranged around a glass-topped table and as she sat down a middle-aged woman bustled into her line of vision, as though summoned by some kind of whistle audible only to her.

Tea, Alessio instructed; something cold for him, a few things to eat.

Orders given, he sat down on one of the chairs facing her and leaned forward with his elbows resting on his knees.

'So the man my guy went to is a friend of your father's?'

'That's right. Stan grew up with my dad and when I moved down to London after university... Well, he and his wife took me under their wing. Made room for me in their house until I was settled—even paid the three months' deposit on my first rental property because they knew that it would be a struggle for my dad to afford it. So, yeah, I owe Stan a lot and it's why I took this job, Mr Baldini.'

'Alessio, please. And you work as…?'

'I design websites but occasionally I work as a freelance hacker. Companies employ me to see if their firewalls are intact and secure. If something can be hacked, then I can do it.'

'Not a job I immediately associate with a woman,' he murmured and raised his eyebrows as she bristled. 'That's not meant as an insult. It's purely a statement of fact. There are a couple of women in my IT department, but largely they're guys.'

'Why didn't you get one of your own employees to sort out your problem?'

'Because it's a sensitive issue and, the less my private life is discussed within the walls of my offices, the better. So you design websites. You freelance and you claim you can get into anything.'

'That's right. Despite not being a man.'

Alessio heard the defensive edge to her voice and his curiosity was piqued. His life had settled into a predictable routine when it came to members of the opposite sex. His one mistake, made when he was eighteen, had been enough for him to develop a very healthy scepticism when it came to women. The fairer sex, he had concluded, was a misconception of stunning magnitude.

'So if you could explain the situation…' Lesley looked at him levelly, her mind already flying ahead to the thrill of solving whatever problem lay in store for her. She barely noticed his housekeeper placing a pot of tea in front of her and a plate crammed with pastries, produced from heaven only knew where.

'I've been getting anonymous emails.' Alessio

flushed as he grappled with the unaccustomed sensation of admitting to having his hands tied when it came to sorting out his own dilemma. 'They started a few weeks ago.'

'At regular intervals?'

'No.' He raked his fingers through his hair and looked at her earnest face tilted to one side... A small crease indented her forehead and he could almost hear her thinking, her mind working as methodically as one of the computers she dealt with. 'I ignored them to start with but the last couple have been...how shall I describe them?...a little *forceful*.' He reached for the pitcher of homemade lemonade to pour himself a glass. 'If you looked me up, you probably know that I own several IT companies. Despite that, I confess that my knowledge of the ins and outs of computers is scant.'

'Actually, I have no idea what companies you own or don't own. I looked you up because I wanted to make sure that there was nothing dodgy about you. I've done this sort of thing before. I'm not looking for background detail, I'm generally looking for any articles that might point a suspicious finger.'

'Dodgy? You thought I might be *dodgy*?'

He looked so genuinely shocked and insulted that she couldn't help laughing. 'You might have had newspaper cuttings about suspect dealings, mafia connections...you know the sort of thing. I'd have been able to find even the most obscure article within minutes if there had been anything untoward about you. You came up clean.'

Alessio nearly choked on his lemonade. 'Mafia dealings...because I'm Italian? That's the most ridiculous thing I've ever heard.'

Lesley shrugged sheepishly. 'I don't like taking chances.'

'I've never done a crooked thing in my entire life.' He flung his arms wide in a gesture that was peculiarly foreign. 'I even buck the trend of the super-rich and am a fully paid-up member of the honest, no-offshore-scams, tax-paying club! To suggest that I might be linked to the Mafia because I happen to be Italian...'

He sat forward and stared at her and she had to fight off the very feminine and girlish response to wonder what he thought of her, as a woman, as opposed to a talented computer whizz-kid there at his bidding. Suddenly flustered, she gulped back a mouthful of hot tea and grimaced.

Wondering what men thought of her wasn't her style. She pretty much *knew* what they thought of her. She had lived her whole life knowing that she was one of the lads. Even her job helped to advance that conclusion.

No, she was too tall, too angular and too mouthy to hold any appeal when it came to the whole sexual attraction thing. Least of all when the guy in question looked like Alessio Baldini. She cringed just thinking about it.

'No, you've been watching too many gangster movies. Surely you must have heard of me?' He was always in the newspapers. Usually in connection with big business deals—occasionally in the gossip columns with a woman hanging onto his arm.

He wasn't sure why he had inserted that irrelevant question but, now that he had, he found that he was awaiting her answer with keen curiosity.

'Nope.'

'No?'

'I guess you probably think that everyone's heard of you, but in actual fact I don't read the newspapers.'

'You don't read the newspapers…not even the gossip columns?'

'Especially not the gossip columns,' she said scathingly. 'Not all girls are interested in what celebs get up to.' She tried to reconnect with the familiar feeling of satisfaction that she wasn't one of those simpering females who became embroiled in silly gossip about the rich and famous, but for once the feeling eluded her.

For once, she longed to be one of those giggly, coy girls who knew how to bat their eyelashes and attract the cute guys; she wanted to be part of the prom set instead of the clever, boyish one lurking on the sidelines; she wanted to be a member of that invisible club from which she had always been excluded because she just never seemed to have the right code words to get in.

She fought back a surge of dissatisfaction with herself and had to stifle a sense of anger that the man sitting opposite her had been the one to have generated the emotion. She had conquered whatever insecurities she had about her looks a long time ago and was perfectly content with her appearance. She might not be to everyone's taste, and she certainly wouldn't be to *his*, but her time would come and she would find someone. At the age of twenty-seven, she was hardly over the hill and, besides, her career was taking off. The last thing she needed or wanted was to be side-tracked by a guy.

She wondered how they had ended up talking about something that had nothing at all to do with the job for which she had been hired.

Was this part of his 'getting to know her' exercise? Was he quietly vetting her the way she had vetted him, when she had skimmed over all that information about him on the computer, making sure that there was nothing worrying about him?

'You were telling me about the emails you received...' She brought the conversation back to the business in hand.

Alessio sighed heavily and gave her a long, considering look from under his lashes.

'The first few were innocuous enough—a couple of one-liners hinting that they had information I might be interested in. Nothing worrying.'

'You get emails like that all the time?'

'I'm a rich man. I get a lot of emails that have little or nothing to do with work.' He smiled wryly and Lesley felt that odd tingling feeling in her body once again. 'I have several email accounts and my secretary is excellent when it comes to weeding out the dross.'

'But these managed to slip through?'

'These went to my personal email address. Very few people have that.'

'Okay.' She frowned and stared off into the distance. 'So you say that the first few were innocuous enough and then the tenor of the emails changed?'

'A few days ago, the first request for money came. Don't get me wrong, I get a lot of requests for money, but they usually take a more straightforward route. Someone wants a sponsor for something; charities asking for hand-outs; small businesses angling for investment...and then the usual assortment of nut cases who need money for dying relatives or to pay lawyers before they can claim their inheritance, which they would happily share with me.'

'And your secretary deals with all of that?'

'She does. It's usually called pressing the delete button on the computer. Some get through to me but, in general, we have established charities to which we give healthy sums of money, and all requests for business investment are automatically referred to my corporate finance division.'

'But this slipped through the net because it came to your personal address. Any idea how he or she could have accessed that information?' She was beginning to think that this sounded a little out of her area of expertise. Hackers usually went for information or, in some cases tried to attack the accounts, but this was clearly... personal. 'And don't you think that this might be better referred to the police?' she inserted, before he could answer.

Alessio laughed drily. He took a long mouthful of his drink and looked at her over the rim of the glass as he drank.

'If you read the papers,' he drawled, 'you might discover that the police have been having a few off-months when it comes to safeguarding the privacy of the rich and famous. I'm a very private man. The less of my life is splashed across the news, the better.'

'So my job is to find out who is behind these emails.'

'Correct.'

'At which point you'll...?'

'Deal with the matter myself.'

He was still smiling, with that suggestion of amusement on his lips, but she could see the steel behind the lazy, watchful dark eyes. 'I should tell you from the offset that I cannot accept this commission if there's any suggestion that you might turn...err...*violent* when it comes to sorting out whoever is behind this.'

Alessio laughed and relaxed back in his chair, stretching out his long legs to cross them at the ankle and loosely linking his fingers on his stomach. 'You have my word that I won't turn, as you say, violent.'

'I hope you're not making fun of me, Mr Baldini,' Lesley said stiffly. 'I'm being perfectly serious.'

'Alessio. The name's Alessio. And you aren't still under the impression that I'm a member of the Mafia, are you? With a stash of guns under the bed and henchmen to do my bidding?'

Lesley flushed. Where had her easy, sassy manner gone? She was seldom lost for words but she was now, especially when those dark, dark eyes were lingering on her flushed cheeks, making her feel even more uncomfortable than she already felt. A burst of shameful heat exploded somewhere deep inside her, her body's acknowledgment of his sexual magnetism, chemistry that was wrapping itself around her like a web, confusing her thoughts and making her pulses race.

'Do I strike you as a violent man, Lesley?'

'I never said that. I'm just being…cautious.'

'Have you had awkward situations before?' The soft pink of her cheeks when she blushed was curiously appealing, maybe because she was at such pains to project herself as a tough woman with no time for frivolity.

'What do you mean?'

'You intimated that you checked me out to make sure that I wasn't *dodgy*…and I think I'm quoting you here. So are you cautious in situations like these… when the computer doesn't go to you but you're forced to go to the computer…because of bad experiences?'

'I'm a careful person.' Why did that make her sound like such a bore, when she wasn't? Once again weirdly conscious of the image she must present to a guy like him, Lesley inhaled deeply and ploughed on. 'And yes,' she asserted matter-of-factly, 'I *have* had a number of poor experiences in the past. A few months ago, I was asked to do a favour for a friend's friend only to find that what he wanted was for me to hack into his ex-wife's bank account and see where her money was being spent. When I refused, he turned ugly.'

'Turned ugly?'

'He'd had a bit too much to drink. He thought that if he pushed me around a bit I'd do what he wanted.' And just in case her awkward responses had been letting her down, maybe giving him the mistaken impression that she was anything but one hundred per cent professional, she concluded crisply, 'Of course, it's annoying, but nothing I can't handle.'

'You can handle men who turn ugly.' Fascinating. He was in the company of someone from another planet. She might have the creamiest complexion he had ever seen, and a heart-shaped face that insisted on looking ridiculously feminine despite the aggressive get-up, but she was certainly nothing like any woman he had ever met. 'Tell me how you do that,' he said with genuine curiosity.

Absently, he noticed that she had depleted the plate of pastries by half its contents. A hearty appetite; his eyes flicked to her body which, despite being well hidden beneath her anti-fashion-statement clothing, was long and slender.

On some subliminal level, Lesley was aware of the shift in his attention, away from her face and onto her body. Her instinct was to squirm. Instead, she clasped her hands tightly together on her lap and tried to force her uncooperative body into a position of relaxed ease.

'I have a black belt in karate.'

Alessio was stunned into silence. 'You do?'

'I do.' She shrugged and held his confounded gaze. 'And it's not that shocking,' she continued into the lengthening silence. 'There were loads of girls in my class when I did it. 'Course, a few of them fell by the wayside when we began moving up the levels.'

'And you did these classes…when, exactly?'

In passing, Lesley wondered what this had to do with her qualifications for doing the job she had come to do. On the other hand, it never hurt to let someone know that you weren't the sort of woman to be messed with.

'I started when I was ten and the classes continued into my teens with a couple of breaks in between.'

'So, when other girls were experimenting with make-up, you were learning the valuable art of self-defence.'

Lesley felt the sharp jab of discomfort as he yet again unwittingly hit the soft spot inside her, the place where her insecurities lay, neatly parcelled up but always ready to be unwrapped at a moment's notice.

'I think every woman should know how to physically defend herself.'

'That's an extremely laudable ambition,' Alessio murmured. He noticed that his long, cold drink was finished. 'Let's go inside. I'll show you to my office and we can continue our conversation there. It's getting a little oppressive out here.' He stood up, squinted towards his gardens and half-smiled when he saw her automatically reach for the plate of pastries and whatever else she could manage to take in with her.

'No need.' He briefly rested one finger on her outstretched hand and Lesley shot back as though she had been scalded. 'Violet will tidy all this away.'

Lesley bit back an automatic retort that it was illuminating to see how the other half lived. She was no inverted snob, even though she might have no time for outward trappings and the importance other people sometimes placed on them, but he made her feel defensive. Worse, he made her feel gauche and awkward, sixteen all over again, cringing at the prospect of having to wear a frock to go to the school leaving dance, knowing that she just couldn't pull it off.

'I'm thinking that your mother must be a strong woman to instil such priorities in her daughter,' he said neutrally.

'My mother died when I was three—a hit-and-run accident when she was cycling back from doing the shopping.'

Alessio stopped in his tracks and stared down at her until she was forced uncomfortably to return his stare.

'Please don't say something trite like *I'm sorry to hear that.*' She tilted her chin and looked at him unblinkingly. 'It happened a long time ago.'

'No. I wasn't going to say that,' Alessio said in a low, musing voice that made her skin tingle.

'My father was the strong influence in my life,' she pressed on in a high voice. 'My father and my five brothers. They all gave me the confidence to know that I could do whatever I chose to do, that my gender did not have to stand in the way of my ambition. I got my degree in maths—the world was my oyster.'

Heart beating as fast as if she had run a marathon, she stared up at him, their eyes tangling until her defensiveness subsided and gave way to something else, something she could barely comprehend, something that made her say quickly, with a tight smile, 'But I don't see how any of this is relevant. If you lead the way to your computer, it shouldn't take long for me to figure out who your problem pest is.'

CHAPTER TWO

THE OFFICE TO which she was led allowed her a good opportunity to really take in the splendour of her surroundings.

Really big country estates devoured money and consequently were rarely in the finest of conditions. Imposing exteriors were often let down by run-down, sad interiors in want of attention.

This house was as magnificent inside as it was out. The pristine gardens, the splendid ivy-clad walls, were replicated inside by a glorious attention to detail. From the cool elegance of the hall, she bypassed a series of rooms, each magnificently decorated. Of course, she could only peek through slightly open doors, because she had to half-run to keep up with him, but she saw enough to convince her that serious money had been thrown at the place—which was incredible, considering it was not used on a regular basis.

Eventually they ended up in an office with book-lined walls and a massive antique desk housing a computer, a lap-top and a small stack of legal tomes. She looked around at the rich burgundy drapes pooling to the ground, the pin-striped sober wallpaper, the deep sofa and chairs.

It was a decor she would not have associated with

him and, as though reading her mind, he said wryly,
'It makes a change from what I'm used to in London.
I'm more of a modern man myself but I find there's
something soothing about working in a turn-of-the-
century gentleman's den.' He moved smoothly round
to the chair at the desk and powered up his computer.
'When I bought this house several years ago, it was
practically derelict. I paid over the odds for it because of
its history and because I wanted to make sure the owner
and her daughter could be rehoused in the manner to
which they had clearly once been accustomed. Before,
that is, the money ran out. They were immensely grateful and only suggested one thing—that I try and keep a
couple of the rooms as close as possible to the original
format. This was one.'

'It's beautiful.' Lesley hovered by the door and
looked around her. Through the French doors, the lawns
outside stretched away to an impossibly distant horizon.
The sun turned everything into dazzling technicolour.
The greens of the grass and the trees seemed greener
than possible and the sky was blindingly turquoise. Inside the office, though, the dark colours threw everything into muted relief. He was right; the space was
soothing.

She looked at him frowning in front of the computer, sitting forward slightly, his long, powerful body
still managing to emanate force even though he wasn't
moving.

'There's no need to remain by the door,' he said without looking at her. 'You'll actually need to venture into
the room and sit next to me if you're to work on this
problem. Ah. Right. Here we go.' He stood up, vacat-
ing the chair for her.

The leather was warm from where he had been sitting, and the heat seemed to infiltrate her entire body as she took his place in front of the computer screen. When he leaned over to tap on the keyboard, she felt her breathing become rapid and shallow and she had to stop herself from gasping out loud.

His forearm was inches away from her breasts and never had the proximity of one person's body proved so rattling. She willed herself to focus on what he was calling up on the screen in front of her and to remember that she was here in a professional capacity.

Why was he getting to her? Perhaps she had been too long without a guy in her life. Friends and family were all very good, but maybe her life of pleasant celibacy had made her unexpectedly vulnerable to a spot of swarthy good looks and a wicked smile.

'So...'

Lesley blinked herself back into the present to find herself staring directly into dark, dark eyes that were far too close to her for comfort.

'So?'

'Email one—a little too familiar, a little too chatty, but nothing that couldn't be easily ignored.'

Lesley looked thoughtfully at the computer screen and read through the email. Her surroundings faded away as she began studying the series of emails posted to him, looking for clues, asking him questions, her fingers moving swiftly and confidently across the keyboard.

She could understand why he had decided to farm out this little problem to an outside source.

If he valued his privacy, then he would not want his IT division to have access to what appeared to be vaguely menacing threats, suggestions of something that could harm his business or ruin his reputation. It would be fodder for any over-imaginative employee, of which there were always a few in any office environment.

Alessio pushed himself away from the desk and strolled towards one of the comfortable, deep chairs facing her.

She was utterly absorbed in what she was doing. He took time out to study her and he was amused and a little surprised to discover that he enjoyed the view.

It wasn't simply the arrangement of her features that he found curiously captivating.

There was a lively intelligence to her that made a refreshing change from the beautiful but intellectually challenged women he dated. He looked at the way her short chocolate-brown hair spiked up, as though too feisty and too wilful to be controlled. Her eyelashes were long and thick; her mouth, as he now saw, was full and, yes, sexy.

A sexy mouth, especially just at this very moment, when her lips were slightly parted.

She frowned and ran her tongue thoughtfully along her upper lip and, on cue, Alessio's body jerked into startling life. His libido, which had been unusually quiet since he'd ended his relationship with a blonde with a penchant for diamonds two months ago, fired up.

It was so unexpected a reaction that he nearly groaned in shock.

Instead, he shifted on the chair and smiled politely as her eyes briefly skittered across to him before resuming their intent concentration on the computer screen.

'Whoever's sent this knows what they're doing.'

'Come again?' Alessio crossed his legs, trying to maintain the illusion that he was in complete control of himself.

'They've been careful to make themselves as untraceable as possible.' Lesley stretched, then slumped back into the chair and swivelled it round so that she was facing him.

She stuck out her legs and gazed at her espadrilles. 'That first email may have been chatty and friendly but he or she knew that they didn't want to be traced. Why didn't you delete them, at least the earlier ones?'

'I had an instinct that they might be worth hanging onto.' He stood up and strolled towards the French doors. He had intended this meeting to be brief and functional, a blip that needed sorting out in his hectic life. Now, he found that his mind was stubbornly refusing to return to the matter in hand. Instead, it was relentlessly pulled back to the image he had of her sitting in front of his computer concentrating ferociously. He wondered what she would look like out of the unappealing ensemble. He wondered whether she would be any different from all the other naked women who had lain across his bed in readiness for him.

He knew she would—instinct again. Somehow he couldn't envisage her lying provocatively for him to take her, passive and willing to please.

No. That wasn't what girls with black belts in karate and a sideline in computer hacking did.

He played with the suddenly tempting notion of prolonging her task. Who knew what might happen between them if she were to be around longer than originally envisaged?

'What would you suggest my next step should be? Because I'm taking from the expression on your face that it's not going to be as straightforward as you first thought.'

'Usually it's pretty easy to sort something like this

out,' Lesley confessed, linking her hands on her stomach and staring off at nothing in particular. The weird, edgy tension she had felt earlier on had dissipated. Work had that effect on her. It occupied her whole mind and left no room for anything else. 'People are predictable when it comes to leaving tracks behind them, but obviously whoever is behind this hasn't used his own computer. He's gone to an Internet café. In fact, I wouldn't be surprised if he goes to a variety of Internet cafés, because we certainly would be able to trace the café he uses if he sticks there. And it wouldn't be too much of a headache finding out which terminal is his and then it would be a short step to identifying the person… I keep saying *he* but it might very well be a *she*.'

'How so? No, we'll get to that over something to drink—and I insist you forfeit the tea in favour of something a little more exciting. My housekeeper makes a very good Pimm's.'

'I couldn't,' Lesley said awkwardly. 'I'm not much of a drinker and I'm…err…driving anyway.'

'Fresh lemonade, in that case.' Alessio strolled towards her and held out his hand to tug her up from the chair to which she seemed to be glued.

For a few seconds, Lesley froze. When she grasped his hand—because frankly she couldn't think of what else to do without appearing ridiculous and childish—she felt a spurt of red-hot electricity zap through her body until every inch of her was galvanised into shrieking, heightened awareness of the dangerously sexy man standing in front of her.

'That would be nice,' she said a little breathlessly. As soon as she could she retrieved her scorching hand and resisted the urge to rub it against her trousers.

Alessio didn't miss a thing. She was a different person when she was concentrating on a computer. Looking at a screen, analysing what was in front of her, working out how to solve the problem he had presented, she oozed self-confidence. He idly wondered what her websites looked like.

But without a computer to absorb her attention she was prickly and defensive, a weird, intriguing mix of independent and vulnerable.

He smiled, turning her insides to liquid, and stood aside to allow her to pass by him out of the office.

'So we have a he or a she who goes to a certain Internet café, or more likely a variety of Internet cafés, for the sole reason of emailing me to, well, purpose as yet slightly unclear, but if I'm any reader of human motivation I'm smelling a lead-up to asking for money for information he or she may or may not know. There seem to be a lot of imponderables in this case.'

They had arrived at the kitchen without her being aware of having padded through the house at all, and she found a glass of fresh lemonade in her hands while he helped himself to a bottle of mineral water.

He motioned to the kitchen table and they sat facing one another on opposite sides.

'Generally,' Lesley said, sipping the lemonade, 'This should be a straightforward case of sourcing the computer in question, paying a visit to the Internet café—and usually these places have CCTV cameras. You would be able to find the culprit without too much bother.'

'But if he's clever enough to hop from café to café...'

'Then it'll take a bit longer but I'll get there. Of course, if you have no skeletons in the cupboard, Mr Baldini, then you could just walk away from this situation.'

'Is there such a thing as an adult without one or two skeletons in the cupboard?'

'Well, then.'

'Although,' Alessio continued thoughtfully, 'Skeletons imply something…wrong, in need of concealment. I can't think of any dark secrets I have under lock or key but there are certain things I would rather not have revealed.'

'Do you honestly care what the public thinks of you? Or maybe it's to do with your company? Sorry, but I don't really know how the big, bad world of business operates, but I'm just assuming that if something gets out that could affect your share prices then you mightn't be too happy.'

'I have a daughter.'

'You *have a daughter*?'

'Surely you got that from your search of me on the Internet?' Alessio said drily.

'I told you, I just skimmed through the stuff. There's an awful lot written up about you and I honestly just wanted to cut to the chase—any articles that could have suggested that I needed to be careful about getting involved. Like I said, I've fine-tuned my search engine when it comes to picking out relevant stuff or else I'd be swamped underneath useless speculation.' *A daughter?*

'Yes. I forgot—the "bodies under the motorway" scenario.' He raised his eyebrows and once again Lesley felt herself in danger of losing touch with common sense.

'I never imagined anything so dramatic, at least not really,' she returned truthfully, which had the effect of making that sexy smile on his face even broader. Flustered, she continued, 'But you were telling me that you have a daughter.'

'You still can't erase the incredulity from your voice,' he remarked, amused. 'Surely you've bumped into people who have had kids?'

'Yes! Of course! But…'

'But?'

Lesley stared at him. 'Why do I get the feeling that you're making fun of me?' she asked, ruffled and red-faced.

'My apologies.' But there was the echo of a smile still lingering in his voice, even though his expression was serious and contrite. 'But you blush so prettily.'

'That's the most ridiculous thing I've ever heard in my life!' And it was. Ridiculous. 'Pretty' was something she most definitely was *not.* Nor was she going to let this guy, this *sex God* of a man—who could have any woman he wanted, if you happened to like that kind of thing—get under her skin.

'Why is it ridiculous?' Alessio allowed himself to be temporarily side-tracked.

'I know you're probably one of these guys who slips into flattery mode with any woman you happen to find yourself confined with, but I'm afraid that I don't go into meltdown at empty compliments.' *What on earth was she going on about?* Why was she jumping into heated self-defence over nonsense like this?

When it came to business, Alessio rarely lost sight of the goal. Right now, not only had he lost sight of it, but he didn't mind. 'Do you go into meltdown at compliments you think are genuine?'

'I…I…'

'You're stammering,' he needlessly pointed out. 'I don't mean to make you feel uncomfortable.'

'I don't…err…feel uncomfortable.'

'Well, that's good.'

Lesley stared helplessly at him. He wasn't just sinfully sexy. The man was beautiful. He hadn't looked beautiful in those pictures, but then she had barely taken them in—a couple of grainy black-and-white shots of a load of businessmen had barely registered on her consciousness. Now, she wished she had paid attention so that she at least could have been prepared for the sort of effect he might have had on her.

Except, she admitted truthfully to herself, she would still have considered herself above and beyond being affected by any man, however good-looking he might happen to be. When it came to matters of the heart, she had always prided herself on her practicality. She knew her limitations and had accepted them. When and if the time came that she wanted a relationship, then she had always known that the man for her would not be the sort who was into looks but the sort who enjoyed intelligence, personality—a meeting of minds as much as anything else.

'You were telling me about your daughter...'

'My daughter.' Alessio sighed heavily and raked his fingers through his dark hair.

It was a gesture of hesitancy that seemed so at odds with his forceful personality that Lesley sat up and stared at him with narrowed eyes.

'Where is she?' Lesley looked past him, as though half-expecting this unexpected addition to his life suddenly to materialise out of nowhere. 'I thought you mentioned that you had no family. Where is your wife?'

'No *sprawling* family,' Alessio amended. 'And no wife. My wife died two years ago.'

'I'm so sorry.'

'There's no need for tears and sympathy.' He waved aside her interruption, although he was startled at how easily a softer nature shone through. 'When I say *wife*, it might be more accurate to say *ex-wife*. Bianca and I were divorced a long time ago.'

'How old is your daughter?'

'Sixteen. And, to save you the hassle of doing the maths, she was, shall we say, an unexpected arrival when I was eighteen.'

'You were a *father* at eighteen?'

'Bianca and I had been seeing each other in a fairly loose fashion for a matter of three months when she announced that her contraceptive pill had failed and I was going to be a father.' His lips thinned. The past was rarely raked up and when it was, as now, it still brought a sour taste to his mouth.

Unfortunately, he could see no way around a certain amount of confidential information exchanging hands because he had a gut feeling that, whatever his uninvited email correspondent wanted, it involved his daughter.

'And you weren't happy about that.' Lesley groped her way to understanding the darkening of his expression.

'A family was not something high on my agenda at the time,' Alessio imparted grimly. 'In fact, I would go so far as to say that it hadn't even crossed my radar. But, naturally, I did the honourable thing and married her. It was a match approved by both sides of the family until, that is, it became apparent that her family's wealth was an illusion. Her parents were up to their eyes in debt and I was a convenient match because of the financial rewards I brought with me.'

'She married you for your *money*?'

'It occurred to no one to do a background check.' He shrugged elegantly. 'You're looking at me as though I've suddenly landed from another planet.'

His slow smile knocked her sideways and she cleared her throat nervously. 'I'm not familiar with people marrying for no better reason than money,' she answered honestly.

Alessio raised his eyebrows. 'In that case, we really *do* come from different planets. My family is extremely wealthy, as am I. Believe me, I am extremely well versed in the tactics women will employ to gain entry to my bank balance.' He crossed his legs, relaxing. 'But you might say that, once bitten, twice shy.'

She made an exceptionally good listener. Was this why he had expanded on the skeleton brief he could have given her? Had gone into details that were irrelevant in the grand scheme of things? He hadn't been lying when he had told her that his unfortunate experience with his ex had left him jaded about women and the lengths they would go to in order to secure themselves a piece of the pie. He was rich and women liked money. It was therefore a given that he employed a healthy amount of caution in his dealings with the opposite sex.

But the woman sitting in front of him couldn't have been less interested in his earnings.

His little problem intrigued her far more than *he* did. It was a situation that Alessio had never encountered in his life before and there was something sexy and challenging about that.

'You mean you don't intend to marry again? I can understand that. And I guess you have your daughter. She must mean the world to you.'

'Naturally.' Alessio's voice cooled. 'Although I'll be the first to admit that things have not been easy between us. I had relatively little contact with Rachel when she was growing up, thanks to my ex-wife's talent for vindictiveness. She lived in Italy but travelled extensively, and usually when she knew that I had arranged a visit.

She was quite happy to whip our daughter out of school at a moment's notice if only to make sure that my trip to Italy to visit would be a waste of time.'

'How awful.'

'At any rate, when Bianca died Rachel naturally came to me, but at the age of fourteen she was virtually a stranger and a fairly hostile one. Frankly, a nightmare.'

'She would have been grieving for her mother.' Lesley could barely remember her own mother and yet *she* still grieved at the lack of one in her life. How much more traumatic to have lost one at the age of fourteen, a time in life when a maternal, guiding hand could not have been more needed.

'She was behind in her schoolwork thanks to my ex-wife's antics, and refused to speak English in the classroom, so the whole business of teaching her was practically impossible. In the end, boarding school seemed the only option and, thankfully, she appears to have settled in there with somewhat more success. At least, there have been no phone calls threatening expulsion.'

'Boarding school...'

Alessio frowned. 'You say that as though it ranks alongside "prison cell".'

'I can't imagine the horror of being separated from my family. My brothers could be little devils when I was growing up but we were a family. Dad, the boys and me.'

Alessio tilted his head and looked at her, considering, tempted to ask her if that was why she had opted for a male-dominated profession, and why she wore clothes better suited to a boy. But the conversation had already drifted too far from the matter at hand. When he glanced down at his watch, it was to find that more time had passed than he might have expected.

'My gut feeling tells me that these emails are in some way connected to my daughter,' Alessio admitted. 'Reason should dictate that they're to do with work but I can't imagine why anyone wouldn't approach me directly about anything to do with my business concerns.'

'No. And if you're as above board as you say you are…'

'You doubt my word?'

Lesley shrugged. 'I don't think that's really my business; the only reason I mention it is because it might be pertinent to finding out who is behind this. 'Course, I shall continue working at the problem, but if it's established that the threat is to do with your work then you might actually be able to pinpoint the culprit yourself.'

'How many people do you imagine work for me?' Alessio asked curiously, and Lesley shrugged and gave the matter some thought.

'No idea.' The company she worked for was small, although prominent in its field, employing only a handful of people on the creative side and slightly fewer on the admin side. 'A hundred or so?'

'You really skimmed through those articles you called up on your computer, didn't you?'

'Big business doesn't interest me,' she informed him airily. 'I may have a talent for numbers, and can do the maths without any trouble at all, but those numbers only matter when it comes to my work. I can work things out precisely but it's really the artistic side of my job that I love. In fact, I only did maths at university because Shane, one of my brothers, told me that it was a man's subject.'

'Thousands.'

Lesley looked at him blankly for a few seconds. 'What are you talking about?'

'Thousands. In various countries. I own several companies and I employ thousands, not hundreds. But that's by the by. This isn't to do with work. This is to do with my daughter. The only problem is that we don't have a great relationship and if I approach her with my suspicions, if I quiz her about her friends, about whether anyone's been acting strangely, asking too many questions…well, I don't anticipate a good outcome to any such conversation. So what would you have done if you hadn't done maths?'

Time had slipped past and they were no nearer to solving the problem, yet he was drawn to asking her yet more questions about herself.

Lesley—following his lead and envisaging the sort of awkward, maybe even downright incendiary conversation that might ensue in the face of Alessio's concerns, should he confront a hostile teenager with them—was taken aback by his abrupt change of topic.

'You said that you only did maths because your brother told you that you couldn't.'

'He never said that I *couldn't*.' She smiled, remembering their war of words. Shane was two years older than her and she always swore that his main purpose in life was to annoy her. He was now a barrister working in Dublin but he still teased her as though they were still kids in primary school. 'He said that it was a man's field, which immediately made me decide to do it.'

'Because, growing up as the only girl in a family of all males, it would have been taken as a given that, whatever your brothers could do, you could as well.'

'I'm wondering what this has to do with the reason I've come here.' She pulled out her mobile phone, checked the time on it and was surprised to discover how much of the day had flown by. 'I'm sorry I haven't been able to sort things out for you immediately. I'd understand perfectly if you want to take the matter to someone else, someone who can devote concentrated time to working on it. It shouldn't take too long, but longer than an hour or two.'

'Would you have done art?' He overrode her interjection as though he hadn't heard any of it and she flung him an exasperated look.

'I did, actually—courses in the town once a week. It was a good decision. It may have clinched me my job.'

'I have no interest in farming out this problem to someone else.'

'I can't give it my full-time attention.'

'Why not?'

'Because,' she said patiently, 'I have a nine-to-five job. And I live in London. And by the time I get back to my place—usually after seven, what with working overtime and then the travel—I'm exhausted. The last thing I need is to start trying to sort your problem out remotely.'

'Who said anything about doing it remotely? Take time off and come here.'

'I beg your pardon?'

'A week. You must be able to take some holiday time? Take it off and come here instead. Trying to sort this out remotely isn't the answer. You won't have sufficient time to do it consistently and also, while this may be to do with unearthing something about my own past, it may also have to do with something in my daughter's life. Something this person thinks poses a risk, should it be exposed. Have you considered that?'

'It had crossed my mind,' Lesley admitted.

'In which case, there could be a double-pronged attack on this problem if you moved in here.'

'What do you mean?'

'My daughter occupies several rooms in the house, by which I mean she has spread herself thin. She has a million books, items of clothing, at least one desktop computer, tablets... If this has to do with anything Rachel has got up to, then you could be on hand to go through her stuff.'

'You want me to *invade her privacy* by searching through her private things?'

'It's all for the greater good.' Their eyes locked and she was suddenly seduced by the temptation to take him up on his offer, to step right out of her comfort zone.

'What's the point of having misplaced scruples? Frankly, I don't see the problem.'

In that single sentence, she glimpsed the man whose natural assumption was that the world would fall in line with what he wanted. And then he smiled, as if he had read her mind, and guessed exactly what was going through it. 'Wouldn't your company allow you a week off? Holiday?'

'That's not the point.'

'Then what is? Possessive boyfriend, perhaps? Won't let you out of his sight for longer than five minutes?'

Lesley looked at him scornfully. 'I would never get involved with anyone who wouldn't let me out of his sight for longer than five minutes! I'm not one of those pathetic, clingy females who craves protection from a big, strong man.' She had a fleeting image of the man sitting opposite her, big, strong, powerful, protecting his woman, making her feel small, fragile and delicate. She had never thought of herself as delicate—too tall, too boyish, too independent. It was ridiculous to have that squirmy sensation in the pit of her stomach now and she thanked the Lord that he really couldn't read her mind.

'So, no boyfriend,' Alessio murmured, cocking his head to one side. 'Then explain to me why you're finding reasons not to do this. I don't want to source anyone else to work on this for me. You might not have been what I expected, but you're good and I trust you, and if my daughter's possessions are to be searched it's essential they be searched by a woman.'

'It wouldn't be ethical to go through someone else's stuff.'

'What if by doing that you spared her a far worse situation? Rachel, I feel, would not be equipped to deal with unpleasant revelations that could damage the foundations of her young life. Furthermore, I won't be looking over your shoulder. You'll be able to work to your own timetable. In fact, I shall be in London most of the time, only returning here some evenings.'

Lesley opened her mouth to formulate a half-hearted protest, because this was all so sudden and so out of the ordinary, but with a slash of his hand he cut her off before any words could leave her mouth.

'She also returns in a few days' time. This is a job that has a very definite deadline; piecemeal when you get a chance isn't going to cut it. You have reservations—I see that—but I need this to be sorted out and I think you're the one to do it. So, please.'

Lesley heard the dark uncertainty in his voice and gritted her teeth with frustration. In a lot of ways, what he said made sense. Even if this job were to take a day or two, she would not be able to give it anything like her full attention if she worked on it remotely for half an hour every evening. And, if she needed to see whether his daughter had logged on to other computer devices, then she would need to be at his house where the equipment was to hand. It wasn't something she relished doing—everyone deserved their privacy—but sometimes privacy had to be invaded as a means of protection.

But moving in, sharing the same space as him? He did something disturbing to her pulse rate, so how was she supposed to live under the same roof?

But the thought drew her with the force of the forbidden.

Watching, Alessio smelled his advantage and lowered his eyes. 'If you won't do this for me…and I realise it would be inconvenient for you…then do it for my daughter, Lesley. She's sixteen and vulnerable.'

CHAPTER THREE

'THIS IS IT...'

Alessio flung back the door to the suite of rooms and stood to one side, allowing Lesley to brush past him.

It was a mere matter of hours since he had pressed home his advantage and persuaded her to take up his offer to move into the house.

She had her misgivings, he could see that, but he wanted her there at hand and he was a man who was accustomed to getting what he wanted, whatever the cost.

As far as he was concerned, his proposition made sense. If she needed to try and hunt down clues from his daughter's possessions, then the only way she could do that would be here, in his house. There was no other way.

He hadn't anticipated this eventuality. He had thought that it would be a simple matter of following a trail of clues on his computer which would lead him straight to whoever was responsible for the emails.

Given that it was not going to be as straightforward as he first thought, it was a stroke of luck that the person working on the case was a woman. She would understand the workings of the female mind and would know where to locate whatever information she might find useful.

Added to that...

He looked at Lesley with lazy, brooding eyes as she stepped into the room.

There was something about the woman. She didn't pull her punches and, whilst a part of him was grimly disapproving of her forthright manner, another part of him was intrigued.

When was the last time he had been in the company of a woman who didn't say what she wanted him to hear?

When had he *ever* been in the company of any woman who didn't say what she wanted him to hear?

He was the product of a life of privilege. He had grown up accustomed to servants and chauffeurs and then, barely into adulthood, had found himself an expectant father. In a heartbeat, his world had changed. He'd no longer had the freedom to make youthful mistakes and to learn from them over time. Responsibility had landed on his doorstep without an invitation and then, on top of that, had come the grim realisation that he had been used for his money.

Not even out of his teens, he had discovered the bitter truth that his fortune would always be targeted. He would never be able to relax in the company of any woman without suspecting that she had her eye to the main chance. He would always have to be on his guard, always watchful, always making sure that no one got too close.

He was a generous lover, and had no problem splashing out on whatever woman happened to be sharing his bed, but he knew where to draw the line and was ruthless when it came to making sure that no woman got too close, certainly not close enough ever to harbour notions of longevity.

It was unusual to find himself in a situation such as

this. It was unusual to be in close personal confines with a woman where sex wasn't on the menu.

It was even more unusual to find himself in this situation with a woman who made no effort to try and please him in any way.

'I was expecting a bedroom.' Lesley turned to look at him. 'Posters on the walls, cuddly toys, that sort of thing.'

'Rachel occupies one wing of the house. There are actually three bedrooms, along with a sitting room, a study, two bathrooms and an exercise room.' He strolled towards her and looked around him, hands shoved in the pockets of his cream trousers. 'This is the first time I've stepped foot into this section of the house since my daughter returned from boarding school for the holidays. When I saw the state it was in, I immediately got in touch with Violet, who informed me that she, along with her assistants, were barred from entry.'

Disapproval was stamped all over his face and Lesley could understand why. The place looked as though a bomb had been detonated in it. The tiled, marble floor of the small hallway was barely visible under discarded clothes and books and, through the open doors, she could see the other rooms appeared to be in a similar state of chaos.

Magazines were strewn everywhere. Shoes, kicked off, had landed randomly and then had been left there. School books lay open on various surfaces.

Going through all of this would be a full-time job.

'Teenagers can be very private creatures,' Lesley said dubiously. 'They hate having their space invaded.' She picked her way into bedroom number one and then continued to explore the various rooms, all the time conscious of Alessio lounging indolently against the wall and watching her progress.

She had the uneasy feeling of having been manipulated. How had she managed to end up here? Now she felt *involved*. She was no longer doing a quick job to help her father's pal out. She was ensconced in the middle of a family saga and wasn't quite sure where to begin.

'I will get Violet to make sure that these rooms are tidied first thing in the morning,' Alessio said as she finally walked towards him. 'At least then you will have something of a clean slate to start on.'

'Probably not such a good idea.' Lesley looked up at him. He was one of the few men with whom she could do that and, as she had quickly discovered, her breathing quickened as their eyes met. 'Adolescents are fond of writing stuff down on bits of paper. If there is anything to be found, that's probably where I'll find it, and that's just the sort of thing a cleaner would stick in the bin.' She hesitated. 'Don't you communicate with your daughter *at all*? I mean, how could she get away with keeping her room—her *rooms*—as messy as this?'

Alessio took one final glance around him and then headed for the door. 'Rachel has spent most of the summer here while I have been in London, only popping back now and again. She's clearly intimidated the cleaners into not going anywhere near her rooms and they've obeyed.'

'You've just *popped back here now and again* to see how she's doing?'

Alessio stopped in his tracks and looked at her coolly. 'You're here to try and sort out a situation involving computers and emails. You're not here to pass judgement on my parenting skills.'

Lesley sighed with obvious exasperation. She had been hustled here with unholy speed. He had even come with her to her office, on the pretext of having a look at what her company did, and had so impressed her boss that Jake had had no trouble in giving her the week off.

And now, having found herself in a situation that somehow didn't seem to be of her own choosing, she wasn't about to be lectured to in that patronising tone of voice.

'I'm not passing opinions on your parenting skills,' she said with restraint. 'I'm trying to make sense of a picture. If I can see the whole picture, then I might have an idea of how and where to proceed.' She had not yet had time since arriving to get down to the business of working her way through the emails and trying to trace the culprit responsible for them.

That was a job for the following day. Right now, she would barely have time to have dinner, run a bath and then hit the sack. It had been a long day.

'I mean,' she said into an unresponsive silence, 'If and when I do find out who is responsible for those emails, we still won't know why he's sending them. He could clam up, refuse to say anything, and then you may still be left with a problem on your hands in con- nection with your daughter.'

They had reached the kitchen, which was a vast space dominated by a massive oak table big enough to seat ten. Everything in the house was larger than life, including all the furnishings.

'They may have nothing to do with Rachel. That's just another possibility.' He took a bottle of wine from the fridge and two wine glasses from one of the cup- boards. There was a rich smell of food and Lesley looked around for Violet, who seemed to be an invis- ible but constant presence in the house.

'Where's Violet?' she asked, hovering.

'Gone for the evening. I try and not keep the hired help chained to the walls at night.' He proffered the glass of wine. 'And you can come inside, Lesley. You're not entering a lion's den.'

It felt like it, however. In ways she couldn't put her finger on, Alessio Baldini felt exciting and dangerous at the same time. Especially so at night, here, in his house with no one around.

'She's kindly prepared a casserole for us. Beef. It's in the oven. We can have it with bread, if that suits you.'

'Of course,' Lesley said faintly. 'Is that how it works when you're here? Meals are prepared for you so that all you have to do is switch the oven on?'

'One of the housekeepers tends to stick around when Rachel's here.' Alessio flushed and turned away.

In that fleeting window, she glimpsed the situation with far more clarity than if she had had it spelled out for her.

He was so awkward with his own daughter that he preferred to have a third party to dilute the atmosphere. Rachel probably felt the same way. Two people, father and daughter, were circling one another like strangers in a ring.

He had been pushed to the background during her formative years, had found his efforts at bonding repelled and dismantled by a vengeful wife, and now found himself with a teenager he didn't know. Nor was he, by nature, a people person—the sort of man who could joke his way back into a relationship.

Into that vacuum, any number of gremlins could have entered.

'So you're *never* on your own with your daughter? Okay. In that case you really wouldn't have a clue what was happening in her life, especially as she spends most of the year away from home. But you were saying that this may not have anything directly to do with Rachel. What did you mean by that?'

She watched him bring the food to the table and re-fill their glasses with more wine.

Alessio gave her a long, considered look from under his lashes.

'What I am about to tell you stays within the walls of this house, is that clear?'

Lesley paused with her glass halfway to her mouth and looked at him over the rim with astonishment.

'And you laugh at me for thinking that you might have links to the Mafia?'

Alessio stared at her and then shook his head and slowly grinned. 'Okay, maybe that sounded a little melodramatic.'

Lesley was knocked sideways by that smile. It was so full of charm, so lacking in the controlled cool she had seen in him before. It felt as though, the more time she spent in his company, the more intriguing and complex he became. He was not simply a mega-rich guy employing her to do a job for him, but a man with so many facets to his personality that it made her head spin.

Worse than that, she could feel herself being sucked in, and that scared her.

'I don't do melodrama,' Alessio was saying with the remnants of his smile. 'Do you?'

'Never.' Lesley licked her lips nervously. 'What are you going to tell me that has to stay here?'

His dark eyes lingered on her flushed face. 'It's un-likely that our guy would have got hold of this informa-tion but, just in case, it's information I would want to protect my daughter from knowing. I certainly would not want it in the public arena.' He swigged the remainder of his wine and did the honours by dishing food onto the plates which had already been put on the table, along with glasses and cutlery.

Mesmerised by the economic elegance of his movements, and lulled by the wine and the creeping darkness outside, Lesley cupped her chin in her hand and stared at him.

He wasn't looking at her. He was concentrating on not spilling any food. He had the expression of someone unaccustomed to doing anything of a culinary nature for themselves—focused yet awkward at the same time.

'You don't look comfortable with a serving spoon,' she remarked idly and Alessio glanced across to where she was sitting, staring at him. She wore a thin gold chain with a tiny pendant around her neck and she was playing with the pendant, rolling it between her fingers as she looked at him.

Suddenly and for no reason, his breathing thickened and heat surged through his body with unexpected force. His libido, that had not seen the light of day for the past couple of months, reared up with such urgency that he felt his sharp intake of breath.

She was not trying to be seductive but somehow he could feel her seducing him.

'I bet you don't do much cooking for yourself.'

'Come again?' Alessio did his best to get his thoughts back in order. An erection was jamming against the zipper of his trousers, rock-hard and painful, and it was a relief to sit down.

'I said, you don't look as though handling pots and pans comes as second nature to you.' She tucked into the casserole, which was mouth-wateringly fragrant. They should be discussing work but the wine had made her feel relaxed and mellow and had allowed her curiosity about him to come out of hiding and to take centre stage.

Sober, she would have chased that curiosity away, because she could feel its danger. But pleasantly tipsy, she wanted to know more about him.

'I don't do much cooking, no.'

'I guess you can always get someone else to do it for you. Top chefs or housekeepers, or maybe just your girlfriends.' She wondered what his girlfriends looked like. He might have had a rocky marriage that had ended in divorce, but he would have lots of girlfriends.

'I don't let women near my kitchen.' Alessio was amused at her disingenuous curiosity. He swirled his wine around in the glass and swallowed a mouthful.

With a bit of alcohol in her system, she looked more relaxed, softer, less defensive.

His erection was still throbbing and his eyes dropped to her mouth, then lower to where the loose neckline of her tee-shirt allowed a glimpse of her shoulder blades and the soft hint of a cleavage. She wasn't big breasted and the little she had was never on show.

'Why? Don't you ever go out with women who like to cook?'

'I've never asked whether they like to cook or not,' he said wryly, finishing his wine, pouring himself another glass and keeping his eyes safely away from her loose-limbed body. 'I've found that, the minute a woman starts eulogising about the joys of home-cooked food, it usually marks the end of the relationship.'

'What do you mean?' Lesley looked at him, surprised.

'It means that the last thing I need is someone trying to prove that they're a domestic goddess in my kitchen. I prefer that the women I date don't get too settled.'

'In case they get ideas of permanence?'

'Which brings me neatly back to what I wanted to say.' That disturbing moment of intense sexual attraction began to ebb away and he wondered how it had arisen in the first place.

She was nothing like the women he dated. Could it be that her intelligence, the strange role she occupied as receiver of information no other woman had ever had, the sheer difference of her body, had all those things conspired against him?

There was a certain intimacy to their conversation. Had that entered the mix and worked some kind of passing, peculiar magic?

More to the point, a little voice inside him asked, what did he intend to do about it?

'I have a certain amount of correspondence locked away that could be very damaging.'

'Correspondence?'

'Of the non-silicon-chip variety,' Alessio elaborated drily. 'Correspondence of the old-fashioned sort—namely, letters.'

'To do with business?' She felt a sudden stab of intense disappointment that she had actually believed him when he had told her that he was an honest guy in all his business dealings.

'No, not to do with business, so you can stop thinking that you've opened a can of worms and you need to clear off as fast as you can. I told you I'm perfectly straight when it comes to my financial dealings and I wasn't lying.'

Lesley released a long sigh of relief. Of course, it was because she would have been in a very awkward situation had he confessed to anything shady, especially considering she was alone with him in his house.

It definitely wasn't because she would have been disappointed in him as a man had he been party to anything crooked.

'Then what? And what is the relevance to the case?'

'This could hurt my daughter. It would certainly be annoying for me should it hit the press. If I fill you in, then you might be able to join some dots and discover if this is the subject of his emails.'

'You have far too much confidence in my abilities, Mr Baldini.' She smiled. 'I may be good at what I do but I'm not a miracle worker.'

'I think we've reached the point where you can call me Alessio. It occurred to me that there may have been stray references in the course of the emails that might point in a certain direction.'

'And you feel that I need to know the direction they may point in so that I can pick them up if they're there?'

'Something like that.'

'Wouldn't you have seen them for yourself?'

'I only began paying attention to those emails the day you were hired. Before that, I had kept them, but hadn't examined them in any depth and I haven't had the opportunity to do so since. It's a slim chance but we can cover all bases.'

'And what if I do find a link?'

'Then I shall know what options to take when it comes to dealing with the perpetrator.'

Lesley sighed and fluffed her short hair up with her fingers. 'Do you know, I have never been in this sort of situation before.'

'But you've had a couple of tricky occasions.'

'Not as complicated as this. The tricky ones have usually involved friends of friends imagining that I can unearth marital affairs by bugging computers, and then

I have to let them down. If I can even be bothered to see what they want in the first place.'

'And this?'

'This feels as though it's got layers.' And she wasn't sure that she wanted to peel them back to see what was lying underneath. It bothered her that he had such an effect on her that he had been able to entice her into taking time off work to help him in the first place.

And it bothered her even more that she couldn't seem to stop wanting to stare at him. Of course he was good-looking, but she was sensible when it came to guys, and this one was definitely off-limits. The gulf between them was so great that they could be living on different planets.

And yet her eyes still sought him out, and that was worrying.

'I had more than one reason for divorcing my wife,' he said heavily, after a while. He hesitated, at a loss as to where to go from there, because sharing confidences was not something he ever did. From the age of eighteen, he had learnt how to keep his opinions to himself—first through a sense of shame that he had been hoodwinked by a girl he had been seeing for a handful of months, a girl who had conned him into thinking she had been on the pill. Later, when his marriage had predictably collapsed, he had developed a forbidding ability to keep his emotions and his thoughts under tight rein. It was what he had always seen as protection against ever making another mistake when it came to the opposite sex.

But now…

Her intelligent eyes were fixed on his face. He reminded himself that this was a woman against whom he needed no protection because she had no ulterior agenda.

'Not only did Bianca lie her way into a marriage but she also managed to lie her way into making me believe that she was in love with me.'

'You were a kid,' Lesley pointed out, when he failed to elaborate on that remark. 'It happens.'

'And you know because...?'

'I don't,' she said abruptly. 'I wasn't one of those girls anyone lied to about being in love with. Carry on.'

Alessio tilted his head and looked at her enquiringly, tempted to take her up on that enigmatic statement, even though he knew he wouldn't get anywhere with it.

'We married and, very shortly after Rachel was born, my wife began fooling around. Discreetly at first, but that didn't last very long. We moved in certain circles and it became a bore to try and work out who she wanted to sleep with and when she would make a move.'

'How awful for you.'

Alessio opened his mouth to brush that show of sympathy to one side but instead stared at her for a few moments in silence. 'It wasn't great,' he admitted heavily.

'It can't have been. Not at any age, but particularly not when you were practically a child yourself and not equipped to deal with that kind of disillusionment.'

'No.' His voice was rough but he gave a little shrug, dismissing that episode in his life.

'I can understand why you would want to protect your daughter from knowing that her mother was... promiscuous.'

'There's rather more.' His voice was steady and matter-of-fact. 'When our marriage was at its lowest ebb, Bianca implied, during one of our rows, that I wasn't Rachel's father at all. Afterwards she retracted her words and said that she hadn't been thinking straight. God knows, she probably realised that Rachel was her lifeline to money, and the last thing she should do was to jeopardise that lifeline, but the words were out and as far as I was concerned couldn't be taken back.'

'No, I can understand that.' Whoever said that money could buy happiness? she thought, feeling her heart constrict for the young boy he must have been then—deceived, betrayed, cheated on; forced to become a man when he was still in his teens.

'One day when she was out shopping, I returned early from work and decided, on impulse, to go through her drawers. By this time, we were sleeping in separate rooms. I found a stash of letters, all from the same guy, someone she had known when she was sixteen. Met him on holiday somewhere in Majorca. Young love. Touching, don't you think? They kept in contact and she was seeing him when she was married to me. I gathered from reading between the lines that he was the son of a poor fisherman, someone her parents would certainly not have welcomed with open arms.'

'No.'

'The lifestyles of the rich and famous,' he mocked wryly. 'I bet you're glad you weren't one of the privileged crowd.'

'I never gave it much thought, but now that you mention it…' She smiled and he grudgingly returned the smile.

'I have no idea whether the affair ended when her behaviour became more out of control but it certainly made me wonder whether she was right about our daughter not being biologically mine. Not that it would have made a scrap of difference but…'

'You'd have to find out that sort of thing.'

'Tests proved conclusively that Rachel is my child but you can see why this information could be highly destructive if it came to light, especially considering the poor relationship I have with my daughter. It could be catastrophic. She would always doubt my love for her if she thought that I had taken a paternity test to prove she was mine in the first place. It would certainly destroy the happy memories she has of her mother and, much as Bianca appalled me, I wouldn't want to deprive Rachel of her memories.'

'But if this information was always private and historic, and only contained in letter form, then I don't see how anyone else could have got hold of it.' But there were always links to links to links; it just took one person to start delving and who knew what could come out in the wash? 'I'll see if I can spot any names or hints that this might be the basis of the threats.'

And at the same time, she would have her work cut out going through his daughter's things, a job which still didn't sit well with her, even though a part of her know that it was probably essential.

'I should be heading up to bed now,' she said, rising to her feet.

'It's not yet nine-thirty.'

'I'm an early-to-bed kind of person,' she said awkwardly, not knowing whether to leave the kitchen or remain where she was, then realising that she was behaving like an employee waiting for her boss to dismiss her. But her feet remained nailed to the spot.

'I have never talked so much about myself,' Alessio murmured, which got her attention, and she looked at him quizzically. 'It's not in my nature. I'm a very private man, hence what I've told you goes no further than this room.'

'Of course it won't,' Lesley assured him vigorously. 'Who would I tell?'

'If someone could consider blackmailing me over this information, then it might occur to you that you could do the same. You would certainly have unrivalled proof of whatever you wanted to glean about my private life in the palm of your hand.'

It was a perfectly logical argument and he was, if nothing else, an extremely logical man. But Alessio still felt an uncustomary twinge of discomfort at having spelled it out so clearly.

He noticed the patches of angry colour that flooded her cheeks and bit back the temptation to apologise for being more blunt than strictly necessary.

She worked with computers; she would know the value of logic and reason.

'You're telling me that you don't trust me.'

'I'm telling you that you keep all of this to yourself. No girly gossip in the toilets at work, or over a glass of wine with your friends, and certainly no pillow talk with whoever you end up sharing your bed with.'

'Thank you for spelling it out so clearly,' Lesley said coldly. 'But I know how to keep a confidence and I fully understand that it's important that none of this gets out. If you have a piece of paper, you can draft something up right here and I'll sign it!'

'Draft something up?' Under normal circumstances, he certainly would have had that in place before hiring her for the job, but for some reason it simply hadn't occurred to him.

Perhaps it had been the surprise of opening the front door to a girl instead of the man he had been expecting.

Perhaps there was something about her that had worked its way past his normal defences so that he had failed to go down the predicted route.

'I'm happy to sign whatever silence clause you want.

One word of what we've spoken about here, and you will have my full permission to fling me into jail and throw away the key.'

'I thought you said that you weren't melodramatic.'

'I'm insulted that you think I'd break the confidence you have in me to do my job and keep the details of it to myself.'

'You may be insulted, but are you surprised?' He rose to his feet, towering over her, and she fell back a couple of steps and held onto the back of the kitchen chair.

Alessio, on his way to make them some coffee, sensed the change in the atmosphere the way a big cat can sense the presence of prey in the shift of the wind. Their eyes met and something inside him, something that operated on an instinctual level, understood that, however scathing and derisive her tone of voice had been, she was tuned in to him in ways that matched his.

Tuned in to him in ways that were sexual.

The realisation struck him from out of nowhere and yet, as he held her gaze a few seconds longer than was necessary, he actually doubted himself because her expression was so tight, straightforward and openly annoyed.

'I am a man who is accustomed to taking precautions,' he murmured huskily.

'I get that.' Especially after everything he had told her. Of course he would want to make sure that he didn't leave himself open to exploitation of any kind. That was probably one of the rules by which he lived his life.

So he was right; why should she be surprised that he had taken her to task?

Except she had been lulled into a false sense of confidences shared, had warmed to the fact that he had

opened up to her, and in the process had chosen to ignore the reality, which was that he had decided that he
had no choice. He hadn't opened up to her because she
was special. He had opened up to her because it was
necessary to make her task a little easier.

'Do you?'

'Of course I do,' she said on a sigh. 'I'm just not used
to people distrusting me. I'm one of the most reliable
people I know when it comes to keeping a secret.'

'Really?' Mere inches separated them. He could feel
the warmth radiating from her body out towards his and
he wondered again whether his instincts had been right
when they had told him that she was not as unaffected
by him as she would have liked to pretend.

'Yes!' She relaxed with a laugh. 'When I was a teenager, I was the one person all the lads turned to when it
came to confidences. They knew I would never breathe
a word when they told me that they fancied someone,
or asked me what I thought it would take to impress
someone else...'

And all the while, Alessio thought to himself, you
were taking lessons in self-defence.

Never one to do much prying into female motiva-
tions, he was surprised to find that he quite wanted to
know more about her. 'You've won your argument,' he
said with a slow smile.

'You mean, you won't be asking me to sign something?'

'No. So there will be no need for you to live in fear
that you will be flung into prison and the key thrown
away if the mood takes me.' His eyes dipped down to
the barely visible swell of her small breasts under the
baggy tee-shirt.

'I appreciate that,' Lesley told him sincerely. 'I don't
know how easy I would have found it, working for some-

one who didn't trust me. So I shall start first thing in the morning.' She suddenly realised just how close their bodies were to one another and she shuffled a couple of discreet inches back. 'If it's all the same to you, you can point me in the direction of your computer and I'll spend the morning there, and the afternoon going through your daughter's rooms just in case I find anything of interest. And you needn't worry about asking your housekeeper to prepare any lunch for me. I usually just eat on the run. I can fill you in when you return from London or else I can call you if you decide to stay in London overnight.'

Alessio inclined his head in agreeable assent—except, maybe there would be no need for that.

Maybe he would stay here in the country—so much more restful than London and so much easier were he to be at hand.

CHAPTER FOUR

LESLEY WAS NOT finding life particularly restful. Having been under the impression that Alessio would be commuting to and from London, with a high possibility of remaining in London for at least part of the time, she'd been dismayed when, two days previously, he'd informed her that there had been a change of plan.

'I'll be staying here,' he had said the morning after she had arrived. 'Makes sense.'

Lesley had no idea how he had reached that conclusion. How did it make sense for him to be around: bothering her; getting under her skin; just *being* within her line of vision and therefore compelling her to look at him?

'You'll probably have a lot of questions and it'll be easier if I'm here to answer them.'

'I could always phone you,' she had said, staring at him with rising panic, because she'd been able to see just how the week was going to play out.

'And then,' he had continued, steamrollering over her interruption, 'I would feel guilty were I to leave you here on your own. The house is very big. My conscience wouldn't be able to live with the thought that you might find it quite unsettling being here with no one around.'

He had directed her to where she would be working

and she'd been appalled to find that she would be sharing office space with him.

'Of course, if you find it uncomfortable working in such close proximity to me, then naturally I can set up camp somewhere else. The house has enough rooms to accommodate one of them being turned into a makeshift work place.'

She had closed her mouth and said nothing, because what had there been to say? That, yes, she *would* find it uncomfortable working in such close proximity to him, because she was just too *aware* of him for her own good; because he made her nervous and tense; because her skin tingled the second he got too close?

She had moved from acknowledging that the man was sexy to accepting that she was attracted to him. She had no idea how that could be the case, given that he just wasn't the sort of person she had ever envisaged herself taking an interest in, but she had given up fighting it. There was just something too demanding about his physicality for her to ignore.

So she had spent her mornings in a state of rigid, hyper-sensitive awareness. She had been conscious of his every small move as he'd peered at his computer screen, reached across his desk to get something or swivelled his chair so that he could find a more comfortable position for his long legs.

She had not been able to block out the timbre of his deep voice whenever he was on the phone. She wouldn't have been able to recall any of the conversations he had had, but she could recall exactly what that voice did to her.

The range of unwanted physical sensations he evoked in her was frankly exhausting.

So she had contrived to have a simple routine of disappearing outside to communicate with her office on the pretext that she didn't want to disturb him.

Besides, she had added, making sure to forestall any objections, she never got the chance to leave London. She had never been to stay at a country estate in her life before. It would be marvellous if she could take advantage of the wonderful opportunity he had given her by working outdoors so that she could enjoy being in the countryside, especially given that the weather was so brilliant.

He had acquiesced although when he had looked at her she had been sure that she could detect a certain amount of amusement.

Now, in a break with this routine, Lesley had decided to start on Rachel's rooms.

She had gone over all of the emails with a fine toothcomb and had found no evidence that the mystery writer was aware of Bianca's past.

She looked around room number one and wondered where to begin.

As per specific instructions, Violet had left everything as it was and Lesley, by no means a neat freak, was not looking forward to going through the stacks of dispersed clothes, books, magazines and random bits of paper that littered the ground.

But she dug in, working her way steadily through the chaos, flinging clothes in the stainless-steel hamper she had dragged from the massive bathroom and marvelling that a child of sixteen could possess so much designer clothing.

This was what money bought: expensive clothes and jewellery. But no amount of expensive clothes and jewellery could fix a broken relationship and, over the past two days, she had seen for herself just how broken the relationship between father and daughter was.

He kept his emotions under tight control but every so often there were glimpses of the man underneath who was confused at his inability to communicate with his daughter and despairing of what the future held for them.

And yet, he wanted to protect her, and would do anything to that end.

She began rifling through the pockets of a pair of jeans, her mind playing with the memory of just how weirdly close the past couple of days had brought them.

Or, at least, *her*.

But then, she thought ruefully, she was handicapped by the fact that she found him attractive. She was therefore primed to analyse everything he said, to be super-attentive to every stray remark, to hang onto his every word with breathless intensity.

Thank God he didn't know what was going through her head.

It took her a couple of seconds before the piece of paper she extracted from the jeans pocket made sense and then a couple more seconds before the links she had begun to see in the emails began to tie up in front of her.

More carefully now, she began feeling her way through the mess, inspecting everything in her path. She went over the clothes she had carelessly chucked into the hamper just in case she had missed something.

Had she expected to find anything at all like this, searching through a few rooms? No; maybe when she got to the computer or the tablet, or whatever other computer gadgets might be lying around.

But scribbles on a bit of paper? No. She thought that teenagers were way beyond using pens and paper by way of communication.

What else might she find?

She had lost that initial feeling of intruding in someone else's space. Something about the messiness made her search more acceptable.

No attempts had been made to hide anything and nothing was under lock and key.

Did that make a difference? In a strange way it did, as did the little things lying about that showed Rachel for the child she still was, even if she had entered the teenage battleground of rebellion and disobedience.

Her art book was wonderful. There were cute little doodles in the margins of her exercise books. Her stationery was very cute, with lots of puppy motifs on the pencil cases and folders. It was at odds with the rest of what was to be found in the room.

An hour and a half into the search, Lesley opened the first of the wardrobes and gasped at the racks of clothes confronting her.

You didn't need to be a connoisseur of fine clothing to know that these were the finest money could buy. She ran her hands through the dresses, skirts and tops and felt silk, cashmere and pure cotton. Some of them were youthful and brightly coloured, others looked far too grown-up for a sixteen-year-old child. Quite a few things still had tags attached because they had yet to be used.

As she pushed the clothes at the front aside, she came across some dresses at the back that were clearly too old for a sixteen-year-old; they must have belonged to Rachel's mother. Lesley gently pulled a demure black dress from the selection and admired the fine material and elegant cut of the design. She knew that it was wrong to try on someone else's clothes but she lost her head for a moment and suddenly found herself slipping into the gorgeous creation. As she turned to look at herself in the mirror, she gasped.

Usually she was awkward, one of the lads, at her most comfortable when she was exchanging banter; yet the creature staring back at her wasn't that person at all. The creature staring back at her was a leggy, attractive young woman with a good figure, good legs and a long neck.

She spun away from the mirror suddenly as she heard the door open and saw Alessio look at her in shock.

'What are you doing here?' She felt naked as his eyes slowly raked over her, from the top of her head, along her body and then all the way back again.

Alessio couldn't stop looking at her. He had left the office to stretch his legs and had decided to check on how Lesley's search was coming along. He hadn't expected to find her in a stunning cocktail dress, her legs seeming to go on for ever.

'Well?' Lesley folded her arms defensively, although what she really wanted to do was somehow reach down and cover her exposed thighs. The skirt should have been a couple of inches above the knee but, because she was obviously taller than Rachel's mother had been, it was obscenely short on her.

'I've interrupted a catwalk session,' he murmured, walking slowly towards her. 'My apologies.'

'I was… I thought…'

'It suits you, just in case you're interested in what I think. The dress, I mean. You should reveal your legs more often.'

'If you would please just go, I'll get changed. I apologise for having tried on the dress. It was totally out of order, and if you want to give me my marching orders then I would completely understand.' She had never felt so mortified in her entire life. What must he be thinking? She had taken something that didn't belong to her and put it on, an especially unforgivable offence, considering she was under his roof in the capacity of a paid employee.

His 'catwalk' comment struck her as an offensive insult but there was no way she was going to call him out on that. She just wanted him to leave the room but he showed no signs of going.

'Why would I give you your marching orders?' She was bright red and as stiff as a plank of wood.

Any other woman would have been overjoyed to be the centre of his attention, as she now was, but instead she was staring straight ahead, unblinking, doing her utmost to shut him out of her line of vision.

He had never wanted a woman as much as he wanted this one right now. Mind and body fused. This wasn't just another of his glamorous, sex-kitten women. This thinking, questioning, irreverent creature was in a different league.

The attraction he had felt for her, which had been there from the second they had met, clarified into the absolute certainty that he wanted her in his bed. It was a thought he had flirted with, dwelled on; rejected because she'd challenged him on too many levels and he liked his women unchallenging.

But, hell...

'Please leave.'

'You don't have to take off the dress,' he said in a lazy drawl. 'I'd quite like to see you working in that outfit.'

'You're making fun of me and I don't like it.' She had managed to blank him out, so that she was just aware of him on the periphery of her vision, but she could still feel his power radiating outwards, wrapping around her like something thick, suffocating and tangible.

She felt like something small and helpless being circled by a beautiful, dangerous predator.

Except he would never hurt her. No; his capacity for destruction lay in his ability to make her hurt herself by believing what he was saying, by allowing her feelings for him get the better of her. She had never realised that lust could be so overwhelming. Nothing had prepared her for the crazy, inappropriate emotions that rode roughshod over her prized and treasured common sense.

'I'll pretend I didn't hear that,' Alessio said softly. Then he reached out and ran his hand along her arm, feeling its soft, silky smoothness. She was so slender. For a few seconds, Lesley didn't react, then the feel of his warm hand on her skin made her stumble backwards with a yelp.

His instincts had been right. How could he have doubted himself? The electricity between them flowed both ways. He stepped back and looked at her lazily. Her eyes were huge and she looked very young and very vulnerable. And she was still wobbling in the high stilettos; that was how uncomfortable she was in a pair of heels. He was struck with a pressing desire to see her dolled up to the nines and, with an even more contradictory one, to have her naked in his arms.

'I'll leave you to get back into your clothes,' he said with the gentleness of someone trying to calm a panicked, highly strung thoroughbred. 'And, to answer your question as to what I'm doing here, I thought I would just pop in and see if your search up here was being fruitful.'

Relieved to have the focus off her and onto work, Lesley allowed some of the tension to ooze out of her body.

'I *have* found one or two things you might be interested in,' she said with staccato jerkiness. 'And I'll come right down to the office.'

'Better still, meet me outside. I'll get Violet to bring us out some tea.' He smiled, encouraging her to relax further. It was all he could do not to let his eyes wander over her, drink her in. He lowered his eyes and reluctantly spun round, walking towards the door and knowing that she wouldn't move a muscle until he was well and truly out of the suite of rooms and heading down the staircase.

Once outside, he couldn't wait for her to join him. He was oblivious to his surroundings as he stared off into the distance, thinking of how she had looked in that outfit. She had incredible legs, an incredible body and it was all the more enhanced by the fact that she was so unaware of her charms.

Five brothers; no mother; karate lessons when the rest of her friends were practising the feminine skills that would serve them well in later life. Was that why she was so skittish around him? Was she skittish around *all* men, or was it just him? Was that why she chose to dress the way she did, why she projected such a capable image, why she deliberately seemed to spurn feminine clothes?

He found himself idly trying to work out what made her tick and he was enjoying the game when he saw her walking towards him with a sheaf of papers in her hand, all business as usual.

'Thank you.' Lesley sat down, taking the glass that was offered to her. She had been so hot and bothered after he had left that she had taken time out to wash her face in cold water and gather herself. 'First of all—and I'm almost one-hundred-per-cent sure about this—our emailing friend has no idea about your wife or the sort of person she was.'

Alessio leant closer, forearms resting on his thighs. 'And you've reached that conclusion because…?'

'Because I've been through each and every email very carefully, looking for clues. I've also found a couple of earlier emails which arrived in your junk box and for some reason weren't deleted. They weren't significant. Perhaps our friend was just having a bit of fun.'

'So you think this isn't about a blackmail plot to do with revelations about Bianca?'

'Yes, partly from reading through the emails and partly common sense. I think if they involved your ex-wife there would have been some sort of guarded reference made that would have warned you of what was to come. And, whilst he or she knew what they were doing and were careful to leave as few tracks behind them as they could, some of those emails are definitely more rushed than others.'

'Woman's intuition?' There was genuine curiosity in his voice and Lesley nodded slowly.

'I think so. What's really significant, though, is that the Internet cafés used were all in roughly the same area, within a radius of a dozen miles or so, and they are all in the general vicinity of where Rachel goes to school. Which leads me to think that she is at the centre of this in some way, shape or form because the person responsible probably knows her or knows of her.'

Alessio sat back and rubbed his eyes wearily. Lesley could see the strain visible beneath the cool, collected exterior when he next looked at her. He might have approached this problem with pragmatism and detachment, as a job to be done—but his daughter was involved and that showed on his face now, in the worry and the stress.

'Any idea of what could be going on? It could still

be that our friend, as you call him, has information on Bianca and wants me to pay him for not sharing that information with Rachel.'

'Does Rachel know anything about what her mother was like as…err…a young girl? I mean, when she was still married to you? I know your daughter would have been a toddler with no memories of that time, but you know how it is: overheard conversations between adults, bits and pieces of gossip from friends or family or whatever.'

Alessio leaned back in the chair and closed his eyes.

'As far as I am aware, Rachel is completely in the dark about Bianca, but who knows? We haven't talked about it. We've barely got past the stage of polite pleasantries.'

Lesley stared at his averted profile. Seeing them in repose, as now, she felt the full impact of his devastating good looks. His sensual mouth lost its stern contours; she could appreciate the length and thickness of his eyelashes, the strong angle of his jaw, the tousled blackness of his slightly too-long hair. His fingers were linked loosely on his stomach; she took in the dark hair on his forearms and then burned when she wondered where that dark hair was replicated.

She wondered whether she should tell him about those random scribbles she had found and decided against it. They formed part of the jigsaw puzzle but she would hang on until more of the pieces came together. It was only fair. He was a desperately concerned father, worried about a daughter he barely knew; to add yet more stress to his situation, when she wasn't even one-hundred per cent sure whether what she had found would prove significant in the end, seemed downright selfish.

The lingering embarrassment she had brought with her after the mini-skirt-wearing episode faded as the silence lengthened between them, a telling indication of his state of mind.

It would have cost him dearly to confide the personal details of his situation with his ex-wife. No matter that he had been practically a child at the time. No one enjoyed being used and Alessio, in particular, was a proud man today and would have been a proud boy all those years ago.

Her heart softened and she resisted the temptation to reach out and stroke the side of his cheek.

'I'm making you feel awkward,' Alessio murmured, breaking the silence, but not opening his eyes or turning in her direction.

Lesley buried the wickedly tantalising thought of touching his cheek. 'Of course not!'

'I don't suppose you banked on this sort of situation when you agreed to the job.'

'I don't suppose you banked on it either when you decided to hire me.'

'True,' he admitted with a ghost of a smile. 'So, where do you suggest we go from here? Quiz Rachel when she gets home day after tomorrow? Try and find out if she has any idea what's going on?' He listened as she ran through some options. He liked hearing her talk. He liked the soft but decisive tone of her voice. He liked the way she could talk to him like this, on his level, with no coy intonations and no irritating indications that she wanted the conversation to take any personal detours.

Mind you, she had so much information about him that personal detours were pretty much an irrelevance:

there really weren't that many nooks and crannies left to discover.

His mind swung back to when he had caught her wearing that dress and his body began to stir into life.

'Talk to me about something else,' he ordered huskily when there was a pause in the conversation. This was as close to relaxation he had come in a long time, despite the grim nature of what was going on. He had his eyes closed, the sun was on his face and his body felt lazy and nicely lethargic.

'What do you want me to talk about?' She could understand why he might not want to dwell ad infinitum on a painful subject, even one that needed to be discussed.

'You. I want you to talk about you.'

Even though he wasn't looking at her, Lesley still reddened. That voice of his; had he any idea how sexy it was? No, of course not.

'I'm a very boring person,' she half-laughed with embarrassment. 'Besides, you know all the basic stuff: my brothers; my dad bringing us all up on his own.'

'So let's skip the basics. Tell me what drove you to try on that dress.'

'I don't want to talk about that.' Lesley's skin prickled with acute discomfort. The mortification she had felt assailed her all over again and she clenched her fists on her lap. 'I've already apologised and I'd really rather we drop the subject and pretend it never happened. It was a mistake.'

'You're embarrassed.'

'Of course I am.'

'No need to be, and I'm not prying. I'm really just trying to grasp anything that might take my mind off what's happening right now with Rachel.'

Suddenly Lesley felt herself deflate. While she was on her high horse, defending her position and beating back his very natural curiosity, he was in the unenviable position of having had to open the door to his past and let her in.

Was it any wonder that he was desperate to take his mind off his situation? Talking relentlessly about something worrying only magnified the worry and anxiety.

'I—I don't know why I tried it,' Lesley offered haltingly. 'Actually, I do know why I tried it on. I was never one for dresses and frocks when I was a teenager. That was stuff meant for other girls but not for me.'

'Because you lacked a mother's guiding hand,' Alessio contributed astutely. 'And even more influential was the fact that you had five brothers.' He grinned and some of the worry that had been etched on his face lifted. 'I remember what I was like and what my friends were like when we were fourteen—not sensitive. I bet they gave you a hard time.'

Lesley laughed. 'And the rest of it. At any rate, I had one embarrassing encounter with a mini-skirt and I decided after that that I was probably better off not going down that road. Besides, at the age of fourteen I was already taller than all the other girls in my class. Downplaying my height didn't involve wearing dresses and short skirts.'

Alessio slowly opened his eyes and then inclined his head so that he was looking directly at her.

Her skin was like satin. As far as he knew, she had yet to make use of the swimming pool, but sitting outside for the past couple of afternoons in the blazing sun had lent a golden tint to her complexion. It suited her.

'But you're not fourteen any longer,' he said huskily. Lesley was lost for words. Drowning in his eyes, her throat suddenly went dry and her body turned to lead. She couldn't move a muscle. She could just watch him, watching her.

He would physically have to get out of his chair if he were to come any closer, and he made no move to do anything of the sort, but she was still overwhelmed by the feeling that he was going to kiss her. It was written in the dark depths of his eyes, a certain intent that made her quiver and tremble inside.

'No, I don't suppose I am,' she choked out.

'But you still don't wear short skirts...'

'Old habits die hard.' She gave up trying to look away. She didn't care what he thought—not at this moment in time, at any rate. 'I... There's no need to dress up for the sort of job that I do. Jeans and jumpers are what we all wear.'

'You don't do justice to your body.' He glanced at his watch. He had broken off working in part, as he had said, to check on Lesley and see whether she had managed to find anything in Rachel's quarters; but also in part because he was due in London for a meeting.

The time had run away. It was much later than he had imagined...something about the sun, the slight breeze, the company of the woman sitting next to him, the way she had frozen to the spot... He wondered whether any man had ever complimented her about the way she looked or whether she had spent a lifetime assuming that no one would, therefore making sure that she carved her own niche through her intelligence and ambition.

He wondered what she would do if he touched her, kissed her.

More than ever, he wanted to have her. In fact, he was tempted to abandon the meeting in London and spend the rest of this lazy afternoon playing the game of seduction.

Already she was standing up, all of a fluster, telling him that she was feeling a little hot and wanted to get back into the shade. With an inward, rueful sigh of resignation, he followed suit.

'You're doing a brilliant job, trying to unravel what the hell is going on with these emails,' he said, uncomfortably aware of his body demanding a certain type of attention that was probably going to make his drive down to London a bit uncomfortable.

Lesley put some much-needed physical distance between them.

What had happened just then? He seemed normal enough now. Had it been her imagination playing tricks on her, making her think that he was going to kiss her? Or was it her own forbidden attraction trying to find a way to become a reality?

It absolutely terrified her that she might encourage him to think that she was attracted to him. It was even more terrifying that she might be reading all sorts of nonsense into his throwaway remarks. The guy was the last word in eligible. He was charming, highly intelligent and sophisticated, and he probably had that sexy, ever so slightly flirty manner with every woman he spoke to. It was just the kind of person he was and misinterpreting anything he said in her favour would be something she did at her own peril.

'Thank you. You're paying me handsomely to do just that.'

Alessio frowned. He didn't like money being brought into the conversation. It lowered the tone.

'Well, carry on the good work,' he said with equal politeness. 'And you'll have the house all to yourself until tomorrow to do it. I have an important meeting in London and I'll be spending the night there in my apartment.' He scowled at her immediate look of relief. Hell, she was attracted to him, but she was determined to fight it, despite the clear signals he had sent that the feeling was reciprocated. Didn't she know that for a man like him, a man who could snap his fingers and have any woman he wanted, her reticence was a challenge?

And yet, was he the type to set off in pursuit of some-one who was reluctant—even though she might be as hot for him as he was for her?

A night away might cool him down a bit.

He left her dithering in the hall, seeing him off, but with a look of impatience on her face for him to be gone.

She needed this. Her nerves were getting progressively more shot by the minute; she couldn't wait for him to leave. She went to see him off, half-expecting him suddenly to decide that he wasn't going anywhere after all, and sagged with relief when the front door slammed behind him and she heard the roar of his car diminishing as he cleared the courtyard and disappeared down the long drive.

She couldn't stay. Certainly, she wanted to be out by the time his daughter arrived. She just couldn't bear the tension of being around him: she couldn't bear the loss of self-control, the way her eyes wanted to seek him out, the constant roller-coaster ride of her emotions. She felt vulnerable and confused.

Well, she had found rather more searching through Rachel's room than she had told him. Not quite enough, but just a little bit more information and she would have sufficient to present to him and leave with the case closed.

She had seen the desk-top computer and was sure

that there would be a certain amount of helpful information there.

She had an afternoon, a night and hopefully part of the day tomorrow, and during that time she would make sure that everything was sorted, because she desperately needed to return to the safety of her comfort zone...

CHAPTER FIVE

LESLEY FLEXED HER fingers, which were stiff from working solidly on Rachel's desk-top for the past two and a half hours.

Alessio had given her the green light to look through anything and everything in his daughter's room and she knew that he was right to allow her to do so. If Rachel was under some sort of threat, whatever that threat was, then everything had to be done to neutralise the situation, even if it meant an invasion of her privacy.

However, Lesley had still felt guilty and nervous when she had sat down in front of the computer to begin opening files.

She had expected to find lots of personal teenage stuff. She had never been one of those girls who had sat around giggling and pouring her heart out to all her friends. She and her friends had mostly belonged to the sporting set, and the sporting set had only occasionally crossed over into the cheerleader set, which was where most of the giggling about boys and confiding had taken place.

However, the computer seemed largely to store school work. Lesley had assumed that the more personal information was probably carried on Rachel's tablet, or else her mobile phone, neither of which were in the house.

But she had found a couple of little strands that added to the building jigsaw puzzle.

Most of the really important information, however, had been gathered the old-fashioned way: pockets of jeans; scraps of paper; old exercise books; margins of text books; letters tossed carelessly in the drawer by the bed.

There had been no attempt to hide any of the stuff Lesley had gathered, and that made her feel much better.

Rachel might have given orders to a very pliant housekeeper not to go anywhere near her rooms, but had there been a little part of her that maybe wanted the information to be found? Was that why she had not destroyed notes that were definitely incriminating?

Lesley could only speculate.

By six that evening, she was exhausted. She ached all over, but she knew that she would be able to hand everything she had found over to Alessio and be on her way.

She felt a little panicky when she thought about getting into her little car and driving away from him for ever, then she told herself that it was just as well she was going to do that, because panicking at the prospect of not seeing him was a very dangerous place to be.

How had he managed to get under her skin so thoroughly and so fast?

When it came to men, she was a girl who had always taken things slowly. Friendships were built over a reasonable period of time. Generally speaking, during that protracted build-up any prospect of the friendship developing into something more serious was apt to fizzle out, which always reassured her that the relationship had not been destined.

But the speed with which Alessio had succeeded in filling her head was scary.

She found that even being alone in his house for a few hours was an unsettling business because she missed his presence!

In the space of only a couple of days, she had become accustomed to living life in the emotional fast lane; had become used to a heightened state of awareness, knowing that he was *around*. When she sat outside in the garden—working on her lap-top, enjoying the peace of the countryside, telling herself what a relief it was that she was not in the same room as him—she was still *conscious* of the fact that he was in the house. Somewhere.

With a little sigh of frustration, she decided that she would have a swim.

She hadn't been near the pool since she had arrived. She hadn't been able to deal with the prospect of him suggesting that he join her, even less with the prospect of him seeing just how angular, flat-chested and boyish her figure was.

He might have made the occasional flirty remark, but she had seen the sort of women he was attracted to. He had handed over his computer files to her and within them were photos of him with various busty, curvaceous, five-foot-two blonde bombshells. They all looked like clones of Marilyn Monroe.

But he wasn't here now, and it was still so hot and muggy, even at this hour of the evening.

When she looked at herself in the mirror, she was startled at how much it changed her appearance. However, she had seen herself in her navy-blue bikini sufficient times to be reassured that she was the same lanky Lesley she had always been.

Without bothering to glance at her reflection, she grabbed a towel from the bathroom and headed downstairs for the pool.

She should have felt wary venturing out with no one around, and just acres upon acres of fields and open land stretching away into the distance, but she didn't. In fact, she felt far more cautious in London, where she was constantly surrounded by people and where there was no such thing as complete darkness even in the dead of night in the middle of winter.

She dived cleanly into the water, gasping at the temperature, but then her body acclimatised as she began swimming.

She was a good swimmer. After being cooped up in front of a computer for several hours, it felt good to be exercising, and she swam without stopping, cutting through the water length after length after length.

She wasn't sure exactly how long she swam; maybe forty-five minutes. She could feel the beginning of that pleasant burn in her body that indicated that her muscles were being stretched to their limit.

At this point, she pulled herself up out of the pool, water sluicing down her body, her short, dark hair plastered down…and it was only then that she noticed Alessio standing to one side, half-concealed in the shadow of one of the trees fringing the side of the veranda.

It took a few seconds for her brain to register his presence there at all because she hadn't been expecting him.

And it took a few seconds more for her to realise that, not only was he standing there, but she wasn't even sure how long he had been standing there looking at her.

With an outraged yelp she walked quickly over to where she had dumped her towel on one of the chairs by the pool and, by the time she had secured it around her, he had walked lazily to where she was standing.

'I hope I didn't interrupt your workout,' he murmured without a hint of an apology in his voice.

'You're not supposed to be here!'

'There was a slight change of plan.'

'You should have warned me that you were going to be coming back!'

'I didn't think I needed to inform you that I would be returning to my own home.'

'How long have you been standing there?' She couldn't bring herself to meet those amused dark eyes. She was horribly conscious of what she must look like, with her wet hair like a cap on her head and her face completely bare of make-up—not that she ever wore much, but still.

'Long enough to realise that it's been a while since I used that pool. In fact, I can't remember the last time I stepped foot in it.' Water droplets were like tiny diamonds on her eyelashes and he wished she would look at him so that he could read the expression in her eyes. Was she genuinely annoyed that he had disturbed her, shown up unexpectedly? Or was she all of a dither because she had been caught off-guard, because he was seeing her for the first time without her armour of jeans, flats and faded tee-shirts? Clothes that neutralised her femininity.

He wondered what she would say if he told her just how delicious she looked, standing there dripping wet with only a towel that barely covered her.

He also wondered what she would say if he told her that he had been standing there for the better part of fifteen minutes, mesmerised as he'd watched her swimming, as at home in the water as a seal. He had been so wrapped up in the sight that he had completely forgotten why he had been obliged to drive back from London.

'Wait right here,' he urged suddenly. 'I'm going to join you. Give me ten minutes. It'll do me good to get rid of the London grime.'

'Join me?' Lesley was frankly horrified.

'You don't have a problem with that, do you?'

'No...err...'

'Good. I'll be back before you can get back in the water.'

Lesley was frozen to the spot as she watched him disappear back through the sprawling triple-fronted French doors that led into the conservatory.

Then, galvanised into action—because diving in while he watched was just out of the question—she hurried back into the water. What choice did she have? To have told him that she was fed up swimming and wanted to go inside, just as he was about to join her in the pool, would have been tantamount to confessing just how awkward he made her feel. The last thing she wanted was for him to know the effect he had on her. He might have some idea that she wasn't as impartial to his presence as she liked to pretend but her feelings were more confused than that and ran a lot deeper.

That was something she was desperate to keep to herself. She could just about cope if he thought that she fancied him; half the female population in the country between the ages of eighteen and eighty would have fancied the man, so it would be no big deal were he to include her in that category.

But it was more than that. Not only was she not the type to randomly fancy guys because of the way they looked, but her reactions to him pointed to something a lot more complex than a simple case of lust which could easily be cured by putting some distance between them.

She had just reached the shallow end of the pool

when Alessio emerged back out in the mellow evening sunshine.

Lesley thought that she might faint. Only now did she fully comprehend how much time she had spent daydreaming about him, about what he might look like under those expensive, casual designer clothes he was fond of wearing.

What would his body look like?

Now she knew: lean, bronzed and utterly beautiful. His shoulders were broad and muscled and his torso tapered to a narrow waist and hips.

He was at home with his body, that much was evident from the way he moved with an easy, casual grace.

Lesley sat on one of the steps at the shallow end of the pool, so that she was levered into a half-sitting position on her elbows while her long legs and most of her body remained under the surface of the water. She felt safer that way.

He dived into the water, as straight as an arrow, and swam steadily and powerfully towards her. It took every ounce of will power not to flinch back as he reared up out of the water and joined her on the step.

'Nice,' he said appreciatively, wiping his face with the palm of his hand, then leaning back just as she did.

'You haven't explained what you're doing here.' Lesley eyed the proximity of his body nervously.

'And I shall do that as soon as we're inside. For the moment, I just want to enjoy being out here. I don't get much by way of time out. I don't want to spoil it by launching into the unexpected little problem that's cropped up.' He glanced across to her. 'You're a good swimmer.'

'Thank you.'

'Been swimming a long time?'

'Since I was four.' She paused and then continued, because talking seemed a bit less stressful than remaining silent and concentrating all her energies on what he was doing to her. 'My father had always been a good swimmer. All my brothers were as well. After my mother died, he got it into his head that he would channel all his energy into getting me into competitive swimming. The boys were all a bit older and had their own hobbies, but he's fond of telling me that I was fertile ground for him to work on.' Lesley laughed and relaxed a little. 'So he made sure to take me down to the local swimming baths at least twice a week. I was out of arm bands and swimming by the time I was five.'

'But you didn't end up becoming a professional swimmer.'

'I didn't,' Lesley admitted. 'Although I entered lots of competitions right up until I went to secondary school, then once I was in secondary school I began to play lots of different types of sport and the swimming was put on the back burner.'

'What sport did you play?' Alessio thought of his last girlfriend, whose only stab at anything energetic had involved the ski slope. He had once made the mistake of trying to get her to play a game of squash with him and had been irritated when she had shrieked with horror at the thought of getting too sweaty. Her hair, apparently, would not have been able to cope. He wondered whether she would have submerged herself in the pool the way Lesley had or whether she would have spent her time lying on a sun lounger and only dipping her feet in when the heat became unbearable.

Any wonder he had broken up with her after a couple of months?

'Squash, tennis, hockey, and of course in between I had my self-defence classes.'

'Energetic.'

'Very.'

'And in between all of that vigorous exercise you still had time for studying.'

Hence no time at all for what every other teenage girl would have been doing. Lesley read behind that mild observation. 'How else would I have ever been able to have a career?' Lesley responded tartly. 'Playing sport is all well and good but it doesn't get you jobs at the end of the day.' She stood up. 'I've been out here for long enough. I should really get back inside, have a shower. Please don't let me keep you from enjoying the pool. It's a shame to have this and not make use of it, especially when you think that it's so rare for the weather to be as good as it has been recently.' She didn't give him time to answer. Instead, she headed for her towel and breathed a sigh of relief when she had wrapped it around her.

When she turned around, it was to find him standing so close to her that she gave a little stumble back, almost crashing into the sun lounger behind her.

'Steady.' Alessio reached out and gripped her arms, then left his hands on her arms. 'I should really talk to you about what's brought me back here. I've got quite a bit of work to catch up on and I'll probably work through the night.'

Lesley found that she couldn't focus on anything while he was still holding her.

'Of course,' she eventually managed to croak. 'I'll go and have a shower, and then shall I meet you in the office?' She could smell him—the clean, chlorinated scent of the swimming pool combined with the heady aroma of the sun drying him as he stood there, practically naked.

'Meet me in the kitchen instead.' Alessio released her abruptly. Just then every instinct inside him wanted to pull her towards him and kiss her, taste her, see whether she would be as delectable as his imagination told him she would be. The intensity of what had shot through him was disturbing.

'I...I didn't expect you to return; I told Violet that there was no need to prepare anything for me before she left. In fact, I let her go early. I do hope you don't mind but I'm accustomed to cooking for myself. I was only going to do myself a plate of pasta.'

'Sounds good to me.'

'Right, then,' Lesley said faintly. She pushed her fingers through her hair, spiking it up.

She left him watching her and dashed upstairs for a very quick shower.

She should have found his unexpected arrival intensely annoying. It had thrown her whole evening out of sync. But there was a dark excitement swirling around inside her and she found that she was looking forward to having dinner with him, stupidly thrilled that he was back at the house.

She told herself that it was simply because she would be able to fill him in on all sorts of discoveries she had made and, the faster she filled him in, the sooner she would be able to leave and the quicker her life would return to normal. Normality seemed like a lifetime away.

He wasn't in the kitchen when she got there half an hour later, with all her paperwork in a folder, so she poured herself a glass of wine and waited for him.

She couldn't think what might have brought him back to his country estate. Something to do with his daughter, she was sure, but what? Might he have discovered something independently? Something that would make it easier for her to tell him what she thought this whole situation was about?

He strolled in when she was halfway through her glass of wine and proceeded to pour himself a whisky and soda.

'I need this,' Alessio said heavily, sinking onto the chair at the head of the table and angling it so that he could stretch his legs out whilst still facing her. 'My mother-in-law called when I was in the middle of my meetings.'

'Is that unusual?'

'Extremely. We may well be on cordial terms but not so cordial that she telephones out of the blue. There's still that ugly residue of their manipulation, although I will concede that Bianca's mother was not the one behind it. And it has to be said that, for the duration of our divorce, it was only thanks to Claudia that I ever got to see Rachel at all. I can count the number of times that happened on the fingers of one hand, but then Claudia never was a match for her daughter.' He caught himself in the act of wanting to talk more about the destructive marriage that had made him the cynical man he was today. How had that happened?

'What did she want?' Lesley eventually asked.

'Rachel has been staying with her for the past four weeks. Pretty much as soon as her school ended, she decided that she wanted to go over there. She doesn't know a great deal of people around here and only a handful in London. The down side of a boarding school out in the country, I suppose.' He sighed heavily and tipped the remainder of his drink down before resting the empty glass on the table and staring at it in brooding silence.

'Yes,' Lesley contributed vaguely. 'It must be difficult.'

'At any rate, the upshot appears to be that my daughter is refusing to return to the UK.'

Lesley's mouth fell open and Alessio smiled crookedly at her. 'She's refusing to speak to me on the telephone. She's dug her heels in and has decided to set up camp with Claudia and, Claudia being Claudia, she lacks the strength to stand up to my daughter.'

'You must be a little put out.'

'That's the understatement of the hour.' He stood up and signalled to her that they should start preparing something to eat. He needed to move around. For a small window, he had been so preoccupied with her, with arriving back and surprising her in the swimming pool, that he had actually put the gravity of the situation to the back of his mind, but now it had returned in full force.

Strangely, he was thankful that Lesley was there.

As if knowing that he would return to the topic in his own time, Lesley began preparing their meal. She had earlier piled all the ingredients she would need on the counter and now she began chopping mushrooms, tomatoes, onions and garlic.

For once, his silence didn't send her into instant meltdown. Rather, she began chatting easily and pleasantly. She told him about her lack of cooking experience. She joked that her brothers were all better cooks than she was and that two of them had even offered to show her the basics. She could sense him begin to unwind, even though she wasn't looking at him at all and he wasn't saying anything, just listening to her rabbit on aimlessly about nothing in particular.

It was soothing, Alessio thought as he watched her

prepare the vegetables slowly and with the painstaking care of someone who wasn't comfortable in the arena of the kitchen.

Nor was he feeling trapped at the thought of a woman busying herself in his kitchen. He cleared as she cooked. It was a picture-perfect snapshot of just the sort of domesticity he avoided at all costs.

'So…' They were sitting at the kitchen table with bowls of pasta in front of them. She had maintained a steady flow of non-threatening conversation, and it had been surprisingly easy, considering she was always a bundle of nervous tension whenever she was in his presence. 'When you say that Rachel is digging her heels in and doesn't want to return to the UK, are you saying *for ever*, or just for the remainder of the summer holidays?'

'I'm saying that she's decided that she hates it over here and doesn't want to return at all.'

'And your mother-in-law can't talk her out of that?'

'Claudia has always been the pushover in the family. Between her bullying husband and Bianca, she was the one who got dragged into their plot and now, in this situation, well, it's probably a mixture of not wanting to hurt or offend her only grandchild and wanting to go down the path of least resistance.'

'So what are you going to do about that?'

'Well, there's simply no question of Rachel staying out there and going to school.' He pushed his empty plate to one side and sat back to look at her. 'I could have waited until tomorrow to come back here and tell you this but…'

'But…?' Lesley rested her chin in the palm of her hand and looked at him. The kitchen lights hadn't been switched on. It had still been bright when they had started preparing dinner, but the sun had suddenly faded, giving way to a violet twilight that cast shadows and angles across his face.

'I have a favour to ask of you.'

'What is it?' Lesley asked cautiously. She began standing to clear the table and he circled her wrist with his hand.

'Sit. Tidying can come later, or not at all. Violet will do it in the morning. I need to ask you something and I will need your undivided attention when I do so.'

She subsided back into the chair, heart beating madly.

'I want you to accompany me to Italy,' Alessio said heavily. 'It's a big ask, I know, but my fear is that, short of dragging Rachel to the plane and forcibly strapping her to the seat, she will simply refuse to listen to a word I have to say.'

'But I don't even know your daughter, Alessio!'

'If I cannot persuade my daughter to return to the UK, this will spell the end of any chance of a relationship I will ever have with her.' He rubbed his eyes wearily and then leaned back and stared blankly up at the ceiling.

Lesley's heart went out to him. Was that how it would be? Most likely. And yet…

'There's something you should see.' She stood up and went to the folder which she had brought down with her. This was the point at which she should now point out that she had gathered as much information as she could and it was up to him to do what needed to be done. In the end, it had been fiddly, but not impossible.

'You've found something?' Alessio was suddenly alert. He sat forward and pulled his chair towards her as she began smoothing out the various bits of paper she had found and the pages she had printed out over the past couple of days she had been at the house.

She had only given him a rough, skeleton idea of her findings before, not wanting to build any pictures that might be incorrect.

'I collated all of this and, well, okay, so I told you that I didn't think that this had anything to do with your wife...'

'Ex-wife.'

'Ex-wife. Well, I was right. I managed to trace our friend. He jumped around a bit, used a few different Internet cafés to cover his tracks, but the cafés, as I told you, were all in the vicinity of your daughter's school. It took a bit of time, but I eventually identified the one he used most frequently. Most importantly, though, in one of the very early emails—one of the emails you never identified as coming from him—he used his own computer. It was a little bit tougher than I thought but I got through to the identity of the person.'

Alessio was listening intently. 'You know who he is?'

'It would have been a bit more difficult to piece together conclusively if I hadn't discovered those very early emails when he'd obviously just been testing the ground. They were very innocuous, which is why he probably thought that they would have been deleted. I guess he didn't figure that they would still be uncovered and brought out of hiding.' She shoved the stack of printed emails across to Alessio and watched as he read them one by one. She had highlighted important bits, phrases, certain ways of saying things that pointed to the same writer behind them.

'You're brilliant.'

Lesley flushed with pleasure. 'I was only doing what you paid me to do.'

'So, build me the picture,' he said softly.

She did and, as she did so, she watched his expression darken and change.

'So now you pretty much have the complete story,' she finished. 'I gathered all this so that I could actually present it to you tomorrow when you returned. I was going to tell you that there's really nothing left for me to do now.'

'I still want you to come with me to Italy.'

'I can't,' Lesley said quickly, with a note of desperation in her voice.

'You've sorted all of this out, but there is still the problem of my daughter. Bringing her back over here with this information, it's going to be even more difficult.'

That was something Lesley had not taken into account when she had worked out her plan to present him with her findings and leave while common sense and her instinct for self-preservation were still intact.

'Yes, but it all remains the same. She's going to be—I can't imagine—certainly not warm and welcoming to the person who brought the whole thing to light.'

'But you have no personal axe to grind with her.' Would she come? It suddenly seemed very important that she was at his side. He was uneasily aware that there was an element of need there. How and why had that happened? He swept aside his discomfort.

'I also have my job, Alessio.' She was certain that she should be feeling horrified and indignant at his nerve in asking her to go way beyond the bounds of what she had been paid to do. Especially when she had made such a big effort to wrap everything up so that she could escape the suffocating, dangerous effect he had on her.

'You can leave that to me,' he murmured.

'Leave that to you? How do you work that one out?'

'I've just concluded a deal to buy a string of luxury boutique hotels in Italy. Failing business, mismanagement, feuding amongst the board members; that's what the trip to London was all about. I needed to be there to finalise the details with lawyers.'

'How exciting,' Lesley said politely.

'More so than you might imagine. It's the first time I shall be dabbling in the leisure industry and, naturally, I will want a comprehensive website designed.'

'You have your own people to do that.'

'They're remarkably busy at the moment. This will be a job that will definitely have to be outsourced. Not only could it be worth a great deal of money to the company lucky enough to get the job, but there's no telling how many other jobs will come in its wake.'

'Are you *coercing* me?'

'I prefer to call it *persuasion.*'

'I don't believe it.'

'I usually get what I want,' Alessio said with utter truth. 'And what I want is for you to come with me to Italy and, if this proves a helpful lever, then that's all to the good. I'm sure when I explain to your boss the size and scale of the job, and the fact that it would be extremely useful to have you over there so that you can soak up the atmosphere and get a handle on how best to pitch the project…' He gave an elegant shrug and a smile of utter devastation; both relayed the message that she was more or less trapped.

Naturally she could turn down his offer but her boss might be a little miffed should he get to hear that. They were a thriving company but, with the current economic climate, potential setbacks lurked round every corner. Whatever work came their way was not to be sniffed at, especially when the work in question could be highly lucrative and extensive.

'And if you're concerned about your pay,' he continued, 'Rest assured that you will be earning exactly the same rate as you were for the job you just so successfully completed.'

'I'm not concerned about the money!'

'Why don't you want to come? It'll be a holiday.'

'You don't need me there, not really.'

'You have no idea what I need or don't need,' Alessio murmured softly.

'You might change your mind when you see what else I have to show you.' But already she was trying to staunch the wave of anticipation at the thought of going abroad with him, having a few more days in his company, feeding her silly addiction.

She rescued papers from the bottom of the folder, pushed them across to him and watched carefully as he rifled through them.

But then, the moment felt too private, and she stood up and began getting them both a couple of cups of coffee.

What would he be thinking? she wondered as he looked at the little collection of articles about him which she had found in a scrap book in Rachel's room. Again, no attempt had been made to conceal them. Rachel had collected bits and pieces about her father over the years; there were photographs as well, which she must have taken from an album somewhere. Photos of him as a young man.

Eventually, when she could no longer pretend to be taking her time with the coffee, she handed a mug to him and sat back down.

'You found these...' Alessio cleared his throat but he couldn't look her in the eyes.

'I found them,' Lesley said gently. 'So, you see, your daughter isn't quite as indifferent to you as you might believe. Having the conversation you need to have with her might not be quite so difficult as you imagine.'

CHAPTER SIX

'THIS IS QUITE a surprise.' This was all Alessio could find
to say and he knew that it was inadequate. His daughter had been collecting a scrap book about him. That
reached deep down to a part of him he'd thought no longer existed. He stared down at the most recent cutting
of him printed off the Internet. He had had an article
written in the business section of the *Financial Times*
following the acquisition of a small, independent bank
in Spain. It was a poor picture but she had still printed
it off and shoved it inside the scrap book.

What was he to think?

He rested his forehead against his clenched fist and
drew in a long breath.

A wave of compassion washed over Lesley. Alessio
Baldini was tough, cool, controlled. If he hadn't already
told her, his entire manner was indicative of someone
who knew that they could get what he wanted simply
by snapping his fingers. It was a trait she couldn't abide
in anyone.

She hated rich men who acted as though they owned
the world and everything in it.

She hated men who felt that they could fling money
at any problem and, lo and behold, a solution would be
forthcoming.

And she hated anyone who didn't value the importance of family life. Family was what grounded you, made you put everything into perspective; stopped you from ever taking yourself too seriously or sacrificing too much in pursuit of your goals.

Alessio acted as he if he owned the world and he certainly acted as though money was the root of solving all problems. If he was a victim of circumstances when it came to an unfortunate family life, then he definitely did not behave as though now was the time when he could begin sorting it out.

So why was she now reaching out to place her hand on his arm? Why had she pulled her chair just that little bit nearer to his so that she could feel the heat radiating from his body?

Was it because the vulnerability she had always sensed in him whenever the subject of his daughter came up was now so glaringly obvious?

Rachel was his Achilles heel; in a flash of comprehension, Lesley saw that. In every other area, Alessio was in complete control of his surroundings, of his *life*, but when it came to his daughter he floundered.

The women he had dated in the past had been kept at a distance. Once bitten, twice shy, and after his experiences with Bianca he had made sure never to let any other woman get past the steel walls that surrounded him. They would never have glimpsed the man who was at a loss when it came to his daughter. She wondered how many of them even *knew* that he had a daughter.

But here she was. She had seen him at his most naked, emotionally.

That was a good thing, she thought, and a bad thing. It was good insofar as everyone needed a sounding board when it came to dark thoughts and emotions.

Those were burdens that could not be carried single-handed. He might have passed the years with his deepest thoughts locked away, but there was no way he would ever have been able to eradicate them, and letting them out could only be a good thing.

With this situation, he had been forced to reveal more about those thoughts to her than he ever had to anyone else. She was certain of that.

The down side was that, for a proud man, the necessity of having to confide thoughts normally hidden would eventually be seen as a sign of weakness.

The sympathetic, listening ear would only work for so long before it turned into a source of resentment.

But did that matter? Really? They wouldn't be around one another for much longer and right here, right now, in some weird, unspoken way, he needed her. She *felt* it, even though it was something he would never, ever articulate.

Those cuttings had moved him beyond words. He was trying hard to control his reaction in front of an audience; that was evident in the thickness of the silence.

'You'll have to return that scrap book to where you found it,' he said gruffly when the silence had been stretched to breaking point. 'Leave it with me overnight and I'll give it to you in the morning.'

Lesley nodded. Her hand was still on his arm and he hadn't shrugged it away. She allowed it to travel so that she was stroking upwards, feeling the strength of his muscles straining under the shirt and the definition of his shoulders and collarbone.

Alessio's eyes narrowed on her.

'Are you feeling sorry for me?' His voice was less cold than it should have been. 'Is that a pity caress?'

He had never confided in anyone. He certainly had

never been an object of pity to anyone, any woman, ever. The thought alone was laughable. Women had always hung onto his every word, longed for some small indication that they occupied a more special role in his life than he was willing to admit to them.

Naturally, they hadn't.

Lesley, though…

She was in a different category. The pity caress did not evoke the expected feelings of contempt, impatience and anger that he would have expected.

He caught her hand in his and held on to it.

'It's not a *pity caress*.' Lesley breathed. Her skin burned where he was touching it, a blaze that was stoked by the expression in his eyes: dark, thoughtful, insightful, amused. 'But I know it must be disconcerting, looking through Rachel's scrap book, seeing pictures of yourself there, articles cut out or printed off from the Internet.' He still wasn't saying anything. He was still just staring at her, his head slightly to one side, his expression brooding and intent.

Her voice petered out and she stared right back at him, eyes wide. She could barely breathe. The moment seemed as fragile as a droplet of water balancing on the tip of a leaf, ready to fall and splinter apart.

She didn't want the moment to end. It was wrong, she knew that, but still she wanted to touch his face and smooth away those very human, very uncertain feelings she knew he would be having; feelings he would be taking great care of to conceal.

'The scrap book was just lying there,' she babbled away as she continued to get lost in his eyes. 'On the bed. I would have felt awful if I had found it hidden under the mattress or at the bottom of a drawer somewhere, but it was just there, waiting to be found.'

'Not by me. Rachel knew that I would never go into her suite of rooms.'

Lesley shrugged. 'I wanted you to see that you're important to your daughter,' she murmured shakily, 'Even if you don't think you are because of the way she acts. Teenagers can be very awkward when it comes to showing their feelings.' He still wasn't saying anything. If he thought that she felt sorry for him, then how was it that he was staying put, not angrily stalking off? 'You remember being a teenager.' She tried a smile in an attempt to lighten the screaming tension between them.

'Vaguely. When I think back to my teenage years, I inevitably end up thinking back to being a daddy before I was out of them.'

'Of course,' Lesley murmured, her voice warm with understanding. At the age of fourteen, not even knowing it, he would have been a mere four years away from becoming a father. It was incredible.

'You're doing it again,' Alessio said under his breath.

'Doing what?'

'Smothering me with your sympathy. Don't worry. Maybe I like it.' His mouth curved into a wolfish smile but underneath that, he thought with passing confusion, her sympathy was actually very welcome.

He reached out and touched her face, then ran two fingers along her cheek, circling her mouth then along her slender neck, coming to rest at the base of her collarbone.

'Have you felt what I've been feeling for the past couple of days?' he asked.

Lesley wasn't sure she was physically capable of answering his question. Not with that hand on her collarbone and her brain reliving every inch of its caress as it had touched her cheek and moved sensuously over her mouth.

'Well?' Alessio prompted. He rested his other hand on her thigh and began massaging it, very gently but very thoroughly, just the one spot, but it was enough to make the breath catch in her throat.

'What do you mean? What are you talking about?' As if she didn't know. As if she wasn't constantly aware of the way he unsettled her. And was she conscious that the electricity flowed both ways? Maybe she was. Maybe that was why the situation had seemed so dangerous.

She had thought that she needed to get out because her attraction to him was getting too much, was threatening to become evident. Maybe a part of her had known that the real reason she needed to get out was because, on some level, she knew that he was attracted to her as well. That underneath the light-hearted flirting there was a very real undercurrent of mutual sexual chemistry.

And that was not good, not at all. She didn't do one-night stands, or two-day stands, or 'going nowhere so why not have a quick romp?' stands.

She did *relationships*. If there had been no guy in her life for literally years, then it was because she had never been the kind of girl who had sex just for the sake of it.

But with Alessio something told her that she could be that girl, and that scared her.

'You know exactly what I mean. You want me. I want you. I've wanted you for a while...'

'I should go up to bed.' Lesley breathed unevenly, nailed to the spot and not moving an inch despite her protestations. 'Leave you to your thoughts...'

'Maybe I'm not that keen on being alone with my thoughts,' Alessio said truthfully. 'Maybe my thoughts are a black hole into which I have no desire to fall.

Maybe I want your pity and your sympathy because they can save me from that fall.'

And what happens when you've been saved from that fall? What happens to me? You're in a weird place right now and, if I rescue you now, what happens when you leave that weird place and shut the door on it once again?

But those muddled thoughts barely had time to settle before they were blown away by the fiercely exciting thought of being with the man who was leaning towards her, staring at her with such intensity that she wanted to moan.

And, before she could retreat behind more weak protestations, he was cupping the back of her neck and drawing her towards him, very slowly, so slowly that she had time to appreciate the depth of his dark eyes; the fine lines that etched his features; the slow, sexy curve of his mouth; the length of his dark eyelashes.

Lesley fell into the kiss with a soft moan, part resignation, part despair; mostly intense, long-awaited excitement. She spread her hand behind his neck in a mirror gesture to how he was holding her and, as his tongue invaded the soft contours of her mouth, she returned the kiss and let that kiss do its work—spread moisture between her legs, pinch her nipples into tight, sensitive buds, raise the hairs on her arms.

'We shouldn't be doing this,' she muttered, breaking apart for a few seconds and immediately wanting to draw him back towards her again.

'Why not?'

'Because this isn't the right reason for going to bed with someone.'

'Don't know what you're talking about.' He leaned

to kiss her again but she stilled him with a hand on his chest and met his gaze with anxious eyes.

'I don't pity you, Alessio,' she said huskily. 'I'm sorry that you don't have the relationship with your daughter that you'd like, but I don't pity you. And when I showed you that scrap book it was because I felt the contents were something you needed to know about. What I feel is…understanding and compassion.'

'And what I feel is that we shouldn't get lost in words.'

'Because words are not your thing?' But she smiled and felt a rush of tenderness towards this strong, powerful man who was also capable of being so wonderfully *human*, hard though he might try to fight it.

'You know what they say about actions speaking louder…' He grinned at her. His body was on fire. She was right—words weren't his thing, at least not the words that made up long, involved conversations about feelings. He scooped her up and she gave a little cry of surprise, then wriggled and told him to put her down immediately; she might be slim but she was way too tall for him to start thinking he could play the caveman with her.

Alessio ignored her and carried her up the stairs to his bedroom.

'Every woman likes a caveman.' He gently kicked open his bedroom door and then deposited her on his king-sized bed.

Night had crept up without either of them realising it and, without the bedroom lights switched on, the darkness only allowed them to see one another in shadowy definition.

'I don't,' Lesley told him breathlessly as he stood in front of her and began unbuttoning his shirt.

She had already seen him barely clothed in the pool. She should know what to expect when it came to his body and yet, as he tossed his shirt carelessly on the ground, it was as if she was looking at him for the first time.

The impact he had on her was as new, as raw, as powerful.

But then, this was different, wasn't it? This wasn't a case of watching him covertly from the sidelines as he covered a few lengths in a swimming pool.

This was lying on his bed, in a darkened room, with the promise of possession flicking through her like a spreading fire.

Alessio didn't want to talk. He wanted to take her, fast and hard, until he heard her cry out with satisfaction. He wanted to pleasure her and feel her come with him inside her.

But how much sweeter to take his time, to taste every inch of her, to withstand the demands of his raging hormones and indulge in making love with her at a more leisurely pace.

'No?' he drawled, hand resting on the zipper of his trousers before he began taking those off as well, where they joined the shirt in a heap on the ground, leaving him in just his boxers. 'You think I'm a caveman because I carried you up the stairs?'

He slowly removed his boxers. He regretted not having turned some lights on because he would have liked to really appreciate the expression on her face as he watched her watching him. He strolled towards the side of the bed and stood there, then he touched himself lightly and heard her swift intake of breath.

'I just think you're a caveman in general,' Lesley feasted her eyes on his impressive erection. When he held it in his hand, she longed to do the same to herself, to touch herself down there. Her nerves were stretched to breaking point and she wished she was just a little more experienced, a little more knowing about what to do when it came to a man like him, a man who probably knew everything there was to know about the opposite sex.

She sat up, crossed her legs and reached out to touch him, replacing his hand with hers and gaining confidence as she felt him shudder with appreciation.

It was a strange turn-on to be fully clothed while he was completely naked.

'Is that right?'

As she took him into her mouth, Alessio grunted and flung his head back. He had died and gone to heaven. The wetness of her mouth on his hard erection, the way she licked, teased and tasted, his fingers curled into her short hair, made him breathe heavily, well aware that he had to come down from this peak or risk bringing this love-making session to an extremely premature conclusion, which was not something he intended to do.

With a sigh of pure regret, he eased her off him.

Then he joined her on the bed. 'Would I be a caveman if I stripped you? I wouldn't...' he slipped his fingers underneath the tee-shirt and began easing it over her head '...want to...' Then came the jeans, which she wriggled out of so that she remained in bra and pants, white, functional items of clothing that looked wonderfully wholesome on her. 'Offend your feminist sensibilities.'

For the life of her, Lesley couldn't find where she had misplaced those feminist sensibilities which he had mentioned. She reached behind to unhook her bra but he gently drew her hands away so that he could accomplish the task himself.

He half-closed his eyes and his nostrils flared with rampant appreciation of her small but perfectly formed breasts. Her nipples were big, brown, circular discs. She had propped herself up on both elbows and her breasts were small, pointed mounds offering themselves to him like sweet, delicate fruit.

In one easy movement, he straddled her, and she fell back against the pillow with a soft, excited moan.

She was wet for him. As he reached behind him to slip his hand under the panties, she groaned and covered her eyes with one hand.

'I want to see you, my darling.' Alessio lowered himself so that he was lightly on top of her. 'Move your hand.'

'I don't usually do this sort of thing,' Lesley mumbled. 'I'm not into one-night stands. I never have been. I don't see the point.'

'Shh.' He gazed down at her until she was burning all over. Then he gently began licking her breast, moving in a concentric circle until his tongue found her nipple. The sensitised tip had peaked into an erect nub, and as he took her whole nipple into his mouth so that he could suckle on it she quivered under him, moving with feverish urgency, arching back so that not a single atom of the pleasurable sensations zinging through her was lost.

She had to get rid of her panties, they were damp and uncomfortable, but with his big body over hers she couldn't reach them. Instead she clasped her hand to the back of his head and pressed him down harder on her breasts, giving little cries and whimpers as he carried on sucking and teasing, moving between her breasts and then, when she was going crazy from it, he trailed his tongue over her rib cage and down to the indentation of her belly button.

His breath on her body was warm and she was breathing fast, hardly believing that what was happening really was happening and yet desperate for it to continue, desperate to carry on shamelessly losing herself in the moment.

He felt her sharp intake of breath as he slipped her underwear down, and then she was holding her breath as he gently parted her legs and flicked his tongue over her core.

Lesley groaned. This was an intimacy she had not experienced before. She curled her fingers into his dark hair and tugged him but her body was responding with a shocking lack of inhibition as he continued to taste her, teasing her swollen bud until she lost the ability to think clearly.

Alessio felt her every response as if their bodies had tuned into the same wavelength. In a blinding, revelatory flash, he realised that everything else that had come before with women could not compete with what was happening right now, because this woman had just seen far more of him than anyone else ever had.

This had not been a simple game of pursuit and capture. She hadn't courted this situation, nor had he anticipated it. Certainly, there had come a point when he had looked at her and liked what he had seen; had wanted what he had seen; had even vaguely *planned* on having her because, when it came to him and women, wanting and having were always the same side of the coin.

But he knew that he hadn't banked on what was happening between them now. For the first time, he had the strangest feeling that this wasn't just about sex.

But the sex was great.

He swept aside all his unravelling thoughts and lost himself in her body, in her sweet little whimpers and her broken groans as she wriggled under him, until at last, when he could feel her wanting to reach her orgasm, he broke off to fumble in the bedside cabinet for a condom.

Lesley could hardly bear that brief pause. She was alive in a way she had never been before and that terrified her. Her relationships with the opposite sex had always been guarded and imbued with a certain amount of defensiveness that stemmed from her own private insecurities.

Having been raised in an all-male family, she had developed brilliant coping skills when it came to standing her ground with the opposite sex. Her brothers had toughened her up and taught her the value of healthy competition, the benefits of never being cowed by a guy, of knowing that she could hold her own.

But no one had been able to help her during those teenage years when the lines of distinction between boys and girls were drawn. She had watched from the sidelines and decided that lipstick and mascara were not for her, that sport was far more enjoyable. It wasn't about how you looked, it was about what was inside you and what was inside her—her intelligence, her sense of humour, her capacity for compassion—did not need to be camouflaged with make-up and sexy clothes.

The only guys she had ever been attracted to were the ones who'd seen her for the person she was, the ones whose heads hadn't swivelled round when a busty blonde in a short skirt had walked past.

So what, it flashed through her head, was she doing with Alessio Baldini?

She sighed and reached up to him as he settled back on her, nudging her legs apart, then she closed her eyes and was transported to another planet as he thrust into her, deep and hard, building a rhythm that drove everything out of her mind.

She flung her head back and succumbed to loud, responsive cries as he continued to fill her.

She came on a tidal wave of intense pleasure and felt her whole body shudder and arch up towards him in a wonderful fusing of bodies.

The moment seemed to last for ever and she was only brought back down to earth when he withdrew from her and cursed fluently under his breath.

'The condom has split.'

Lesley abruptly surfaced from the pleasant, dreamy cloud on which she had been happily drifting, and the uncomfortable thoughts which had been sidelined when he had begun touching her returned with double intensity.

What on earth had she done? How could she have allowed herself to end up in bed with this man? Had she lost her mind? This was a situation that was going nowhere and would never go anywhere. She was Lesley Fox, a practical, clever, not at all sexy woman who should have known better than to be sweet talked into sleeping with a man who wouldn't have looked twice at her under normal circumstances.

On every level, he was just the sort of man she usually wouldn't have gone near and, had he seen her passing on the street, she certainly would not have been the sort of woman he would have noticed. She would literally have been invisible to him because she just wasn't his type.

Fate had thrown them together and an attraction had built between them but she knew that she would be a complete fool not to recognise that that attraction was grounded in novelty.

'How the hell could that have happened?' Alessio said, his voice dark with barely contained anger. 'This is the last thing I need right now.'

Lesley got that. He had found himself tricked into marriage by a pregnancy he had not courted once upon a time and his entire adult life had been affected. Of course he would not want to repeat that situation.

Yet, she couldn't help but feel the sting of hurt at the simmering anger in his voice.

'It won't happen,' she said stiffly. She wriggled into a sitting position and watched as he vaulted upright and began searching around for his boxers, having disposed of the faulty condom.

'And you know that because?'

'It's the wrong time of month for that to happen.' She surreptitiously crossed her fingers and tried to calculate when she had last had her period. 'And, rest assured, the last thing I would want would be to end up pregnant, Alessio. As it stands, this was a very bad idea.'

In the process of locating a tee-shirt from a chest of drawers, he paused and strolled back to the bed. The condom had split and there was nothing he could do about that now. He could only hope that she was right, that they were safe.

But, that aside, how could she say that making love had been a very bad idea? He was oddly affronted.

'You know what. This. Us. Ending up in bed together. It shouldn't have happened.'

'Why not? We're attracted to one another. How could it have been a bad idea? I was under the impression that you had actually enjoyed the experience.' He looked down at her and felt his libido begin to rise once again.

'That's not the point.' She swung her legs over the side of the bed and stood up, conscious of her nudity, gritting her teeth against the temptation to drag the covers off the bed and shield herself from him.

'God, you're beautiful.'

Lesley flushed and looked away, stubbornly proud, and refusing to believe that he meant a word of that. Novelty was a beautiful thing but became boring very quickly.

'Well?' He caught her wrist and tilted her face so that she had no option but to look at him.

'Well what?' Lesley muttered, lowering her eyes.

'Well, let's go back to bed.'

'Didn't you hear a word I just said?'

'Every word.' He kissed her delicately on the corner of her mouth and then very gently on her lips.

In a heartbeat, and to her disgust, Lesley could feel her determination begin to melt away.

'You're not my type,' she mumbled, refusing to cave in, but his lips were so soft against her jaw that her disobedient body was responding in all sorts of stupidly predictable ways.

'Because I'm a caveman?'

'Yes!' Her hands crept up to his neck and she protested feebly as he lifted her off her feet and back towards the bed to which she had only minutes previously sworn not to return.

'So, what are you looking for in a man?' Alessio murmured.

This time, he drew the covers over them. It was very dark outside. Even with the curtains open, the night was black velvet with only a slither of moon penetrating the darkness and weakly illuminating the bedroom.

He could feel her reluctance, her mind fighting her body, and it felt imperative that her body win the battle because he wanted her, more than he had ever wanted any woman in his life before.

'Not someone like you, Alessio,' Lesley whispered, pressing her hands flat against his chest and feeling the steady beat of his heart.

'Why? Why not someone like me?'

'Because…' *Because safety was not with a man who looked like him, a man who could have anyone he wanted.* She knew her limits. She knew that she was just not the sort of girl who drew guys to her like a magnet. She never had been. She just didn't have the confidence; had never had the right preparation; had never had a mother's guiding hand to show her the way to all those little feminine wiles that went into the mix of attraction between the sexes.

But bigger than her fear of involvement with him was her fear of *not* getting involved, *not* taking the chance.

'You're just not the sort of person I ever imagined having any kind of relationship with, that's all.'

'We're not talking marriage here, Lesley, we're talking about enjoying each other.' He propped himself up on one elbow and traced his finger along her arm. 'I'm not looking for commitment any more than you probably are.'

And certainly not with someone like you; Lesley reluctantly filled in the remainder of that remark.

'And you still haven't told me the sort of man you would call "your type".' She was warm and yielding in his arms. She might make a lot of noises about this being a mistake, but she wanted him as much as he wanted her, and he knew that if he slipped his fingers into her he would feel the tell-tale proof of her arousal.

He could have her right here and right now, despite whatever she said about him not being her type. And who, in the end, cared whether he was her type or not? Hadn't he just told her that this wasn't about commitment and marriage? In other words, did it really matter if he wasn't her type?

But he was piqued at the remark. She was forthright and spoke her mind; he had become accustomed to that very quickly. But surely what she had said amounted to an unacceptable lack of tact! He thought that there was nothing wrong in asking her to explain exactly what she had meant.

His voice had dropped a few shades.

'You're offended, aren't you?' Lesley asked and Alessio was quick to deny any such thing.

Lesley could have kicked herself for asking him that question. Of course he wouldn't be offended! To be offended, he would actually have had to care about her and that was not the case here, as he had made patently clear.

'That's a relief!' she exclaimed lightly. 'My type? I guess thoughtful, caring, sensitive; someone who believes in the same things that I do, who has similar interests…maybe even someone working in the same field. You know—artistic, creative, not really bothered about the whole business of making money.'

Alessio bared his teeth in a smile. 'Sounds a lot of fun. Sure someone like that would be able to keep up with you? No, scrap that—too much talk. There are better things to do and, now that we've established that you can't resist me even though I'm the last kind of person you would want in your life, let's make love.'

'Alessio…'

He stifled any further protest with a long, lingering kiss that released in her a sigh of pure resignation. So this made no sense, so she was a complete idiot…

Where had the practical, level-headed girl with no illusions about herself gone? All she seemed capable of doing was giving in.

'And,' he murmured into her ear. 'In case you think that Italy is off the agenda because I'm not a touchy-feely art director for a design company, forget it. I still want you there by my side. Trust me, I will make it worth your while.'

CHAPTER SEVEN

EVERYTHING SEEMED TO happen at the speed of light after that. Of course, there was no inconvenient hanging around for affordable flights or having to surf the Internet for places to stay. None of the usual headaches dogged Alessio's spur-of-the-moment decision to take Lesley to Italy.

Two days after he had extended his invitation, they were boarding a plane to Italy.

It was going to be a surprise visit. Armed with information, they were going to get the full story from his daughter, lay all the cards on the table and then, when they were back in the UK, Alessio would sort the other half of the equation out. He would pay an informal visit to his emailing friend and he was sure that they would reach a happy conclusion where no money changed hands.

Lessons, he had assured her, would regrettably have to be learnt.

Lesley privately wondered what his approach to his daughter would be. Would similar lessons also 'regrettably have to be learnt'? How harsh would those lessons be? He barely had a relationship with Rachel and she privately wondered how he intended ever to build on it if he went in to 'sort things out' with the diplomacy of a bull in a china shop.

That was one of the reasons she had agreed to go to Italy with him.

Without saying it in so many words, she knew that he was looking to her for some sort of invisible moral back-up, even though he had stated quite clearly that he needed her there primarily to impart the technicalities of what she had discovered should the situation demand it.

'You haven't said anything for the past half an hour.' Alessio interrupted her train of thought as they were shown into the first class cabin of the plane. 'Why?'

Lesley bristled. 'I was just thinking how fast everything's moved,' she said as they were shown to seats as big as armchairs and invited to have a glass of champagne, which she refused.

She stole a glance at his sexy face, lazy and amused at the little show of rebellion.

'I came to do a job for you, thinking that I would be in and out of your house in a matter of a few hours and now here I am, days later, boarding a plane for Italy.'

'I know. Isn't life full of adventure and surprise?' He waved aside an awe-struck air hostess and settled into the seat next to her. 'I confess that I myself am surprised at the way things unfolded. Surprised but not displeased.'

'Because you've got what you wanted,' Lesley complained. She was so accustomed to her independence that she couldn't help feeling disgruntled at the way she had been railroaded into doing exactly what he had wanted her to do.

Even though, a little voice inside her pointed out, this rollercoaster ride was the most exciting thing she had ever done in her life—even though it was scary, even though it had yanked her out of her precious comfort zone, even though she knew that it would come to nothing and the fall back to Planet Earth would be painful.

'I didn't force your hand,' Alessio said comfortably.

'You went into the office and talked to my boss.'

'I just wanted to point out the world of opportunity lying at his feet if he could see his way to releasing you for one week to accompany me to Italy.'

'I dread to think what the office grapevine is going to make of this situation.'

'Do you care what anyone thinks?' He leant against the window so that he could direct one hundred per cent of his undivided attention on her.

'Of course I do!' Lesley blushed because she knew that, whilst she might give the impression of being strong, sassy and outspoken, she still had a basic need to be liked and accepted. She just wasn't always good at showing that side of herself. In fact, she was uncomfortably aware of the fact that, whilst Alessio might have shown her more of himself than he might have liked, she had likewise done the same.

He would not know it, but against all odds she had allowed herself to walk into unchartered territory, to have a completely new experience with a man knowing that he was not the right man for her.

'Relax and enjoy the ride,' he murmured.

'I'm not going to enjoy confronting your daughter with all the information we've managed to uncover. She's going to know that I went through her belongings.'

'If Rachel had wanted to keep her private life private, then she should have destroyed all the incriminating evidence. The fact is that she's still a child and she has no vote when it comes to us doing what was necessary to protect her.'

'She may not see it quite like that.'

'She will have to make a very big effort to, in that case.'

Lesley sighed and leaned back into the seat with her eyes shut. What Alessio did with his daughter was really none of her business. Yes, she'd been involved in bringing the situation to light, but its solutions and whatever repercussions followed would be a continuing saga she would leave behind. She would return to the blessed safety of what she knew and the family story of Alessio and his daughter would remain a mystery to her for ever.

So there was no need to feel any compunction about just switching off.

Yet she had to bite back the temptation to tell him what she thought, even though she knew that he would have every right to dismiss whatever advice she had to offer about the peculiarity of their relationship, if a 'relationship' was what it could be called. She was his lover, a woman who probably knew far too much about his life for his liking. She had been paid to investigate a personal problem, yet had no right to have any discussions about that problem, even though they were sleeping together.

In a normal relationship, she should have felt free to speak her mind, but this was not a normal relationship, was it? For either of them. She had sacrificed her feminist principles for sex and she still couldn't understand herself, nor could she understand how it was that she felt no regrets.

In fact, when he looked at her the way he was looking at her right now, all she felt was a dizzying need to have him take her.

If only he could see into her mind and unravel all her doubts and uncertainties. Thank goodness he couldn't. As far as he was concerned, she was a tough career woman with as little desire for a long-term relationship as him. They had both stepped out of the box, drawn to each other by a combination of proximity and the pull of novelty.

'You're thinking,' Alessio said drily. 'Why don't you spit it out and then we can get it out of the way?'

'Get what out of the way?'

'Whatever disagreements you have about the way I intend to handle this situation.'

'You hate it when I tell you what I think,' Lesley said with asperity. Alessio shrugged and continued looking at her in the way that made her toes curl and her mouth run dry.

'And I don't like it when I can see you thinking but you're saying nothing. "Between a rock and a hard place" comes to mind.' He was amazed at how easily he had adapted to her outspoken approach. His immediate instinct now was not to shove her back behind his boundary lines and remind her about overstepping the mark.

'I just don't think you should confront Rachel and demand to know what the hell is going on.' She shifted in the big seat and turned so that she was completely facing him.

The plane was beginning to taxi in preparation for taking off, and she fell silent for a short while as the usual canned talk was given about safety exits, but as soon as they were airborne she looked at him worriedly once again.

'It's hard to know how to get answers if you don't ask for them,' he pointed out.

'We know the situation.'

'And I want to know how it got to where it finally got. It's one thing knowing the outcome but I don't intend to let history repeat itself.'

'You might want to try a little sympathy.'

Alessio snorted.

'You said yourself that she's just a kid,' Lesley reminded him gently.

'You *could* always spare me the horror of making a mess of things by talking to Rachel yourself,' he said.

'She's not my daughter.'

'Then allow me to work this one out myself.' But he knew that she was right. There was no tactful way of asking the questions he would have to ask, and if his daughter disliked him now then she was about to dislike him a whole lot more when he was finished talking to her.

Of course, there were those photos, cuttings of him— some indication, as Lesley had said, that she wasn't completely indifferent to the fact that he was her father.

But would that be enough to take them past this little crisis? Unlikely. Especially when she discovered that the photos and cuttings had been salvaged in an undercover operation.

'Okay.'

Alessio had looked away, out through the window to the dense bank of cloud over which they were flying. Now, he turned to Lesley with a frown.

'Okay. I'll talk to Rachel if you like,' she said on a reluctant sigh.

'Why would you do that?'

Why would she? Because she couldn't bear to see him looking the way he was looking now, with the hopeless expression of someone staring defeat in the face.

And why did she care? she asked herself. But she shied away from trying to find an answer to that.

'Because I'm on the outside of this mess. If she directs all her teenage anger at me, then by the time she gets to you some of it may have diffused.'

'And the likelihood of that is…?' But he was touched at her generosity of spirit.

'Not good odds,' Lesley conceded. 'But worth a try, don't you think?' He was staring at her with an expression of intense curiosity and she continued quickly, before he could interrupt with the most obvious question: *why?* A question to which she had no answer. 'Besides, I'm good at mediating. I got a lot of practice at doing that when I was growing up. When there are six kids in a family, a dad worked off his feet, and five of those six are boys, there's always lots of opportunity to practise mediation skills.'

But just no opportunity to practise *being a girl*. And that was why she was the way she was now: hesitant in relationships; self-conscious about whether she had what it took to make any relationship last; willing not to get into the water at all rather than diving in and finding herself out of her depth and unable to cope.

Only since Alessio had appeared on the scene had she really seen the pattern in her behaviour, the way she kept guys, smiling, at arm's length.

He was so dramatically different from any man she had ever been remotely drawn to that it had been easy to pinpoint her own lack of self-confidence. She was a clever career woman with a bright life ahead of her and yet that sinfully beautiful face had reduced all those achievements to rubble.

She had looked at him and returned to her teenage years when she had simply not known how to approach a boy because she had had no idea what they were looking for.

For her, Alessio Baldini was not the obvious choice

when it came to picking a guy to sleep with, yet sleep with him she had, and she was glad that she had done so. She had broken through the glass barrier that had stood between her and the opposite sex. It was strange, but he had given her confidence she hadn't really even known she had needed.

'And mediation skills are so important when one is growing up,' Alessio murmured.

Basking in her new-found revelations, Lesley smiled. 'No, they're not,' she admitted with more candour than she'd ever done to anyone in her life before. 'In fact, I can't think of any skill a teenage girl has less use for than mediation skills,' she mused. 'But I had plenty of that.' She leaned back and half-closed her eyes. When she next spoke it was almost as though she was talking with no audience listening to what was being said.

'My mum died when I was so young, I barely remember her. I mean, Dad always told us about her, what she was like and such, and there were pictures of her everywhere. But the truth is, I don't have any memories of her—of doing anything with her, if you see what I mean.'

She glanced sideways at him and he nodded. He had always fancied himself as the sort of man who would be completely at sea when it came to listening to women pour their hearts out, hence it was a tendency that he had strenuously discouraged.

Now, though, he was drawn to what she was saying and by the faraway, pensive expression on her face.

'I never thought that I missed having a mother. I never knew what it was like to have one and my dad was always good enough for me. But I can see now that growing up in a male-only family might have given me confidence with the opposite sex but only when it came to things like work and study. I was encouraged to be as good as they were, and I think I succeeded, but I wasn't taught, well...'

'How to wear make-up and shop for dresses?'

'Sounds crazy but I do think girls need to be taught stuff like that.' She looked at him gravely. 'I can see that it's easy to have bags of confidence in one area and not much in another,' she said with a rueful shake of her head. 'When it came to the whole game-playing, sexual attraction thing, I don't think I've ever had loads of confidence.'

'And now?'

'I feel I have, so I guess I should say thank you.'

'*Thank you?* What are you thanking me for?'

'For encouraging me to step out of the box,' Lesley told him with that blend of frankness and disingenuousness which he found so appealing.

Alessio was momentarily distracted from the headache awaiting him in Italy. He had no idea where she was going with this but it had all the feel of a conversation heading down a road he would rather not explore.

'Always happy to oblige,' he said vaguely. 'I hope you've packed light clothes. The heat in Italy is quite different from the heat in England.'

'If I hadn't taken on this job, there's not a chance in the world that I would ever have met you.'

'That's true enough.'

'Not only do we not move in the same circles, we have no interests in common whatsoever.'

Alessio was vaguely indignant at what he thought might be an insult in disguise. Was she comparing him to the 'soul mate' guy she had yet to meet, the touchy-feely one with the artistic side and a love of all things natural?

'And if we *had* ever met, at a social do or something like that, I would never have had the confidence to approach you.'

'I'm not sure where you're going with this.'

'Here's what I'm saying, Alessio. I feel as though I've taken huge strides in gaining self-confidence in certain areas and it's thanks in some measure to you. I could say that I'm going to be a completely different person when I get back to the UK and start dating again.'

Alessio could not believe what he was hearing. He had no idea where this conversation had come from and he was enraged that she could sit there, his lover, and talk about going back on the dating scene!

'The dating scene.'

'Is this conversation becoming a little too deep for you?' Lesley asked with a grin. 'I know you don't do deep when it comes to women and conversations.'

'And how do you know that?'

'Well, you've already told me that you don't like encouraging them to get behind a stove and start cooking a meal for you, just in case they think, I don't know, they have somehow managed to get a foot through the door. So I'm guessing that meaningful conversations are probably on the banned list as well.'

They were. It was true. He had never enjoyed long, emotional conversations which, from experience, always ended up in the same place—invitations to meet the parents, questions about commitment and where the relationship was heading.

In fact, the second that type of conversation began rearing its head, he usually felt a pressing need to end the relationship. He had been coerced into one marriage and he had made a vow never to let himself be railroaded into another similar mistake, however tempting the woman in question might be.

He looked into her astute, brown eyes and scowled. 'I may not be looking for someone to walk down the aisle with, but that doesn't mean that I'm not prepared to have meaningful discussions with women. I'm also insulted,' he was driven to continue, 'That I've been used as some kind of trial run for the real thing.'

'What do you mean?' Lesley was feeling good. The vague unease that had been plaguing her ever since she had recognised how affected she was by Alessio had been boxed away with an explanation that made sense.

Sleeping with him had opened her eyes to fears and doubts she had been harbouring for years. She felt that she had buried a lack of self-confidence in her own sexuality under the guise of academic success and then, later on, success in her career. She had dressed in ways that didn't enhance her own femininity because she had always feared that she lacked what it took.

But then she had slept with him, slept with a man who was way out of her league, had been wanted and desired by him, and made to feel proud of the way she looked.

Was it any wonder that he had such a dramatic effect on her? It was a case of lust mixed up with a hundred other things.

But the bottom line was that he was no more than a learning curve for her. When she thought about it like that, it made perfect sense. It also released her from the disturbing suspicion that she was way too deep in a non-relationship that was going nowhere, a relationship that meant far more to her than it did to him.

Learning curves provided lessons and, once those lessons had been learnt, it was always easy to move on.

Learning curves didn't result in broken hearts.

She breathed in quickly and shakily. 'Well?' she flung at him, while her mind continued to chew over the notion that her involvement with him had been fast and hard. She had been catapulted into a world far removed from hers, thrown into the company of a man who was very, very different from the sort of men she was used to, and certainly worlds apart from the sort of man she would ever have expected herself to be attracted to.

But common sense had been no match for the power of his appeal and now here she was.

When she thought about never seeing him again, she felt faintly, sickeningly panicked.

What did that mean? Her thoughts became muddled when she tried to work her way through what suddenly seemed a dangerous, uncertain quagmire.

'I mean that you used me,' Alessio said bluntly. 'I don't like being used. And I don't appreciate you talking about jumping back into the dating scene, not when we're still lovers. I expect the women I sleep with to only have eyes for me.'

The unbridled arrogance of that statement, which was so fundamentally *Alessio,* brought a reluctant smile to her lips.

She had meant it when she had told him that under normal circumstances they would never have met. Their paths simply wouldn't have crossed. He didn't mix in the same circles as she did. And, even if by some freak chance they *had* met, they would have looked at one another and quickly looked away.

She would have seen a cold, wealthy, arrogant cardboard cut-out and he would have seen, well, a woman who was nothing like the sort of women he went out with and therefore she'd have been invisible. But the circumstances that had brought them together had uniquely provided them with a different insight into one another.

She had seen beneath the veneer to the three-dimensional man and he had seen through the sassy, liberal-minded, outspoken woman in charge of her life to the uncertain, insecure girl.

She was smart enough to realise, however, that that changed nothing. He was and always would be uninterested in any relationship that demanded longevity. He was shaped by his past and his main focus now was his daughter and trying to resolve the difficult situation that had arisen there. He might have slept with her because she was so different from what he was used to and because she was there, ready and willing but, whereas he had fundamentally reached deep and changed her, she hadn't done likewise with him.

'You're smiling.' Alessio was reluctant to abandon the conversation. When, he thought, was this dive back into the dating scene going to begin? Had she put time limits on what they had? Wasn't he usually the one to do that?

'I don't want to argue with you.' Lesley kept that smile pinned to her face. 'Who will you introduce me as when we get to Italy?'

'I haven't given it any thought. Where is all this hectic dating going to take place?'

'I beg your pardon?'

'You can't start conversations you don't intend to finish. So, where will you be going to meet Mr Right? I'm taking it you intend to start hunting when we return to England, or will you be looking around Italy for any suitable candidates?'

'Are you upset because I said what I said?'

'Why would I be upset?'

'I have no idea,' Lesley said as flippantly as she could. 'Because we both know that what we have isn't going to last.' She allowed just a fraction of a second in which he could have contradicted her, but of course he said nothing, and that hurt and reinforced for her the position she held in his life. 'And of course I'm not going to be looking around Italy for suitable candidates. I haven't forgotten why I'll be there in the first place.'

'Good,' Alessio said brusquely.

But the atmosphere between them had changed, and when he flipped open his lap-top and began working Lesley took the hint and excavated her own lap-top so that she too could begin working, even though she couldn't concentrate.

What she had said had put his nose out of joint, she decided. He wanted her to be his, to belong to him for however long he deemed it suitable, until the time came when he got bored of her and decided that it was time for her to go. For her to talk to him about dating other men would have been a blow to his masculine pride, hence his reaction. He wasn't upset, nor was he jealous of these imaginary men she would soon be seeking out. If they existed.

Her thoughts drifted and meandered until the plane began its descent. Then they were touching down at the airport in Liguria and everything vanished, except the reason why they were here in the first place.

Even the bright sunshine vanished as they stepped out and were ushered into a chauffeur-driven car to begin the journey to his house on the peninsula.

'I used to come here far more frequently in the past,'

he mused as he tried to work out the last time he had visited his coastal retreat.

'And then what happened?' It was her first time in Italy and she had to drag her eyes away from the lush green of the backdrop, the mountains that reared up to one side, the flora which was eye-wateringly exuberant.

'Life seemed to take over.' He shrugged. 'I woke up to the fact that Bianca had as little to do with this part of Italy as she possibly could and, of course, where she went, my daughter was dragged along. My interest died over a period of time and, anyway, work prohibited the sort of lengthy holidays that do this place justice.'

'Why didn't you just sell up?'

'I had no pressing reason to. Now I'm glad I hung onto the place. It may have been a bit uncomfortable had we been under the same roof as Rachel and Claudia, given the circumstances. I hadn't planned on saying anything to my mother-in-law about our arrival, but in all events I decided to spare her the shock of a surprise visit—although I've told her to say nothing to Rachel, for obvious reasons.'

'Those reasons being?'

'I can do without my teenage daughter scarpering.'

'You don't think she would, do you? Where would she go?'

'I should think she knows Italy a lot better than I do. She certainly would have friends in the area I know nothing about. I think it's fair to say that my knowledge of the people she hangs out with isn't exactly comprehensive.' But he smiled and then stared out of the window. 'I shudder to think of Claudia trying to keep control of my daughter on a permanent basis.'

The conversation lapsed. The sun was setting by the time they finally made it to his house, which they

approached from the rear and which was perched on
a hill top.

The front of the house overlooked a drop down to
the sea and the broad wooden-floored veranda, with
its deep rattan-framed sofas, was the perfect spot from
which you could just sit and watch the changing face
of the ocean.

Only when they had settled in, shown to their bedroom by a housekeeper—yet another employee keeping
a vacant house going—did Alessio inform her that he
intended visiting his mother-in-law later that evening.

'It won't be too late for her,' he said, prowling
through the bedroom and then finally moving to the
window to stare outside. He turned to look at her. In
loose-fitting trousers and a small, silky vest, she looked
spectacular. It unsettled him to think that, even with this
pressing business to conclude, she had still managed to
distract him to the point where all he could think of was
her returning to London and joining the singles scene.

He wouldn't have said that his ego was so immense
that it could be so easily bruised, but his teeth clamped
together in grim rejection of the thought of any man
touching her. Since when had he been the possessive
type, let alone jealous?

'It will also allow Rachel to sleep on everything, give
her time to put things into perspective and to come to
terms with returning with us on the next flight over.'

'You make it sound as though we'll be leaving tomorrow.' Lesley hovered by the bed, sensing his mood
and wondering whether it stemmed from parental concern at what was to come. She wanted to reach out and
comfort him but knew, with unerring instinct, that that
would be the last thing he wanted.

Yet hadn't he implied that they would be in the country for at least a week? She wondered why the rush was suddenly on to get out as quickly as possible. Did he really think that she had been using him? Had he decided that the sooner he was rid of her, the better, now that she had bucked the trend of all his other women and displayed a lack of suitable clinginess?

Pride stopped her from asking for any inconvenient explanations.

'Not that it matters when we leave,' she hastened to add. 'Would I have time to have a shower?'

'Of course. I have some work I need to get through anyway. I can use the time to do that and you can meet me downstairs in the sitting room. Unlike my country estate, you should be able to find your way around this villa without the use of a map.'

He smiled, and Lesley smiled back and muttered something suitable, but she was dismayed to feel a lump gathering at the back of her throat.

The sex between them was so hot that she would have expected him to have given her that wolfish grin of his, to have joined her in the shower, to have forgotten what they had come here for...just for a while.

Instead, he was vanishing through the door without a backward glance and she had to swallow back her bitter disappointment.

Once showered, and in a pair of faded jeans and a loose tee-shirt, she found him waiting for her in the sitting room, pacing while he jangled car keys in his pocket. The chauffeur had departed in the saloon car in which they had been ferried and she wondered how they were going to get to Claudia's villa, but there was a small four-wheel-drive jeep tucked away at the side of the house.

She had all the paperwork in a backpack which she

had slung over her shoulder. 'I hope I'm not under-dressed,' she said suddenly, looking up at him. 'I don't know how formal your mother-in-law is.'

'You're fine,' Alessio reassured her. A sudden image of her naked body flashed through his head with such sudden force that his heart seemed to skip a beat. He should have his mind one hundred per cent focused on the situation about to unravel, he told himself impatiently, instead of thinking about her and whatever life choices she decided to make. 'Your dress code isn't the issue here,' he said abruptly and Lesley nodded and turned away.

'I know that,' she returned coolly. 'I just wouldn't want to offend anyone.'

Alessio thought that that was rather shutting the door after the horse had bolted, considering she had had no trouble in offending *him*, but it was such a ridiculous thought that he swept it aside and offered a conciliatory smile.

'Don't think that I don't appreciate what you're doing,' he told her in a low voice. 'You didn't have to come here.'

'Even though you made sure I did by dangling that carrot of a fabulous new big job under my boss's nose?' She was still edgy at his dismissive attitude towards her but, when he looked at her like that, his dark eyes roving over her face, her body did its usual thing and leapt into heated response.

As if smelling that reaction, Alessio felt some of the tension leave his body and this time when he smiled it was with genuine, sexy warmth.

'I've always liked using all the tools in my box,' he murmured and Lesley shot him a fledgling grin.

His black mood had evaporated. She could sense it.

Perhaps now that they were about to leave some of his anxiety about what lay ahead was filtering away, replaced by a sense of the inevitable.

At any rate, she just wanted to enjoy this return to normality between them. For that little window when there had been tension between them, she had felt awful. She knew that she had to get a grip, had to put this little escapade into perspective.

She would give herself the remainder of what time was left in Italy and then, once they returned to the UK, whatever the outcome of what happened here, she would return to the life she had temporarily left behind. She had already laid the groundwork for a plausible excuse, one that would allow her to retreat with her dignity and pride intact.

It was time to leave this family saga behind her.

CHAPTER EIGHT

The drive to Claudia's villa took under half an hour. He told her that he hadn't been back to Portofino for a year and a half, and then it had been a flying visit, but he still seemed to remember the narrow roads effortlessly.

They arrived at a house that was twice the size of Alessio's. 'Bianca always had a flair for the flamboyant,' he said drily as he killed the engine and they both stared at an imposing villa fronted by four Romanesque columns, the middle two standing on either side of a bank of shallow steps that led to the front door. 'When we were married and she discovered that money was no object, she made it her mission to spend. As I said, though, she ended up spending very little time here—too far from the action. A peaceful life by the sea was not her idea of fun.'

Lesley wondered what it must be like to nip out at lunchtime and buy a villa by the sea for no better reason than *you could*. 'Is your mother-in-law expecting me?'

'No,' Alessio admitted. 'As far as Claudia is concerned, I am here on a mission to take my wayward daughter in hand and bring her back with me to London. I thought it best to keep the unsavoury details of this little visit to myself.' He leaned across to flip open the passenger door. 'I didn't think,' he continued, 'That

Rachel would have appreciated her grandmother knowing the ins and outs of what has been going on. Right. Let's get this over and done with.'

Lesley felt for him. Underneath the cool, composed exterior she knew that he would be feeling a certain dread at the conversation he would need to have with his daughter. He would be the Big, Bad Wolf and, for a sixteen-year-old, there would be no extenuating circumstances.

The ringing of the doorbell reverberated from the bowels of the villa. Just when Lesley thought that no one was in despite the abundance of lights on, she heard the sound of footsteps, and then the door was opening and there in front of them was a diminutive, timid looking woman in her mid-sixties: dark hair, dark, anxious eyes and a face that looked braced for an unpleasant surprise until she registered who was at the door and the harried expression broke into a beaming smile.

Lesley faded back, allowing for a rapid exchange of Italian, and only when there was a lull in the conversation did Claudia register her presence.

Despite what Alessio had said, Lesley had expected someone harder, tougher and colder. Her daughter, after all, had not come out of Alessio's telling of the story as an exemplary character, but now she could see why he had dismissed Claudia's ability to cope with Rachel.

Their arrival had been unannounced; they certainly had not been expected for supper. Alessio had been vague, Claudia told her, gripping Lesley's arm as she led them towards one of myriad rooms that comprised the ground floor of the ornately decorated house.

'I was not even sure that he would be coming at all,' she confided. 'Far less that he would be bringing a lady friend with him…'

Caught uncomfortably on the outside of a conversation she couldn't understand, Lesley could only smile weakly as Alessio fired off something in Italian and then they were entering the dining room where, evidently, dinner had been interrupted.

Standing a little behind both Claudia and Alessio, Lesley nervously looked around the room, feeling like an intruder in this strange family unit.

For a house by the coast, it was oddly furnished with ornate, dark wooden furniture, heavy drapes and a patterned rug that obscured most of the marble floor. Dominating one of the walls was a huge portrait of a striking woman with voluptuous dark good looks, wild hair falling over one shoulder and a haughty expression. Lesley assumed that it was Bianca and she could see why a boy of eighteen would have been instantly drawn to her.

The tension in the room was palpable. Claudia had bustled forward, but her movements were jerky and her smile was forced, while Alessio remained where he was, eyes narrowed, looking at the girl who had remained seated and was returning his stare with open insolence.

Rachel looked older than sixteen but then Lesley knew by now that she was only a few weeks away from her seventeenth birthday.

The tableau seemed to remain static for ages, even though it could only have been a matter of seconds. Claudia had launched into Italian and Rachel was pointedly ignoring her, although her gaze had shifted from Alessio, and now she was staring at Lesley with the concentration of an explorer spotting a new sub-species for the first time.

'And who are *you*?' She tossed her hair back, a mane of long, dark hair similar to the woman's in the portrait, although the resemblance ended there. Rachel had her father's aristocratic good looks. This was the gangly teenager whose leather mini-skirt Lesley had stealthily tried on. She reminded Lesley of the cool kids who had ruled the school as teenagers, except now a much older and more mature Lesley could see her for what she really was: a confused kid with a lot of attitude and a need to be defensive. She was scared of being hurt.

'Claudia.' Alessio turned to the older woman. 'If you would excuse us, I need to have a quiet word with my daughter.'

Claudia looked relieved and scuttled off, shutting the door quietly behind her.

Immediately Rachel launched into Italian and Alessio held up one commanding hand.

'English!'

It was the voice of complete and utter authority and his daughter glared at him, sullenly defiant but not quite brave enough to defy him.

'I'm Lesley.' Lesley moved forward into the simmering silence, not bothering to extend a hand in greeting because she knew it wouldn't be taken, instead sitting at the dining room table where she saw that Rachel had been playing a game on her phone.

'I helped to create that.' She pointed to the game with genuine pleasure. 'Three years ago.' She dumped the backpack onto the ground. 'I was seconded out to help design a website for a starter computer company and I got involved with the gaming side of things. It made a nice change. If I had only known how big that game would have become, I would have insisted on putting my name to it and then I would be getting royalties.'

Rachel automatically switched off the phone and turned it upside down.

Alessio had strolled towards his daughter and adopted the chair next to her so that she was now sandwiched between her father and Lesley.

'I know why you've come.' Rachel addressed her father in perfect, fluent English. 'And I'm not going back to England. I'm not going back to that stupid boarding school. I hate it there and I hate living with you. I'm staying here. Grandma Claudia said she's happy to have me.'

'I'm sure,' Alessio said in a measured voice, 'That you would love nothing more than to stay with your grandmother, running wild and doing whatever you want, but it is not going to happen.'

'You can't make me!'

Alessio sighed and raked his fingers through his hair. 'You're still a minor. I think you will find that I can.'

Looking between them, Lesley wondered if either realised just how alike they were: the proud jut of their chins, their stubbornness, even their mannerisms. Two halves of the same coin waiting to be aligned.

'I don't intend to have a protracted argument with you about this, Rachel. Returning to England is inevitable. We are both here because there is something else that needs to be discussed.'

He was the voice of stern authority and Lesley sighed as she reached down to the backpack and began extracting her folder, which she laid on the shiny table.

'What's that?' But her voice was hesitant under the defiance.

'A few weeks ago,' Alessio said impassively, 'I started getting emails. Lesley came to help me unravel them.'

Rachel was staring at the folder. Her face had paled and Lesley saw that she was gripping the arms of the chair. Impulsively she reached out and covered the thin, brown hand with hers and surprisingly it was allowed to remain there.

'It's thanks to me,' she said quietly, 'That all this stuff was uncovered. I'm afraid I looked through your bedroom. Your father, of course, would have rather I didn't, but it was the only way to compile the full picture.'

'You looked *through my things*?' Dark eyes were now focused accusingly on her, turned from Alessio. Lesley had become the target for Rachel's anger and confusion and Lesley breathed a little sigh of relief because, the less hostility directed at Alessio, the greater the chance of him eventually repairing his relationship with his daughter. It was worth it.

It was worth it because she loved him.

That realisation, springing out at her from nowhere, should have knocked her for six, but hadn't she already arrived that conclusion somewhere deep inside her? Hadn't she known that, underneath the arguments about lust and learning curves, stepping out of comfort zones and finding her sexuality, the simple truth of the matter was that she had been ambushed by the one thing she had never expected? It had struck her like a lightning bolt, penetrating straight through logic and common sense and obliterating her defences.

'You had no right,' Rachel was hissing.

Lesley let it wash over her and eventually the vitriol fizzled out and there was silence.

'So, tell me,' Alessio said in a voice that brooked no argument, 'About a certain Jack Perkins.'

Lesley left them after the initial setting out of the information. It was a sorry story of a lonely teenager, unhappy at boarding school, who had fallen in with the wrong crowd—or, rather, fallen in with the wrong boy. Piecing together the slips of paper and the stray emails, Lesley could only surmise that she had smoked a joint or two and then, vulnerable, knowing that she would be expelled from yet another school, she had become captive to a sixteen-year-old lad with a serious drug habit.

The finer details, she would leave for Alessio to discover. In the meantime, not quite knowing what to do with herself, she went outside and tried to get her thoughts in order.

Where did she go from here? She had always been in control of her life; she had always been proud of the fact that she knew where she was heading. She hadn't stopped for a minute to think that something as crazy as falling in love could ever derail her plans because she had always assumed that she would fall in love with someone who slotted into her life without causing too much of a ripple. She hadn't been lying when she had told Alessio that the kind of guy she imagined for herself would be someone very much like her.

How could she ever have guessed that the wrong person would come along and throw everything into chaos?

And what did she do now?

Still thinking, she felt rather than saw Alessio behind her and she turned around. Even in the darkness he had the bearing of a man carrying the weight of the world on his shoulders, and she instinctively walked towards him and wrapped her arms around his waist.

Alessio felt like he could hold onto her for ever. Wrong-footed by the intensity of that feeling, he pulled her closer and covered her mouth with his. His hand crept up underneath the tee-shirt and Lesley stepped back.

'Is sex the *only* thing you ever think about?' she

asked sharply, and she answered the question herself, providing the affirmative she knew was the death knell to any relationship they had.

He wanted sex, she wanted more—it was as simple as that. Never had the gulf between them seemed so vast. It went far beyond the differences in their backgrounds, their life experiences or their expectations. It was the very basic difference between someone who wanted love and someone who only wanted sex.

'How is Rachel?' She folded her arms, making sure to keep some space between them.

'Shaken.'

'Is that all you have to say? That she's *shaken*?'

'Are you deliberately trying to goad me into an argument?' Alessio looked at her narrowly. 'I'm frankly not in the mood to soothe whatever feathers I've accidentally ruffled.' He shook his head, annoyed with himself for venting his stress on her, but he had picked something up—something stirring under the surface—even though, for the life of him, he couldn't understand what could possibly be bugging her. She certainly hadn't spent the past hour trying and failing to get through to a wayward teenager who had sat in semi-mute silence absorbing everything that was being said to her but responding to nothing.

He was frustrated beyond endurance and he wondered if his own frustration was making him see nuances in her behaviour that weren't there.

'And I'm frankly amazed that you could talk to your daughter, have this awkward conversation, and yet have so little to report back on the subject.'

'I didn't realise that it was my duty to *report back* to you,' Alessio grated and Lesley reddened.

'Wrong choice of words.' She sighed. Here were the

cracks, she thought with a hollow sense of utter dejection. Things would go swimmingly well just so long as she could disentangle sex from love, but she was finding that she couldn't now. She spiked her fingers through her short hair and looked away from him, out towards the same black sea which his villa down the road overlooked.

She could see the way this would play out: making love would become a bittersweet experience; she would be the temporary mistress, making do, wondering when her time would be up. She suspected that that time would come very quickly once they returned to England. The refreshing, quirky novelty of bedding a woman with brains, who spoke her mind, who could navigate a computer faster than he could, would soon pall and he would begin itching to return to the unchallenging women who had been his staple diet.

Nor would he want a woman around who reminded him of the sore topic of his daughter and her misbehaviour, which had almost cost him a great deal of money.

'Would it be okay if I went to talk to her?' Lesley asked, and Alessio looked at her in surprise.

'What would you hope to achieve?'

'It might help talking to someone who isn't you.'

'Even though she sees you as the perpetrator of the "searching the bedroom" crime? I should have stepped in there and told her that that was a joint decision.'

'Why?' Lesley asked with genuine honesty. 'I guess you had enough on your plate to deal with and, besides, I will walk away from this and never see either of you again. If she pins the blame on me, then I can take it.'

Alessio's jaw hardened but he made no comment. 'She's still in the dining room,' he said. 'At least, that's where I left her. Claudia has disappeared to bed, and frankly I don't blame her. In the morning, I shall tell her that my daughter has agreed that the best thing is to return to England with me.'

'And school?'

'As yet to be decided, but it's safe to say that she won't be returning to her old stamping ground.'

'That's good.' She fidgeted, feeling his distance and knowing that, while she had been responsible for creating it, she still didn't like it. 'I won't be long,' she promised, and backed away.

Like a magnet, his presence seemed to want to pull her back towards him but she forced herself through to the dining room, little knowing what she would find.

She half-expected Rachel to have disappeared into another part of the house, but the teenager was still sitting in the same chair, staring vacantly through the window.

'I thought we might have a chat,' Lesley said, approaching her warily and pulling a chair out to sit right next to her.

'What for? Have you decided that you want to apologise for going through my belongings when *you had no right*?'

'No.'

Rachel looked at her sullenly. She switched on her mobile phone, switched it off again and rested it on the table.

'Your dad's been worried sick.'

'I'm surprised he could take the time off to be worried,' Rachel muttered, fiddling with the phone and then eventually folding her arms and looking at Lesley with unmitigated antagonism. 'This is all your fault.'

'Actually, it's got nothing to do with me. I'm only

here because of you and you're in this position because of what you did.'

'I don't have to sit here and listen to some stupid employee preach to me.' But she remained on the chair, glaring.

'And I don't have to sit here, but I want to, because I grew up without a mum and I know it can't be easy for you.'

'Oh puh…lease….' She dragged that one word out into a lengthy, disdainful, childish snort of contempt.

'Especially,' Lesley persevered, 'As Alessio—your father—isn't the easiest person in the world when it comes to touchy-feely conversations.'

'*Alessio*? Since when are you on first-name terms with my father?'

'He wants nothing more than to have a relationship with you, you know,' Lesley said quietly. She wondered if this was what love did, made you want to do your utmost to help the object of your affections, to make sure they were all right, even if you knew that they didn't return your love and would happily exit your life without much of a backward glance.

'And that's why he never bothered to get in touch when I was growing up? *Ever*?'

Lesley's heart constricted. 'Is that what you really believe?'

'It's what I was told by my mum.'

'I think you'll find that your father did his best to keep in touch, to visit… Well, you'll have to talk to him about that.'

'I'm not going to be talking to him again.'

'Why didn't you come clean with your dad, or even one of the teachers, when that boy started threatening you?' She had found a couple of crumpled notes and had quickly got the measure of a lad who had been happy to extort as much of Rachel's considerable pocket money as he could by holding it over her head that he had proof of the one joint she had smoked with him and was willing to lie to everyone that it had been more than that. When the pocket money had started running out, he must have decided to go directly to the goose that was laying the golden eggs: pay up or else he would go to the press and disclose that one of the biggest movers and shakers in the business world had a druggie teenage daughter. 'You must have been scared stiff,' she mused, half to herself.

'That's none of your business.'

Some of the aggression had left her voice. When Lesley looked at her, she saw the teenage girl who had been bullied and threatened by someone willing to take advantage of her one small error of judgement.

'Well, you dad's going to sort all of that out. He'll make the whole thing go away.' She heard the admiring warmth in her voice and cleared her throat. 'You should give him a chance.'

'And what's it to you?'

Lesley blushed.

'Oh, right.' She gave a knowing little laugh and sniffed. 'Well, I'm not about to give anyone a chance, and I don't care if he sorts that thing out or not. So. He dumped me and I had to traipse around with my mum and all her boyfriends.'

'You *knew* your mum…err…? Well, none of my business.' She stood up. 'You should give your dad a chance and at least listen to what he has to say. He tried very hard to keep in touch with you but, well, you should let him explain how that went—and you should go get some sleep.'

She exited the room, closing the door quietly behind her. Had she got through to Rachel? Who knew? It would take more than one conversation to break down some of those teenage walls, but several things had emerged.

Aside from the fact that everything was now on the table—and, whether she admitted it or not, that would have come as a huge relief to Rachel—it was clear that the girl had had no idea just how hard her father had tried to keep in touch with her, how hard he had fought to maintain contact.

And Alessio had no idea that his daughter was aware of Bianca's wild, promiscuous temperament.

Join those two things together, throw into the mix the fact that Rachel had kept a scrapbook of photos and cuttings, and Lesley suspected that an honest conversation between father and daughter would go some distance to opening the door to a proper relationship.

And if Rachel was no longer at a boarding school, but at a day school in London, they would both have the opportunity to start building a future and leaving the past behind.

She went outside to find Alessio still there and she quietly told him what she had learned during the conversation with his daughter.

'She thinks you abandoned her,' she reinforced bluntly. 'And she would have been devastated at the thought of that. It might explain why she's been such a rebel, but she's young. You're going to have to take the lead and lower your defences if you want to get through to her.'

Alessio listened, head tilted to one side, and when she had finished talking he nodded slowly and then told her in return what he intended to do to sort the small matter of a certain Jack Perkins. He had already contacted someone he trusted to supply him with information about the boy and he had enough at his disposal to pay a visit to his parents and make sure the matter was resolved quickly and efficiently, never again to rear its ugly head.

'When I'm through,' Alessio promised in a voice of steel, 'That boy will think twice before he goes near an Internet café again, never mind threatening anyone.'

Lesley believed him and she didn't doubt that Jack Perkins' life of crime was about to come crashing down around his head. It had transpired that his family was well-connected. Not only would they be horrified at what their son had done, and the drug problems he was experiencing, but his father would know that Alessio's power stretched far; if he were to be crossed again by a delinquent boy, then who knew what the repercussions would be?

The problem, Alessio assured her, would wait until he returned to the UK. It wasn't going anywhere and, whilst he could hand over the business of wrapping it up to a trusted advisor and friend, he would much rather do it himself.

'When I'm attacked,' he said softly, 'Then I prefer to retaliate using my own fists rather than relying on my bodyguards.'

Everything, Lesley thought, had been neatly wrapped up and she was certain that father and daughter would eventually find their way and become the family unit they deserved to be.

Which left her...the spectator whose purpose had been served and whose time had come to depart.

They drove in silence back to Alessio's villa. He planned on returning to his mother-in-law's the following morning and he would talk to his daughter once again.

He didn't say what that conversation would be, but Lesley knew that he had taken on board what she had said, and he would try and grope his way to some sort of mutual ground on which they could both converse.

Alessio knew that, generally speaking, the outcome to what could have been a disaster had been good.

Jack Perkins had revealed problems with his daughter that would now be addressed, and Lesley's mediation had been pretty damn fantastic. How could his daughter not have known that he had tried his hardest? He would set her straight on that. He could see that Rachel had been lost and therefore far too vulnerable in a school that had clearly allowed too much freedom. He might or might not take them to task on that.

'Thanks,' he suddenly said gruffly as they pulled up into the carport at the side of the villa. He killed the engine and looked at Lesley. 'You didn't just sort out who was behind this but you went the extra mile, and we both know, gentle bribe or no gentle bribe, you didn't have to do that.' Right now, all he wanted to do was get inside the villa, carry her upstairs to the bedroom and make love to her. Take all night making love to her. He had never felt as close to any woman.

No, Lesley thought with a tinge of bitterness, she really had had no need to go the extra mile, but she had, and it had had nothing to do with bribes, gentle or otherwise.

'We should talk,' she said after a while.

Alessio stilled. 'I thought we just had.'

Lesley hopped out of the car, slammed the door behind her and waited for him. Just then, in the car, it had felt way too intimate. Give it just a few more seconds sitting there, breathing him in, hearing that lazy, sexy drawl, and all her good intentions would have gone down the drain.

'Want to tell me what this is all about?' was the first thing he asked the second they were inside his villa. He threw the car keys on the hand-carved sideboard by the front door and led the way into the kitchen where he helped himself to a long glass of water from a bottle in the fridge. Then he sat down and watched as she took the seat furthest away from him.

'How long,' she finally asked, 'Do you plan on staying here?'

'Where is that question leading?' For the first time, he could feel quicksand underneath his feet and he didn't like it. He wished he had had something stronger to drink; a whisky would have gone down far better than a glass of water. He didn't like the way she had sat a million miles across the room from him; he didn't like the mood she had been in for the past few hours; he didn't like the way she couldn't quite seem to meet his eyes. 'Oh, for God's sake,' he muttered when she didn't say anything. 'At least until the end of the week. Rachel and I have a few things to sort out, not to mention a frank discussion of where she will go to school. There are a lot of fences to be mended and they won't be mended overnight; it'll take a few days before we can even work out where the holes are. But what has that got to do with anything?'

'I won't be staying on here with you.' She cleared her throat and took a deep breath. 'I do realise that I promised I would stay the week, but I think my job here is done, and it's time for me to return to London.'

'Your job here *is done*?' Alessio could not believe what he was hearing.

'Yes, and I just want to say that there's every chance that you and your daughter will find a happy solution to the difficulties you've been experiencing in your relationship.'

'Your job here...*is done*? So you're *heading back*?'

'I don't see the point of staying on.'

'And I don't believe I'm hearing this. What do you mean you don't *see the point of staying on*?' He point-blank refused to ask *what about us?* That was not a question that would ever pass his lips. He remembered what she had said about wanting to head back out there, get into the thick of the dating scene—now that she had used him to reintroduce her to the world of sex; now that she had overcome her insecurities, thanks to him.

Pride slammed in and he looked at her coldly.

'What we have, Alessio, isn't going anywhere. We both agreed on that, didn't we?' She could have kicked herself for the plaintive request she heard in her voice, the request begging him to contradict her. 'And I'm not interested in having a fling until we both run out of steam. Actually, probably until we get back to London. I'm not in the market for a holiday romance.'

'And what are you in the market for?' Alessio asked softly.

Lesley tilted her chin and returned his cool stare. Was she about to reveal that she was in the market for a long-term, for ever, happy-ever-after, committed relationship? Would she say that so that he could naturally assume that she was talking about *him*? Wanting that relationship *with him*? It would be the first conclusion he would reach. Women, he had told her, always seemed to want more than he was prepared to give. He would assume that she had simply joined the queue.

There was no way that she would allow her dignity to be trampled into the ground.

'Right now…' her voice was steady and controlled, giving nothing away '…all I want is to further my career. The company is still growing. There are loads of opportunities to grow with it, even perhaps to be transferred to another part of the country. I want to be there to take advantage of those opportunities.' She thought she sounded like someone trying to sell themselves at an interview, but she held her ground and her eyes remained clear and focused.

'And the career opportunities are going to disappear unless you hurry back to London as fast as you can?'

'I realise you'll probably pull that big job out from under our feet.' That thought only now struck her, as did the conclusion that she wasn't going to win employee of the week if her boss found out that she had been instrumental in losing a job that would bring hundreds of thousands of pounds to the company and extend their reach far wider than they had anticipated.

Alessio wondered whether her thirst for a rewarding career would make her change her mind about not staying on, about not continuing what they had. It revolted him to think that it might. He had never had to use leverage to get any woman into his bed and he wasn't about to start now.

Nor had he ever had to beg any woman to stay in his bed once she was there, and he certainly wasn't about to start *that* now.

'You misjudge me,' he said coldly. 'I offered that job to your boss and I am not a man who would renege on a promise, least of all over an affair that goes belly up. Your company has the job and everything that goes with it.'

Lesley lowered her eyes. He was a man of honour. She had known that. He just wasn't a man in love.

'I also think that when I decide to embark on another relationship.'

'You mean after you've launched yourself back into the singles scene.'

She shrugged, allowing him to think something she knew to be way off mark. She could think of nothing less likely than painting the town red and clubbing.

'I just feel that, if I decide to get involved with anyone, then it should be with the person who is right for me. So, I think we should call it a day for us.'

'Good luck with your search,' Alessio gritted. 'And, now that you've said your piece, I shall go and do some work downstairs. Feel free to use the bedroom where your suitcase has been put; I shall sleep in one of the other bedrooms and you can book your return flight first thing in the morning. Naturally, I will cover the cost.' He stood up and walked towards the door. 'I intend to go to Claudia's by nine tomorrow. If I don't see you before I go, have a safe flight. The money I owe you will be in your bank account by the time you land.' He nodded curtly and shut the kitchen door behind him.

This is all for the best, Lesley thought, staring at the closed door and trying to come to terms with the thought that she would probably never see him again.

It was time for her to move on…

CHAPTER NINE

LESLEY PAUSED IN front of the towering glass house and stared up and up and up. Somewhere in there, occupying three floors in what was the most expensive office block in central London, Alessio would be hard at work. At least, she hoped so. She hoped he wasn't out of the country. She didn't think she could screw up her courage and make this trip to see him a second time.

A month ago, she had walked out on him and she hadn't heard from him since. Not a word. He had duly deposited a wad of money into her account, as he had promised—far too much, considering she had bailed on their trip a day in.

How had his talk with his daughter turned out? Had they made amends, begun the protracted process of repairing their relationship? Where was she at school now?

Had he found someone else? Had he found her replacement?

For the past few weeks, those questions had churned round and round in her head, buzzing like angry hornets, growing fat on her misery until… Well, until something else had come along that was so big and so overwhelming that there was no room left in her head for those questions.

She took a deep breath and propelled her reluctant feet forward until she was standing in the foyer of the building, surrounded by a constant river of people coming and going, some in snappy suits, walking with an air of purpose; others, clearly tourists, staring around them, wondering where they should go to get to the viewing gallery or to one of the many restaurants.

In front of her a long glass-and-metal counter separated a bank of receptionists from the public. They each had a snazzy, small computer screen in front of them and they were all impeccably groomed.

She had worked out what she was going to say, having decided beforehand that it wasn't going to be easy gaining access to the great Alessio Baldini—that, in fact, he might very well refuse to see her at all. She had formulated a borderline sob story, filled with innuendo and just enough of a suggestion that, should she not be allowed up to whatever floor he occupied, he would be a very angry man.

It worked. Ten minutes after she had arrived, a lift was carrying her up to one of the top floors, from which she knew he would be able to overlook all of London. She had no idea how much the rent was on a place like this and her head spun thinking about it. She had been told that she would be met at the lift, and she was, but it was only as they were approaching his office that nerves really truly kicked in and she had to fight to keep her breathing steady and even and not to hyperventilate.

She was aware of his personal assistant asking concerned questions and she knew that she was answering those questions in a reassuring enough voice, but she felt sick to the stomach.

By the time they reached his office suite, she was close to fainting.

She didn't even know if she was doing the right thing. The decision to come here had been taken and then rejected and then taken again so many times that she had lost count.

The outer office, occupied by his personal assistant, was luxurious. In one corner, a massive semi-circular desk housed several phones and a computer terminal. Against one of the walls was a long, grey bench-like sofa that looked very uncomfortable. Against the other wall was a smooth, walnut built-in cupboard with no handles, just a bank of smooth wood.

It was an intimidating office, but not as intimidating as the massive door behind which Alessio would be waiting for her.

And waiting for her he most certainly was. He had been in the middle of a conference call when he had been buzzed by his secretary and informed that a certain Lesley Fox was downstairs in reception and should she be sent away or brought up?

Alessio had cut short his conference call without any preamble. His better self had told him to refuse her entry. Why on earth would he want to have anything further to do with a woman who had slept with him, had not denied having slept with him as part of her preparations for entering the world of hectic dating and then walked out of his life without a backward glance? Why would he engage in any further conversation with someone who had made it perfectly clear that he was not the sort of man she was looking for, even though they had slept together? Even though there had been no complaints there!

He had made sure that the money owed to her was deposited into her bank account, and had had no word from her confirming whether she had received it or not, despite the fact that he had paid her over and above the agreed amount, including paying her for time she had not worked for him at all.

The time he had wasted waiting for a phone call or text from her had infuriated him.

Not to mention the time he had wasted just *thinking* about her. She was hardly worth thinking about and yet, in the past few weeks, she had been on his mind like a background refrain he just couldn't get out of his head.

And so, when he had been called on his internal line to be told that she was there in the building, that she wanted to see him, there had been no contest in his head.

He had no idea what she could possibly want, and underwriting his curiosity was the altogether pleasant day dream that she had returned to beg for him back. Perhaps the wild and wonderful world of chatting up random men in bars and clubs had not quite lived up to expectation. Maybe having fun with the wrong guy was not quite the horror story she had first thought. Maybe she missed the sex; she had certainly seemed to enjoy every second of being touched by him.

Or, more prosaically, maybe her boss had sent her along on something to do with the job he had put their way. It made sense. She knew him. Indeed, they had landed that lucrative contract without even having to tender for it because of her. If anything needed to be discussed, her boss would naturally assume that she should be the one to do it and there would be no way that she could refuse. At least, not unless she started pouring out the details of her private life, which he knew she would never do.

He frowned, not caring for that scenario, which he immediately jettisoned so that he could focus as he waited for her on more pleasurable ones.

By the time his secretary, Claire, announced her arrival, through the internal line to which she exclusively had access, Alessio had come to the conclusion that he was only mildly curious as to the nature of her surprise visit—that he didn't care a whit what she had to say to him and that the only reason he was even allowing her entry into his office was because he was gentlemanly enough not to have her chucked out from the foyer in full view of everyone.

Still, he made her wait a while, before sitting back in his leather chair and informing Claire that his visitor could be ushered in—cool, calm and screamingly forbidding.

Lesley felt the breath catch jaggedly in her throat as she heard the door close quietly behind her. Of course, she hadn't forgotten what he looked like. How could she when his image had been imprinted in her brain with the red-hot force of a branding iron?

But nothing had prepared her for the cold depths of those dark eyes or the intimidating silence that greeted her arrival in his office.

She didn't know whether to keep standing or to confidently head for one of the leather chairs in front of his desk so that she could sit down. She certainly felt as though her legs didn't have much strength left in them.

Eventually, she only scuttled towards one of the chairs when he told her to sit, simultaneously glancing at his watch as though to remind her that, whilst she might have been offered a seat, she should make sure that she didn't get too comfortable because he didn't have a lot of time for her.

This was the guy she had fallen in love with. She knew she would have dented his pride when she had walked out on him, but still she had half-hoped that he might contact her in some way, if only to ask whether she had received the money he had deposited into her account.

Or else to fill her in on what had happened in his family drama. Surely that would have been the polite thing to do?

But not a word, and she knew that had she not arrived on his doorstep, so to speak, then she would never have seen him again. Right now, those brooding dark eyes were surveying her with all the enthusiasm of someone contemplating something the cat had inadvertently brought in.

'So,' Alessio finally drawled, tapping his rarely used fountain pen on the surface of his desk. 'To what do I owe this unexpected pleasure?' To his disgust, he couldn't help but think that she looked amazing.

He had made one half-hearted attempt to replace her with one of the women he had dated several months ago, a hot blonde with big breasts and a face that could turn heads from a mile away, but he had barely been able to stick it out for an evening in her company.

How could he when he had been too busy thinking of the woman slumped in the chair in front of him? Not in her trademark jeans this time but a neat pair of dark trousers and a snug little jacket that accentuated the long, lean lines of her body.

On cue, he felt himself begin to respond, which irritated the hell out of him.

'I'm sorry if I'm disturbing you,' Lesley managed. Now that she was here, she realised that she couldn't just drop her bombshell on him without any kind of warning.

'I'm a busy man.' He gesticulated widely and shot her a curving smile that contained no warmth. 'But never let it be said that I'm rude. An ex-lover deserves at least a few minutes of my time.'

Lesley bit her tongue and refrained from telling him that that remark in itself was the height of rudeness.

'I won't be long. How is Rachel?'

'You made this journey to talk about my daughter?'

Lesley shrugged. 'Well, I became quite involved in what was going on. I'm curious to know how things turned out in the end.'

Alessio was pretty sure that she hadn't travelled to central London and confronted him at his office just to ask one or two questions about Rachel, but he was willing to play along with the game until she revealed the true reason for showing up.

'My daughter has been…subdued since this whole business came out in the open. She returned to London without much fuss and she seems relieved that the boarding school option is now no longer on the cards. Naturally, I have had to lay down some ground rules for her—the most important of which is that I don't want to hear from anyone in the school that she's been acting up.' Except he had been far less harsh in delivering that message than it sounded.

Rachel might have been a complete idiot, led astray for reasons that were fairly understandable, but he had to accept his fair share of the blame as well. He had taken his eye off the ball.

Now, there was dialogue between them, and he had high hopes that in time that dialogue would turn into fluent conversation. Would that be asking too much?

He had certainly taken the unfortunate affair by the horns and sorted it all out, personally paying a visit to the boy's parents and outlining for them in words of one syllable what would happen if he ever had another email from the lad.

He had shied away from taking the full hard line, however, confident that the boy's parents, who had seemed decent but bewildered, would take matters in hand. They both travelled extensively and only now had it dawned on them that in their absence they had left behind a lonely young man with a drug problem that had fortunately been caught in the bud.

Rachel had not commented on the outcome, but he had been shrewd enough to see the relief on her face. She had found herself caught up in something far bigger than she had anticipated and, in the end, he had come to her rescue, although that was something he had taken care not to ram home.

'That's good.' Lesley clasped her hands together.

'So is there anything else you want? Because if that's all…' He looked at the slender column of her neck, her down-bent head, the slump of her shoulders, and wanted to ask her if she missed him.

Where the hell had *that* notion come from?

'Just one other thing.' She cleared her throat and looked at him with visible discomfort.

And, all at once, Alessio knew where she was going with this visit of hers. She wanted back in with him. She had walked away with her head held high and a load of nonsense about needing to find the right guy, wherever the hell he might be. But, having begun her search, she had obviously fast reached the conclusion that the right guy wasn't going to be as easy to pin down as she had thought and, in the absence of Mr Right, Mr Fantastic Sex would do instead.

Over his dead body.

Although, it had to be said that the thought of her

begging for him was an appealing one. He turned that pleasant fantasy over in his head and very nearly smiled.

He was no longer looking at his watch. Instead, he pushed the chair away from the desk and relaxed back, his fingers lightly linked together on his flat, hard stomach.

Should he rescue her from the awkwardness of what she wanted to say? Or should he just wait in growing silence until her eventual discomfort propelled her into speech? Both options carried their own special appeal.

Eventually, with a rueful sigh that implied that far too much of his valuable time had already been wasted, he said, shaking his head, 'Sorry. It's a little too late for you.'

Lesley looked at him in sudden confusion. She knew that this was an awkward situation. She had appeared at his office and demanded to see him, and now here she was, body as stiff as a plank of wood, sitting in mute silence while she tried to work how best to say what she had come to say. No wonder he wanted to shuffle her out as fast as he could. He must be wondering what the hell she was doing, wasting his time.

'You're—you're busy,' she stammered, roused into speech as her brain sluggishly cranked back into gear just enough to understand that he wanted her out because he had more important things to do.

Once again, she wondered whether she had been replaced. Once again, she wondered whether he had reverted to type, back to the sexy blondes with the big breasts and the big hair.

'Have you been busy?' she blurted out impulsively, almost but not quite covering her mouth with her hand in an instinctive and futile attempt to retract her words.

Alessio got her drift immediately. No matter that the

question hadn't been completed. He could tell from the heightened colour in her cheeks and her startled, embarrassed eyes that she was asking him about his sex life, and he felt a groundswell of satisfaction.

'Busy? Explain.'

'Work. You know.' When she had thought about having this conversation, about seeing him again, she had underestimated the dramatic effect he would have on her senses. In her head, she had pictured herself cool, composed—a little nervous, understandably, but strong enough to say her piece and leave.

Instead, here she was, her thoughts all over the place and her body responding to him on that deep, subterranean level that was so disconcerting. The love which she had hoped might have found a more settled place— somewhere not to the forefront—pounded through her veins like a desperate virus, destroying everything in its path and making her stumble over her words.

Not to mention she'd hoped not to ask questions that should never have left her mouth, because she could tell from the knowing look in those deep, dark eyes that he knew perfectly well what she had wanted to know when she had asked him whether he had been 'busy'.

'Work's been…work. It's always busy. Outside of work…' Alessio thought of his non-date with a non-contender for a partner and felt his hackles rise that the woman staring at him with those big, almond-shaped brown eyes had driven him into seeking out someone for company simply to try and replace the images of her he had somehow ended up storing in his head. He shrugged, letting her assume that his private life was a delicate place to which she was not invited—hilarious, considering just how much she knew about him. 'What about you?' He smoothly changed the subject. 'Have you found your perfect soul-mate as yet?'

'What did you mean when you said that it was a little too late for me?' The remark had been playing at the back of her mind and she knew that she needed him to spell it out in words of one syllable.

'If you think that you can walk back into my life because you had a bit of trouble locating Mr Right, then it's not going to happen.'

Pride. But then, what the hell was wrong with pride? He certainly had no intention of telling her the truth, which was that he was finding it hard to rid his system of her, even though she should have been no more than a blurry memory by now.

He was a man who moved on when it came to women. Always had been—never mind when it came to moving on from a woman who had dumped him!

Just thinking about that made his teeth snap together in rage.

'I don't intend walking back into your life,' Lesley replied coolly. So, now she knew where she stood. Was she still happy that she had come here? Frankly, she could still turn around and walk right back through that door but, yes, she was happy she was here, whatever the outcome.

Alessio's eyes narrowed. He noticed what he had failed to notice before—the rigid way she was sitting, as though every nerve in her body was on red-hot alert; the way she was fiddling with her fingers; the determined tilt of her chin.

'Then why are you here?' His voice was brusque and dismissive. Having lingered on the pleasant scenario of her pleading to be a part of his life once again, he was irrationally annoyed that he had misread whatever signals she had been giving off.

'I'm here because I'm pregnant.'

There. She had said it. The enormous thing that had been absorbing every minute of every day of her life since she had done that home pregnancy test over three days ago was finally out in the open.

She had skipped a period. It hadn't even occurred to her that she could be pregnant; she had forgotten all about that torn condom. She had had far too much on her mind for that little detail to surface. It was only as she'd tallied the missed period with tender breasts that she remembered the very first time they had made love...and the outcome of that had been very clear to see in the bright blue line on that little plastic stick.

She hadn't bothered to buy more, to repeat the test. Why would she do that, when in her heart she knew that the result was accurate?

She had had a couple of days to get used to the idea, to move from feeling as though she was falling into a bottomless hole to gradually accepting that, whatever the landing, she would have to deal with it; that the hole wouldn't be bottomless.

She had had time to engage her brain in beginning trying to work out how her life would change, because there was no way that she would be getting rid of this baby. And, as her brain had engaged, her emotions had followed suit and a flutter of excitement and curiosity had begun to work their way into the equation.

She was going to be a mum. She hadn't banked on that happening, and she knew that it would bring a host of problems, but she couldn't snuff out that little flutter of excitement.

Boy or girl? What would it look like? A miniature

Alessio? Certainly, a permanent reminder of the only man she knew she would ever love.

And should she tell him? If she loved him, would she ruin his life by telling him that he was going to be a father—again? Another unplanned and unwanted pregnancy. Would he think that she was trapping him, just like Bianca had, into marriage for all the wrong reasons?

Wouldn't the kindest thing be to keep silent, to let him carry on with his life? It was hardly as though he had made any attempt at all to contact her after she had left Italy! She had been a bit of fun and he had been happy enough to watch her walk away. Wouldn't the best solution be to let him remember her as a bit of fun rather than detonate a bomb that would have far-reaching and permanent ramifications he would not want?

In the end, she just couldn't bring herself to deny him the opportunity of knowing that he was going to be a father. The baby was half his and he had his rights, whatever the outcome might be.

But it was still a bomb she'd detonated, and she could see that in the way his expression changed from total puzzlement to dawning comprehension and then to shock and horror.

'I'm sorry,' she said in a clear, high voice. 'I know this is probably the last thing you were expecting.'

Alessio was finding it almost impossible to join his thoughts up. Pregnant. She was pregnant. For once he couldn't find the right words to deal with what was going through his head, to express himself. In fact, he actually couldn't find any words at all.

'It was that first time,' Lesley continued into the lengthening silence. 'Do you remember?'

'The condom split.'

'It was a one in a thousand chance.'

'The condom split and now you're pregnant.' He leant forward and raked his fingers through his hair, keeping his head lowered.

'It was no one's fault,' Lesley said, chewing her lower lip and looking at his reaction, the way he couldn't even look at her. Right now he hated her; that was clear. He was listening to the sound of his life being derailed and, whether down to a burst condom or not, he was somehow blaming her.

'I wasn't going to come here...'

That brought his head up, snapping to attention, and he looked at her in utter disbelief. 'What, you were just going to disappear with my baby inside you and not tell me about it?'

'Can you blame me?' Lesley muttered defensively. 'I know the story about how you were trapped into a loveless marriage by your last wife; I know what the consequences of that were.'

'Those consequences being...?' When Bianca had smiled smugly and told him that he was going to be a father, he had been utterly devastated. Now, strangely, the thought that this woman might have spared him devastation second time round didn't sit right. In fact, he was furious that the thought might even have crossed her mind although, in some rational part of himself, he could fully understand why. He also knew the answer to his own stupid question, although he waited for her to speak while his thoughts continued to spin and spin, as though they were in a washing machine with the speed turned high.

'No commitment,' Lesley said without bothering to dress it up. 'No one ever allowed to get too close. No woman ever thinking that she could get her foot through the door, because you were always ready to bang that door firmly shut the minute you smelled any unwanted advances in that direction. And please don't look at me as though I'm talking rubbish, Alessio. We both know I'm not. So excuse me for thinking that it might have been an idea to spare you the nightmare of…of this…'

'So you would have just disappeared?' He held onto that tangible, unappealing thought and allowed his anger to build up. 'Walked away? And then what—in sixteen years' time I would have found out that I'd fathered a child when he or she came knocking on my door asking to meet me?'

'I hadn't thought that far into the future.' She shot him a mutinous look from under her lashes. 'I looked into a future a few months away and what I saw was a man who would resent finding himself trapped again.'

'You can't speculate on what my reactions might or might not have been.'

'Well, it doesn't matter. I'm here now. I've told you. And there's something else—I want you to know straight off that I'm not asking you for anything. You know the situation and that's my duty done.' She began standing up and found that she was trembling. Alessio stared at her with open-mouthed incredulity.

'Where do you think you're going?'

'I'm leaving.' She hesitated. This was the right time to leave. She had done what she had come to do. There was no way that she intended to put any pressure on him to do anything but carry on with his precious, loveless existence, free from the responsibility of a clinging woman and an unwanted baby.

Yet his presence continued to pull her towards him like a powerful magnet.

'You're kidding!' Alessio's voice cracked with the

harshness of a whip. 'You breeze in here, tell me that you're carrying my child, and then announce that you're on your way!'

'I told you, I don't want anything from you.'

'What you want is by the by.'

'I beg your pardon?'

'It's impossible having this sort of conversation here. We need to get out, go somewhere else. My place.'

Lesley stared at him in utter horror. Was he mad? The last thing she wanted was to be cooped up with him on his turf. It was bad enough that she was in his office. Besides, where else was the conversation going to go?

Financial contributions; of course. He was a wealthy man and in possession of a muddy conscience; he would salve it by flinging money at it.

'I realise you might want to help out on the money front,' she said stiltedly. 'But, believe it or not, that's not why I came here. I can manage perfectly well on my own. I can take maternity leave and anyway, with what I do, I should be able to work from home.'

'You don't seem to be hearing me.' He stood up and noticed how she fell back.

She might want him out of her life but it wasn't going to happen. Too bad if her joyful hunt for the right guy had crashed and burned; she was having his baby and he was going to be part of her life whether she liked it or not.

The thought was not as unwelcome as he might have expected. In fact, he was proud of how easily he was beginning to take the whole thing on board.

It made sense, of course. He was older and wiser. He had mellowed over time. Now that sick feeling of having an abyss yawn open at his feet was absent.

'If you want to discuss the financial side of things,

then we can do that at a later date. Right now, I'll give you time to digest everything.'

'I've digested it. Now, sit back down.' This was not where he wanted to be. An office couldn't contain him. He felt restless, in need of moving. He wanted the space of his apartment. But there was no way she would go there with him; he was astute enough to decipher that from her dismayed reaction to the suggestion. And he wasn't going to push it.

It crossed his mind that this might have come as a bolt from the blue for him, turning his life on its axis and sending it spiralling off in directions he could never have predicted, but it would likewise have been the same for her. Yet here she was, apparently in full control. But then, hadn't he always known that there was a thread of absolute bravery and determination running through her?

And when she said that she didn't want anything from him, he knew that she meant it. This situation could not have been more different from the one in which he had found himself all those years ago.

Not that that made any difference. He was still going to be a presence in her life now whether she liked it or not.

Lesley had reluctantly sat back down and was now looking at him with a sullen lack of enthusiasm. She had expected more of an explosion of rage, in the middle of which she could have sneaked off, leaving him to calm down. He seemed to be handling the whole thing a great deal more calmly than she had expected.

'This isn't just about me contributing to the mother and baby fund,' he said, in case she had got it into her head that it might be. 'You're having my baby and I intend to be involved in this every single step of the way.'

'What are you talking about?'

'Do you really take me for a man who walks away from responsibility?'

'I'm not your ex-wife!' Lesley said tightly, fists clenched on her lap. 'I haven't come here looking for anything and you certainly don't owe me or this baby anything!'

'I'm not going to be a part-time father,' Alessio gritted. 'I was a part-time father once, not of my own choosing, and it won't happen again.'

Not once had Lesley seen the situation from that angle. Not once had she considered that he would want actual, active involvement, yet it made perfect sense. 'What are you suggesting?' she asked, bewildered and on the back foot.

'What else is there to suggest but marriage?'

For a few frozen seconds, Lesley thought that she might have misheard him, but when she looked at him his face was set, composed and unyielding.

She released a hysterical laugh that fizzled out very quickly. 'I don't believe I'm hearing this. Are you mad? Get married?'

'Why so shocked?'

'Because…' *Because you don't love me. You probably don't even like me very much right now.* 'Because having a baby isn't the right reason for two people to get married,' she said in as controlled a voice as she could muster. 'You of all people should know that! Your marriage ended in tears because you went into it for all the wrong reasons.'

'Any marriage involving my ex-wife would have ended in tears.' Alessio was finding it hard to grapple with the notion that she had laughed at his suggestion of marriage. Was she *that* intent on finding Mr Right that she couldn't bear the thought of being hitched to him? It was downright offensive! 'You're not Bianca, and you need to look at the bigger picture.' Was that overly aggressive? He didn't think so but he saw the way she stiffened and he tempered what he was going to say with a milder, more conciliatory voice. 'By which I mean that this isn't about us as individuals but about a child that didn't ask to be brought into the world. To do the best for him or her is to provide a united family.'

'To do the best for him or her is to provide two loving parents who live separately instead of two resentful ones joined in a union where there's no love lost.' Just saying those words out loud made her feel ill because what she should really have said was that there was no worse union than one in which love was given but not returned. What she could have told him was that she could predict any future where they were married, and what she could see was him eventually loathing her for being the other half of a marriage he might have initiated but which had eventually become his prison cell.

There was a lot she could have told him but instead all she said was, 'There's no way I would ever marry you.'

CHAPTER TEN

THE PAIN STARTED just after midnight. Five months before her due date. Lesley awoke, at first disorientated, then terrified when, on inspection, she realised that she was bleeding.

What did that mean? She had read something about that in one of the many books Alessio had bought for her. Right now, however, her brain had ceased to function normally. All she could think of doing was getting on her mobile phone and calling him.

She had knocked him back, had told him repeatedly that she wasn't going to marry him, yet he had continued to defy her low expectations by stealthily becoming a rock she could lean on. He was with her most evenings, totally disregarding what she had said to him about pregnancy not being an illness. He had attended the antenatal appointments with her. He had cunningly incorporated Rachel into the picture, bringing his daughter along with him many of the times he'd visited her, talking as though the future held the prospect of them all being a family, even though Lesley had been careful to steer clear of agreeing to any such sweeping statements.

What was he hoping to achieve? She didn't know. He didn't love her and not once had he claimed to.

But, bit by bit, she knew that she was beginning to rely on him—and it was never so strongly proved as now, when the sound of his deep voice over the end of the phone had the immediate effect of calming her panicked nerves.

'I should have stayed the night,' was the first thing he told her, having made it over to her house in record time.

'It wasn't necessary.' Lesley leaned back and closed her eyes. The pain had diminished but she was still in a state of shock at thinking that something might be wrong. That she might lose the baby. Tears threatened close to the surface but she pushed them away, focusing on a good outcome, despite the fact that she knew she was still bleeding.

And then something else occurred to her, a wayward thought that needled its way into her brain and took root, refusing to budge. 'I shouldn't have called you,' she said more sharply than she had intended. 'I wouldn't have if I'd thought that you were going to fret and worry.' But she hadn't thought of doing anything *but* picking up that phone to him. To a man who had suddenly become indispensable despite the fact that she was not the love of his life; despite the fact that he wouldn't be in this car here with her now if she had never visited him in his office.

She had never foreseen the way he had managed to become so ingrained into the fabric of her daily life. He brought food for her. He stocked her up with pregnancy books. He insisted they eat in when he was around because it was less hassle than going out. He had taken care of that persistent leak in the bathroom which had suddenly decided to act up.

And not once had she sat back and thought of where all this was leading.

'Of course you should have called me,' Alessio said softly. 'Why wouldn't you? This baby is mine as well. I share all the responsibilities with you.'

And share them he had, backing away from trying to foist his marriage solution onto her, even though he had been baffled at her stubborn persistence that there was no way that she was going to marry him.

Why not? He just didn't get it. They were good together. They were having a baby. Hell, he had made sure not to lay a finger on her, but he still burned to have her in his bed, and the memory of the sex they had shared still made him lose concentration in meetings. And, yes, so maybe he had mentioned once or twice that he had learnt bitter lessons from being trapped into marriage by the wrong woman for the wrong reasons, but hadn't that made his proposal even more sincere—the fact that he was willing to sidestep those unfortunate lessons and re-tread the same ground?

Why couldn't she see that?

He had stopped thinking about the possibility that she was still saving herself for Mr Right. Just going down that road made him see red.

'I hate it when you talk about responsibilities,' she snapped, looking briefly at him and then just as quickly looking away. 'And you're driving way too fast. We're going to crash.'

'I'm sticking to the speed limit. Of course I'm going to talk about responsibilities. Why shouldn't I?' Would she rather he had turned his back on her and walked away? Was that the sort of modern guy she would have preferred him to be? He hung onto his patience with difficulty, recognising that the last thing she needed was to be stressed out.

'I just want you to know,' Lesley said fiercely, 'That if anything happens to this baby…'

'Nothing is going to happen to this baby.'

'You don't know that!'

Alessio could sense her desire to have an argument with him and he had no intention of allowing her to indulge that desire. A heated row was not appropriate but he shrewdly guessed that, if he mentioned that, it would generate an even bigger row.

What the hell was wrong? Of course she was worried. So was he, frankly. But he was here with her, driving her to the hospital, fully prepared to be right there by her side, so why the need to launch into an attack?

Frustration tore into him but, like his impatience, he kept it firmly in check.

Suddenly she felt that it was extremely important that she let him know this vital thing. 'And I just want you to know that, if something does, then your duties to me are finished. You can walk away with a clear conscience, knowing that you didn't dump me when I was pregnant with your child.'

Alessio sucked in his breath sharply. Ahead, he could see the big, impersonal hospital building. He had wanted her to have private medical care during the pregnancy and for the birth of the baby, but she had flatly refused, and he had reluctantly ceded ground. If, indeed, there was anything at all amiss, that small victory would be obliterated because he would damn well make sure that she got the best medical attention there was available.

'This is not the time for this sort of conversation.' He screeched to a halt in front of the Accident and Emergency entrance but, before he killed the engine, he looked at her intently, his eyes boring into her. 'Just try and relax, my darling. I know you're probably scared stiff but I'm here for you.' He brushed her cheek lightly and the tenderness of that touch brought a lump to her throat.

'You're here for the baby, not for me,' Lesley muttered under her breath. But then any further conversation was lost as they were hurried through, suddenly caught up in a very efficient process, channelled to the right place, speeding along the quiet hospital corridors with Lesley in a wheelchair and Alessio keeping pace next to her.

There seemed to be an awful lot of people around and she clasped his hand tightly, hardly even realising that she was doing that.

'If something happens to the baby...' he bent to whisper into her ear as they headed towards the ultrasound room '...then I'm still here for you.'

An exhausting hour later, during which Lesley had had no time to think about what those whispered words meant, she finally found herself in a private room decorated with a television on a bracket against the wall and a heavy door leading, she could see, to her own en-suite bathroom.

Part of her wondered whether those whispered words had actually been uttered or had they been a fiction of her fevered imagination?

She covertly watched as he drew the curtains together and then pulled a chair so that he was on eye-level with her as she lay on the bed.

'Thank you for bringing me here, Alessio,' she said with a weak smile that ended up in a yawn.

'You're tired. But everything's going to be all right with the baby. Didn't I say?'

Lesley smiled with her eyes half-closed. The relief

was overwhelming. They had pointed out the strongly beating heart on the scan and had reassured her that rest was all that was called for. She had been planning to work from home towards the beginning of the third trimester. That would now have to be brought forward.

'You said.'

'And—and I meant what I said when we were rushing you in.'

Lesley's eyes flew open and she felt as though her heart had skipped a beat. She had not intended to remind him of what he had said, just in case she had misheard, just in case he had said what he somehow thought she wanted to hear in the depths of her anxiety over her scare.

But now his eyes held hers and she just wanted to lose herself in possibilities.

'What did you say? I can't quite...um...remember.' She looked down at her hand which had somehow found its way between his much bigger hands.

'What I should say is that there was a moment back then when it flashed through my mind—what would I do if anything happened to *you*? It scared the living daylights out of me.'

'I know you feel very responsible...with me being pregnant.' She deliberately tried to kill the shoot of hope rising inside her and tenaciously refusing to go away.

'I'm not talking about the baby. I'm talking about you.' He felt as though he was looking over the side of a very sheer cliff, but he wanted to jump; he didn't care what sort of landing he might be heading for.

So far she hadn't tried to remind him that he wasn't her type and that they weren't suited for one another. That surely had to be a good sign?

'I don't know what I'd do if anything happened to

you because you're the love of my life. No, wait, don't say a thing. Just listen to what I have to say and then, if you want me to butt out of your life, I'll do as you say. We can go down the legal route and have the papers drawn up for custody rights, and an allowance to be made for you, and I'll stop pestering you with my attention.' He took a deep breath and his eyes shifted to her mouth, then to the unappealing hospital gown which she was still wearing, and then finally they settled on their linked fingers. It seemed safer.

'I'm listening.' *The love of his life*? She just wanted to repeat that phrase over and over in her head because she didn't think she could possibly get used to hearing it.

'When you first appeared at my front door, I knew you were different to every single woman I had ever met. I knew you were sharp, feisty, outspoken. I was drawn to you, and I guess the fact that you occupied a special place of intimate knowledge about certain aspects of my private life not usually open to public view fuelled my attraction. It was as though the whole package became irresistible. You were sexy as hell without knowing it. You had brains and you had insight into me.'

Lesley almost burst out laughing at the 'sexy as hell' bit but then she remembered the way he had looked at her when they had made love, the things he had said. *She* might have had insecurities about how she looked, but she didn't doubt that his attraction had been genuine and spontaneous. Hadn't he been the one to put those insecurities to bed, after all?

'It just felt so damned right between us,' he admitted, stealing a surreptitious look at her face, and encouraged that she didn't seem to be blocking him out. 'And the more we got to know one another the better it felt. I thought it was all about the sex, but it was much bigger than that, and I just didn't see it. Maybe after Bianca I simply assumed that women could only satisfy a certain part of me before they hit my metaphorical glass ceiling and disappeared from my life. I wasn't looking for any kind of involvement and I certainly didn't bank on finding any. But involvement found me without my even realising it.'

He laughed under his breath and, when he felt the touch of her hand on his cheek, he held it in place so that he could flip it over and kiss the palm of her hand. He relaxed, but not too much.

'Thanks to you, my relationship with Rachel is the healthiest it's ever been. Thanks to you, I've discovered that there's far more to life than trying to be a father to a hostile teenager and burying myself in my work. I never stopped to question how it was that I wasn't gutted when you told me about the pregnancy. I knew I felt different this time round from when Bianca had presented me with a future of fatherhood. If I had taken the time to analyse things, I might have begun to see what had already happened. I might have seen that I had fallen hopelessly in love with you.'

All his cards were on the table and he felt good. Whatever the outcome. He carried on before she could interrupt with a pity statement about him not really being the one for her.

'And I may not cry at girlie movies or bake bread but you can take me on. I'm a good bet. I'm here for you; you know that. I'll always be here for you because I'm nothing without you. If you still don't want to marry me, or if you want to put me on probation, then I'm willing to go along because I feel I can prove to you that I can be the sort of man you want me to be.'

'Probation?' The concept was barely comprehensible.

'A period of time during which you can try me out for size.' He had never thought he would ever in a million years utter such words to any woman. But he just had and he didn't regret any of them.

'I know what the word means.' The thoughts were rushing round in her head, a mad jumble that filled every space. She wanted to fling her arms around him, kiss him on the mouth, pull him right into her, jump up and down, shout from the rooftops—all of those things at the same time.

Instead, she said in a barely audible voice, 'Why didn't you say sooner? I wish you had. I've been so miserable, because I love you so much and I thought that the last thing you needed was to be trapped into marriage to someone you never wanted to see out your days with.' She lay back and smiled with such pure joy that it took her breath away. Then she looked at him and carried on smiling, and smiling, and smiling. 'I knew I was falling for you but I knew you weren't into committed relationships.'

'I never was.'

'That should have stopped me but I just didn't see it coming. You really weren't the sort of guy I ever thought I could have fallen in love with, but who said love obeys rules? By the time I realised that I loved you, I was in so deep that the only way out for me was to run as fast as I could in the opposite direction. It was the hardest thing I ever did in my entire life but I thought that, if I stayed, my heart would be so broken that I would never recover.'

'My darling... My beautiful, unique, special darling.' He kissed her gently on the lips and had the wonderful feeling of being exactly where he was meant to be.

'Then I found out that I was pregnant, and after the

shock had worn off a bit, I felt sick at the thought of telling you—sick at the thought of knowing that you would be horrified, your worst nightmare turned into reality.'

'And here we are. So I'm asking you again, my dearest—will you marry me?'

They were married in Ireland a month before their baby was born, with all her family in attendance. Her father, her brothers and her brothers' partners all filled the small local church. And, when they retired to the hotel which they had booked into, the party was still carrying on, as he was told, in typical Irish style. And just as soon as the baby was born, he was informed, they would throw a proper bash—the alcohol wouldn't stop flowing for at least two days. Alessio had grinned and told them that he couldn't wait but that, before the baby discovered the wonders of an Irish bash, she or he would first have to discover the wonders of going on honeymoon, because they had both agreed that wherever they went their baby would come as well.

And their baby, Rose Alexandra, a little girl with his dark hair and big, dark eyes, was born without fuss, a healthy eight pounds four ounces. Rachel, who was over the moon at the prospect of having a sibling she could thoroughly spoil, could barely contain her excitement when she paid her first visit to the hospital and peered into the little tilted cot at the side of Lesley's bed.

The perfect family unit, was the thought that ran through Alessio's mind as he looked at the snapshot picture in front of him. His beautiful wife, radiant but tired after giving birth, smiling down at the baby in her arms while Rachel, the daughter he had once thought lost to him but now found, stood over them both, her dark hair falling in a curtain as she gently touched her sister's small, plump, pink cheek.

If he could have bottled this moment in time, he would have. Instead, still on cloud nine, he leaned into the little group and knew that this, finally, was what life should be all about.

* * * * *

'I can see only one way to secure their happiness...' Georgina paused, refusing to be drawn. **'And to satisfy your insatiable need for business success.'**

Santos leant forward at his desk. 'And that is?'

'You get married first, inherit the business, leaving them to enjoy a happy married life together.'

He looked at her, his handsome face set in a mask so emotionless she blinked in shock. Did this man not have any compassion in his heart?

'As you seem to have it all worked out, who do you suggest I marry?' The question came out slowly, as if he was sure he'd foiled her plan.

She took a deep breath and looked directly into his eyes. She mustn't show any nerves, any fear. He was like a predatory lion and she knew he'd smell it.

'Me.'

Rachael Thomas was born in Cheltenham, but grew up in Worcester. As a young child she loved to read and make up stories. For as long as she can remember she's wanted to be a writer. As a teenager she became an avid reader of Mills & Boon®, borrowing endless copies from her local library—a place she loved to be.

In her early twenties she moved to Wales, where she met and married her own hero—which meant embarking on the biggest learning curve of her life as she settled in to her new role as a farmer's wife. When her two children were in primary school she decided it was time to rekindle her dreams of being a writer.

It took almost seven years to realise those dreams, but along the way she's met some wonderful people, travelled to amazing places and had a fabulous time. When she entered her story into Harlequin's *So You Think You Can Write* contest she never for one moment imagined a publishing contract would be the result. Now she's thrilled to have achieved her dream, and to be writing for her favourite Mills & Boon line is the icing on the cake.

She loves to contrast her daily life on the farm by spending time creating irresistible heroes and determined heroines whose love affairs play out in glamorous settings. You can visit her website at www.rachaelthomas.co.uk

**This is Rachael's debut story—
we hope you love it as much as we do!**

A DEAL
BEFORE THE ALTAR

BY
RACHAEL THOMAS

MILLS &
BOON

Published in Great Britain 2014
by Mills & Boon, an imprint of Harlequin (UK) Limited,
Eton House, 18-24 Paradise Road, Richmond, Surrey, TW9 1SR

© 2014 Rachael Thomas

ISBN: 978-0-263-24999-6

Harlequin (UK) Limited's policy is to use papers that are natural,
renewable and recyclable products and made from wood grown in
sustainable forests. The logging and manufacturing processes conform
to the legal environmental regulations of the country of origin.

Printed and bound in Spain
by Blackprint CPI, Barcelona

A DEAL
BEFORE THE ALTAR

To my family and friends, who have supported me always
as I've pursued my dream,
and to the wonderful friendships I've made along the way.

CHAPTER ONE

GEORGINA ENTERED THE sleek luxury of the office and knew she was being watched. Her every step scrutinised by a man who was revered and feared by businessmen and women alike.

'Ms Henshaw.' His deep voice, with a hint of accent, was firm and commanding. 'I don't think I need to ask why you are here.'

He leant against his desk, arms folded across his broad chest, as if he'd already decided he didn't want to hear what she had to say. His black hair gleamed, but the intensity in his eyes nearly robbed her of the ability to speak.

'I'm sure you don't, Mr Ramirez.' She injected as much firmness into her voice as she could, determined she wouldn't be dismissed before she'd said all she had to say. 'You are, after all, the cause of the problem.'

'Am I indeed?' Santos Lopez Ramirez locked his gaze with hers and for a moment she almost lost her nerve. Almost.

She studied his face, looking for a hint of compassion, but there was nothing. His mouth was set in a firm line that highlighted the harsh angles of his cheekbones, softened only slightly by his tanned complexion. His jaw was cleanshaven, but she didn't miss the way he clenched it, as if biting back his words.

'You know you are.' She paused briefly before continuing. 'You are the one person who is preventing Emma and Carlo from doing what they want.'

'So what are you going to do about it, Ms Henshaw?'

As he raised his brows in question a flutter of nerves took flight in her stomach. But now was the time to be the woman the world thought she was—the cold and manipulative woman who took exactly what she wanted in life and discarded what she didn't.

'I will do whatever it takes to make it happen, Mr Ramirez.'

The butterflies dissipated as she thought of Emma, of all the dreams of a fairytale wedding her younger sister so often spoke about. Her own ideas of love and happiness had long since been shattered, but she wanted her sister to find that dream.

'That's a very bold statement.'

Bold. Stupid. It didn't matter what he thought. All she cared about was Emma's happiness—happiness was something neither of them had experienced much of in recent years.

'I'm a very bold woman, Mr Ramirez.'

He smiled. An indolent smile that tugged at the corners of his mouth. Her breath caught in her throat and nerves almost swarmed over her as he unfolded his arms and took a purposeful step towards her.

'I admire that in a woman.'

Tall and unyielding, he stood before her. And despite the spacious office, the wall of windows and the sparse furnishings, he dominated the room.

She stood her ground, refusing to move, to be intimidated. 'Your admiration is not the reason I'm here.'

'I don't have time for games, Ms Henshaw.'

'I have a deal to put to you, Mr Ramirez.' He couldn't

dismiss her yet. It had been hard enough getting past his secretary, and she didn't intend to waste the opportunity.

'A deal?'

'I meant what I said.' She spoke firmly, determined he should never know just how anxious she was, how desperate to achieve her aim. 'I will do whatever it takes.'

Santos took in the determined jut of the brunette's chin. She looked so arrogantly sure of herself that he wondered if she was going to start the Paso Doble right there in his office.

Lust hurtled through his body at the images such thoughts brought to mind.

'And why would you want to do that?'

Santos returned to his chair and sat down, his gaze running over her body. The charcoal skirt and jacket, although professional and businesslike, did little to disguise her womanly figure. The tantalising hint of a lace camisole beneath the jacket caught his eye, but it was the heels she wore that stole the show. Her designer leopard print heels not only spoke volumes about the real woman, but showcased the most fantastic pair of legs he'd seen in ages. He was entranced, but it was the attitude radiating from her glorious body that really intrigued him.

'Emma is my sister and I want her to be happy.'

The intensity of her gaze as she spoke only aroused his interest further.

'I'll do anything to achieve that.'

He rose from his chair, his body suddenly restless, to stand in front of the floor-to-ceiling windows of his office. He surveyed the view of London glinting in the autumn sunshine, recalling all he'd discovered about the sister of quiet and demure Emma, the woman his half-

brother Carlo was currently dating. A situation that had
thrown everything into turmoil.

This woman certainly had a reputation. Widowed
at twenty-three, and having been left a substantial fortune, she now led a socialite lifestyle and was never short
of male company. A mercenary woman, if the circumstances of her marriage were to be believed.

'And just how far are you prepared to go in the name
of sisterly love?'

Behind him he heard her intake of breath and knew
he'd touched a nerve. A stab of desire shot through him
as he imagined her sighing in pleasure as he kissed her.
Quickly he regained control. Now was not a good time
to find himself attracted to a woman—especially one
with such a tarnished and scandalous reputation. He had
a business to run. One that was a contentious issue between himself and Carlo. One he had to find a solution
to quickly. Time was running out.

'As I have already said, Mr Ramirez, I will do whatever it takes.' Her voice had a slightly husky quality to
it, which threatened to undo his control, so he remained
focused on the view of London a moment longer.

Finally he turned to face her, strode across the thick
carpet until he stood at her side, his right arm almost
touching her shoulder. He looked sideways down at her,
catching her light floral scent as he did so. Not the sort
usually favoured by a woman of her reputation—it was
soft and very feminine.

'So you agree with their plans to marry...your sister
and my brother?'

She stood firm, like a soldier on parade being in-
spected by a commanding officer. He walked slowly
round behind her, admiration building. She didn't flinch,
didn't move. His gaze was drawn to the streaks of fiery

red which entwined in her hair and again he thought of
her in his bed, hair wildly fanned out across the pillow.

'Why shouldn't they get married?'

Her words drew him sharply back. 'They are young,'
he said quietly, and walked away from her. Being close
distracted him, took his mind from the current problem
to more primal matters. 'Too young.'

'They are in love.' The words flew at him across the
room with such passion that he stopped to look at her,
wondering if she was as indifferent and in control as she
wanted him to think. He looked at her beautiful face, the
firm set of her full lips and the haughty rise of her brows.
Had he just imagined that spark of passion? Conjured it
up because of the direction his thoughts had gone? He
must have done. As she stood before him she was not
only sculpted from ice but frozen to the core.

A challenge indeed.

'And you believe in love, do you?' All through his
younger years he'd been introduced to an endless stream
of his father's girlfriends. Then as a teenager he'd watched
from the sidelines as his father had fallen under the spell
of a younger woman. The love they'd shared and later
bestowed on Carlo, his new brother, had been incompre-
hensible to him. It had done little to instil ideas of love
and happiness in him.

'About as much as you do.'

Her gaze met his, stubbornly holding it, provoking
him to deny it.

'Very perceptive, Ms Henshaw. We are, then, kindred
spirits, able to enjoy the opposite sex without the drama
of emotional attachment.'

This was always the attitude he'd adopted, and one
that had begun to feel less and less favourable. But the
idea of being so captivated by a woman, so completely

under her spell it would make a man turn his back on his son, was even less appealing.

'Put like that, then, yes, I suppose we are.'

Georgina cringed inwardly, knowing exactly what he was referring to. Was he really going to drag up her past, use it as a reason to stop his brother from marrying Emma? She wouldn't let him—not when she now knew the real reason he didn't want them to marry. She had to change his mind.

For a moment her nerves almost got the better of her. There was only one option she could think of to secure her sister's happiness, and although it didn't sit well with her she had to persuade him it was possible.

'What exactly is it you want, Ms Henshaw?'

A distanced, almost bored tone had entered his voice and she watched him stalk back to the windows, looking more like a caged animal than a businessman.

'I want to put a business proposition to you.'

He turned instantly, his interest piqued, and she stifled a smile of triumph. She was now talking his language. Business was what made this man tick. That was obvious.

'A proposition? You?'

He moved back to his desk and gestured her to sit, the muscles of his arm rippling beneath his white shirt snagging her attention. Mentally she shook herself. Getting distracted by his good looks would not help her through this. And hadn't she told herself months ago that relationships were not what she needed?

'I'd prefer to stand,' she said firmly, not missing the quirk of his dark brows.

'As you wish.'

He sat behind his desk, his dark eyes watching her. She wouldn't let him intimidate her. She had to remain as calm and detached as possible. So much was riding on her being able to deliver her proposition in an efficient, businesslike manner.

'I want my sister to be happy, and Carlo makes her happy.' She tried to keep her voice steady and devoid of emotion. This hard businessman obviously believed all that was written about her in the press. He believed she was cast from the same mould as him. 'From my understanding of the situation, there is only one solution.'

He didn't say a word, waiting for her to continue. His silence unnerved her, but she had to stay strong, remain focused.

Quickly she pressed on. 'I know about the condition in your father's will.'

'You are very well informed of my affairs, Ms Henshaw, but I fail to see what business of yours that is.'

His hard expression gave her a glimpse of the formidable businessman he was. She'd done her research on him. 'I know you have built your business up to the international concern it is today since your father passed away, and that once either you or Carlo marry the business will pass solely to that brother.' She paused, almost wanting to give up as she looked at him, his dark eyes as bleak as a starless night.

'Full marks for research,' he said, his voice as emotionless as she hoped hers was.

It had been Emma who had told her about the condition of the will. She'd sobbed for the loss of her dreams of marrying the man she loved, dreams of living happily ever after with Carlo, just because of the greed of his elder brother.

'I also know Carlo doesn't share your appetite for success. He has little or no interest in the business, wanting only to live a normal life married to my sister.'

'A *normal* life?'

She knew he was stalling, being evasive. Wouldn't she hate it if he picked apart her private affairs? But she had to carry on before she lost all confidence in her plan. For Emma she had to do it, just as she'd had to five years ago.

'A life that isn't centred on a business but one that is centred on a happy family home.' The words flowed from her with practised ease.

'And an example of that would be your own family, would it?'

She felt her eyes widen, shocked he'd brought it up. 'I see you have done your own research, Mr Ramirez, but my parents' marriage has nothing to do with Emma and Carlo.'

'I have no wish for my family name to be joined by marriage to a woman's whose mother is an alcoholic and whose father has been absent so long nobody knows where he is.'

'So it has nothing to do with your power-hungry need to take the business from Carlo by preventing this marriage?' Her heartbeat was rising and her emotions were beginning to take over. She had to remain composed.

'They have sent you here to plead their case, have they?'

He glowered at her. But her last words seemed only to have bounced off his tough exterior. She took a deep breath, wanting to appear poised before she spoke again.

He laced his long tanned fingers together in front of him on the desk in a relaxed fashion, but Georgina knew he was anything but relaxed. The firm set of his broad shoulders gave that away. He was confident, self-assured and powerful.

'On the contrary, Mr Ramirez, they have no idea I'm here and I want it to stay that way.'

One dark brow quirked up, but he said nothing.

'I can see only one way to secure their happiness...' She paused, refusing to be drawn. 'And to satisfy your insatiable need for business success.'

He leant forward at his desk. 'And that is?'

'You get married first, inherit the business, and leave them to enjoy a happy married life together.'

As he looked at her his handsome face set in a mask so emotionless she blinked in shock. Did this man not have any compassion in his heart?

'As you seem to have it all worked out, who do you suggest I marry?' The question came out slowly, as if he was sure he'd foiled her plan.

She took a deep breath and looked directly into his eyes. She mustn't show any nerves, any fear. He was like a predatory lion and she knew he'd smell it.

'Me.'

There—she'd said it. And now she had she wanted to bolt like a frightened animal. He didn't say a word. Not a trace of emotion could be seen on his face. Silence hung between them, and a tension so taut she thought it was going to snap with a crack at any moment.

Shock rocked through Santos as he listened to her ridiculous proposition. It was the last thing he'd expected to hear, but then her reputation should have given him forewarning. She already had one marriage behind her—one that had made her a very wealthy woman indeed. And if rumour was to be believed it had not been a love-match.

'Why, exactly, would I wish to get married? And to you, of all women?'

His voice was hard, his accent suddenly more pronounced. He sounded dangerous.

Briefly Santos saw pain flash across her face, saw the

curling of her manicured fingers and wished the words unsaid. Marriage was the one thing he wanted to avoid at all costs, but even though his legal team were working on a solution he had to consider the option. If he wanted to save his business, and the last five years of hard work since his father had first become ill, he might actually have to take a wife. So wouldn't this woman, who had so willingly walked into the lion's den, be the perfect choice? Costly, maybe, if her track record was anything to go by, but he could deal with that.

'It wouldn't be a marriage in the true sense of the word.'

Her words, spoken with conviction, dragged his attention back to her face.

'And what is that?'

'A marriage for love, of course—like the one your brother and my sister wish to make. A commitment for life.' Her words flowed freely, and once again he thought he heard a spark of passion.

Suspiciously he looked at her as he sat back again in his chair. 'You are not looking for love, Ms Henshaw?'

'Not at all, Mr Ramirez. I only want my sister's happiness. I will do anything to achieve that. Once they are married we can annul our marriage and go separate ways.

Santos considered this wild suggestion more seriously. Would it hurt to go along with it for now—to have another option if his legal team were unable to sort out an alternative?

'And you would want what, exactly, from this *marriage*?' His mind raced. On a business level it made perfect sense. He would finally have the security of inheriting the business he'd built up and would have done his duty by his brother, freeing Carlo of obligations he had little or no interest in.

'I want nothing from you other than our names on a marriage certificate. Once that is done we need not see each other. We just apply for an annulment.'

Her voice had hardened and his past rushed back at him. He saw the teenager who had hardly grieved for his controlling mother. Felt the pain as his father eventually remarried and moved on with a loving and kind woman whom Santos had resented. A woman who had changed his father, almost taking him away from his firstborn with the power of her love.

'I find that hard to believe. You must want something.' Experience had taught him that. Everyone wanted something. Everyone had a price.

'Nothing more than I've already stated.'

Her cool, calm words sounded believable.

Santos thought of the conditions of the will and gritted his teeth against the memory of the day he'd realised what his manipulative father had done. It seemed this attractive woman knew a lot about the will, but she didn't know it all. She hadn't mentioned the other conditions that he would have to meet before finally inheriting. It wasn't as simple as marriage.

'I require more than that. My wife, when I take one, will be a wife in every sense of the word.'

Did she really think he was going to accept her proposition meekly, without attaching his own conditions? If he had to get married he'd rather do it for business than become as vulnerable as his father had after his second marriage. There was also the matter that he was a hot-blooded male and this woman had stirred his blood the second she'd walked proudly into his office.

Santos watched as realisation dawned on her pretty face, followed by defeat. But he said nothing more. To do so now would be to show his hand. He would never

give away the fact that he actually saw her proposition
as a serious option—his back-up plan.

'I can't do that.' She gasped the words out, her face
whitening before his eyes.

'Then your very first words to me were lies.'

Part of him felt relieved. She hadn't really been serious. But another part of him, the deal-chaser, wanted
this—but on his terms. Marriage would not only secure
the business but would put a stop to the endless rounds
of parties. It would enhance his image in the business
world, giving him what appeared to be a happy marriage,
and it would mean he didn't have to get emotionally involved. Something he avoided at all costs.

She still hadn't spoken so he carried on, pushing forward his conditions, turning it completely to his advantage. 'That is the only deal I'm prepared to make.'

Georgina's heart sank. Was he seriously suggesting a
real marriage—one that would entail her being at his
side publicly *and* sleeping in his bed at night?

'We know nothing of each other.' She grabbed at the
first thing that came to mind.

'On the contrary, Georgina. I think we both know
enough.'

The use of her name sent a warm tingle down her
spine. His gaze fixed on hers so intently she felt as if he
was physically holding her captive. Her pulse-rate leapt,
then beat hard as she thought of spending the night in his
bed, of being his wife in every sense of the word.

She couldn't banish the image of him with one of his
model-like women hanging on his arm. Would such a man
as Santos Ramirez even want to be seen publicly with
her? Worse still, would he find her lacking as a lover? No,

lover wasn't the right word. Would he find her lacking as a sexual partner?

'I know that the world would never be fooled into thinking we had married for any other reason than convenience.' She clutched awkwardly at excuses as she still struggled to take in what he wanted.

'And that would be because you have already been married and widowed purely for financial gain.'

Pain lanced through her as she thought of Richard Henshaw—the man she'd married because she had been genuinely fond of him. The same man who had given her stability and security in her life for the first time ever. In that moment she hated Santos more than any other man for bringing Richard into it.

'No.' Her voice filled with entreaty. 'Because I am nothing like the type of woman you date.'

He raised a brow, and a slight smile teased at the corners of his lips. 'As far as people would know I'd have become besotted with you exactly *because* you are not like any woman I have ever dated.'

'Would you really want people to think that instead of thinking we were married in name only to keep your business?'

'I have no intention of anyone ever thinking I have married for business gain only.' He looked steadily at her. 'Especially Carlo.'

Georgina couldn't take it in. Her whole plan had been turned upside down. He'd taken complete and utter control of the situation and turned it into something she just couldn't think of doing.

'How is that achievable?'

She struggled to comprehend how Emma would ever believe she had married such a man simply because she wanted to. Not now Emma knew all about her first marriage and the reasons behind it.

'You said that nobody knows you are here—is that not true?'

'No, nobody,' she replied, trying to grasp where this was leading.

'Good,' he said, and stood up, making her feel small and insignificant as he moved around his desk to stand before her once more. 'I will host a party tomorrow evening, to which you and Emma are invited.'

'How is that going to help?' Georgina couldn't figure out where he was going with this.

He smiled. A lazy smile that did nothing to hide his amusement at the situation. 'We won't be able to leave each other alone; the attraction will be obvious to all there. Then we will spend the entire weekend together, maybe longer, after which we shall make the announcement.'

The tone of his voice had changed, giving it a warm depth, and she had the distinct impression that if he was really attracted to her she would be unable to resist. A tingle shimmied down her spine, causing her pulse-rate to leap—which had nothing to do with anxiety and everything to do with the dark and possibly dangerous man who watched her intently.

'Okay,' she said quickly, aware that her voice had become a husky whisper. She wanted to push on with her plans but hoped she could change his mind later. A real marriage surely wasn't necessary. 'We'll do it your way.'

'There was never any doubt about that, *querida*.'

CHAPTER TWO

GEORGINA'S ANXIETY LEVELS had risen tenfold since entering the hotel where Santos was having his impromptu party. Her sister, who was so excited, believing a party meant there was hope for her and Carlo to be married, had vanished from her side the moment they arrived. Georgina now felt conspicuous as she stood just inside the doorway of the hotel room.

'*Buenas noches*, Ms Henshaw.'

She looked up at Santos, her breath catching as he moved closer to her. He was immaculately dressed in a dark suit and tie, the white of his shirt enhancing his attractive tan. The smile on his lips was warm and welcoming. That same warmth reached his eyes as he took her hand. The touch of his fingers as he lightly held hers made her shiver, as if a feather had been trailed down her spine.

Speak, she told herself firmly. *Don't let his act of attraction distract you.*

'Good evening, Mr Ramirez,' she said, injecting firmness into her voice as she remembered they were not yet supposed to have met. She certainly didn't want Emma to discover what she was about to do. 'It is a pleasure to meet you at last.'

He quirked a brow, and she wondered if she'd gone too far, but around her they were already drawing speculative gazes. It seemed to Georgina that the elite of London society were here—and all at his request.

'Please, call me Santos,' he said as he lifted her hand to his lips.

Her stomach did a strange flutter as those lips brushed sensuously over the back of her hand. Stunned into silence, she was mesmerised by his dark hair as he lowered his head. The barely controlled waves of shiny black hair looked so inviting she wondered what it would feel like to run her fingers through it. Then he straightened, towering over her once more, his gaze locking with hers.

Don't go there, she warned herself, and tried to pull back her hand, but his fingers tightened on hers. A sexy smile spread across his lips and she dragged in a ragged breath, then swallowed hard. What was she doing, allowing this man to get to her?

'The pleasure is mine.' His words were deep and uneven. He didn't let her hand go, instead forcing her to stay, so that she could do nothing other than stand there. She looked into the ever darkening depths of his eyes and felt a sizzle of awareness slide over her like the slow thaw of mountain snow. Shy and flustered was something she'd never felt—but, far worse, she knew she was already out of her depth. How was she ever going to get through the evening when he turned on charm like this?

She would because she had to. She was doing this for Emma's happiness. She clutched her bag, thinking of the few essentials she'd slipped into it, knowing she wasn't going to be returning home that night.

She smiled, more to herself than anyone else, determined not to let this man's charisma knock her off balance. It was all for show, and if he could do it then so could she.

'Something is amusing you?' His fingers traced a slow,

teasing circle on the palm of her hand, making tingles race along her arm. She wanted to pull away, wanted to break the contact, yet couldn't. Somewhere deep inside her something stirred—an emotion long since locked away.

'I was merely admiring your charm.' She smiled up at him, pulling herself closer against him. It felt flirty. Dangerous. 'I'm sure women just drop at your feet.'

He laughed. A soft rumble that made her tremble. Instinctively she tried to pull her hand free. Again his fingers tightened and his eyes darkened, and for a moment her eyes locked with his. She drew in a quick breath as she saw the sparks of desire within those dark depths. Her body responded to the primal call of his as heady heat thundered around her.

'That is always my intention, *querida*.'

He smiled down at her, letting her hand go so that she felt suddenly bereft of his contact—like a ship torn from its anchor to drift in the harbour.

'Champagne?'

She blinked, not quite able to keep up with his train of thought. Glancing around her, she caught her sister's eye as she chatted with other guests, Carlo at her side. Emma looked radiant and happy, and Georgina knew there was no going back now. Just as she had done five years ago, she had to put Emma first. She'd done it once, and she could do it again, but Emma must never know.

'Champagne would be lovely,' she purred, being as flirtatious as she possibly could. Maybe a little champagne was just what she needed to boost her confidence.

With his hand in the small of her back she moved into the room, aware of the curious glances being directed their way. Santos handed her a flute of champagne, but her head was becoming light, as if she'd already had

several glasses of the bubbly liquid. She couldn't quite
believe how this handsome and powerful businessman
was able to make her feel so special, so fresh and alive.
His charm offensive was potent, making her feel unique
and, worse than that, desired. If this was how he was
going to play out their planned public scene of attraction
she would have to be careful, remind herself it was all an
act. Because right now it felt very real. And she liked it.

Santos couldn't help but watch Georgina as she sipped
her champagne. The need to act as if he were attracted
to her had gone out of the window the moment she'd entered the room. He'd heard the hush, felt the ripple of interest, and had been as mesmerised by her as every other
man in the room.

Still looking as proud and defiant as she had yesterday in his office, she'd stood framed in the doorway.
The jade silk of her dress skimmed over her body, neither revealing nor concealing her curves. A black wrap
hung loosely off her shoulders, and he'd been unable to
take his eyes off the creamy expanse of her skin, broken only by the thin jade straps. Her neck was bare of
any jewellery—something many of the women he knew
couldn't carry off.

Even if he hadn't had to go up to her and start the charade of attraction he would have wanted to. The same
kick of lust he'd felt yesterday had stirred in his veins
once again, propelling him towards her. As he'd taken
her hand, enjoying the softness of her skin, he had known
he wanted her.

'Your plan is working.' He leant down and whispered
against her hair, the fresh scent of it invading his senses,
making his pulse throb with unquenched desire.

She pulled back from him, confusion filling her eyes, her fingers clutching tightly to her glass. 'It is?'

He heard the uncertainty in her voice and had the strangest desire to stroke his fingers down her cheek. An affectionate gesture he'd never normally think of making. Just what was it about this woman that stirred something unknown deep within him?

'With your dedication to the role, how could anyone question what they are seeing?' She turned away, exchanging her empty glass for another bubble-filled one.

The brittleness of her words reminded him just who he was dealing with. Georgina Henshaw was an avaricious woman who, with one marriage already behind her, could play his game with as much detachment as he employed.

He watched her beautiful yet emotionless face as she scanned the room, her eyes finally resting on her sister. With a sternness that would have become any teacher her gaze followed Emma as she moved across the room, until she nestled herself against his brother.

Unable to stop himself from watching the loving moment, he saw how his brother looked down at Emma. Saw the open adoration in the young woman's eyes. Even as Carlo dipped his head and kissed her he couldn't avert his gaze. Whatever it was between them was so powerful he felt it from the other side of the room. Just as he had done as a youth, when Carlo's mother had first met his father, he felt excluded. It was almost as if he'd gone back in time, watching Carlo grow strong from his mother's love while he could only look on.

'They make a good couple, don't they?'

Georgina's words dragged him back from a past he rarely visited. For a moment he was disorientated.

'They don't have to marry to prove that.'

He couldn't keep the harshness from his words. Beside him Georgina stiffened, as if she was taking a step back from him. He forced his mind to more pleasant thoughts—like the way the woman at his side stirred his desires like no other.

'I hope you aren't going back on our deal, Mr Ramirez?'

He deflected her sharp-toned words with a smile. 'Santos,' he said softly, placing his arm across her shoulders and pulling her body against his, relishing the warmth of it. 'I think you should call me Santos. If you want this to work.'

He looked down into her upturned face. Her eyes darkened until they reminded him of the depths of a forest. Her full lips parted slightly and he felt the heavy tug of desire.

He wanted her.

Slowly he lowered his head and brushed his lips over hers. Her breath mingled with his, warming his mouth, and he imagined the sensation of her sighing in pleasure. This was going to be a *very* interesting night.

Briefly her lips responded. Softening beneath his. And his whole body suddenly ached for hers. It was stronger than the heady lust that usually coursed through his blood when he kissed a woman. This was potent. Vibrant and alive. It was more powerful than anything he'd known before.

Georgina's body heated as his lips touched hers, the contact so light it almost didn't happen. Involuntarily she closed her eyes as the liquid warmth of desire slid over her. She swayed closer to him, felt his arm, strong and firm, draw her closer.

She knew there and then that he had power over her. He had the ability to stir emotions she never again wanted to explore, and she would have to be on her guard.

Her fingers clutched the stem of the glass in her hand as she hardened herself against what she was feeling. This wasn't for real. This was all an act. And if she didn't keep that in mind she'd make a fool of herself, because at this moment in time she wanted nothing more than to be kissed by Santos.

Not this light, lingering kiss. After several years without experiencing the intimacy of any kiss she knew he'd awakened something deep within her. She wanted more. Her body hungered for passion. To her horror, she realised her body hungered for *him*.

But she couldn't let that happen. She had to stay in control—not just of herself, but of the situation. Never could she allow herself to become a woman so desperate for love that she'd beg a man to stay, as her mother had done to her father. In Santos she recognised the same inability to commit to a relationship her father had possessed. He would be the worst man for her to give her heart to.

No, to allow Santos to know just how easily he could stir her hidden and unexplored desires would be fatal.

She pulled away from him and looked into his smouldering eyes. He was good. Nobody could question what he was thinking right now. He looked as if he wanted to ravish her right there in the middle of the party.

A tingle raced around her at the thought and her breathing deepened. It was as if her body was working in opposition to her heart and her head, and it was winning.

She flirted back at him, ignoring the heavy ache of her limbs and the throb of desire deep inside her. 'Santos, that was...' She paused and looked beyond him into the throng of partygoers who mingled around them, looked to her sister. 'Amazing,' she finished, hoping he'd think the

husky note in her voice was part of her act and not something she had little or no control over—a reaction to him.

'Amazing, huh?'

His voice was deeper and his accent, which had only
been a hint before, much stronger. He sounded sexy. *Too*
sexy.

'Definitely. Emma looks so shocked. I'm certain
she'll believe there is something between us.' She moved
against him as she spoke, felt the firmness of his body
and tried to ignore the sizzle of electricity zipping around
hers.

'And what about you, *querida*? Do you believe it?'

He smiled down at her, pulling her just a little closer,
so that she could feel her breasts pressing against his
chest. Her breath caught in her throat and for a moment
she couldn't say a word.

Focus, she reminded herself. *Focus on why you're
even here with him.*

'I believe we look convincing.' She hated the way her
voice stammered, and to hide it lifted her chin and raised
a brow at him.

He laughed. A soft sound she felt rumbling against
her. It was all too close, too personal. She tried to step
back from him but he pressed his hand firmly into the
small of her back, bringing her hip close against him.

She gasped as she felt the hardness of his arousal, and
nerves made her heart beat wildly—so hard she could feel
the pulse in her neck throbbing. His dark eyes, smouldering with desire, met hers.

'I too am convinced.'

His voice was a harsh whisper as he spoke against
her ear, his breath blowing on her neck, making it tingle.

'I am also convinced that now would be a good time
to leave this damned party.'

She turned her head towards him, intending to speak, to try and douse the fire that had ignited between them. A fire she could never allow to burn. Her cheek touched his as he lowered his head and, following some kind of instinct she'd never before experienced, she moved until his lips were against hers.

Briefly her gaze locked with his, then her eyelids fluttered closed as the pressure of his lips met hers. The kiss was hard, demanding much more. She wound her arms around his neck, one hand still clutching her empty champagne flute, and gave herself up to the mastery of this man's kiss. Her lips and her body asked for more and he responded, making her heart thump hard.

His tongue slid into her mouth, entwining with hers. He tasted wild and untamed. She sighed, making him deepen the kiss, and he began to invade every cell of her body with a heady desire she'd never known before.

Heaven help her, she wanted this man. Wanted him in a way she hadn't known was possible.

Just when she thought she couldn't remain standing against him any longer he broke the kiss. She slid her arms down slowly from his neck and he took the glass from her hand, putting it on a nearby table. Cool air rushed around her as their bodies parted and she felt exposed, naked, as if everyone in the room would be able to see just how much her body wanted his.

Santos's gaze slid over her, just as it had done when she'd entered the room, but this time her skin sizzled. When it lingered on her breasts her knees weakened and breathing was suddenly the hardest thing to do. She was transfixed, unable to move, unable to hide from his open desire.

Around them the noise of the party slowly came back

to her and she was thankful that they were not alone. What would she have done if they were?

She'd have made a big mistake, that was what. She would have allowed passion and champagne to take over, allowed them to destroy everything, exposing emotions and leaving her vulnerable. She'd seen it with her mother, knew the consequences, and had promised herself she'd never allow that to happen to her.

'We leave now.'

His voice, though still deep and throaty, radiated total command and, afraid hers would sound weak and trembling, she nodded in agreement.

With his hand possessively in the small of her back he propelled her towards the door. Partygoers stepped aside for them. Envious glances from women came her way. The cool façade she lived behind slipped firmly back into place. She lifted her chin, smiled, and walked proudly at Santos's side.

What would they think if they knew the truth? Would they gasp in shock at the calculated plan she was acting out?

'Georgie?' Emma's voice filtered through the defensive wall she'd quickly rebuilt, despite the hum of her body.

She looked into her sister's face and saw genuine happiness. It shone from her eyes so brightly that she knew she was doing the right thing. She touched Emma's arm and gave her a secretive smile. The smile of a woman who was being swept away by the most magnetic man she'd ever met.

'I'll call you in the morning.'

Emma's smile widened and she looked from her to Santos and back again. 'Okay.' She grinned and turned to leave, obviously in a hurry to tell Carlo.

'Let's go,' Georgina said, without looking at Santos. The taste of deception was strong in her mouth.

'I like it.'

His voice purred like a big cat content to take it easy for a while. He led her out of the noise of the party into the hotel foyer. The lights were brighter—too bright—as if she was now under his spotlight. His gaze slid down her again, desire still sparking in his eyes despite the latent control in his voice.

'*What* do you like?' she questioned sharply as he began to lead her out onto the streets. She shivered against the cold autumn air.

'Georgie.'

Emma's pet name for her sounded so exotic on his lips—sexy, even. Her body heated despite the wind, which blew her hair quickly into disarray. She combed her fingers through it, gathering it at her neck, trying to prevent herself from becoming a totally dishevelled mess.

'I prefer Georgina,' she said, trying to ignore the way her body hummed as he took her hand and pulled her close against him. Was this what it was like to be protected?

Minutes later she was in the back of his chauffeur-driven car. The light from the streetlamps cast a glow around the interior and she glanced at Santos, startled to find he was watching her intently.

She looked down at her hands clasped in her lap, unable to look into the heat of his eyes.

'You are a very beautiful woman.'

Georgina tensed. This wasn't supposed to be happening. 'You can drop the act now.' Her words were stiff and she looked up at his face. The angles of his cheekbones were severe in the ever-changing light.

'I'm enjoying the role.' His deep voice seemed to ripple around the car, sending pinpricks of heat rushing over her. 'And you never know who may be listening or watching.'

Georgina glanced at the chauffeur, who appeared to be concentrating on driving. She heard Santos laugh softly and her gaze flew to meet his once more. He really was charming—but on a lethal level. Somewhere deep inside her she recognised him as the kind of man who could hurt her or, worse, destroy her. He was the same type of devil-may-care man her mother had fallen for time and time again, and exactly like her father.

'You don't really think I'll buy that, do you?' She raised a brow at him, infusing indifference into her body with each syllable.

Cool and aloof. That was the protection she needed.

'My staff are nothing but discreet,' he replied as the car came to a stop outside some very exclusive riverside apartments.

'That is a relief—but then I suppose I'm just another on a very long list as far as they are concerned.' The haughty demeanour she routinely hid behind sounded in her voice, and from the look on his face, the frown that furrowed his brow, she knew she'd scored a direct hit.

With one final look at her he got out of the car, almost instantly appearing at her door. He held out his hand for her, but the look on his face suggested he was far from happy. For a moment she was worried. Had she pushed things just a little too far, taunting him like that? A man like him was used to people pandering to his ego.

She had the sudden urge to bolt past him and run away. Reason followed swiftly. She wouldn't help her sister like that, and the shoes she was wearing certainly hadn't been created for running.

'If you want to drop this charade you can go home

now.' His voice was rough, edged with exasperation. 'But just remember, *querida,* it was your idea.'

He was right. She had started this and she would finish it—but only when she knew her sister could marry the man she loved without any implications from this power-hungry man who now stood waiting for her, looking devastatingly sexy. Did he really mean to keep this up, even in private?

For a moment she wondered if she'd already done enough. They'd been seen leaving the party together. Then she remembered Emma's smile, the hope that had shone from her eyes. Georgina realised that it didn't matter what anyone else thought, whether they believed their whirlwind romance was real. It only mattered what Emma thought. There was no way she could let her sister think that yet again she was marrying to secure her future. Emma was all she cared about.

She could do this—even if it meant continuing with the charade of attraction.

Taking his hand, she stepped out of the car and looked up at the tall modern building. She'd never given any thought to where he might live, but the clean, precise lines of this apartment block didn't surprise her.

'I suppose you have the top floor, complete with river views?'

'Very perceptive of you.'

His voice had lowered to a steely tone, interwoven with charm, and her stomach fluttered irrationally.

'It seems you *do* know something about me after all.'

Yes, I do. I know too much. I know you have an abundance of charm and the ability to break a woman's heart.

'It was merely an observation.' Georgina kept the words light as he gestured her towards the entrance of the building. She was beginning to feel disorientated by him, by his seductive tone and sexy smiles. She couldn't allow that to happen. As far as she was concerned once his name was on their marriage certificate and her sister was married all contact would be severed. She had no intention of becoming a *real* wife. Whatever motivation was behind that absurd request she would find a way out of it. She had to.

The lift doors closed on them with expensive silence and as they were taken upwards she kept her eyes straight ahead, watching the doors, not daring to look at him or at their reflection, which seemed to mock her from all sides. She could feel the intensity of his gaze, but refused to meet it. She didn't dare. He was still acting the part of an attracted and attentive man and it was beginning to stir emotions she'd long since locked away.

She almost let out a sigh of relief as the lift doors opened. The opulence of the corridor wasn't lost on her. He wrapped his arm around her, so her elbow nestled in the palm of his hand, and she moved towards the door of his apartment, a sense of dread filling her.

'Do we really need to take it this far?' The words left her in a rush, before she'd had time to consider them.

He stopped outside the white double doors to his apartment, his arm still around her, keeping her close. She looked up at him, desperate to keep calm. He mustn't know just how unnerved he made her feel.

'Yes—if you want authenticity you need to be seen leaving here tomorrow morning.' Amusement lightened his eyes before he turned to open the doors.

'We could have just stayed at the hotel…' She clutched at the idea, not daring to cross the threshold, not wanting to be alone with him—especially on his territory.

'On the contrary.' He smiled that heart-stopping smile that could very easily make her think she was the only woman he saw, the only woman he wanted. 'To bring you here gives a clear message to everyone who knows me—including my brother.'

With his arm firmly around her, he walked into the apartment. She had no choice but to go too. Her heels clicked on a marble floor and the low lighting hinted at a very sparse and masculine living space.

'I don't understand...' The words rushed out on an unsteady breath as he finally moved away from her. At least she could breathe properly, now he wasn't so close.

Dropping his keys onto a table, he took off his jacket and tossed it over the back of a large black leather sofa. Unable to keep her eyes off him, she watched as he loosened his tie and unbuttoned the top of his shirt. Dark tanned skin drew her eyes and she had to force herself to look away.

'I *never* bring a woman back to my apartment.'

The implication of his words sank in. He was giving a very clear message—not just to Carlo, but to her. He wanted the business so badly he was prepared not only to accept her proposal of marriage, but to do everything to make it look real. Even appear to cast aside his womanising reputation and ways and take her as his wife.

'I should be honoured, then,' she replied flippantly, in an attempt to hide her thoughts.

He might be able to discard the way he lived for the sake of his business, but she couldn't quite let slip the distant demeanour *she* hid behind. After all, it wasn't a business she was doing it for, but the love of her sister.

'The first woman to spend a night here with you?'

Santos flicked on a light, wanting to see Georgina's face better. In fact he wanted to see more than just her face. All evening her soft skin had teased his senses—so much so that he'd done the one thing he never did with any woman. He'd kissed her publicly. Not just a light brush of lips on lips either, but a desire-laden kiss that held a promise of passion and satisfaction.

'More champagne?'

He should just be showing her to her room, as he'd intended when he'd formed this bizarre back-up plan yesterday. But even then, as she'd stood so proudly in his office, he'd found the cocktail of icy control laced with underlying passion tempting. Too tempting. And challenging. What man could refuse such a challenge?

'No, thanks.'

Her frosty tone made it clear the ice maiden was back. He watched as she walked across the room to look down on the Thames, at the city's lights reflected in the dark water.

Ordinarily, if he'd taken a woman back to a hotel suite, he wouldn't be thinking of any kind of drink. He would be enjoying holding her, kissing her, and thinking only of satisfying their sexual needs. But this was different.

It unnerved him, but he quickly pushed the notion to the back of his mind. It was different simply because of the deal they'd struck. Never before had he spent time with a woman for any other reason than that he wanted to.

'Coffee?'

'No, thanks.' She turned to face him. 'We both know this isn't for real, and there isn't anyone here to witness anything more, so can we just say goodnight and go to bed—separately?'

He raised his brows at that last word and was rewarded with a light flush to her cheeks, giving her an air of innocence. Their eyes met and for a moment it was as if everything hung in the balance. Boldly she held his gaze.

Did she have any idea how magnificent she looked? A glacial beauty with barely concealed simmering passion.

'I'll show you to your room.'

He turned and broke the contact, but could feel her gaze following him. A sizzle of desire zipped through him and he gripped his hands into fists. If she could be so coldly in control, then so could he.

Her heels tapped rhythmically as she walked behind him, out of the vast open space of the living area and into a long corridor. He stopped outside a door, opened it, and reached in to flick on the light. 'I trust this will be comfortable for you?'

Then he looked at her face, saw a moment of hesitancy in eyes which now sparkled like rich mahogany.

'If you need anything I'll be in here.'

He pushed open the door to the master bedroom, where the lights of the city were visible for miles through large windows.

'I won't need anything,' she said, lifting her chin defiantly, and he fought hard the urge to lower his head and capture those full lips beneath his. He wanted to taste her again, to feel her mould to his body as if she were meant to be there.

'I'll see you in the morning, then,' he said, and stepped away from her—away from the temptation of her body, away from the sweet seductive scent that wrapped itself around him.

In that moment he realised he was no better than his father if he couldn't allow this woman to sleep alone. But she fired something deep within him. Something so powerful he didn't want to ignore it.

'Goodnight,' she whispered. and moved into the room, using the door to shield her glorious body from his view, apprehension clear in her eyes.

Anger simmered in his blood, mixing with unquenched desire. He was worse than his father, moving from one woman to the next. Memories from childhood, of watching an endless stream of woman enter his home, surfaced like a tidal wave. Was he now just as bad, if he couldn't walk away from Georgina?

'Goodnight.' His voice was harsh as he battled with emotions long since packed away.

Damn it all—this was a business arrangement, a means to an end. If he couldn't get out of that clause in the will legally, then he would damn well take her up on her proposition. Keeping the business was his priority. Nothing else mattered. And if Georgina had offered herself as a sacrificial lamb, so be it. Soon she would be his wife, and he had no intention of saying goodnight then.

CHAPTER THREE

GEORGINA WOKE WITH a start. Her heart thumped in her chest like a hammer as she tried to blink away the images that had haunted her sleep. Images of Santos kissing her, wanting her. Images that had heated her body as surely as if he had spent the night next to her.

She dragged in a sharp breath and looked around the room, different now the calm light of dawn was casting its glow. Her jade dress was draped over a chair, just where she'd left it, and she pulled the sheet tighter against her, feeling suddenly naked in her underwear.

Waking up in a man's bed, even if it was only the guest bed, was something she wasn't used to. She groaned at the thought of the field-day the press would have if they ever found out.

She hadn't given a thought to the morning as she'd left the party last night. Her mind had been elsewhere, thanks to Santos's charm attack.

In that moment she knew she couldn't face him. There was only one option. She had to leave now.

Could she make a quick getaway? The thought raced into her head and quickly she flung back the sheet and grabbed her dress. The silk was cool against her skin as she stepped into it and embarrassment washed over her as she thought of all those who'd know about this walk of shame.

She would be able to slip away without seeing Santos, she reassured herself, especially at this early hour.

She washed her face in the en-suite bathroom, trying hard to remove the traces of last night's make-up before applying fresh mascara and lipstick—all she'd been able to fit into her evening bag.

At the bedroom door she paused, took a deep breath, forcing her racing heart to calm before slowly opening it. Silence greeted her and she smiled, sure she was going to be able to slip away. With her bag in her hand and sandals dangling from her fingers she closed the door and padded softly along the wooden floor of the hallway, but as she entered the vast open living space the smell of strong coffee greeted her.

Her heart sank.

Someone was up.

Did Santos have a housekeeper who prepared breakfast for him? Yes, that must be it. Could she slip out without whoever it was in the kitchen noticing her? Quietly she walked across the huge room, feeling more like an intruder with every step.

'Going somewhere?'

The deep, seductive tones of Santos's voice halted her in her tracks. She turned to look at him and tried not to react to the sexy image he created in denims and a shirt. Casual suited him. But she didn't want to dwell on that now.

'Home, of course.' She kept her voice bright, as if this scenario was one she was familiar with, and met his gaze. Lifting her chin, she made every effort to appear totally indifferent to him—which was hard when he stood before her, cool and powerful, just like the man who had haunted her through her dreams last night.

'This early?' He pushed back the cuff of his shirt and looked at his watch, a small smile lingering on his lips. 'I think you have time for a coffee first. Even the most hardened shoppers aren't about *this* early on a Saturday.'

'It's not the shoppers I'm worried about,' she said with a huff of exasperation. 'Emma will be wondering where I am.'

'Precisely.'

The curt word made her blink, and despite her need to get away she walked towards him. As she did so Santos turned and headed back into the kitchen, its sleek design as contemporary as the rest of the apartment.

'How do you take your coffee?'

'This is a game to you, isn't it?' She really wasn't in the mood for pleasantries. 'We were seen leaving the party together and your housekeeper will know I've spent the night. I think that is enough, don't you?'

Santos didn't answer, and she found herself mesmerised as he poured the coffee. In her chest her heart was pounding, and a whole stream of butterflies had taken flight in her stomach.

It's not him, she told herself firmly. *It's just that you haven't been in this situation for years.* It was exactly this kind of awkward morning-after she had witnessed her mother and her lovers enduring, and exactly what she'd then gone and done herself as a naive young woman. But she'd changed, and repeating her past wasn't something she wanted to do.

'Try this.' He took her sandals and bag from her and replaced them with a steaming mug of black coffee. 'And even if my housekeeper *had* seen you—assuming she was working, that is—I would expect nothing other than her discretion.'

He smiled at her, and the butterflies in her stomach fluttered ever more wildly, but before she could respond he continued, 'At least no one will know you didn't sleep in my bed. That would really upset our plans.'

Georgina's fingers burned, and she was sure it wasn't just the mug of hot liquid in her hands. His touch, brief as it was, had jolted her with a voltage more powerful than any coffee. She took a sip—anything other than stand and look at him, fearing that if she did he would see just what an effect he was having on her.

'We left the party together. It will have to be enough.' She instilled as much courage into her voice as she could muster, which was difficult given the way her body now tingled.

Purposefully he moved past her, to place her shoes beneath a small ornamental table and drop her bag onto its glossy surface. His expression when he turned back to her was one of guarded control.

'I'm not a man to do things by half, Georgina. If I do something, I do it properly.' He stepped closer to her, the fresh scent of pine and his dark hair still slightly damp evidence that he'd recently showered.

She thought of his kiss last night at the party. The feel of his lips on hers, the way she hadn't been able to do anything other than sway towards him, and knew he was right. He didn't do anything by halves.

'I'm sure you don't, Mr Ramirez—'

'Santos,' he interrupted, his voice firm as he moved towards her.

He was coming so near she had to brace herself against the urge to move closer to him. The desire to experience his kiss just once more was almost overwhelming. She clung to her cup of coffee as if it were a lifeline.

Distance was what she needed. Distance was the safest option. She stepped back, out of the shadow of his power. She didn't know what was the matter with her—she'd never experienced this before. It was insane. Of all the men to find herself attracted to, why did it have to be *this* man? She furrowed her brow.

'If you don't use my name, who is going to believe this charade of yours?'

He raised his brow in question at her. Did he really think he could get the better of her so easily?

'You appear to be taking this far more seriously than me,' she goaded, and took another sip of her coffee before placing it on the table. Then, turning to look directly at him, she added for good measure, 'Santos.'

'You can be assured of that, *querida*.'

His lips—the ones that had set light to a trail of heady need as he'd kissed her last night—spread into a smile of the kind that made his dark eyes sparkle, full of triumph.

'I have as much to gain from this deal as you do.'

'More, if your commitment to it is anything to go by.' The words flew from her before she'd had time to think. She had to remember her goal—the sole reason she'd even approached this man in the first place. Antagonising him could put it all in jeopardy.

He didn't respond with words, but she saw his expression change. The smile still lingered, but granite hardness blazed from his eyes and he folded his arms across his chest, highlighting the breadth of his shoulders.

'Which is why I have made plans for us to go to Spain.'

Shock coursed through her body, leaving her almost gasping for air, as if she'd been plunged into a cold sea. 'Why Spain? We can stay in London. Spend the weekend here together quite easily.' She almost spluttered the last words. 'Why do we need to go to Spain?'

Santos watched as her brown eyes widened in shock and decided he preferred her with less make-up. Her soft skin looked fresh, and he fought hard against that unfamiliar urge to reach out and brush his finger against it, feel its softness.

Mentally he shook himself. The morning after was always a time to be brief—a quick goodbye had never failed him before. So why did he want to keep her here? Was it because this morning wasn't a normal morning-after? His body still fizzed with need, despite the cold shower he'd forced himself to stand under after he'd woken alone, knowing she was there, in his apartment, as untouchable as if she was the other side of the world.

'My home is in Spain, and if we are to be married I can cut through the red tape far more easily there.'

He heard her sharp intake of breath, saw her shoulders stiffen. His gaze was drawn to the way the jade silk clung to her body. She was as desirable in the morning light as she'd looked in the subdued lights of the party last night.

He wanted her more than he'd ever wanted a woman. She wasn't simpering and needy, looking for something that he couldn't give. She was strong and as in control as he was. But underneath all that he sensed a passion that would engulf him, rendering him helpless, and that was a position he would never put himself in.

He would never be as weak as his father had been.

'I still have to go home.'

She reached past him to grab her bag and sandals, her shoulder brushing his arm. He braced himself against the urge to pull her into his arms and kiss her as he had done at the party.

'A girl can't flit off for a weekend with nothing more than her Friday evening outfit.'

Her voice was light, almost lyrical. She was obviously used to loving and leaving. She also appeared used to coping in situations like this, and he'd do well to remember that. He watched as she placed her hand on the table, leaning against it as she lifted one shapely leg and slipped on a sandal. Mesmerised, he watched her fiddle with the straps, her brunette hair cascading over her shoulder, shielding her face from his view.

She straightened, taller now. His gaze locked with hers and a sizzle of something undefinable zipped between them. She blinked, long lashes breaking the connection, and bent to put on her other sandal.

'Okay,' she said softly. 'What do I need for this wedding in Spain?'

He smiled. He hadn't ever thought he would be getting married, and never in his wildest dreams had he imagined such a reluctant bride. Women usually fell over themselves to please him, and he knew if he'd asked the magic question to any one of the glamorous models he'd recently dated they would have been dragging him away.

'Your passport and birth certificate is all you need to bring. I have everything else sorted.'

'To perfection, by the sound of it. I suppose you have organised a pre-nuptial agreement?' She pushed her thick hair behind her ear and looked straight at him, her eyebrows raised in question.

Of *course* he'd arranged a pre-nuptial agreement. Any man in his position would. He'd had his legal team on it since she'd left his office on Thursday—just as they'd been finding out if it would be quicker and easier for them to marry in Spain. Her track record showed an ability to marry for financial gain and, no matter how passionately she declared sisterly love as the reason behind her proposition, he'd decided to safeguard everything.

'It would be foolish not to, *querida*.'

Her eyes sparked with burnished gold and he knew he'd hit a raw nerve. It was well known that she'd become a wealthy woman after her husband died.

'Fine.'

The word crackled between them, and her lips were firmly pressed together, as if she was holding back what she really wanted to say.

He looked at her lovely face, her lips set in a firm line of discontent, and he couldn't help himself. He reached out and brushed his fingers down her cheek. She didn't move, didn't pull away from him, just looked at him with such wide-eyed innocence he wondered if it was the same woman he'd met a few days ago.

'It will protect us both.' Her skin was so soft he wanted more. He stepped closer, the urge to kiss her stronger than anything he'd known.

'I have packing to do.'

Georgina's heart was pounding in her chest so hard she was sure he would be able to hear it. She couldn't do this. Why ever had she thought it was a good idea? Had it *really* been her only option? Offering herself to a man renowned for his ruthless business tactics.

For a moment his gaze locked with hers, the dark depths of his eyes seeming to search hers as if looking into her soul. Just when she thought she couldn't take it any more he dropped his hand and moved away from her. As he'd done a few days ago in his office he walked to the windows and stood looking out over London.

She needed to go home and think. Once she was away from him she could think of other options, but she couldn't do any of that if he was around. Just one smouldering look from his eyes made her pulse leap. She wasn't supposed to feel anything for him, but the attraction that simmered like an undercurrent waiting to snare the unsuspecting unnerved her more than anything else.

'My car will take you to your apartment and wait while you pack.'

'Wait while I pack?' She laughed. 'Have you any idea how long it takes a woman to pack for a trip abroad?' Not that she would count herself among one of those women, but she needed time alone.

'Yes.' He turned to face her. 'As a matter of fact I do—which is why you will find just about anything you need waiting for you in Spain.'

'You've thought of everything, haven't you?' She couldn't believe the calculated way he'd planned all this. From the party where they would first be seen together to the trip away to get married.

'As I said, I do things properly. I cover every eventuality. Which is why my car will wait for you.'

'I made a deal with you, Santos.' Did he actually think she was going to run away? She was made of stronger stuff than that. 'I have no intention of going back on that deal, despite the fact that you have manipulated the situation to your advantage.'

'The "situation", as you call it, will be to the advantage of both of us.'

He smiled and his eyes darkened with the promise of something she didn't want to think of.

'Of that you can be sure.'

CHAPTER FOUR

GEORGINA HAD THOUGHT the private jet was luxurious, but the villa, with its stunning sea view, was beyond anything she could have imagined. White curtains stirred in the breeze, making the sunlight dance across the marble floor. The fashionable furnishings offered every comfort possible, giving the villa the feel of a home.

She stood and looked out of the open doors, which led onto the terrace. The heat of the afternoon sun must be having an effect on her. She'd been here for several hours and still she couldn't get over the world of opulence she'd entered. But, determined that Santos shouldn't know how out of her depth she felt, she kept her awe of her new surroundings hidden.

'We'll eat out tonight.'

Santos's voice brought her thoughts back to the present as he came to stand next to her. Each time he was near, her skin sizzled and anticipation zinged down her spine, but she couldn't and wouldn't go there. This was a business deal and nothing more. She could never allow it to be more.

She dragged her gaze from the sparkling sea and turned to face him. He too had changed. He'd washed away the hours spent travelling and stood before her looking more relaxed then she'd seen him before. She couldn't help herself and allowed her gaze to linger, to take in the latent strength of his body as he walked across the room to the doors of the terrace. The commanding strength he exuded excited her and terrified her at the same time.

'Would that be to keep up the pretence of an affair?' The words slipped from her mouth with practised ease, the facetious tone one she regularly used. 'It's obvious now why we are here.'

'Is it?'

Damn him, he appeared to be laughing at her. His new, relaxed mood made him smile at her prickly demeanour. It was as if he was genuinely flirting with her, teasing her as he might one of his lovers.

'Of course it is. This area is a playground for the rich and famous, and with them come photographers and journalists, all waiting to catch the next big story. I saw them taking photos as we arrived.'

She took a deep breath and forced herself to stop talking. Allowing Santos to see how he unnerved her wasn't going to do any good at all. If he wanted to parade her around as part of the pretence then so be it.

'For a woman who dreamt up this whole idea you're very touchy about it.'

He walked out onto the terrace, where he leant his strong arms on the balustrade. Briefly she remembered how it had felt to be held in their strength, but immediately she dragged her wandering mind back. She had to keep focused. It was almost as if he knew he was distracting her. She was convinced he was using it to his advantage.

'I didn't *dream* this up.' She flung her hands wide, gesturing around them, and pushed to the back of her mind the terms he'd agreed on, hoping it would never have to go that far. 'It's you who took the idea from marriage in name only to this—this pretend love affair.'

He turned back to face her and folded his arms across his chest, the sun behind him making it difficult to read his expression. 'This is the best way.'

'Best for who?'

She realised she'd never questioned his motivation for changing things. She'd been so desperate to achieve her aims she hadn't given it a thought. Yes, she knew he wanted the business—that much Emma had told her—but why would such a wealthy and successful man, who had women falling at his feet, agree so easily to her proposition of marriage?

'It doesn't matter who it's best for. Once we are married your sister can marry Carlo and you will have got what you wanted.'

'Not forgetting what *you* want. You will inherit the business, then we can both get on with our lives. As if this had never happened.' She kept her words firm, as if she believed wholeheartedly in what she was doing. One thing she would never do was let him know her doubts.

The clinking of ice in glasses halted further conversation as drinks were brought out to them. She watched as a petite Spanish girl placed the tray on the table before she slipped away, seeming to melt into the background.

'*Exactamente, querida.*'

He turned to face her as he spoke and a shiver of apprehension slipped over her.

'It all seems too easy, Santos,' she said, realising she'd used his name without having to force herself. 'I can't believe a man like you would agree to my deal so easily. There must be something more in it for you.'

He moved away from the balustrade and came close to her. Too close. Her first reaction was to step back, but she stood her ground and met his gaze head-on, despite the pounding of her heart and the race of her pulse. Something in his expression had changed. He looked more intense, his eyes darker. She couldn't help but look into them and momentarily floundered.

'Yes, there is, *querida*.'

He stepped closer and the air seemed alive with something she'd never experienced before.

'And that is?' She feigned bravado, her words short and sharp.

'I want what we agreed in my office. A wife.'

He was serious, and from the resolute set of his mouth she knew he wasn't going to change his mind any time soon. 'We don't need to make this marriage any more difficult to get out of than need be,' she said

'I have no intention of *getting out* of it, Georgina. I want a real wife—not someone joined to me just because we signed the same bit of paper.'

His gaze dropped from her eyes and lingered on her lips and she realised she was biting her bottom lip. The tension of waiting to hear what he really wanted was too much. As was his proximity. Her stomach fluttered wildly and she had to concentrate hard just to breathe.

'But why me?' She moved backwards, but still the sizzle was there. She could feel it with every pore of her skin. *He's just trying to throw you off balance*, she assured herself, and asked again. 'Why me, Santos? Why now?'

'Because you're the only woman who's asked me to marry them at a time when I need to be married.'

When I need to be married.

Those words rang inside her head like a cathedral choir. He didn't want to be married either, and she clung to the hope that she could persuade him later that separation was the best option.

Images of being with Santos, of spending days and nights with him, filled her mind. She became dizzy at the thought of what the nights would entail. Why did he want her in that way when he could have any one of the glamorous women who always seemed to be in his life?

Santos watched as an array of emotions flashed across her beautiful face. She might well have asked him to marry her, but he could see the idea of a real marriage unsettled her as much as it did him. Marriage was something he'd never wanted to enter into. He hated that he was being forced to marry by his father's ridiculous clause in his will. As a child he'd witnessed the destructive side of marriage—a side he knew lurked beneath every claim of love.

Love. He knew it didn't exist. It was a false and misleading emotion that could destroy any man, woman or child. It was open for exploitation. Never would he allow any woman close enough to manipulate him. Marrying Georgina was a necessity, nothing more.

'Lucky I asked when I did,' she said, and flashed a smile at him. But sadness clouded her eyes.

Was she thinking of her first husband? Had she loved him? Had he been manipulated just as easily? *Fool,* he told himself, fighting back irrational emotions that were completely alien to him. *Don't even go there.*

'Lucky for who, *querida*?' He couldn't resist the urge to provoke her, wanting to see those soft brown eyes spark with passionate fire, as they had done the very first time he'd seen her in his office.

She raised her brows at him. 'For you. I could have just encouraged Emma and Carlo to slip off and get married without anyone knowing. So I suppose you have the most to lose, Santos, and you have the most at stake.'

His name sounded hard on her lips, fierce. He wanted to go over to her and kiss them until they softened, until every last drop of restraint disappeared. Instead he focused his mind, because if one thing was true it was the fact that he *did* have the most to lose.

But he'd never admit that.

'We both have things at stake, Georgina.' Impatience crept into his voice. 'So I have had a mutually beneficial agreement drawn up.'

'Ah, the pre-nup.' She picked up her drink, ice clinking, and took a sip, all the while maintaining eye contact with him. 'I'll sign whatever is needed. I made that clear when I first put the proposition to you.'

'In that case, now would be a good time to do it.'

He saw the colour drain from her face, watched as she took a deep breath and met his gaze.

'Okay.'

That one word shook with fierce determination.

'We can finalise the formalities of our arrangement so that we can enjoy a relaxed evening out.' His business mind took over, insisting he secure everything before going any further with this deal—because a deal was all it was. One struck for the mutual benefit of both parties.

A flicker of guilt flashed into his mind. A moment ago she'd looked vulnerable, outside her comfort zone, but now she was as dignified and collected as she could be. Was she trying to throw him off balance in a bid to secure more for herself out of the marriage?

'Let's just get it done, Santos.' Her shoulders straightened and the spark of fire flared in her eyes, leaving him in no doubt that she meant every word.

He nodded his approval and admired her undaunted tone. 'The agreement is on my desk.'

He led the way to his study. For the first time in his life he was anxious about the outcome of a deal. Normally he would be in total control, able to steer deals his way, manoeuvring people like pieces on a chessboard.

But not with Georgina.

It wasn't her rigid sense of purpose or her defiance that left him second-guessing where their conversations would lead, but the woman herself. The soft curves of her delicious body, the passion in her eyes in those rare unguarded moments, always left him feeling distracted.

He wanted her.

But she was unlike any woman he'd wanted before. He sensed she was different, sensed that he had to play it cool. He knew she was like a proud lioness, knew that she would show her strength, her courage, but if she needed to she'd turn and flee, leaving him in the dust. And if she did that all would be lost. She was, after all, his last hope—his legal team had made that clear—but, like a card player, he'd keep his hand close to his chest and certainly wouldn't be revealing the full extent of the will just yet...not when he was still trying to get his head around it himself.

He clenched his hands and drew in a deep breath. Damn Carlo. His rush to marry had forced him to contemplate things he never would have entertained before.

He gestured to a chair on one side of his desk, taking in the graceful way she sat and noting the guarded expression on her face. He had to handle this as he would with any deal—ruthlessly. It was the only way. Otherwise he risked being weakened by her smile or, worse, by the undercurrent of something passionate that always seemed to surround them. How much of that was an act on her part he wasn't sure, but he had to fight hard against the way his body responded to her.

'My legal team have drawn up an agreement in Spanish and English. I think it will be beneficial to us both.' He kept his voice controlled as he took his seat opposite her, then he turned the document round and slid it across the desk towards her.

Their eyes met and a simmer of tension passed between them. She lowered her lashes and with slender fingers drew the document closer to her. He watched as she read the conditions, certain she'd be happy with his generous terms.

'It looks very comprehensive.'

She glanced up, but he wasn't sure if he was relieved or not to see a teasing smile on her lips.

'You obviously feel the need to protect yourself from my scheming ways.'

'It protects us both.'

He tried unsuccessfully to keep the irritation from his voice. Did she *have* to remind him of her past right at this moment? Was she proud of all the men she'd dated within weeks of her husband passing away? He pushed to the back of his mind all he'd learnt about her after that first visit to his office.

She raised her brows at him suggestively. Damn, was the woman deliberately trying to provoke him?

He stood and walked round the desk and leant down, one hand flat on the hard polished surface, bracing his arm. With pen in hand he pointed at the contract. 'As my wife you will be entitled to a substantial allowance to do with as you please.' Her perfume invaded his senses and he realised his mistake in coming close. 'Any children the marriage produces I will stand by and support, regardless of the outcome of our marriage.'

At least he'd touched on the subject of children. It was hard to believe that he, a man who'd never wanted to be married and certainly hadn't wanted to father a child, now sought both. Or at least was being forced to.

'Children?'

There was no doubting the shock in her voice. He looked down into her eyes, bright and wide. 'Yes. Children.'

He watched her slender throat as she swallowed and guilt sliced at him. He should tell her that a child might well become essential to secure the business, but something kept him silent. He wasn't sure if it was the fear of spooking her or the still raw anger at his father for creating such a clause. He had mentioned he wanted a *real* wife—surely that left her in no doubt.

He hoped he'd never have to go that far. It went against everything he believed in. As a *mistake* himself, he did not want to bring a child into the world unless he could give it love and security. The latter wouldn't be a problem, but love…?

'Do you want children?'

Her hesitant question made him clench his jaw and he saw her gaze dart to the movement, then quickly back to his eyes.

Georgina had asked the question lightly, despite the way her stomach had flipped over and was now churning. Did he really anticipate children? From a short-term marriage contract? She hoped not. Having a child was the one thing she'd never wanted to do. It was simply out of the question.

She looked down at the contract, the words blurring on the page as she fought back memories of her childhood. A childhood that had left her scarred and certain she didn't ever want to be a mother.

'As I said, I have covered all eventualities—to protect both of us.'

She swallowed hard and looked again up into his eyes. Their dark magnetic depths almost made her lose her nerve. For one tiny second she imagined a child with eyes the same colour, but quashed the image before it could manifest itself into anything bigger.

She had to have breathing space. His closeness, the fresh scent of his aftershave and the heat of his body so close to hers, was undoing her last remnants of self-control. She needed space and she needed it now.

'You have covered everything concisely, just as I would have expected from you.' She picked up the pen and with a flowing movement of her wrist signed the contract. The pen dropped to the desk as she pushed back the chair and moved away from him—away from the power he had over her every time he came close. 'There. All signed.'

'You don't have any questions?' He looked startled by her bravado and stood straight, towering over her, leaving her no option but to stand and face him.

'Just one.'

'And that is?'

'When are we going to finalise this deal and get married?'

That isn't the question, her mind screamed as she watched a sexy smile spread across his lips. *You should have asked when you can call Emma*, she scolded herself. She wanted to tell her sister that she could start making plans for her own wedding.

'Tuesday.'

'What?' All the air seemed to have left her lungs, as

if she'd run into a brick wall, and her heart was pounding madly. 'But that is only three days away.'

'Is there a problem with that?' His voice resonated with control and his expression hardened in challenge, the smile of moments before gone.

'No…no,' she stammered, hating herself for doing so. 'I just hadn't expected it to be so soon.'

'I see no reason to delay.'

His eyes hardened and his voice was firm as he spoke and she knew deep down that he was right. The sooner they were married the better. But Tuesday felt all too soon. She hardly knew him. *You don't need to*, a nagging voice inside her chided.

'I'll need to get something to wear. I'm sure you don't want your bride turning up in jeans.' She tried at humour, but her voice sounded brisk even to her ears.

He looked at his watch. 'That wouldn't be the image I was planning—which is why I've arranged for outfits to be brought here this afternoon. Select whichever one you want, and also something suitable for this evening.'

The velvet-edged strength of his voice and sexy accent caused her to drag in a ragged breath.

'What exactly *is* this evening?' In a bid to quell the nauseous tremor in her stomach she lifted her chin, dropped her shoulders and met his gaze.

'Our engagement.'

The words were curt and she watched as he walked back around to his side of the desk. He picked up the pen, pulled the papers towards him and signed next to her signature on the contract before looking back up at her.

'I fully intend for us to be seen out this evening as if we are a couple madly in love.'

'It's only Emma who needs to think we actually *want* to get married. It doesn't matter to me what anyone else thinks—not now.' She couldn't believe he wanted to put on a public engagement.

'I don't want doubt in anyone's mind,' he said as he sat back and looked up at her. 'Least of all people I've known for many years. I want them to think that we are in love.'

'There will be people you *know* there tonight? Not family, surely?'

It was all getting too much. Everything was happening so fast—much faster than she'd ever planned. She was getting deeper and deeper all the time into something she obviously hadn't given enough thought to.

'*Sí,* my cousin.'

Amusement shone from his eyes. Was he enjoying her discomfort?

'Other than that, just friends—but they will talk. I want the right things said.'

Further conversation was halted as the maid Georgina had seen earlier knocked on the door. Spanish words flowed melodiously between her and Santos, and Georgina felt strangely excluded. Her grasp of the language was basic to say the least.

'I shall leave you now to select your wedding gown. Señora Santana is well known in Spain for her gowns.' He turned his attention back to her, the smile that the maid had been treated to still lingering on his lips.

She felt a nervous panic at the thought of being left alone, hardly able to communicate with his staff, let alone whoever was here with wedding outfits. Santos laughed. A soft throaty chuckle that was maddeningly sexy.

'Don't panic. I shall be in here. I have plenty of work to do.'

'I'm not panicking,' she flung at him, and smiled at the maid, who was waiting to show her where to go. How did he always manage to know what she was thinking?

'I'll wait for you on the balcony at seven,' he said as she left the room.

She stopped on the threshold and turned to look at him. His tall frame dominated the study so that he seemed almost dangerous. And he was, if the way she reacted to him was anything to go by.

Georgina was taken to yet another bedroom, as big and airy as the one she'd been shown to on arrival. The only difference was the rail of white and cream silk almost mockingly awaiting her approval. One glance at the dresses and Georgina knew that most of them weren't suitable.

'Buenas tardes, señora.' An immaculately dressed woman in her forties all but glided across the marble floor. 'A little too romantic maybe?' Her accent was heavy and she stroked the dresses lovingly and smiled at Georgina.

'I have already been married....' Georgina began, resenting the need to explain anything, but Señora Santana put up her hand as if to tell her to stop.

'Not a problem. Señor Ramirez has explained,' she said, and walked behind the rail of dresses to another which Georgina hadn't noticed.

Just what had Santos explained? Curiosity piqued, she followed and drew in a breath of awe. These dresses were beautiful. Bold colours of red, green and midnight-blue had been added to frills or even completely forming a bodice.

Georgina couldn't help but smile. These were more like it. A sweet, innocent bride was not the image she was going for. She trailed her fingers over the silk and chiffon. But one dress in particular caught her attention.

She took the dress from the rail and held it against

her. It was perfect. It was everything, and more, that she could want this dress to be.

'*Perfecto.*' Señora Santana smiled and urged Georgina to try it on.

Caught up in the moment, she relished the feel of silk and chiffon against her skin and looked at her image in the mirror. The dress fitted perfectly. As if it had been made for her. She slipped her foot into a dainty strappy sandal, feeling more and more like Cinderella every moment.

'You will need a veil.'

'No,' Georgina replied quickly, and glanced in the mirror at the other lady. 'No veil,' she said more gently, and smiled. She hadn't had a veil for her first wedding—hadn't even had a dress—so she saw no need to go over the top now. Especially as it was, once more, a marriage of convenience.

Señora Santana shrugged. 'Ah, I have the perfect alternative. You will see. But now we choose a dress for dinner. No?'

No was just what Georgina wanted to say. She'd gone along with the wedding dress, knowing it was part of the whole plan and necessary. Photos would almost certainly end up in the glossy magazines, whether she wanted them there or not. But a dress for this evening wasn't necessary. At least not one of this quality.

'No, the wedding dress is enough.'

The woman's eyes widened. 'But Señor Ramirez insisted. You *must* choose one.'

Finally Señora Santana's insistence had worn Georgina down and she'd selected a classic black dress, which now lay on her bed. The hours had just disappeared whilst she was trying dresses on, leaving very little time before she was to meet Santos. Now, after a quick shower, she dried her hair and applied make-up.

Why was she feeling nervous about seeing Santos again? She looked at her watch. Five minutes to seven. He would be waiting on the terrace very soon. She looked again at the dress, feeling almost like a sacrificial lamb.

But wasn't that exactly what she was?

For her sister's happiness she'd once again taken on a role she didn't want. Marrying Richard had been to put Emma through school and a roof over their heads. It had been his suggestion, and even to this day she couldn't believe a man had done that for her. She'd been on tenterhooks during all the three years they were married, just waiting for him to leave her. But she'd never expected him to leave her the way he had. As a widow. She'd known he was ill—but not that ill.

With a heavy heart she picked up the dress, stepped into it. For a moment the zip eluded her and it took several minutes of contortions to pull it up. Flustered by her efforts, she slipped on the new pair of shoes insisted upon by Señora Santana and left the bedroom, her heels sounding loud on the marble.

CHAPTER FIVE

SANTOS WAS LOOKING out at the sea, dressed in a dark suit, as she approached the balcony. When he turned and his gaze met hers her breath caught in her throat. It wasn't right that a man could be so sexy. The cloth of his suit had been cut with precision, emphasising his broad shoulders and strong thighs to perfection.

She swallowed hard, desperate to calm her racing heartbeat. If she carried on like this there wouldn't be any need for pretence. Her attraction to him was becoming stronger, and if he turned on the charm as he had at the party she'd be lost. Worse still, if he kissed her again she didn't think she'd be able to resist him.

'You look beautiful,' he said, his voice deep, with a husky edge to it. 'Exactly what I had in mind.'

Well, if that didn't serve as a reminder that it was all an act, then nothing would.

'I'm glad it meets with your approval,' she said tartly and, desperate to hide her confusion, walked past him to the table, selecting a drink from those prepared. Anger fizzed in her veins at the thought of the way he made her feel: light-headed and soft one minute, then short and sharp the next. In a bid to rein in her rising and very mixed emotions she all but downed her drink in one go.

'Steady, *querida*.' He smiled. A mocking smile. As if he knew her turmoil. 'That drink is pretty potent.'

She looked at the almost empty glass. The remains of the liquid looked more like a soft drink, but its effect on her head was already clear. Whatever was she trying to do to herself? She put the glass down and turned to look at him, holding her hair back as the sea breeze toyed with it just as he was toying with her.

'If you are ready shall we go?'

He didn't wait for her to answer, but placed his hand in the small of her back, its heat scorching through the silk of her dress, and all but propelled her towards the door. Outside, a sleek, gleaming sports car waited, fiery red. Exactly what she'd imagined him driving.

'Suits you,' she said in a cavalier tone, and dropped down into the low seat as he stood by the open door.

He raised his brows and smiled at her. '*Gracias*.'

When Santos climbed in beside her she became all too aware of just how close she was to him. His tanned fingers pulled the gearstick backwards as the car growled into life. She couldn't help but notice that the space beneath the steering wheel seemed almost too compact for his powerful thighs.

A small but insistent fire sparked to life deep inside her as she watched him drive. Each move he made sent a shiver of awareness over her and she bit down hard on her lip against the new wave of emotions that assailed her. She couldn't be falling for him—she *couldn't*.

'Is it far?' Nerves made her voice quiver as she finally acknowledged the attraction she felt for him, and he glanced across at her before returning his attention to the road ahead.

'No, but arriving in style will attract the attention we need.'

'Attention?' Her mind was scrambled as she looked at his profile. The shadow of stubble only added to the sexy appeal he emanated.

'How else is the world going to know we are engaged?' He glanced across at her again, his gaze meeting hers briefly before returning to the task of driving. 'This is what you wanted. Puerto Banus is a renowned favourite of the rich and famous, and with them come the press photographers, hungry for gossip.'

Now she understood his insistence on dressing for dinner. This was Act Two. The next part of their public courtship, played out to perfection. It was time to retreat behind her public persona.

'And tonight, *querida*, we shall give them something to gossip about.'

His voice was laden with promise and as the fire rose higher inside her she looked away.

The car growled into the small harbour town and Georgina couldn't help but take it all in. Cars as sleek and powerful as Santos's lined the narrow streets, parked outside global designer shops. Yachts that looked more like floating palaces were moored all around the harbour, many with lights glinting and parties in full swing on board.

This was most definitely a playground for the wealthy.

Santos parked the car, expertly manoeuvring it into a space in front of one of the bigger yachts. He switched off the engine and silence seemed to cloak them. The leather seat crunched as he turned to face her.

'You look absolutely stunning tonight.' He reached up and pushed her hair back from her face and she trembled.

She didn't say anything. She couldn't. All she could do was look into the mesmerising depths of his eyes.

'You are playing your part well—so well even I'm convinced.'

His voice was a husky whisper and she wished he wouldn't slide his fingers through her hair like that.

'Convinced of what?' She forced the words out, alarmed at the throaty sound of her voice.

'The attraction between us…'

He moved a little closer and she wondered if he was going to kiss her. She wanted him to, but knew it would be her undoing. Then, before she even had a chance to think, his lips claimed hers. Try as she might she couldn't stop her eyes from closing, couldn't help reaching up to touch his cheek, feeling the slight stubble against her fingertips. She was attracted to him, despite all she'd promised herself, and he must never know. That would be to show her weakness. Give him all the power. She'd seen it before.

She pulled back a little from him, her lips still very close to his, and opened her eyes. 'I'm a brilliant actress,' she whispered as her fingers smoothed once more across his face.

The sound that came from him resembled a growl as his hand caught and held hers. 'Don't take your role too far, *querida*. I might just go past the need to act.'

For a moment she sat transfixed by the tension that hung between them. The promised threat of his words was not lost on her. Did her really want her? Did he find himself struggling against the same raw need she was fighting right now?

'It's showtime, Georgina.' His words were firm and sharp as he pulled away from her and got out of the car.

She watched him walk around the front of it, relaxed but masterful. Obviously she didn't have the same effect on him—didn't scramble his emotions until he couldn't think straight.

Okay, showtime it is, she thought as she got out of the

car and walked with him towards the busy street lined with restaurants. She could do this—even if it meant putting on the biggest show of her life.

Suddenly a man's shouts caught her attention and a waiter from one restaurant came out to greet him, hugging Santos and then stepping back to cast an enquiring look her way.

'Georgina, this is my cousin Raul—owner of this restaurant and at our bidding for this evening.'

She felt suddenly shy beneath the man's gaze. He took her hand and with the same charm Santos possessed kissed it. 'I can see why my cousin is so entranced.'

To her horror she blushed, but managed to smile back at him. 'What more could a girl ask for?' She raised her brows, made her voice light and melodious, even a little flirty.

Raul laughed and after a brief look of shock Santos did too. Then he smiled at Georgina, a dangerous light in his eyes.

'Raul, do you have the table I requested?'

'*Sí,*' Raul replied, and continued in Spanish.

Santos put his arm around her shoulders, pulling her close as he followed his cousin to their table. It was private, and candles fluttered in the evening breeze. The sea could be heard lapping gently onto the shore close by.

It was perfectly romantic.

The whole meal was. Each course was divine and all the while Santos exuded what she was fast becoming aware was his lethal charm. She smiled, played her part all through dinner, but reality was beginning to blur. She sipped her wine and looked out at the sea, where the setting sun cast an orange glow across the rippling surface.

'Georgie?'

Her attention swung back to Santos when she heard her

name on his lips. His voice sounded hoarse, as if he was choked with emotion. Oh, he was good at this, she thought, and smiled at him. He'd never used her pet name before.

'Will you marry me?'

'What?' she gasped as he slid a small velvet box across the table. *Calm down. It's probably for his cousin's benefit.*

'Will you make me the happiest man alive and marry me?'

His dark eyes were watching her intently. When she looked into them she thought she saw the same desire she'd seen at the party, the same simmering passion. Just as she'd thought she'd seen it earlier, when they were in the car. But that couldn't be, could it?

She reached for the box, aware of the role she had to play, but he caught her hand in his. The heat of his touch was almost too much.

'Marry me?'

'Yes.' Her whole body quivered, but she couldn't lower her gaze, couldn't break that tenuous connection. 'Yes, I'll marry you.'

Slowly he let her hand go, opened the box and pulled out a glittering diamond ring. As he slid it onto her finger the candlelight made it sparkle, bringing it to life. He lifted her hand to his lips, his gaze holding hers captive, and kissed her fingers.

This was what it would really feel like, she thought as she looked into his dark eyes. This was be the closest she'd ever come to having a real proposal.

Applause erupted around them, making her jump. She hadn't realised they were being watched, and neither had Santos. Even he looked taken aback. She laughed, unable to help herself, and the tension of the moment slipped away as the other diners returned their attention to their meals.

'Let's go,' he said in a throaty growl, sounding as if he really couldn't wait to get her home. Something indefinable skittered over her, making her tummy somersault and her breath tighten in her chest.

Don't do this to yourself. You are just a means to an end. He doesn't really want you.

It was dark as they walked back along the street. Yachts were lit up, giving everything a magical appeal. The warm breeze on her skin felt wonderful, but not as wonderful as Santos's arm about her waist, pulling her against his magnificent body. She savoured the moment, stored it for later. The champagne she'd drunk was making it easier to enjoy being with him like this and easier to let go of her usual anxiety. This wonderful feeling was going to have to last her a lifetime.

By the car Santos stopped. Instinctively she looked up at him, then couldn't help herself as she reached up and kissed his lips. His response was gentle at first, setting her body alight. The fire was fuelled further by his hands sliding down her back, pulling her so very close to him. Whatever it was that had simmered between them at the party was now well and truly alight. As her hips pressed against his aroused body she knew he wanted her. Was it so wrong to give in to it? To enjoy it for what it was? A passing attraction.

'Santos,' she murmured against his lips.

It was all the encouragement he needed and he deepened the kiss, plunging his tongue into her mouth as she sighed in pleasure.

Need rocketed through her body and she almost became incapable of thought as he stepped closer, forcing her back against the side of his car, pressing hard against her and stoking the fire deep within her body. Unleashing an insatiable need for him.

His hand slid down her side, over her hip and down to her bottom. He pulled her hard against him and raw desire tore through her, leaving her gasping against his lips as her arms clung around his neck. It was mind-blowing. She'd never known anything like it.

A flash lit up the world for a second—or so it seemed to Georgina. But in that second she regained her breath, and the control she'd so very nearly lost. She turned her face to the opportunist photographer, knowing he was just what she needed to bring her feet firmly back to the ground.

Beside her Santos spoke in Spanish, his voice thick and hoarse as the photographer snapped another photo. Quickly Santos put some distance between them and opened the car door for her, but she didn't miss the raw desire in his eyes.

Once they were inside she asked, 'What did you tell him?'

'That we'd just got engaged and needed private time.' His voice was husky and heavily accented.

Of course he'd say that. But she couldn't help feeling humiliated. His kiss—which had been part of the act, the charade—had nearly been her undoing. She'd wanted more...wanted him to take her home. More than anything she'd wanted him to take her to his bed. But that could never happen.

Never.

To allow him to know how much her feelings towards him had changed would be the worst possible scenario. With that in mind she retreated to her room as soon as they arrived back at his villa.

The next morning Georgina used the excuse of it being Sunday and stayed in her room. Eventually she ventured out, hoping the quietness of the villa meant Santos was ensconced in his study.

As she strolled through the living area movement in the pool caught her eye. Santos was powering through the water, his strokes effortless. She shouldn't be watching but couldn't help herself, almost unaware of each step towards the pool she took. The afternoon sun shone brightly and she put on her sunglasses, watching as his muscles flexed.

Abruptly he stopped and looked at her, his dark eyes gleaming with amusement. 'Are you coming in?'

The husky depths of his voice made her stomach flutter and she was glad of the sunglasses she could hide behind. 'I'll give it a miss,' she said as she sat down on the edge of a sun lounger, even more drawn to him.

'Pity,' he replied, and swam over to her. His hair was flat against his head and rivulets of water ran down his face. 'It's very relaxing.'

Hardly. The thought of being in the water with him made her pulse race, and inwardly she cursed the attraction she felt for him. It was making things complicated.

'Maybe a walk along the beach?'

'That would be nice,' she said, and stood up, aware that at any moment he would haul his bronzed body from the water. And she wasn't ready for that. 'I'll go and change.'

Not trusting herself to look back at him, she hurried to her room and changed into a cool dress and flat sandals. Regaining her composure, she returned to the terrace and waited.

She knew when he was there as if her body was completely tuned in to his. She turned to face him and that spark of attraction zipped instantly between them.

'Shall we?'

He took her hand and for a moment their eyes met,

his darkening instantly. She remembered his touch last night, his kiss, and could hardly draw breath.

Right now, with his hand holding hers she felt safe. Cherished.

As if he could read her thoughts he held her hand just a little tighter. She smiled a genuine smile, one she couldn't hold back, as he stepped closer and brushed his lips over hers.

Everything around her ceased to exist. It was just the two of them. No deal—nothing. When he pulled back she looked up into his eyes. Was this what she'd been searching for? This strange warm feeling of contentment?

'We won't get very far like this,' she teased lightly, her heart almost melting as he laughed softly.

'*Sí*, you are right. We will walk.'

Sand, warm from the afternoon sun, poured into her sandals, but she didn't care. She just wanted to savour this moment. Because this was what it must be like, that glowing feeling of a new relationship. The first tender stirrings of love. Was it even possible?

'You're smiling,' he said as he pulled her to a stop, his hand not relinquishing its hold on hers. 'For the first time since we met you look happy.'

'I am.' And she meant it. Right now all she wanted was to be herself, to bask in the warmth of this new sensation. Santos made her feel things she'd never thought possible, and knowing those feelings wouldn't last for ever she wanted to relax and enjoy them. 'What about you?'

'In the company of a woman as beautiful as you, how could I not be happy?'

She searched his eyes, looking for a hint of mockery, but found only a heart-rending tenderness. He stroked his fingers down her cheek, lifting her chin as he bent and lightly kissed her lips.

Her heart pounded erratically and a tingle of excitement raced around her. Light-headed and almost giddy, she kissed him back, tentatively at first. This wasn't the needy kiss of last night—this was giving and caressing. It was loving.

She pulled back from him a little, shyness making her look up from under her lashes as heat infused her cheeks. 'You don't have to say and do these things—not now, anyway.'

'What I say is true.'

His voice was husky and raw as he brushed her hair back from her face, sending waves of delicious sensation all over her.

'And I only do what I want.'

It was as if a bond was forming with each gentle caress of his hands and each soft word. He was pulling her towards him. This man was so far removed from the compelling man she'd first felt a spark of attraction for she was lost for words.

Without another word he pulled her against him, holding her so close she could hear his heart thumping as wildly as hers. Was he aware of what was happening? Did he also feel as if he was wading out to sea, getting deeper and deeper, unable to turn back to the safety of shore?

The next morning Santos planned to work, but all he wanted was to be with Georgina. It was as if magic had been in the air last night on the beach and had weaved around them, bringing them closer in a way he'd never been with a woman before.

Was it because she still hadn't shared his bed? Was that one fact making him delusional? Like a man lost in the desert?

A bit of distance, that was what they needed, he decided, and for the best part of the day he shut himself in his study. He tortured himself when he heard her in the pool, but it was more than desire that raced around his blood. Something new, something undefinable, now simmered there too.

Finally, as the sun was setting, he could stand it no longer and went in search of the woman who would tomorrow be his wife. She was curled on the sofa, her phone in her hand. She looked up at him as he stood in front of her.

'I can't get Emma on the phone.' Her words were rushed.

Guilt shot through him, he'd completely forgotten her need to phone her sister.

'I sent a text instead.'

He didn't know how to respond to the obvious anxiety in her voice. Worrying about siblings was not something he'd ever done. Distraction was what she needed, he decided. 'Would you care to join me for a walk?'

'Another walk? Tonight?' She put her phone on a nearby table and smiled at him, the same warm smile she'd given him the night before. 'It's supposed to be bad luck for the bride to see the groom on the eve of her wedding.'

'I won't tell if you don't,' he teased, and held out his hand to her. She hesitated, then laughed softly. It was such a sexy sound he had to brace himself against the onslaught of thudding desire which rushed over him.

'In that case, how can I refuse?' She seemed different, as if all pretence had been abandoned, and he knew this was the real Georgina. The fiery, demanding woman who had burst into his office last week no longer existed.

The sea was calmer than he'd ever known it, with the waves hardly making any sound. They walked along the sand hand in hand, as they had done the previous afternoon. The sky was dark and the stars were shining brightly as he stopped and turned to her.

'I've enjoyed your company,' he said awkwardly. 'It's hard to believe it's only been a few days since we arrived.'

Georgina looked up at him. Was it possible he felt it too? He was so different now, so relaxed, and she knew she was in danger of falling in love with him.

'Don't say any more,' she whispered, putting her finger on his lips. She didn't want him to give her hope if he didn't mean it.

He kissed her fingers and before she knew how she was in his arms, her body pressed close to his. Fire tore through her as she kissed him, giving way to all the new emotions she was battling with. She wanted him with a fierceness that shocked her.

He deepened the kiss, his arms pressing her close against him, leaving her in no doubt that she needed to stop things now. She pulled back from him, her heart racing, and her breathing fast.

'I can't, Santos.'

'Can't what?' His voice was hoarse and he tried to kiss her again.

'This,' she said, moving back from him. 'We shouldn't even be seeing one another tonight. It's bad luck.'

CHAPTER SIX

SANTOS'S PULSE POUNDED in his head and a fire coursed through his veins which had little to do with the punishing early-morning run he'd just completed. After yet another night of trying to douse his need for Georgina he'd given up and, despite it being the morning of his wedding, had gone out to find some kind of release. He wasn't sure how much more he could take.

How could one woman drive him to such distraction?

Refusing to explore the answer to that question, he returned to his villa. As he did so he heard female voices and knew that Señora Santana had arrived, along with the others, to do the bridal hair and make-up. He clenched his hands into fists, fighting hard against the urge to go to Georgina's room, send everyone out and continue what she'd started last night—because start it she most definitely had.

Patience, he reminded himself, and headed for a cold shower instead. His run had not had the desired effect. Heady lust still throbbed through his veins and he knew of only one antidote for that—other than taking Georgina to his bed right now. *Work*. Once he'd showered he would shut himself in his office and work until lunchtime, when he would escort Georgina to the beach to become his wife.

An hour later he admitted it was impossible. The figures blurred before him and all he could think about was that kiss last night. At first so innocent and tender, then passion had taken over. Santos realised he'd been so consumed by need he'd behaved like a teenager, raging hormones taking control of his senses, rendering him completely under her spell.

Just as his father had been with Carlo's mother.

That thought alone had the sobering effect he needed on his body. He could never allow himself to be at the mercy of a woman—wanting her so much that nothing else mattered. Not even his inheritance. He'd never wanted a serious relationship, and certainly didn't want to get married, but his father's interfering had changed that.

In a bid to divert his mind he turned to his laptop, scanning the business pages and the headlines from Spain and England before looking at the celebrity gossip columns. Sure enough, just as he'd expected, he and Georgina were featured leaving the party together. Speculation as to what would happen next had filled the columns for the last two days.

At least now nobody would think him grasping enough to marry purely for financial gain. That sort of reputation wouldn't go down well when making business deals in the future. But if his business rivals thought he had a human side, one touched by love—whatever that was— they would be less guarded with him, giving him the edge he always sought.

He looked up at the clock on the wall. Eleven-thirty. Almost time to seal the hardest deal of his life. He turned off the laptop, put away his papers and headed back to his room to put on his suit.

As he fixed his cufflinks he looked in the mirror. Was he doing the right thing? He thought of the clause in the will, the need for an heir, and knew in that moment he should have told Georgina exactly what might be expected of her unless his legal team could find another way out. So why hadn't he? Because he didn't seriously think it would come to that when he was paying to find a solution. But then he hadn't thought he'd ever have to marry either.

A knock at the door drew his attention and he strode over to open it, knowing he was to be given the message that she was ready. It was time to make Georgina his wife. Guilt shot through him. She didn't know exactly what she'd signed up for. He had to tell her as soon as they were alone. Tell her that his mention of children in the prenuptial agreement might prove vital in the deal she'd come up with. Even *he* wasn't that harsh. Despite everything, he still clung to the hope that it wouldn't be necessary.

She was waiting for him on the terrace, but nothing could have prepared him for that moment if he'd spent several years organising it, instead of several days.

Georgina looked amazing.

Cream chiffon and silk encased her slender figure, but the slit in the floor-length dress drew his eye to her leg as she moved towards him. Her dark hair had been pulled back into a chignon and lace was attached to it, giving her a very Spanish air. The bodice of her dress clung to her breasts lovingly and on the single strap diamonds sparkled.

'I trust this meets your requirements?'

Her chin lifted defiantly, and her voice was as sharp as a razor, but her eyes still blazed with the same desire he'd seen in them last night. Gone was the woman he'd held in his arms as the stars sparkled above them.

'Every bride should look stunning on her wedding

day,' he said firmly, admiring the confidence that radiated from her. 'And you do.'

He fought to stop his mind envisaging removing the gown later as he truly made her his. Because if the attraction that existed between them—the one they had both been trying to deny—finally got the better of them when they were alone, there would be no doubt about consummating their marriage.

'You look very handsome too,' she said, a small blush creeping across her cheeks, her words softer.

'I'm pleased you didn't choose one of those fussy, frilly gowns I saw being brought in.' He tried to lighten the mood with small talk, but each step she took towards him showcased her slender legs and it was having a powerful effect on him. 'Such a daring dress was made for you.'

'Having been married before, I didn't think the usual fairytale image was appropriate.' She followed his lead and kept her voice light.

'It is far better than what you wore the first time,' he said slowly, his gaze holding hers. 'A business suit at a registry office? Hardly the stuff of fairytales.'

'You know that?' Her beautiful dark eyes widened slightly and she drew in a sharp breath.

'I always research my business deals, Georgina, and this one is no exception.' His words sounded firmer than he'd intended as he remembered exactly why they were doing this. The effort of not reaching for her, taking her in his arms and kissing her as he had last night, was almost too much. 'Ready?'

She looked at him for a moment, her brown eyes cool and emotionless, then she swallowed hard, giving away the fact that she wasn't as composed as she wanted him to think.

'I'm ready.' Still her voice was hard, full of determination.

He took her hand and led her from the terrace, down the steps towards the beach, where his cousin and a friend waited to witness their marriage. He glanced at her, smiling at her continued air of defiance.

Pride unexpectedly swelled in his chest as he realised just what was about to happen. He was about to take this gorgeous woman as his wife—a woman any man would be proud to be seen with. She was clever, witty, and incredibly sexy. Her hand in his was small and he clutched it tighter, enjoying the warmth of her.

Georgina's step almost faltered, and it was nothing to do with the grains of sand sliding through her sandals as she made her way across the beach. It was everything to do with the proud and arrogant man at her side.

His hand was warm as it held hers and she risked a quick look at him. He looked as if he'd stepped from her long-ago abandoned dream of a happy-ever-after. He was exactly the image of the man she'd used to dream of marrying: tall, dark, and devastatingly handsome. But this man was also dangerous. The way he could send her senses into overdrive meant she had to guard herself well or risk being hurt.

The waves rolled onto the sand before rushing back to sea and Georgina wished she could slip away with them. Doubts… Surely they were natural for a bride, but they clouded her mind, making her homesick. She wanted to see Emma, to tell her what was happening. This morning she'd nearly called her, but as she'd looked at her sister's number she'd known she didn't have enough strength to conceal the truth.

She wished she had someone here she knew. Someone for *her*. Someone who could reassure her she was doing the right thing.

When Santos stopped, not far from Raul and two others, she knew it was too late.

'I'm sorry there wasn't time to find one of your friends to witness this.'

Santos spoke softly next to her ear, almost making her jump and dragging her from her melancholy. It was as if he knew her thoughts.

She smiled brightly at him—maybe a little too brightly. 'It might have given the game away if you'd started flying my friends out here.'

'If you're sure?'

'I'm sure,' she replied quickly, injecting as much bravado into her voice as possible. 'Let's just get this over and done with.'

He looked shocked, but time for any further discussion was lost as the minister greeted them.

Everything seemed to spin. The minister's words, first in English, then Spanish, blended with the rush of the waves. Santos continued to hold her hand tightly and the heat of his body beside her was matched only by the sun.

She couldn't think—couldn't even grasp the concept of the words that were being said. When she'd walked into Santos's office last week she hadn't envisaged this—a beach ceremony with a man she was finding ever harder to resist. A man who wanted to be married to her about as much as she wanted to be to him.

'Georgie?'

She looked slowly up at him, remembering the need to act like a real bride, and smiled. He smiled back. A smile that reached into the dark depths of his eyes, melting her from the inside out.

He took her hands in his and spoke in Spanish to her.

She had no idea what he was saying, what he was doing. Everything seemed unreal. Then he slid a gold ring on her finger, repeating the words in English, and she realised he was doing exactly what she should be. Acting.

Panic raced through her. She didn't have a ring for him. Should she have got one? A polite cough at her side caught her attention and Raul handed her a ring, his smile full of charm. She smiled and turned back to Santos, slid the ring onto his finger and repeated the words that bound them legally in a marriage neither wanted.

Moments later Santos covered her lips with his, almost knocking the air from her as his arms wrapped around her, pulling her closer. She should resist, but sparks took off inside her like New Year's Eve fireworks and she wound her arms about his neck. It was as if the desire of last night still simmered.

Just as suddenly as the kiss had begun it ended, and Santos pulled away from her, but he kept her hand in his as he thanked Raul, his friend and the minster. Spanish flowed around her and all she could do was stand and wait, trying to come to terms with what she'd done.

It's for Emma. Just as it was last time.

'Now it is time for us.' Santos returned his attention back to her, his dark eyes sparking with fire.

'Us?' she asked as she watched the three people who'd witnessed her marriage walk back across the beach.

'Sí.' He dropped a kiss lightly on her nose and she blinked in shock at the affectionate gesture. 'We have to have at least a few days for our honeymoon before we return to London.'

Honeymoon.

Had he gone mad?

'Is that really necessary?' She couldn't believe he was serious. 'We're married now. You've got your business.

Can't we just go back and tell Emma and Carlo they can get married?'

'This was your idea, Georgina. You wanted to make it look as real as possible.' He frowned and looked down at her, his hand still clasping hers.

'I only wanted our names on a marriage certificate. I didn't want all this *acting*.' She should never have hoped to change things so late in the day. Not when she was dealing with a man like Santos.

His dark eyes narrowed in suspicion. 'You wanted authenticity and you've damn well got it.'

He let go of her hand and stepped back from her, then turned and walked back to the villa. She watched him go, just as she'd watched her father go all those years ago.

What was she doing? She couldn't stay on the beach—an abandoned bride for all to see. Propelled into action, she kicked off her sandals, picked them up and marched after him. They'd been married for only a matter of minutes and were already arguing. Surely that would make him see they needed to go their separate ways?

'Okay,' she said as she caught up with him, injecting as much ferocity as she could into her voice. 'We'll have the honeymoon. But once Emma and Carlo get married this farce ends.'

'Farce?'

He stopped and turned to face her. The fury in his face served only to increase her need to keep what she really felt for him concealed.

Without warning he pulled her into his arms, his lips claiming hers in a demanding and hungry kiss, weakening her body so that she could barely stand. She wanted to respond, wanted to take the pleasure his lips promised, but instead she reminded herself it wasn't real. None of it was. At least not for him.

His hands pressed her ever closer to him, until she had no doubt that although the marriage wasn't real his desire for her was. Her lips parted and his tongue plundered her mouth, entwining with hers in an erotic dance, making her sigh with pleasure.

Heaven help her, she wanted more. She wanted this man in a way she'd never wanted a man before.

He pulled back from her, his breathing deep and ragged. 'Now, deny that, Mrs Ramirez. Deny that you want me. Deny what your body tells me.'

'This wasn't supposed to happen.' Her lips were bruised and her body trembled with unquenched desire as she looked into his eyes, seeing sparks of passion within their depths.

'Come,' he demanded as he took her hand, and the gentleness of yesterday was gone.

Was he about to drag her to his room, take her to his bed? Excitement fizzed in her veins, only to be replaced by disappointment as he walked straight through the villa and out to his car.

'Where are we going?'

He opened the door of the car for her and she got in, hampered by the silk and chiffon of her dress. Mesmerised, she watched his hands expertly gather the silk skirt and bundle it into the car, his fingers brushing against her bare leg where the gown so daringly parted. She shivered as their eyes met. Their gazes remained locked; his hand rested on her leg.

'To my yacht.'

His voice was deep and incredibly seductive. Her heart jolted and her pulse raced as his fingers trailed over her thigh, moving teasingly higher.

'For our honeymoon.'

The smouldering flames she saw in his eyes should

have been warning enough, but she didn't want to listen to sense any more. This man wanted her, desired her, and she wanted him too. All sensible reasoning slipped away as he bent and kissed her thigh, where his fingers had made a blazing trail.

'Santos.' She placed her hands either side of his face, forcing him to look up at her. 'Please don't. At least not here.'

He smiled and stretched up to press his lips to hers, breathing Spanish words against them. She had no idea what he said and neither did she care. She watched, anticipation throbbing in her blood, as he shut the car door and strode around the front to the driver's side. He looked at her as the engine growled to life, his gaze so hot it seemed to melt the chiffon from her body and dissolve the silk of her skirt. And when those dark and dangerous eyes met hers she knew it was already too late. She'd lost. His expert charm and arrogant confidence had won.

She was as good as his.

She sat silently contemplating what had just happened between them as Santos drove. The car sped along the coast road, but she didn't doubt his ability to handle it. The sea glistened in the afternoon sun and she realised that very soon they'd be alone out there.

Tyres screeched as he came to an abrupt halt next to what was probably the biggest yacht in the harbour. She wasn't sure if she felt relieved or disappointed that they weren't going to be alone after all. A yacht this size must have at least a dozen crew members.

As they boarded he fired off rapid instructions in Spanish and everything seemed to come to life around them. A maid stepped forward, offering a glass of champagne, and Georgina took it, grateful to have something to hold other than Santos's hand.

She looked at him and he raised his glass to her. 'To my beautiful wife.'

His gaze openly devoured her and her body tingled.

'To my handsome husband,' she flirted.

Just one sip of champagne was making her braver than she really was. She had to play the game well, so she smiled as he smiled. But her words weren't lies. He was more handsome than she could ever have dreamed of, standing on deck in his designer suit, glass of champagne in hand, passion for her sparking in his eyes. He was everything and more from her abandoned dream of the perfect man.

'As we sail we shall have our wedding breakfast.'

He sipped his champagne and she watched him swallow, mesmerised by the movement of his throat. Food was the last thing she wanted right now, but maybe it would bring her back to her senses, dull the thud of desire in her veins and enable her to think rationally.

Whilst they'd been talking the yacht had slipped away from the harbour and was now sailing past the long stone wall and out into the sea. The small but affluent town of Puerto Banus looked picturesque, nestled below the looming mountains, and Georgina was transfixed by the view.

'So beautiful,' she whispered, unable to drag her eyes from it.

'Beautiful indeed.' Santos's voice was firm and strong as he stood next to her. 'But it is outshone by the beauty of my bride.'

Georgina took another sip of champagne—anything to calm her nerves—and then turned to face him. 'Surely we don't need to keep up the pretence here?'

His hand reached out, his fingers lifting her chin so that she had no option but to look at him. Her legs became unsteady and she wondered if it wasn't more to do with the man next to her than the motion of the yacht.

'Tonight I ask only one thing of you, Georgina.'

Her heart accelerated and pounded in her chest like a drum. Her gaze locked with his, held there by only the smallest touch of his fingers to her chin. Her breathing deepened and she wondered if she'd be able to stand for much longer so close to him.

'And that is…?' She maintained control of her voice, but control of her body was much harder. Heat was building low down in her stomach, spreading slowly and re-lighting the fire that had so nearly consumed her last night.

'No pretence. Not tonight, at least.'

Santos saw her eyes widen, watched as the soft brown of her irises turned darker until they were as black as the night sky. Her full lips, the ones that had kissed him almost into oblivion last night, parted and he fought hard against the urge to crush them beneath his.

'Not even a little bit?' She smiled up at him, and a hint of mischief danced in her eyes.

She was still hiding herself from him.

'No.' He lifted her chin a little higher and brushed his lips against hers, feeling her body tremble as it so nearly touched his. She smelt good, her perfume sweet and light. 'No pretence at all, Georgie.'

He liked calling her that. It made her seem more real—warmer, somehow. Like the woman he'd glimpsed last night. And tonight he was determined to find her again. It was *that* woman he wanted—the woman who'd filled his dreams and every waking moment since.

He took the glass from her hand and without taking his eyes from hers dropped it onto a nearby seat. The yacht lurched as they headed out to sea, pitching her against him, and instinctively he wrapped his arms around her, keeping her close.

'You can let me go now,' she said firmly, her breath feathering against his chin as she looked up at him. 'I wouldn't want you to think I'm throwing myself at you.'

He laughed and let her go. 'I wouldn't ever think that of you.'

She was so vibrant, so beautiful, and she was his wife.

As he faced her he saw shyness spread over her face—an emotion he would never have associated with the demanding woman who'd all but barged into his office last week.

Her fingers brushed his and his pulse raced in anticipation, just as it had been doing every time she came near him. It was almost torture, wanting a woman and not being able to have her. But tonight would be different. Tonight she would be his.

He watched as she walked away from him, the sandals she'd struggled with on the beach long since abandoned. The wind whipped at her dress, lifting the silk around her, allowing him more than a glimpse of long slender legs as she moved inside the yacht.

Pushing back the carnal thoughts that filled his mind, he followed her—and almost stopped in his stride when he saw the sadness on her face as she stood and looked out of the window. Was she thinking of her sister? Missing her?

'I'm sorry there wasn't anyone at the wedding for you.' Uneasy guilt compelled him to say it again, despite her earlier assurances.

She turned and looked at him, blinking her lashes rapidly over her eyes. 'It's not as if it was a real wedding—if it was I'd have insisted on Emma being there.'

She shrugged and looked back out at the retreating coast-line. 'Besides, you only had your cousin.'

'Raul *is* my family.'

'I've never heard Emma or Carlo mention him before.' She rubbed her hands on her arms as if cold.

'He's my mother's brother's son, so not a blood rela-tion to Carlo.' His clipped words caught her attention.

'You make it sound as if having a stepmother and half-brother is a bad thing.'

This was the first window into his life he'd allowed her to see through, and it made him feel vulnerable, but he was strangely compelled to talk and continued.

'My father and I were happy enough after my mother left, but when she died in an accident a few years later my father went to pieces. It was as if he'd been waiting for her to come back to him.'

He'd never told anyone that before. Talking of his childhood was something he just didn't do. But memories rushed back at him now like a sea wind, keen and sharp.

'I'm sorry,' she said softly, touching his arm. 'It hurts when a parent leaves. As a child you feel...' She paused and his heart constricted. 'Responsible, somehow.'

He looked down at her upturned face, at her soft skin glowing in the late afternoon sun, her eyes full of genu-ine concern. When was the last time anyone had been concerned about him? He wanted to talk to her, share his memories with her. After all she knew something of his pain—his research on her had proved that.

'My father had a second youth—dating women as if they were going out of fashion. So when he met the woman who would later be my stepmother it was a re-lief. He settled down again. I just hadn't expected to be excluded from the family when Carlo was born.'

She frowned slightly but said nothing, her steady gaze encouraging him to talk.

'As time went by Carlo became the centre of everything and I stood on the outside, looking in. I refused to compete for my father's attention. When I left university I began to take over the running of the investment business and my father spent more and more time with his *new* family.'

'But surely they loved you?'

He could see pity in her eyes, the image he'd painted for her, and anger surfaced. He did not need her pity. Just as he hadn't needed his father's love as a boy.

'*Love*, Georgina? What is *that*?'

His words were sharper than he'd wanted. He sensed her draw back from him, both physically and emotionally, and was thankful when she didn't say anything else.

'You're cold,' he said when she shivered. 'We will go inside and eat.'

As far as he was concerned the discussion was now closed.

He led her inside and even he was stunned at the intimacy of the small feast that had been prepared for them. The large table was set at one end, just for two, candles glowed and rose petals were scattered across the cream tablecloth. He heard her stifled gasp of shock and smiled.

'Your staff have excelled themselves,' she said softly as she came to stand beside him. 'It looks divine.'

The intimacy only increased once he was seated at the table with her, the soft glow of candlelight casting her face into partial shadow. Her shoulders were bare apart from the one strap of the dress. They looked creamy, soft, and he wanted to touch her skin, to kiss it, taste it.

Food was the last thing he wanted.

* * *

Determined not to be put off by Santos's sudden change of subject, and desperate to keep her traitorous body under control, Georgina spoke. 'I can remember my father walking away late one summer's evening. It was dark and hot, and later there was such a storm I worried all night about him. It sounds like it was tough for you too after your mother died.'

He'd almost opened up to her—almost let her in.

His face hardened and she knew she'd touched on a nerve.

'It was. But I'm not going to talk about such things now.'

He offered her some of the delicacies on the table, his fingers brushing hers, causing her to look up into his eyes.

'There are far better things to talk of on our wedding day.'

Our wedding day.

The words hung in the air between them as his dark eyes held hers. She should say something—anything. But she couldn't. The intensity of the attraction sparking between them was too much.

'You're not eating.'

He glanced quickly at her untouched plate and her pulse-rate leapt as once again his gaze held hers.

'It's looks delicious, but—'

'You're just not hungry?' He cut across her words, then took her hand, his own tanned one covering hers easily, sending shock waves of heat up her arm, and she was glad he'd forgotten the talk of his family.

'No,' she answered boldly, and wondered what he would say if she told him just what she *did* want right now. Would he laugh at her if she told him that all she could think of was kissing him, feeling his arms tight around her? She just couldn't fight the attraction any longer.

'So what *does* my sweet bride want?' He raised her fingers to his lips, dropping lingering kisses to each finger, and all the while he watched her, his eyes darkening with desire. 'Remember,' he teased, his voice deep and heavily accented. 'No pretence—not tonight.'

'I want…' She paused and smiled coyly at him as he waited. 'You.'

Shock laced with excitement fizzed in her veins as he raised his brows, slowly and suggestively. Once more he kissed her fingers, each time lingering longer, until she couldn't stand the anticipation any more.

He stood up from the table, keeping a tight hold on her hand, and pulled her up against him, holding her close.

Music began to drift around the room, reminding her that they were far from alone, that the crew and staff were lingering in the background to do his bidding. The disappointment she felt at not being totally alone with him shocked her. She wanted what they'd shared over the last few days.

'It is a tradition, is it not, for the bride and groom to dance together?'

He was so close now she could smell fresh pine mixed with the musky scent of pure male. It was intoxicating.

'In England it is, yes.' Her voice was little more than a husky whisper.

'Then we dance.'

He walked away from the table, guiding her to the middle of the room as the gentle rhythm of the music continued. When he held her close once more her knees threatened to give way, so intense was the attraction between them. It was an attraction that had been stamped out several times already, but Georgina knew this time it was going to be different—because this time she wanted him with a fever that engulfed her whole body. He was her husband now, and despite trying not to she had feelings for him.

This was how a bride *should* feel, and she pushed back memories of the clinical registry office service when she'd married Richard. It might only be for this one night, but she knew she had to live for the moment—had to surrender herself to it completely. This could be her one chance of sampling such heady romance.

As those thoughts flickered to life in her mind Santos kissed her—a soft, lingering kiss that held the promise of passion, one that awakened every nerve in her body. She deepened the kiss, closing her eyes against the onslaught of pleasure which crashed over her like waves onto the beach as she pressed close against him, feeling the evidence of his desire.

Breaking the kiss, he began to move her slowly around the room to the sound of the music. How could a dance be so erotic, so loaded with sexual tension and the promise of passion? The intensity of it was so much that she longed to give in and rest her head against his shoulder, close her eyes.

No pretence...not tonight.

His deep, husky words replayed in her mind.

Should she allow herself to taste what it might be like to love a man? To feel what it would be like to be loved back? Santos certainly seemed to be playing the part of devoted lover today. She didn't think for one moment it wasn't part of the charade they had created, but right now, as his arms held her close, the idea of happy-ever-after seemed tangibly close.

She laid her cheek against his shoulder, a soft sigh

escaping her as she closed her eyes. He tensed, and she knew he hadn't been able to abandon the idea of pretence completely. He was as on edge as she was, which made her a little less vulnerable—because together they could abandon the carefully constructed façades they each lived behind.

His arms tightened around her body, pulling her closer to him, and heat raced through her. As he pressed his lips into her hair she closed her eyes again, the sensation too much, and focused all her attention on the music instead of the feel of his strong body.

As she moved with him she realised the movement of the yacht had changed and glanced at the shoreline.

'Have we stopped?' Her words were husky. She'd never heard her voice like that.

'*Sí, querida.*'

He brushed his lips over hers as she looked up at him, sending another flurry of tingles skittering over her.

'We are to anchor here tonight. The crew and staff are leaving. They will be back in the morning.'

'So we will be completely alone out here?'

'Very much so.'

He stroked a hand down her face and she fought the urge to turn and kiss it.

'Does that worry you, *querida*?'

It should worry her, but it didn't. She wanted to be with him like this, to feel his body against hers, to taste his kisses. How could she pretend otherwise?

She searched the dark depths of his eyes, dropping her gaze to his lips briefly before looking back into his eyes. 'Should I be worried?' A flirty edge had slipped back into her voice as she struggled to keep her emotions under control and stay behind the safety of the barrier she'd erected long ago.

His voice was deep and incredibly sexy as he rubbed the pad of his thumb over her lips, making her lose those last doubts.

'Only if you don't want me to sweep you up into my arms and carry you to the bedroom.'

CHAPTER SEVEN

RIGHT NOW THAT was all Georgina wanted. It was all she could think about. It was as if the gently lapping sea beyond the yacht and the warm breeze had conspired against her. The luxury of everything was feeding the romantic dream she'd long ago abandoned.

But for tonight at least she could live it. Tonight she *would* live it—would allow herself to taste what she'd never thought possible.

'What more could a girl ask for from her groom?'

Her heart thumped in her chest and her breathing deepened, so that she had to drag every breath in, but still she couldn't quite let go of the bravado she always hid behind even as her body yearned for his.

In one swift movement he swept her feet from the floor to hold her firmly in his arms. The silk of her skirt fell apart at the slit and the heat of his fingers on her thigh scorched her skin, bringing a blush to her cheeks.

He swung round so that the tiny spotlights in the yacht's ceiling blurred behind him as she watched his face. It was set firm, as if his jaw was clenched.

'Then we will waste no more time.'

The depth of his voice, so sensual, laden with intent, sent a ripple of awareness cascading over her.

She felt every step he took as he marched through

the living area. A harsh Spanish curse left his lips as he reached the curving stairs which she guessed led to the bedrooms. Only vaguely aware of her surroundings, she remained focused on his face, but when he looked down at her the intensity of desire burning in his dark eyes made her smile.

He didn't smile back. His face remained set in firm lines. 'Damn stairs,' he growled, and turned his body slightly as he carried her upwards.

She reached up and touched his face, a small sense of triumph shooting through her as he dragged in a ragged breath. His skin was smooth, despite the darkness hinting at fresh stubble growth as her fingers slid down to his neck.

'You can put me down.' Her voice was barely above a whisper.

'Not until I have you where I want you.'

The strength of his words made her shiver with excitement.

As he reached the top of the stairs she looked around her and saw open double doors through which was the most magnificent bedroom she'd ever seen. Briefly she took in the dark mahogany furnishings and the big bed, its cream covers scattered with pink rose petals, as Santos walked briskly towards it.

Gently he placed her on the bed, and she leant back on her arms as he stood like a magnificent bullfighter at the side. She trembled as he looked down at her, his eyes as dark as the depths of the ocean.

Nervousness suddenly washed over her. It had been a long time since she'd been in a situation like this, with a man openly desiring her, his intentions clear. Would he be expecting the practised lover that society thought she was? The temptress she willingly portrayed herself to be?

'And this is exactly where I want you, *querida*.'

As the slow, purposeful words came huskily from his lips she watched him undo his tie and drop it to the floor, his jacket soon following.

Hungry for him, she let her gaze devour the strength in his arms as his white shirt pulled tight across his biceps. She bit her lip as he undid the top buttons, exposing dark chest hair and tanned skin. All the while he watched her with such intensity she knew she would be powerless to resist him.

Keeping her gaze locked with his, she reached up to her chignon, but something in his expression stilled her hand. The smouldering passion she saw in his eyes sent a dizzying current through her.

'Don't.'

His voice was harsh, and the arrogance that surrounded him maddened and excited her at the same time.

'But…' she whispered as he stepped closer to the bed, towering over her, dominating the very air she breathed.

'I've wanted to free your hair all day.'

He knelt on the bed beside her, his weight making her sway towards him as the mattress dipped. Within seconds he'd released the pins that secured her hair and she felt it slide over her shoulders.

'I've wanted to see it around your shoulders in all its glory.'

She closed her eyes against the sensation of his body so close to her, inhaling the intoxicating male scent that was uniquely Santos. When his lips pressed briefly against her shoulder she gasped softly in pleasure.

She opened her eyes and turned to face him, momentarily shocked at how close he was. His handsome face was only inches from hers. 'Santos…' she whispered as he kissed her cheek, her forehead, her nose, stoking the ever growing heat deep inside her.

'I want you, Georgie,' he husked out between each kiss. 'I want to make you mine.'

'I want that too.' And she did. Nothing else seemed to matter now except the two of them.

He silenced her with a long, lingering kiss that drew every ounce of reservation from her body, replacing it with unadulterated need. A small sound of pleasure escaped her lips as he broke the kiss, only to be smothered as his lips claimed hers in another greedy kiss that rocked her to the core.

Santos shook with need as he deepened the kiss. Never before had he felt as if he was on the edge of control with a woman—but then never before had a woman played so hard to get.

Her hand touched the side of his face, her palm pressing his cheek as she kissed him back, need for need, her tongue teasing his. He broke free of the kiss and looked at her full lips, already bruised from his kisses, then to her eyes, darker than he'd ever seen them.

She moved back from him, further up the bed, and a hot stab of lust grabbed him as her slender legs were exposed yet again. Teasing and testing him. He took hold of her foot and slowly undid one sandal, pulling it from her before tossing it to the floor.

She smiled and for a moment he thought he saw shyness in her eyes, but then it was gone as she lifted her other foot. He took it, and again slowly removed the sandal, but this time he didn't let go of her ankle. Unable to help himself, he smoothed his palm up her leg, past her knee, until it slid underneath the silk of her dress. A dress he desperately wanted to remove from her.

She closed her eyes and dropped her head back against the bed, a look of total abandon on her face as his hand slid higher. The warmth of her skin was almost too much for him. *Patience*, he urged himself. This was a night to take it slowly. This was a woman to savour.

He reluctantly moved his hand down her thigh, past her knee and back to her shapely ankle.

'How does a man get his wife out of her wedding gown?'

His voice was uneven and ragged. He was using every last bit of control just to stop himself from taking her right now.

'At the back.'

The words were a tremulous whisper, serving only to excite him further. He was used to his lovers being bold, but he liked this air of innocence she'd adopted.

She sat forward, waiting for him to unzip the gown. Sitting back on his heels, he steadied himself as he reached behind her and undid a clasp, then slid the zip down her back. His anticipation almost boiled over with every breath she breathed against his naked chest. Her scent invaded his senses and he dragged in a deep breath, tasting her.

At last the bodice of the gown sagged around her and he moved back, catching a glimpse of creamy soft breasts as it slipped lower. Part of him wanted to rip the gown from her, but a more disciplined part of him wanted to savour the moment, to make it special for both of them. It was, after all, their wedding night.

He kissed her, pushing her back against the pillows as his tongue delved deeper into her mouth. She tasted of champagne and his senses fizzed like a shaken bottle. Her arms wound their way around his neck, pulling him down to her, pressing against her.

He spread his hand over her bare shoulder, enjoying the feel of her skin, then slowly slid it downwards—until he met the resistance of the gown's bodice and wished he *had* ripped it from her.

She moved beneath him, thrusting her breasts upwards, inviting him to touch them—an invitation he had no trouble in accepting. His hand pushed aside the bodice, cupping her breast, his thumb and finger rubbing over the hardened nipple.

'Oh, Santos,' she whispered against his lips as her body arched even more. Need rocked through him.

Words failed him as he kissed down her throat, over her collarbone and down to her breast, finally taking her nipple in his mouth as her fingers ploughed through his hair. But still it wasn't enough. He wanted more—much more.

He pulled himself away from her, smiling at the disappointment on her face as he did so. 'This has to go.' He took hold of the bodice of her gown and pulled. Her breasts were slowly revealed, and then, almost erotically, her flat stomach and her beautifully shaped hips were laid bare to his hungry gaze. 'So beautiful, *mi esposa.*'

She smiled at him. And again that shyness he'd glimpsed earlier was in her face as she lay partially naked before him.

He kissed her stomach, revelling in his mastery as her body arched towards him again, begging him for more even if the words didn't come from her lips. Still lower his kisses went, until he found the silk of her panties. She bucked wildly beneath him then, almost undoing the control he was desperately hanging on to.

He looked up at her, at her dark hair spread about her on the pillow in sexy disarray, eyes closed as she enjoyed his touch. No sign of shyness now.

Agilely he rose from the bed, amused at the expression on her face as she looked at him, questions in her gorgeous eyes. As he pulled the wedding gown down she lifted her bottom, enabling him to pull it away in one go, leaving her dressed in only cream silk panties.

She looked divine.

And she was his.

'It's not very fair if you remain dressed, is it?' Her smile was coy and teasing as she looked up at him, completely at ease with her near nakedness. An accomplished temptress.

He undid the remainder of his shirt buttons with deft fingers and pulled it from his body. Her gaze roved hungrily over his body before finally meeting his eyes, and passion charged around him as his heart thundered like a herd of wild horses.

The air was electrified and he pulled off the remainder of his clothes without breaking eye contact. Her eyes were sending him a secret message of desire and need. How had he ever thought this woman cold?

Georgina couldn't help but look at him. Arrogantly naked before her, confidence in every move he made. She knew he'd achieved his aim. He'd made her desire him, want him completely. Every nerve in her body ached for his touch and being naked to his gaze excited her. Never before had she wanted a man as she wanted Santos.

Shyness took over once more, but she tried to act as if being naked in front of a man—a man as naked as she was, who so obviously desired her—was something she was more than used to. She watched as he sat back on the bed, his legs astride hers, rendering movement almost impossible. His aroused body was magnificent, and so very tantalisingly close to her, intensifying the rush of need, of raw desire she'd never known before.

He hooked a finger in the top of her panties, his gaze locking with hers. 'These too.'

Before she could say or do anything he'd pulled them down. The silk slid from her effortlessly and, in what she could only guess was a well-practised manoeuvre, he pulled them from her legs and threw them to the floor without moving from her at all.

She was exposed, naked and vulnerable, but for the first time in her life she didn't care. All she cared about right at this moment was satisfying the burning need she had for this man.

Her husband.

Her body ached for the fulfilment of his body. She wanted him in a way she'd never dreamt possible, and sparks of excitement at the prospect of being his shot round her.

He bent low over her and kissed her stomach before moving down further, his breath warm, sending fire gushing through her. She closed her eyes to the pleasure of his exploration. When she thought she couldn't take it any more his kisses moved back up her stomach to her breasts. In turn he kissed each hardened nipple. He pushed first one knee between her legs, then the other and, giving herself up to an instinct as old as time itself, she opened her legs, wanting to feel him deep inside her, desperate to be at one with him.

Her fingers gripped his shoulders as his erection nudged her moistness. He lowered himself onto her, kissing her as his body shook with the effort of holding back. She felt his heated hardness teasing her, and then, just when she thought she couldn't take one more second of it, he thrust deep inside her. She gasped at the pleasure of his possession, her fingers gripping ever tighter to his shoulders as she moved with him. Her legs wrapped around him, pulling him deeper into her, and he groaned in Spanish and thrust harder, deeper.

Their rhythm increased until she couldn't help but cry out in joy. A new and exciting sensation washed over her and she opened her eyes to look out of the sloping windows above the bed, feeling as if she too were flying among the stars that now sparkled above her in the night sky.

Santos's body shook and he cried out before burying his head in her hair, his body pressing hers into the bed. She wrapped her arms tightly around his back, keeping him there, wanting to feel him deep within her.

Finally her heart-rate began to slow and her breathing returned to normal. Santos lifted his head and looked into her eyes. 'Now you're truly my wife, Georgie.'

She didn't know what to say—what to do, even—so she just smiled back, her body still too sluggish with the aftermath of passion.

Santos rolled off and away from her and the cool evening air shocked her naked body, making her shiver. He reached down, grabbed a throw from the bottom of the bed, pulled it up over them and, to her total amazement, pulled her close.

She hadn't expected this. She'd thought he would disappear to the bathroom and come back partially clothed, ready to move on from what they'd just shared. Was this relaxed closeness part of his idea of no pretence? Was this the real man he didn't want the world to see?

'I should have asked this sooner,' he said, his voice sounding strangely unsure, and she wondered what was coming next. 'But we didn't use any contraception.'

'It's okay,' she whispered softly, and trailed her fingers down his arm, feeling a thrill of excitement when he groaned and pulled her close against him. Her mind quickly raced, wondering where her handbag was. Thankfully she'd put her contraceptive pills in there when she'd hurriedly packed for Spain. Not that she'd thought she'd actually need their protection. 'It's sorted.'

He stiffened slightly. 'Even so, I should have at least asked, but—'

'Don't worry. There won't be any repercussion from tonight. Just sleep.' She kissed him lingeringly on the lips, feeling the tension slip from him. Finding herself pregnant was not an option she relished, and she was certain he'd feel the same. 'Relax, Santos, try and sleep.'

He kissed her, pulling her close against his nakedness, stirring slumbering desire again. 'How can I sleep with you naked next to me?'

'At least for a while,' she teased as he kissed her again, his hands smoothing over her back.

She closed her eyes against the rising need for him, determined to play it cool. He must never know just how much she wanted him at this moment.

As he slept his breathing became deeper and steadier, and in the dim light of the bedroom she could see his naked back. Her fingers were desperate to touch him again, to create a trail over his tanned skin. The temptation became too much and she moved, but as soon as she did his relaxed hold on her tightened and he mumbled something in Spanish. It was enough to stop her.

Instead she lay and looked up at the night sky through the sloping windows just above the bed. The motion of the yacht was soothing and finally she relaxed, after what felt like days of being on edge, waiting for Santos to pull out of their agreement. They were married. The deal was well and truly sealed.

Tomorrow she'd call Emma, tell her to make plans for her own wedding. She smiled, remembering the morning she'd first met Santos. His arrogance and undeniable air of authority had almost made her turn and run from his office. Never in her wildest dreams had she thought that the man she'd proposed to as part of a business deal would end up being the first man she'd ever wanted— *really* wanted. The first man to show her just how good loving could be. The first man she could love, if only she let herself.

He didn't love her and had gone to extreme lengths to tell her he couldn't love anyone. He might have discarded pretence for the night, but would tomorrow be different?

Santos murmured again, pulling her against him and kissing her hair, sending a rush of heat through her body. Firmly she closed her eyes against the new wave of desire that was washing over her—because surely tomorrow it would be different.

Tomorrow she had to focus on Emma, on making sure Santos kept his side of the deal.

Santos woke in the early hours of dawn, his body heavy and relaxed in a way he'd never felt before. Georgina's scent lingered on the pillow next to him, reawakening the desire that had coursed like an overflowing river through him last night.

From the other side of the room he heard movement and he propped himself up on his elbow. With amusement he watched as Georgina, sexily naked, appeared to be looking for something to put on. He took in her slender waist, shapely hips and long legs as she stood, her back to him, looking around the room.

'*Buenos dias, mi esposa.*' *My wife*—that was something he'd never thought he'd call a woman.

She turned to face him and despite her nakedness looked as in control as she always did. For him, last night had changed something, softened the way he felt about her, but apparently it was not the same for her. She looked as if finding herself naked in a man's room was perfectly normal. A situation she was well used to.

'Morning,' she replied huskily, a smile playing about her kissable lips. 'I was looking for something to put on.'

'Your bag is in the wardrobe, but you will also find everything else you need in there too.'

Transfixed, he watched as she walked across the room, the swell of her breasts causing the blood to pound in his veins. If she didn't put something on very quickly she'd find herself back in his bed.

'Very convenient.'

The hint of sarcasm in her words was not lost on him. Keeping an array of women's clothes in his villa or on his yacht was not something he'd done before—but then catering for a future wife was not something he'd had to do either.

'I was merely trying to think of your convenience, *querida*.'

She opened the door of the wardrobe, assessed the contents, then opted for a cream silk dressing gown. She slipped it on and pulled it tight around her, knotting the belt at her stomach. The garment should have doused the fire now raging in his body, but it didn't. The outline of her body, still clearly visible, was more teasing than seeing her naked.

'Come here.' His voice was gruff and husky as desire pumped through him.

Instantly she looked shy, a blush creeping over her face, and he wondered which was the act. The bravado he saw more often or the innocent shyness she now displayed.

Slowly she walked towards the bed, her eyes darkening, remaining locked with his. He reached towards her, grabbed her hand and pulled her down to the bed.

'Santos!' she gasped in shock. 'What are you doing?'

'I would have thought that was obvious, *querida*.' As she lay beside him on the bed, her breathing faster, her breasts rising and falling in the most erotic way, he pulled the belt undone and pushed aside the silk, exposing her delicious body. 'I'm going to make love to my wife.'

Those words lit a raging fire inside him.

Unable to analyse those feelings now, he silenced her with a kiss so hard and deep he almost couldn't breathe. His need for her was far greater than last night—as if now he'd tasted her he needed more, like some kind of addict. Her hands explored his body, pushing aside the sheet and touching him until he couldn't stand it any longer. Urgently he pushed her back against the bed, covering her body with his as he thrust hard and deep within her delicious warmth.

It was as if his whole world rocked as he climaxed, relishing the feeling of being deep inside her. She cried out, her body arching towards him as she too found release. As his heartrate slowed and his mind regained the ability to think he realised he'd done the one thing he'd never done before. Early-morning sex. It gave women the wrong message. Made them think he wanted more.

But Georgina was already his wife. What more could she want from him?

He lay back, exhausted and exhilarated at the same time, his breathing and heart-rate finally returning to normal, and contemplated what had happened. Because something had changed, but he just couldn't understand what.

* * *

'I'll just go and shower.' More vulnerable than ever, Georgina wanted to put a little distance between herself and this man's magnetism.

'Don't be too long, *querida*.' He smiled at her, sending her senses into a spin as her heart flipped over.

Instead of answering him, she slipped from the bed with a bold teasing smile, grabbed her abandoned dressing gown and headed for the bathroom.

How on earth was she going to cope with today after what they'd shared last night? Would his rule of no pretence continue into the first day of their married life, or would he return to being the arrogant and controlling man she knew he was?

The hot water of the shower did little to ease her worries and she knew she had to talk to Emma. Just to hear her sister's voice would reaffirm why she'd married Santos.

With a towel wrapped round her body she emerged from the bathroom to find the bedroom empty. Quickly she reached into the wardrobe for her bag and pulled out her phone to see Emma had sent her a message.

OMG Georgie! You and Santos!

As she read the text from her sister she could almost hear her voice, the laughter in it—relief, even—and quickly she called Emma.

'Georgie!' Emma's excited voice was so vibrant it was as if it was on loudspeaker.

'Emma, I *so* wish you could be here, but…' Georgina swallowed. The first lie was about to leave her lips. 'We just had to get away and be alone.'

'You're really happy?'

'Do you think I'd jet off to Spain if not? After all that I've been through?' Thoughts of Richard mixed with the lies she was telling, the web of deceit she was spinning. *It's for Emma*, she reassured herself.

'Then I'm happy for you—but can you do one thing for me?'

'Anything for you, Emma.' That at least was true.

'Don't come back just yet. Carlo and I... Well, we're going to arrange our wedding, and if Santos finds out he's sure to put a stop to it. He's so against us getting married.'

Georgina swallowed hard. She should tell Emma. Instead she lightened her voice. 'We're enjoying our time together.' Was that a lie? she wondered as her body warmed at the memory of last night—her wedding night. 'Do you really think we're going to rush back to London?'

As she ended the call she let out a big sigh—relief that her sister and Carlo were now actually able to plan their wedding. She wished she'd been able to tell Emma that Santos was now her brother-in-law, but that was the kind of news to tell her face to face, when they got back to London.

Anxiety rose up. Just how was she going to convince Santos that heading back to reality was *not* what he wanted to do?

CHAPTER EIGHT

THE SUN WAS hot by the time Georgina came up on deck, to find Santos relaxing, an empty coffee cup on the table. She hadn't yet seen him look quite this relaxed before, so at ease with life.

As if aware of her presence he turned to face her, and she wanted to hug her arms about her body, to shield herself from his appraising gaze. Instead she fought the urge, and when the wind blew the sheer kaftan against her like a second skin, revealing the tiny blue bikini she'd reluctantly put on, she walked towards him. As confident as any of the top models he'd dated, she smiled.

'It's so wonderful out here, away from everybody. I'd love to stay a bit longer.' She slid seductively into the seat opposite him, nerves tingling all over her body.

Anxiety, she told herself, refusing to acknowledge the fact that it was Santos who did that to her.

He looked past her briefly and she wondered if she'd gone too far. But a moment later a tray of breakfast and fresh coffee arrived. The crew were obviously back on board. Once they were alone again he turned his attention to her, his dark eyes sparkling like the sea in the morning sun.

'There would be one condition.' He poured coffee, the aroma reminding her of how little she'd eaten last night.

'And that would be…?' Her voice was flirty—the exact opposite of how she felt.

'The same as last night.'

'Last night…' she breathed, in a husky echo of his words as her body responded to the memory of his touch, his kisses.

He smiled, a dangerously seductive smile, and she all but melted. 'No pretence.'

'None at all?' She teased him with a coy smile, her fingers twining in her hair.

'I like the real Georgie.' He leant forward in his seat, his brows lifting suggestively. 'The Georgina you don't let the world see.'

She laughed a nervous laugh that made him smile even more, which in turn sent her heart thumping erratically. 'You make me sound fake—as if I'm a total fraud.'

'Not fake,' he said, and passed her a coffee.

She sipped it, thankful for something to do other than look into his handsome face.

'Just scared to let anyone know the real you.'

His words hit her with the precision of a marksman. Not letting the world see the real Georgina was just what she'd tried to do for the last five years. For so long that sometimes she forgot who she really was—forgot the woman with dreams of happiness. No, going there wasn't an option.

'Well, I guess we'll just have to spend time together—get to know one another a bit better.' She sipped her coffee and looked out at the sea, its ever-moving waves sparkling like diamonds, before turning her attention back to him.

'*Exactamente.*'

His gaze held hers, dark and passionate, sending shivers down her spine, and she wondered if she could do this. But if Emma was to stand any chance of making her wedding arrangements in peace she had to ensure they stayed in Spain.

'Thank you,' she said, alarmed at how husky her voice had suddenly become, how easily she could slip into the role of seductress.

'We'll sail further along the coast. There is a secluded cove we can stop at—a good place to swim in the sea.'

He smiled at her again. Her heart flipped over and butterflies took flight in her stomach. Perhaps it wouldn't be hard, keeping him occupied, because she really did want to. He was so very different from the man she'd first met in his office, the man her sister had talked of. This man consumed her very soul—made her want him and the dreams she'd long since forgotten.

'I'd like that.' A blush crept over her cheeks as she met his gaze before it slid down over her body, taking in all that the bikini did very little to hide.

'For my beautiful bride—anything.' He stood and leant down over her, his lips hovering tantalisingly close to hers as she looked up at him.

His breath was warm on her face and she resisted the need to close her eyes, wanting to see his. With excruciating slowness he brought his lips down onto hers, the sensation sending sparks of awareness all over her until she could only close her eyes, give in to the pleasure of his lips as they brushed gently over hers.

The kiss ended and he stood upright, dominating the sheltered outside area of the yacht. 'I will go and make arrangements while you enjoy breakfast.'

She watched him stride away, his casual jeans hugging his long legs to perfection. She shook her head briefly, trying to stop the images of last night, memories of his tanned body against her pale skin.

In a bid to quell her rising desire she turned her attention to the breakfast, not sure if she could eat anything. But the array of fresh fruit and the lure of warm croissants soon won her appetite over.

She became aware of the coastline receding, the yacht moving smoothly through gently rolling waves. Excitement fizzed inside her. It was like being young again.

She'd been happy before life had plunged her into a situation she really hadn't wanted. Her whole outlook on life had been carefree and full of adventure until the night her father had left. Now those memories were the reason she'd promised herself she'd never have children—because what would happen if she became like her mother? What would happen if she too went from one man to the next, looking endlessly for something that didn't exist, ignoring her children to the point of neglect?

'Why so sad, *querida*?'

Santos's accented voice shattered her thoughts as surely as if she'd been viewing them through a mirror.

'I was just remembering.' Quickly she tried to hide her emotions, recreate the impenetrable wall she hid behind, because right now her defences were low. Too low. And Santos was watching her with such unexpected sympathy she almost couldn't look at him.

'We all have things we shouldn't remember, but sometimes it helps to talk.'

His tone was soothing and reassuring. He sat next to her, taking her hand, his thumb stroking over the back of it gently. His concern as genuine as a lover's. She wanted to pull away, to distance herself from him. She felt utterly exposed, as if every emotion was completely visible to him.

'It was just my excitement as I realised the yacht was

moving,' she said, aware of the hoarseness in her voice. 'It's like being young again.'

He nodded once, his eyes full of understanding. 'What happened?'

'My mother found solace in the bottle after my father left.' Her heart thumped hard as pent-up anger flowed through her like a tidal wave—one that couldn't be halted now as it roared towards the shore. 'I had no choice but to care for Emma, try and shield her from it all. I had to grow up very quickly.'

'Shield her from what, Georgie?'

She looked up at him. His voice was now hard and controlled, his eyes narrowed and his brows pulling together in concentration.

She shouldn't be telling him this. It had nothing to do with him, and would serve no purpose whatsoever, but it was liberating to finally share it with someone.

'What was it, Georgina?' he urged as her silence lengthened.

He reached out and pushed back the hair from her face and she dropped her gaze, not wanting to see the sympathy in his eyes. How could a man as ruthless and in control as Santos possibly understand?

'Tell me, Georgie.'

One hand stroked her hair whilst the other held firmly onto her hand. She had no means of escape, no way out.

What would he think of her if she told him?

'At first she was just incapable of looking after us— that was unless she was in the throes of a new affair— but soon it was down to me to get Emma to school, to put a meal on the table.'

He stopped stroking her hair, his hand resting on her shoulder, warm and comforting. 'Go on.'

Those first words had unleashed all her hurt and she

knew she should stop. She shrugged, not wanting to allow him any closer emotionally.

'So I got out as soon as an opportunity presented itself. I had to. It was the only way of keeping a roof over our heads and food on the table. Any money my mother had was spent on what she considered important—not on what actually *was*, like food and rent.'

He sat back from her, his hands falling to his thighs, silent for a moment as he took in what she'd said. 'That opportunity being your marriage to Richard Henshaw?' His voice was hard, a slight growl in his throat.

She looked up at him. He really did think she'd married purely for the money and status Richard had given her. Words of defence were on the tip of her tongue, but something stopped her, froze them as if the warm sea breeze had changed to a bitter winter wind. Instead she wanted to tell him—wanted him to know.

'He offered me everything I wanted—and more.'

She sat taller in her seat and looked him in the eye. For a moment she'd almost told him the truth—told him how Richard had literally rescued her, offering her security for Emma and asking for nothing other than that she took his name. But sense had prevailed. If he wanted to think of her as a gold-digging socialite then he could.

'And, yes,' she added, with the haughty tone she knew made her sound so like the woman he thought she was resounding in her voice, 'I married him for his money and his status. But you can't accuse me of hiding that from you. Not when it is common knowledge.'

Santos's stomach hardened as his breath came fast. He clenched his teeth against an attack of jealousy as he imagined Georgina with another man—one she'd just admitted she'd had no feelings for. She hadn't attempted to hide the fact that she'd used a man who must have known he was ill when he married her.

She'd used Richard and she sat there now with the innocence of a child and waited for his reaction. He was angry with himself—angry at the irrational jealousy that raged inside him just thinking of her with another man. She was his wife, and what he felt for her now surpassed anything he'd felt for previous lovers.

'We all have a past, *querida*.' He kept his tone as nonchalant as possible, regretting having started the conversation. He'd known of her reputation when he'd agreed to their ludicrous deal, so why did it matter so much?

Control, he reminded himself. Whatever happened he had to be in control, and for a moment there he'd almost lost it—almost given in to the temptations of the devil. This whole episode was about getting what he wanted, not about emotions. Never emotions.

He stood up and walked to the side of the yacht, checking their location, almost relieved to see they had arrived at his chosen bay. He breathed deeply, enjoying the salty tang in his mouth, trying to revitalise himself before he turned back to look at the woman who was now his wife.

'Yes, we do. Including you.'

The accusation in her voice was clear and he couldn't help but smile at her pretence at fury. Her expression was severe, but her eyes were telling a different story.

'It's called life, Georgie.' He put out a hand and stepped towards her. 'And right now ours is for living. What about a swim in the sea? Wash all your troubles away?'

For a moment he thought she was going to refuse. Confusion furrowed her brow, then she regained her composure, took his hand and smiled up at him, openly flirting.

'A swim sounds delicious.'

Delicious. She was delicious, with the wind wrapping the almost see-through kaftan close to her glorious body, the blue bikini showcasing just what a figure she had. Lust thudded in his veins and he cursed his wayward thoughts.

'Something wrong?' A hint of a playful smile tugged her full lips up at the corners.

She knew exactly what was wrong, damn her.

'No. Unless it's wrong for a man to want to drag his wife back to bed instead of going swimming?' His voice was deep and guttural with the effort of reining in his libido.

She blushed and, as he had many times in the last few days, he wondered how she managed that little trick—how she managed to appear so innocent. 'I think we should swim first. It's not even midday yet.'

First.

She wanted him as much as he wanted her. Her darkening eyes were smouldering, giving him the message, setting fire to the embers of desire that had scorched his body last night. Never before had a woman affected him so much, made him want her so badly—but then never before had he had to wait so long to get a woman into his bed. And he certainly hadn't had to marry her to do so.

The irony of it wasn't lost on him as he felt her hand in his. It felt surprisingly good, as if it was right. 'I'll hold you to that,' he managed, despite the heat that raged within him. A swim in cold water was exactly what he needed.

He led her to the platform that had been lowered once the yacht was anchored and slipped off his deck shoes. Her gaze heated his blood as he pulled off his shirt, the sun instantly warm on his skin.

'Not joining me?' he teased, tugging off his jeans, amused by the blush that crept over her cheeks as her gaze slid down his body, resting on the evidence of just how aroused he had become at her loaded promise of what was to follow their swim.

The air crackled around them, their attraction as overpowering as if he hadn't touched her, hadn't tasted her skin or made her his. It was like the first time all over again, with anticipation raging in him like a bull.

He dived into the blue waters, and the rush of cold over his body was just what he needed. As he broke the surface he wiped water from his face and looked back up at Georgina, now sitting on the edge, feet dangling in the water, wearing only that very sexy blue bikini.

'It's cold!'

She laughed, her face lighting up, giving her an air of playful innocence, tugging at something deep within him.

'Only at first. Come on—you'll never know how good it is until you try it.' He trod water as he spoke, energised by the exercise and cold water.

Georgina watched, mesmerised, as his strong arms kept him exactly where he wanted to be. His strength and power were undeniable. She was behaving like a lovestruck teenager. Her heart was still pounding after that moment when he'd stood before her in his trunks, his tanned skin gleaming in the sun, the hardness of his arousal obvious. She wanted him with a ferocious need so alien that her breath had caught in her throat, and she'd been relieved when he'd expertly dived into the clear water. Relieved he had taken the temptation from her.

Cautiously she slipped into the water, gasping and laughing at the same time. 'It's so cold!' She tried hard to be sophisticated and serene, but all she managed was a fumbling splash.

'Only for a while,' Santos said, and in one stroke he moved towards her, encircling her body with his arm, keeping her safe and close. 'Like *you* were the day you propositioned me in my office.'

Shocked that he'd brought that up, she stopped moving her arms and immediately sank below the surface. His arm around her body pulled her back up, spluttering like a child.

'How dare you?' She tried to move away from him, back to the platform.

'Oh, I dare, *querida*—because it's true. You want everyone to think you are carved from ice, but you're not, are you?

She clutched the platform, gained a foothold on the ladder and pulled herself out of the water, then turned to face him as he looked up at her from the blue waves. 'Neither are you.'

'Can you blame me when you stand there like a sea goddess, water dripping from you in a most inviting way?'

'You're impossible.' The words rushed out, her frustration making her want to march away, but she couldn't tear her gaze from Santos as in one swift movement that made the muscles in his arms flex he hauled himself out of the sea.

Water ran down his tanned chest, trickling among his dark hair, heading downwards. She knew she shouldn't be looking, but she couldn't help herself. His thighs were strong and more dark hair lay flat against his wet skin, creating patterns all the way to his ankles. He was magnificent as he stood, sunlight gleaming on his skin.

He grabbed her hand and without a word headed back inside the yacht, leaving her little option but to follow. She couldn't say anything. The same sexual tension that had last night completely robbed her of the ability to think, let alone speak, raged around them.

In seconds they were alone in their suite, and only then did he let go of her hand. For a moment they looked at one another, gazes locked in some sort of primal dance. His chest rose and fell with the effort of breathing, just as hers did, and she knew instantly where this was going to end—and, worse, where she wanted it to end. He was an addiction.

With a muttered Spanish curse he turned and opened the door to the bathroom, and she watched through the doorway as he turned on the shower. She swallowed hard as he turned back to her, his expression almost fierce with control.

'Santos…' She managed a croaky whisper as he held out his hand to her. She took it and he pulled her hard against his wet body. Only then did she realise she was trembling.

'You're cold,' he said quietly, but she didn't miss the intensity in his voice.

She wasn't cold—not enough to tremble like this. It was him, and the electrified air that seemed to surround them.

'Come on.' He led her into the steam-filled bathroom and into the shower—one that had definitely been designed for two.

His hands slowly untied the bikini where it fastened at her neck, and each time his fingers touched her she had to suppress a shiver of pleasure. He let the thin straps go and peeled the wet material slowly away from her breasts, his gaze lingering enticingly on them.

He made a signal with his hands for her to turn around and slowly she did so, meeting the jets of warm water. Behind her she felt his hands as he released the final clasp of the bikini top and it dropped to the shower floor. Seconds later it was joined by his black trunks and her knees nearly buckled beneath her. Desire flooded her as he pressed his naked body against her back.

Instinctively her chin tilted up and she leant her head back against his shoulder, turning her face towards his. Hot, urgent lips claimed hers with such force she staggered forward, taking them both under the hot jets of water. His hands cupped her breasts and fire engulfed her, making her cry out with pleasure.

'You are the most desirable woman ever, *mi esposa.*'

He kissed down her neck, uttering words she didn't understand. But she did understand the desire and passion entwined with each one. A desire and passion that raged as wildly inside her.

'Santos, I want you.' Her voice was husky as his hands slid down her stomach, his fingers tugging at the ties on the side of the bikini briefs. As the material fell away his fingers moved towards the heated centre of her need for him and she arched away from him, trying to fight the ripple of pleasure from his touch.

With a suddenness that knocked all the breath from her body he turned her around, grasped her thighs, lifting her against him.

'Santos, it's never been like this before,' she gasped between ragged breaths as he lowered her onto him, plunging deeply and urgently inside her. She didn't care that she was telling him too much, giving away just how inexperienced she really was and how she was falling in love with him.

'Never?' The question rasped from him, halting her thoughts, as his fingers dug into her thighs, holding her where he wanted her.

She moved with him, encouraging him in this hot,

hard and primal dance. 'Never,' she gasped out as stars shattered around her so that instead of water coursing all over her it was stardust. 'Never. *Never.*'

As he found his release she clung to his body, trembling more now than she had when she'd stood before him in the bedroom just moments ago. He was breathing hard, his chest heaving against her tender breasts, one arm braced against the shower wall.

'At least we agree on something.' His voice, heavily accented, was a ragged whisper.

He released his vice-like grip on her thighs and she slid down, her legs so weak she wondered if she'd be able to stand. She couldn't. Her knees crumpled, but his arms were about her and in seconds he'd swept her up off her feet and left the shower.

Pausing briefly to grab a towel, he made his way to the bed. As if she were the most precious thing in the world he let her down to stand in front of him and then wrapped the white towel around her, heedless of his own wet body. Then he bent and kissed her lips so tenderly she thought she might actually cry. This was exactly what she'd abandoned all hope of ever finding, this warm, loving feeling.

Except this wasn't for real. This was just part of a deal, satisfying the attraction that had been arcing between them since that very first meeting. It was also the only way she knew of keeping Santos from heading back to the villa and maybe London.

'You're still wet,' she whispered, not wanting to analyse her motives or question her dreams now.

He stepped back from her and started rubbing his hands over the towel to dry her. This was getting too intense, too close to being like a proper romance, so great was the attraction she felt for him. Her breath shuddered as he pulled the towel from her and dried himself off.

And all the while his gaze held hers, the passion and desire still flowing between them evident in the depths of his eyes.

He picked her dressing gown off the bed, now remade after their night of passion, and handed it to her. 'You must care for your sister very much.'

Instantly her senses were on high alert. What was he suggesting? 'She's all I have.'

He handed her the cream silk garment. 'But to marry just so that your sister can marry for love?' His voice rose with incredulity as he took fresh clothes from the wardrobe and hastily got dressed.

'Maybe I love my sister as much as you hate your brother.' Was he referring to their marriage or her first one? It made no difference; both had been made out of love for her sister.

Tension filled the room and his eyes sparked with anger as he stood in front of her, all the passion and desire of moments ago forgotten.

'Half-brother.' The words were harsh and staccato.

She pulled on the dressing gown, no longer wanting him to see her naked now he was clothed, as if it somehow weakened her. He turned and paced across the room towards the door, but she couldn't let him go, couldn't let him walk out now, even if it meant killing the loving moments they'd shared.

'Coward.' The word rushed from her lips, provoking him.

Instantly he whirled round and fixed her with a fierce glare, his face a hardened and angry mask. 'I don't do emotions, Georgina. Hate or love. I don't do them.'

'And because of that two people who love one another are suffering.'

'How?' He strode back across the room, but she stood

her ground. 'And how do you know they are in love? How do they even know?'

'You must have loved someone, Santos, despite what you just said.'

'Love is for weak-willed fools.' His voice was like granite and his eyes glittered dangerously as he looked at her.

'You don't really believe that?' she whispered in disbelief.

She'd vowed she'd never love anyone other than Emma, never give her heart to a man as her mother had time and time again. But somehow she'd become dangerously close to loving Santos.

'Isn't that why you made this damn deal, Georgina, because you don't believe in love?' He was like an angry lion, caged up and looking for a way out as he strode across the room to glance out of the window. He turned and looked at her, waiting for her reply.

'I did it *for* love.' She rallied against his contempt. 'I did it for the love of my sister.'

'Ha!' He laughed, so arrogantly she almost cringed. 'You did it for money, for all you could get from it—just as you did the first time around.'

How dared he bring Richard into this? The man who had seen she needed a lifeline and offered one without expecting anything in return? Well, if that was what he thought of her, so be it. Attack was the best form of defence.

'Yes, just as I did the first time.'

For a moment he looked at her in stunned silence, his jaw grinding hard. He looked for all the world as if he was jealous of Richard. How could a powerful man like Santos be jealous of anything or anyone?

He glared at her. 'Get dressed,' he snapped after what seemed like an eternity. 'We're going back to the villa.'

Panic tore at her. She'd promised Emma she'd keep him out of the way, and here on the yacht was the perfect place.

'So soon?' She hated the nervous edge to her voice, but knew any attempts at flattering him would be futile.

His eyes narrowed. 'I have work to do. Playing at this newlywed game has gone on for long enough.'

With that he strode from the room and she sank onto the bed. Last night they had made love for the first time, been given pleasure so intense it still lingered in her body. Only minutes ago they had been consumed by desire and need for one another. How could the man who kissed her so passionately be the same man who'd just left the room?

She dragged in a deep breath, pressing her fingertips to her lips, bruised from his hard kisses in the shower. How could she, a woman who'd renounced love, feel such desolation as the man she'd given herself to last night with total completeness walked out on her?

CHAPTER NINE

SANTOS'S MOOD WAS as dark as the storm clouds rolling down from the mountains. He'd thought Georgina was different, thought she could keep emotions out of things. Instead she'd proved beyond doubt that she was as clingy as any woman, unable to resist the urge to delve into his past.

He'd thought he'd met his match—a woman who could share his passion without the need for anything more.

But he'd been wrong, damn it, very wrong.

'I have business matters to attend to.'

Unable to keep the frustration from reverberating in his voice as they arrived back at the villa, he swung the car in through the gates without giving the photographers loitering there a second glance and powered up the driveway.

Georgina was silent next to him, but he could feel her watching him. He couldn't look at her now. She'd already proved just what an effect she had on him, proved how easily she could distract him.

'I'll get ready to go back to London.' Her voice was quiet, but firm.

'London?' The car halted abruptly as he fought for control. His fingers curled hard around the leather of the steering wheel as he gripped it even harder. One thing was for certain: she was not going back to London. Not yet.

'It's what I'd planned once the world knew we were married.' Her voice still had a husky edge to it, but strength and determination echoed there too.

That unsettled him even more. She seemed able to shut off and return to icy control much more easily than he was able to do. The carefree hours they'd spent on the yacht meant his usual detached approach to relationships was eluding him. And he didn't like it.

Santos looked at her lips, full and still very kissable. Fire leapt to life deep within him—a ferocious burning need to take her straight to his bed once more. It was more than lust, this need to be with her. He gritted his teeth; he had to be as collected as she was right now.

'That is what you *originally* planned, Georgina.' He tossed the words carelessly at her, trying to appear as unaffected by her as possible as he turned off the engine and got out of the car. 'But it is not what we finally agreed on.'

She got out of the car, all elegance and poise, then faced him across the shiny red roof. She looked stunning, sexy, and very different from the woman he'd brought here just a few days ago. Her eyes were bright, her skin lightly tanned and her hair looked tousled, as if she'd just got out of his bed.

'I'm going home, Santos.' Her words were clipped as she slammed the car door shut.

'You *are* home. You agreed to live as my wife, to be by my side, and right now I'm here.'

Not wanting to discuss it further, he locked the car and marched into the house, heading straight for his study. The sound of her footsteps on the marble floor would have told him she was following even if his body hadn't tingled so wildly, alerting him to her presence.

'Look, Santos…' She practically purred as she followed him into the sanctuary of his study. Hell, she was good at this—good at putting on a show of whatever she wanted people to see. Anger, gentleness or hot desire, it didn't matter—she was an accomplished actress through and through. 'Is there really a need to keep up this pretence?'

He thought of the clause of his father's will, the way it had pushed him into not only marrying but considering having a child, an heir. Frustration mixed with his anger and he pushed the thought roughly aside.

'It was in the agreement.' He kept his words firm as he headed to the filing cabinet and the file containing copies of their pre-nuptial agreement.

'I did not sign anything to say I would stay by your side like a faithful puppy dog. You must be mistaken, Santos.' Her eyes sparked fury at him, their colour lightening to a brilliant bronze, and her voice had a sharp edge to it, but she still looked sexy, still made his body ache for her.

If she continued to stand there like that, her hand on her hip, her lips almost pouting, he'd have to kiss her. And if he did that he'd never stop. She was like an addiction.

He turned his back on her, opened the cabinet drawer and pulled out the folder, tossing it on the desk so that the contents slipped from it, spreading across the table like a pack of cards. 'Take a look.'

Her gaze dropped from his face to the documents, then back to his. 'I know what I signed.' Her voice wavered slightly. 'But we've done what we set out to do. If I have to stay here then at least let me ring Emma, tell her she and Carlo can set a date.'

He inhaled deeply. He had to tell her just what else he needed from the marriage.

Her phone rang and she delved into her bag and pulled it out. For a moment she looked at it, then at him. 'It's Emma,' she said as the ringing ceased. 'What do I tell her? That we are happily married so they can be the same?'

He cursed harshly and paced to his window, taking in the view of the mountains almost obscured by dark clouds laden with the promise of a storm. The air was heavy and he knew that at any moment it would break.

He cursed again and dragged his fingers through his hair with an unaccustomed feeling of tumultuous emotions. What the hell had happened to him to make him feel so out of control?

He'd got married. One of the two things in the world he'd never wanted to do. The second was to become a father, and now it seemed his hand was to be forced there too unless he could find another way.

Again he raked his hands through his hair. He couldn't think straight. The air was becoming heavier and more oppressive by the minute and he could feel Georgina's gaze fully on him, expectantly waiting for an answer.

'Tell her to arrange their wedding.' His words were sharp, and it was an effort to keep his frustration at the situation he now found himself in from showing. Damn it, he still couldn't tell her why she had to stay.

Her gaze locked with his, the soft brown eyes that had almost melted his soul as he'd made her his now burnished like copper, angry and glittering. He clenched his hands and met her challenging gaze.

'This is what you wanted all along, isn't it?' What was she waiting for now? His blessing for the marriage?

'You know it is…'

A *but* seemed to linger in the air with as much threat as the storm he could feel waiting to erupt.

He raised a brow at her, finally slipping back into his professional mode. 'Anything else?'

She shook her head, a look of disappointment crossing her face and he bit down hard on the sudden urge to go to her, to hold her and make everything right. Because he couldn't. He would never be able to make this right—for Georgina or himself.

She stood tall and resolute for a few more seconds, her gaze fixed to his, then she left, taking with her some of the pressure that dominated the room.

He needed to contact his legal team. There just had to be a way out of that final clause. Satisfied he'd sorted the situation for now, he turned on his laptop. He had far too many emails to answer, but the first one snared his attention with such ferocity he dropped down into his chair.

It was offering him congratulations on his marriage. Just what they had planned. But it was the last line that almost made his heart stop. He and Georgina weren't the only couple to have got married.

Blood pounded in his ears, the sound so loud it almost masked the first rumble of thunder as the storm finally broke.

It couldn't be true.

Quickly he scanned the headlines and within minutes found confirmation that, yes, it was true. He'd been tricked, manipulated, and totally played for a fool. He wanted to rage and shout, but one thing life had taught him was that rushing in without first knowing all the facts could leave him in a weak position.

No, this had to be approached with caution. He had to know what part Georgina had played in this. Instinct told him it was a very big part. He was angry he'd lowered his defences enough for her to see the man he really was. For the first time ever he'd felt the stirrings of something he'd shut out of his life long ago and had almost been fooled into opening that door.

Georgina slipped outside to the pool. The clouds were dark and heavy. It looked as if a storm was brewing, and she hated storms—she'd never shaken off her childhood fear of them. Despite the dark clouds that hung low in the sky she settled on a lounger by the pool, her need to speak with Emma greater than her desire to hide from the storm. She could hardly wait to hear her sister's squeal of delight when she told her they could set a date.

'Georgie.' Emma sounded different somehow as she answered the phone. 'Where are you?'

'I'm still in Spain, and you can get set a date for your wedding.' She took a breath, putting on an air of jubilation—one she was far from feeling. 'Santos and I—we're married.'

Emma hesitated, and a shiver of apprehension slipped down Georgina's spine as the silence lengthened down the phone connection.

Finally Emma spoke, sounding oddly far away. 'I know. It's all over town.'

At least her plan had worked, Georgina consoled herself. All she could hope for now was that Emma would believe that she and Santos had married because of the attraction they had for one another, after the whirlwind romance that had started at the party.

'Georgie…'

Emma's voice sounded nervous, and as the silence lengthened still further Georgina heard the first rumble of thunder. 'Georgie, Carlo and I…we got married a few days ago.'

Georgina almost dropped the phone with shock. Her

quiet, biddable sister had gone against everyone and married in secret, without even telling *her*. Hurt lanced through her as she thought of the day she'd always imagined for Emma—a day when she would be there to see her married, not on a yacht off the coast of Spain.

A flash of lightning made Georgina's heart-rate accelerate wildly, but she tried to keep it under control. She didn't want Emma to worry—didn't want her to know of the ramifications her actions.

'Georgie, are you still there?'

She could hear the unease in her sister's voice and tried to focus her mind. How could Emma have betrayed her?

'I have to go, Emma, there's a storm coming. I'll call you later.'

She cut the connection as the full implications of what this meant hit home.

And Santos. What would *he* think?

A low rumble of thunder followed by the first heavy drops of rain made her retreat to the safety of the villa. Her fear of the storm outweighed the fact that Santos was himself like a brewing storm—one she didn't want to be around when it broke. From the doorway she watched the raindrops falling into the pool, disturbing its smooth surface. Deep down she knew she had more than a storm to fear.

The temperature dropped and a cool wind picked up. The white curtains billowed into the room where she stood, watching the increasingly heavy rain. Lightning lit up the darkening sky and she shuddered in a breath, as tense as the air around her. The clap of thunder was so loud she had to suppress a scream as she beat a hasty retreat further into the villa, feeling as shaken by Emma's revelation as by the storm itself. The trembling of her hands was very real.

'Scared of the storm?' Santos's voice was clipped and hard. 'Or is this another of your wonderful acting roles?'

She frowned, blinking in confusion as he came to stand before her. His dark eyes were full of fury and as he folded his arms across his chest and looked down at her she saw visible tension in his neck and shoulders.

'A little,' she lied, and rubbed her hands up and down her arms as if she were cold, refusing to rise to the bait of his last comment.

His gaze darted to the movement, watching through narrowed eyes, then moved back to her face. She fought the way her body responded to him, despite her apprehension about telling him what she'd just found out. She took a deep breath and tried to focus herself, curb her fear of the storm and deny the need to be held by him, to feel safe in his arms.

He marched past her and closed the doors to the terrace. The curtains ceased their wild dance but the tension of the storm remained, wrapping itself around them, drawing them towards each other. His dark gaze met hers and defiantly she lifted her chin, straightened her back, determined not to show him her fear.

There were two storms raging, she realised with a sinking feeling. Two storms she was going to have to ride out, no matter what. There wasn't any escape from either now.

'Your plan worked,' he said as he stood with his back to the doors and the lashing rain.

The dark clouds behind him only intensified the image of anger he projected.

'My plan was for Emma to think we were lovers so she wouldn't question our marriage.' Her voice didn't sound as firm as she wanted, and anxiety made her stomach flutter. She had to regain her composure.

'And why was that so important, Georgina?'

The use of her full name hurt, somehow, and the light sarcasm in his voice was unmistakable.

'You openly admit to marrying for financial security once already—why would she question *our* marriage?'

She watched his jaw tighten as he took in a deep breath, as if he was holding back what he really wanted to say. 'She never knew I married Richard so that I could fund her education and give her a secure home. My first marriage isn't part of this, Santos.'

Thunder cracked overhead, the villa seeming to shake with the force of it. Georgina glanced anxiously around the room, thankful that she was no longer out at sea.

'It damn well is when your reputation precedes you.' His voice was hard and echoed the aggression of the storm. The expression on his face was as dark and brooding as the sky.

'My reputation?' Lightning lit the room and her heart thudded almost as loudly as the thunder. 'If by that you mean that I married Richard, an older and unwell man, because he offered me lifelong security in return for a few years of companionship, then, yes, my reputation does precede me.'

She glared at him, hardly able to believe they were discussing her first marriage when it was the marriage of his brother to her sister that should take precedence. That was the one that affected them both, whether they liked it or not.

She had to tell him, but anxiously kept the conversation on its current course. As the next crack of thunder threatened to shake the foundations of the villa she stood her ground, glaring at Santos.

'A companionship so loving that you were dating other

men just weeks after his funeral.' He practically snarled the words at her, so intense was his anger.

'It was what he wanted,' she said, softly but firmly, remembering how insistent Richard had been that she should move on in life, find herself a man she could love.

She'd dated a few men just to do as Richard had wanted, to honour the memory of the man who'd given her a future. But she hadn't enjoyed their company and very quickly gossip had started.

After the initial shock of being at the centre of everyone's speculation she'd soon realised it provided a wall to hide behind.

'I found out very quickly that seeing a man once or twice only was the best way.' Let him think the worst of her. She had other worries right now. Besides, if he believed that of her it would keep him at arm's length—something she had to do now no matter what. She couldn't dwell on the closeness they'd shared.

Santos's brow furrowed. 'Best way for what?' The words snapped from him.

'For doing what *you* do,' she flung at him as another rumble of thunder, just as intense, reverberated around the room. 'For keeping the world at bay, keeping the gossips with something to get their teeth into, because ultimately it meant I could be on my own. I never wanted to be married the first time and I certainly don't want to be married now.'

She flopped down onto the sofa, unable to fight any longer. Remaining indifferent to what was being said about her and the shock of what Emma had done was finally too much.

How could her sister have said nothing? How could she have sneaked away the moment she'd left for Spain? It was a complete and utter betrayal. Emma had as good as thrown everything she'd ever done for her back in her face.

Santos walked across the marble floor. A hint of softness entered his tone as he crouched before her, forcing her to look into his eyes. 'Then why offer yourself to me?'

She swallowed down the urge to cry, to collapse into an emotional heap, and looked into his eyes. Their dark depths were almost unreadable. He was so close, and the spark of attraction passing between them was as strong as ever, but she mustn't let that cloud her mind and muddle her judgement.

'Why, Georgina?' he prompted, his voice a little firmer, and she realised the anger she'd seen in him earlier was still simmering beneath the surface.

She took a breath to tell him what she'd just learnt, but couldn't. The look in his glittering eyes halted those words

'For Emma,' she began, trying to put off the moment just a little longer. 'She believes in the dream of love, the happy-ever-after, and it's Carlo—your brother—who is that dream for her. When she told me about the will it seemed the most obvious deal to make. I'd married for convenience for Emma's benefit once before. I could do it again.'

Georgina was emotionally wrung out, but she had to tell him. She didn't want to—didn't want to rouse his anger—but she knew she had to. She couldn't keep it from him. He had a right to know.

'They are already married.'

The words were out before he had a chance to say anything.

He studied her for a moment, crouching in front of her as if he was talking to a child, making her think he'd be good with children. An image of her holding a baby with Santos's dark eyes and complexion rushed into her mind, not for the first time in recent days, but she pushed it harshly away. Marrying him was one thing, but she'd never have his child. She could never have a child, full-stop. She didn't want to risk being as useless as her own mother.

'When did you know?' His words, although cajoling, still reverberated with anger.

She looked down at the phone she still clutched in her hand and sighed. 'Minutes ago.'

Betrayal ripped through her again at the thought of what Emma and Carlo had done, but she knew Emma would never have done it alone—never.

'I can't believe it,' she whispered, more to herself than Santos.

'They married on Saturday.'

He stood up and looked down on her, his height making her feel small, his words like hailstones raining down on her. Another rumble of thunder followed, echoing his anger.

'Saturday?' She blinked back tears as she thought of Emma getting married whilst she'd been flying out to Spain. Then it hit her. 'That means Carlo married first.'

He nodded, folding his arms across his chest once more.

'So our marriage was for nothing. Carlo inherits the business and I miss the biggest day of my sister's life.' She wanted to jump up, to stand and face him, but her knees were too weak so she just buried her face in her hands.

What was she going to do now? Santos probably thought she'd conspired with them to outsmart him. There was only one thing she could do. Go home. Get far away from Santos.

'I'll go and pack,' she said, finally finding the strength to stand as another rumble filled the room, this time sounding as if it was finally receding.

'No.'

Santos grabbed her arm as she made to leave and she looked up into his face. A small part of her wanted to see the gentleness she'd seen on their wedding night. She wanted to feel as special as he'd made her feel that night. But instead his eyes were brittle with hardness.

'You are my wife. You will stay here.'

She shook her head. 'No, Santos, I can't. Their marriage changes everything.'

'Your scheming, meaning that Carlo married first, has changed nothing. We are still married.'

He held her arm tight, pulling her against his body. She could feel the heat of it and, despite the anger and tension in the air, her body responded traitorously to his.

'It's all about the business for you, isn't it?' Accusation rang in her voice as she lifted her chin, finding her defiant streak once more, denying the burning need that raged inside her. 'You can't bear it that you've lost it.'

He shook his head and his voice was hard. 'I haven't lost it. Not yet. And we will remain married.'

'Why?' Her breath was heaving in her chest.

His eyes darkened, the brittleness of earlier replaced with hot desire.

'Because of this.'

Before she could question him further his mouth claimed hers in a hot, searing kiss. She gasped in a mixture of annoyance and pleasure as his hand cupped her breast, making her arch against him, only being held upright by the firm grasp of his hand on her arm. She had no escape. Neither did she want an escape. She wanted his touch, his kiss. Damn it, she wanted *him*. She wanted him because she loved him—and that was exactly why she had to go.

She could hardly think straight, let alone put coherent words together, as he broke the kiss and looked down at her.

'This undeniable attraction that exists between us. We can't fight it for ever.'

'No,' she managed in a croaky voice. 'But it can't last for ever.'

He shrugged, relinquishing his grip on her arm to hold her hand instead. 'True, but we can explore it while it lasts.'

'Why would I want to do that?' Indignation at his knowing glance leapt through her.

'Because we are man and wife,' he said in a smooth tone that rippled over her heightened senses like velvet. 'Truly man and wife.'

She shook her head. 'Not really, we aren't. It was just a deal. Just a marriage of convenience.'

'Was our wedding night on the yacht just part of the deal?'

His self-satisfied smile made her blush at the memory of just how abandoned she'd been. He kissed her—a brief but intense one.

'I thought not.'

'No, Santos.' She pushed at his chest, needing space to think. 'This isn't what I wanted. Neither of us did. And now Emma and Carlo have married there is no need for us to be together.'

'That's where you are wrong, because Carlo hasn't yet inherited the business.'

'Of course he has. He's married—before you.' She almost froze with shock. Some of his earlier words were now making sense, like his accusation of her acting. He'd been playing with her.

'Yes, they are married.' The smile didn't reach his eyes this time. 'But, *querida*, that doesn't change anything.'

'What do you mean?' Confused, she stopped pushing him away. She didn't understand. Emma and Carlo had got married before she and Santos had even arrived in Spain, making Carlo the first son to marry. 'Why doesn't it change anything?'

Santos struggled with his conscience. Her act of being the wounded party was very convincing, just as her act of fear of the storm had been, but he didn't believe she'd known nothing of their plans. Why else would she have asked so seductively to stay on the yacht longer, or even agreed to leave London with him, if not to make it as difficult as possible for him to contact the outside world? She'd practically thrown herself at him, used all that a woman could to snare his interest and keep him from going back to the villa. She'd made him want her, teased and dallied with his desire since that first kiss at the party, and there was only one reason as far as he was concerned.

She'd planned it all along.

True, she'd wanted him as much as he'd wanted her. He'd have to be blind and stupid not to see how her body responded to his slightest touch. And each time he'd kissed her the attraction between them had intensified, until they couldn't ignore it any longer.

She'd deceived him, duped him, like all females did, with her body. And just like his father he'd ignored everything to be with her, to make her his. He'd been like a man possessed, unable to think of anything else other than Georgina. Thoughts of her had been all-consuming.

He enjoyed being with women, but never had he been so completely under a woman's spell.

Even now, when her kisses tasted of deceit, he wanted her. Passion burned in her eyes as she stood and glared at him. How dared she look so wounded? There could only be one winner in this game of passion and deceit she'd started. And that would be him.

'It isn't the first son to marry who inherits.' The words slipped out effortlessly. Finally he'd got her attention. 'But the first married son to produce an heir.'

He watched as his words slowly filtered through, like water permeating through limestone, until finally the expression on her face told him she understood the full implications.

She shook her head, backing away from him as if he was evil itself, her beautiful face ashen white, her eyes wide with disbelief. Oh, but she was a good actress. He almost believed it. Almost.

CHAPTER TEN

THE FIRST MARRIED son to produce an heir.

No, she screamed in her head, whilst outwardly the shutters came down, cocooning her behind a safe barrier.

'How long have you known this?' How could he stand there so calmly and tell her that? He might as well say her whole plan had been a waste of time. He'd lied all this time, but she couldn't see a trace of remorse.

'Long enough.'

His words sent a shiver down her spine.

'So what were you hoping for? A honeymoon baby?' She wanted to close her eyes against the pain of shattered dreams as they splintered around her. For just one night she'd thought she could sample that dream. She hadn't expected her attraction for him to turn into something deeper. Now it was spoilt by his admissions. His deceit. 'No wonder you were so—what was it?—unusually *relaxed* about contraception.'

'That's absurd.'

His eyes looked dark and hostile but she stood tall, remaining as defiant as she could manage.

A ray of sunlight speared the gloom and she glanced out at the clearing sky, glad that at least one storm was over.

'Not absurd, Santos.' She looked directly at him, something akin to anger and disappointment flitting through her. 'Not when you consider the clause of the will and that you knew Carlo wanted to get married. He loves my sister. Just by marrying he was a threat to you—because not only would he be the first married son, but probably the first married son to have the required heir.'

It was like a puzzle, and finally she was putting it together. She still had a few pieces to find, but it was all beginning to make sense now.

'Why are you so against Carlo?' She felt frustrated by those missing pieces. 'When you could have married any one of the women you've dated in the past and inherited everything you believe is yours.'

She watched as he paced the room—long, lean strides that drew her attention. As if needing escape, he opened the doors to the terrace and strode out. The fresh smell of dampness after the rain rushed into the room as he left. For a moment she stood and watched him, saw his pain, his frustration, with every move he made, and something deep inside her tugged at her emotions.

She knew that kind of pain, that kind of emptiness.

She walked to the door. Santos stood looking out to sea, his broad shoulders tense and the muscles in his arms taut as he leant on the balustrade. She longed to go to him, to touch him and soothe his pain. But sense prevailed. This was all of his making. She couldn't let him know how she felt—not when he'd used everyone as pawns in his power game.

It rushed at her so hard she almost stumbled. All her breath momentarily left her body and her heart raced like a wild horse fleeing captivity.

It couldn't be true—it just couldn't.

She loved him. Completely and utterly.

She pressed her fingertips to her lips to stifle a cry of distress. She didn't want to love anyone. She *couldn't* love anyone. And certainly not Santos Ramirez. Since the day her father had turned his back on them she'd watched her mother take a path of self-destruction. Her parents' actions proved beyond doubt that love was all-consuming, but also that it hurt, left you alone and killed all joy in life when it went wrong. It was a gamble she'd never wanted to take, so how had it happened? How had she fallen in love with Santos?

'I'm not against Carlo.'

His harsh words dragged her mind back from the pain of her past.

'Just the marriage.'

She sensed his vulnerability as he remained with his back to her, looking out to sea, at the sky clearing and brightening after the storm. Knowing she shouldn't, but unable to stop herself, she crossed the terrace and stood by him, her shoulder almost touching his arm as she stood surveying the view.

'Why did your father put such a clause in his will, forcing you to marry?' This was something that had niggled at her since Emma had first mentioned it. She'd imagined two young boys vying for their father's attention. A man who didn't deserve any from either of them as far as she was concerned.

'It's a family business, started by my grandfather— my mother's father. I suppose he assumed that as I was older by nine years I'd marry and have a family a long time before Carlo did.'

He sounded resigned and it tugged at her heart to hear him, almost as if he was admitting defeat.

'He must have thought he was being fair to us both, putting that clause in his will.'

'So why didn't you marry?' The question just had to

be asked. He'd never been short of female company. She'd very quickly learnt that.

He turned to face her and she held her breath as he looked down at her. His eyes searched her face as if looking for answers to questions he didn't even know. She watched as his face set into hard lines, shutting her out.

'To avoid the mess we are in now.' The angry words all but barked out at her.

She shivered despite the sun. 'It's easy to sort out.' Her words were curt as she lifted her chin in defiance and challenge, the softer emotions quashed by his frozen expression. 'I leave and you file for divorce.'

In one swift stride he came towards her, his hand holding her arm firmly. 'You are not going anywhere unless I do—and as for a divorce...'

He spoke with a voice so stern and disapproving she blinked in shock.

'There will not be a divorce. Your meddling has made sure of that.'

'But—' she began, wondering what she wanted to try and tell him, even what she didn't. 'There isn't any reason to remain married—not now.'

'You are forgetting, *mi esposa*, that an heir may yet still be needed.' He let go of her, keeping her where she stood with just the fixed glare of his dark eyes.

'No,' she snapped, and backed away from him, bumping against the chair she'd sat in to call her sister earlier. 'Even you're not so cold and callous that you'd bring a child into the world just to inherit a business.'

'I had hoped not even to marry to inherit. When you so kindly offered yourself I believed it would be enough, that I could find a way out of the clause long before Carlo married. But your meddling has changed everything.'

His eyes glittered furiously at her but she held her

ground, squared her shoulders and met his accusation head on.

Her *meddling*? 'What do you mean?'

'Don't play the innocent with me.'

His eyes glittered dangerously but she refused to be intimidated, refused to back down.

'Not when you've led me on, driven me wild with need for you since the night of the party.'

'I did not lead you on.' Indignation flared to life in her and she almost stamped her foot in frustration.

Santos knew he was losing his patience, reaching the boiling point that very few people managed to push him to. All he wanted was to prevent her from leaving. He needed her, yes, but he wanted her more.

'So what was our wedding night if not to divert my attention and keep me out of the way?'

She gasped at him, a blush creeping over her cheeks, and she looked as if she was struggling for words.

'You must have been delighted when I took you to the yacht. What better place to keep me out of the way?' Humiliation burned through him like a forest fire. He'd been used, played for a fool, and it wounded him even more to think that he'd relaxed. He'd wanted to open up to her, wanted to be who he really was, when all along she'd been as fake as snow in the desert. 'You flirted yourself at me in an attempt to stay longer on the yacht.'

Her brow furrowed and pain and confusion swirled in her eyes. For a moment he wanted to reach for her, wanted to kiss it all away. But kissing had got him into this mess. Kissing and much more had left him emotionally exposed and vulnerable.

'If that's what you think, Santos, it would be much better if you just let me go home. Alone.' Her words were firm and devoid of any emotion.

'That,' he snapped, instantly reining himself back, 'is not negotiable. You will stay here with me now I know where Carlo and Emma are.'

'Where they are?' She spoke rapidly, shock sounding in her tone. 'You mean they're not in London?'

Was it possible he'd got it all wrong? That she'd known nothing of their marriage plans?

He moved away from her—away from the intensity of her eyes and the questions deep within them. Maybe sending her back to London alone would be for the best, enable him to think clearly. Because his need for her had increased since they'd spent the night together and each time she came close his body remembered, even if his mind refused to acknowledge what he was beginning to feel for her.

'Perhaps you can tell me.' He tossed the words across the terrace as he made his way back inside the villa. 'You can explain everything to me on our way out this evening.'

'There's only one place I'm going this evening and that's the airport—with or without your help.' He knew she had followed him inside. He could feel her, sense her.

He sat down on the sofa, stretching his arm along the back of the black leather, and watched as she stood, fury blazing from her, in the centre of the room. A smile twitched the corners of his lips despite the bitter taste of humiliation. She looked stunningly sexy, a little fireball of passion.

'Tonight we are expected at a party my cousin has arranged for us and I have no intention of arriving without my bride.'

'Well, I'm sorry to disappoint you, Santos, but your bride is leaving. Right now.'

He clenched his jaw as his mind raced. 'You can't. You signed the agreement. You have legally agreed to live as my wife for twelve months.'

Her eyes widened in shock. 'I don't believe you actually put that in. You're barbaric.'

'I need an heir, Georgina.'

Right there in front of him she seemed to deflate. All the fire and fury drained from her and he sat forward, his elbows on his knees. Was she actually going to faint?

'I can't give you what you want.'

The anguish in her voice alarmed him and he leapt up and stood before her.

'I can't have a baby—I can't.'

Can't have a baby.

He hadn't considered this. He'd assumed that, like almost every woman, she'd want to become a mother.

'Why not?'

This threw everything into turmoil. If Carlo and Emma returned from Vegas as parents-to-be he would have lost everything—exactly what he'd promised his mother he'd never do the last time he saw her. Although he still didn't know what kind of misguided loyalty made him want to keep that promise.

Large tears welled up in Georgina's eyes. One broke free and ran down her cheek. Santos didn't know what to do. He hadn't considered the possibility that she couldn't have children. She'd been so adamant that she'd do anything to enable her sister to marry. He'd seen her as a viable back-up plan—a marriage of convenience to a woman who would be the mother of his child, should that drastic step be needed.

'I can't...I just can't,' she croaked in a whisper, tugging at something deep inside him so much that he wanted to hold her close, to soothe her.

Instead he clenched his hands into fists and marched away from her. 'This changes nothing. You are my wife. You agreed to it for one year and I'm not going to allow you to publicly humiliate me any further. I don't need my wife deserting me within days of our supposed whirlwind romance. It's bad enough that Carlo and Emma have run off to Vegas…'

'Vegas?' Incredulity made her tear-laden eyes widen and he steeled himself against the need to hold her.

'As if you didn't know.'

Attack was the only way he could control the myriad of strange new emotions running riot inside him. He wanted her with him, yet he didn't. Above all he wanted to punish her for her part in deceiving him, but even *he* wasn't so callous that in the face of what she'd just told him he'd actually do that.

Vegas. Emma had gone to Las Vegas to get married.

'I didn't know,' Georgina whispered, betrayal rushing through her.

They must have planned it for weeks. Why hadn't Emma said something? Taken her into her confidence?

He took her hand, his mood softened. 'It seems we are both victims of their deception.'

His deep voice sent shivers of awareness down her spine, but she remained firm and resolute, not trusting him.

'Have you spoken to Carlo?' She pulled back, watching his face as she asked the question.

'No, but the gossip columns are full of it. When we left for Spain they must have gone straight to Vegas. They must have left as soon as we'd left the party. Damn it, they knew all along.'

He let go of her as his frustration built again and she felt strangely alone. The touch of his hand had been grounding, somehow. He blamed her for what Emma and Carlo had done, that much was obvious, yet still she wanted his comfort, wanted to feel his arms around her.

If she was going to survive the next few days she had to push her emotions right to the back of her mind—had to ignore them before they exposed her to the biggest pain of all. One thing she was sure of: she couldn't remain his wife for a year—not if it meant living with him.

Twice in her life she had trusted and loved a man and twice he had let her down. Her father, whom she'd adored, had walked away one stormy night without a backward glance, leaving her in tears, clinging to the front door. Then Richard, whom she'd loved in a gentle, appreciative way, had left her alone in the world—more alone than she cared to admit.

Now Santos.

She'd fallen in love with him so passionately and deeply she couldn't even think properly any more. Her usual unemotional demeanour was smashed into icy crumbs.

'Emma would never have done it if she'd thought it would end like this.' She tried to think back to all they'd spoken off when they'd been getting ready for the party Santos had thrown. She shook her head in disbelief. 'She just wouldn't.'

'It would seem your sister isn't as loyal to you as you are to her.' Santos's voice was hard as he paced the room. 'Whatever possessed them to run off and get married?'

'Love,' Georgina whispered.

Santos rounded on her. 'Love is for fools. It destroys lives.'

'How can you say that?' Her frustration matched his fury and she glared at him, daring him to answer. 'You must have loved once.'

An echo of a previous conversation filled her mind.

He closed the distance between them in long strides, dominating the room with his volatile mood. 'Your father walked out on you, no?' His accent was stronger than ever as he battled with his emotions.

Her breath caught in her throat as he brought up her past, made the memories of that night—already too fresh after the storm—rush back. 'My father has nothing to do with it.'

'If he'd loved you he wouldn't have left. That's what you think, no?'

His eyes locked with hers, holding her prisoner, forcing her to face things she didn't want to face.

Before she could answer his harsh words came at her again, as if he no longer cared what he was saying. 'It's the same for me. Love will never be a part of how I think of my mother, or she of me.' He whirled around and marched back outside, as if needing more space to vent his anger.

Cautiously she followed him outside. 'What happened with your mother?' Her words were a whisper as she watched him drag in a deep breath.

He turned to look at her once more, his face set in firm lines.

'I was a mistake.' He swallowed as if the words tasted bitter and her heart tugged for him. 'A mistake that forced her to marry my father. A mistake she always made me pay for.'

'But your father loved her, didn't he?' She scanned her

mind for the little snippets of his life he'd told her about, trying to piece things together.

'And that love was rewarded with my being ignored as a young boy.' Pain resounded in his voice and he sighed and turned to look out to sea.

He was turning his back not only on her but on the conversation. It was what he always did, she realised. Right from that first time in his office when he'd looked out over London. It seemed a lifetime ago instead of less than a week.

'But your father moved on and you have a brother now.'

She heard him inhale deeply, saw his shoulders lift and then fall. She'd said the wrong thing again.

'Half-brother.' The words were grated out, and still he kept his back resolutely turned. 'One who has just proved how little he thinks of me. Just as always, he's got what he wants.'

Georgina thought again of all Emma had told her about Carlo. 'I'm sure it's not like that. In fact I'd go as far as to say he doesn't want to inherit the business. He wants to do his own thing, make his own way in life.'

Santos turned round to face her, questions in his dark eyes. 'You're wrong. How could any man not want to inherit his father's business?'

'Not everyone is as motivated by power as you are, Santos. Carlo and Emma just want to make a life together—a normal life.' Without thinking she reached out and touched his arm, her fingers heating as they felt the firmness of his muscles.

'What is that, Georgina?' He sounded drained and tired.

'They want to be together. They're in love, Santos. Is that so hard to accept?' She moved closer to him, trying to quash the surge of love she felt for him as he opened up and let her see his pain.

He looked down into her eyes, his darkening. She thought he might kiss her as he moved closer, with his head dropping lower. But then he stopped, the abruptness of it sending a chill through her.

'No, Georgina, no.' He moved away from her and for the first time ever he looked at a loss for what to say.

This powerful all-controlling man that she'd fallen in love with couldn't and wouldn't accept that love even existed. If that didn't staunch the love that was rapidly growing for him, then nothing would.

'No to what, Santos? Can't you just accept that they love one another and there aren't any ulterior motives at work?'

He changed as he stepped away, as if the distance was enabling him to regain his power, his authority. 'You engineered this whole thing—encouraged them to fly off to Vegas, kept me busy in the way only a woman of your reputation can, and secured a big financial settlement for yourself along the way.'

Hurt raced through her, stinging like a thousand bees. 'You can keep your money, tear up the agreement—anything.' She rounded on him, angry at herself for feeling for him, for wanting to reach out to him, for wanting to love him. 'I don't even know why you haven't just bought Carlo out. It would have been much less complicated than getting married.'

'Don't insult my business management. You know nothing about it—about the way Carlo has refused my generous offer, not once but twice, holding out for the ultimate prize.'

His voice was fierce but she didn't pay any heed to it

at all. Her emotions were running so high she no longer cared what happened.

'No, I *don't* know anything about it. All I know is that I should never have got involved.' She hissed the words at him as his dark eyes accused her. 'I should have just helped them get married.'

'You did.'

'No!' Exasperation made her voice sharp.

He really believed she'd done this for money, for her own gain as well as Emma's. Enraged beyond comprehension, she marched to his study. Her thoughts were beyond rational as she barged into the room, and when she saw the file holding their agreement on his desk she picked it up.

Santos entered the study just as she took hold of the agreement they'd both signed such a short time ago, his face as dark as the thunderclouds had been earlier. She looked at him, smiled sarcastically. Challenging him. Then she tore up the agreement into as many tiny pieces as her shaking hands could manage.

'You can do what you like, *mi esposa*, but you will still be my wife.'

'I'm leaving, Santos, as your wife or not. I don't care, but I'm going back to London.'

She pushed past him and almost ran to her room. Without pausing she grabbed her handbag, checked for her passport and spun on her heel, not wanting anything from him.

She'd get a taxi to the airport and sit there all night if she had to, but one thing was for sure: she'd be on the next flight back to London. With that plan of action in mind she headed for the front door of the villa, glad Santos was nowhere to be seen.

Anger and frustration still raced in her veins as she pulled open the heavy ornate door—but Santos stood there, hands folded across his powerful body.

CHAPTER ELEVEN

'I HAVE TO go, Santos,' she fired at him, her heart thudding so loudly she thought he might hear it. 'We should never have married. I was stupid to think it could work.'

'Stupid to try and deceive me—that's what you mean, is it not, *querida*?' His words were slow and very deliberate.

The setting sun cast an orange glow around him as he stood firm and resolute before her. Despite the pain in her heart, her body responded to the image of him—the man she loved. The man she must never think of again once she'd got back to London. Perhaps she'd move away, get a small place in the country, live simply and quietly. Anything not to have to see him again.

'I'm not even going to deny it.' Her temper flared. 'You're determined to think the worst so you can go ahead and do it, just like you have with your brother and his mother. Even your father.'

He inhaled deeply, his handsome face becoming sharper than she'd ever seen. His eyes hardened until they resembled polished obsidian, with glittering hints of the lava that formed it hidden in their depths.

'Get in the car, Georgina.' His tone brooked no rebuke and she stiffened at the challenge. There was no way she was going to let him stop her. She had to get away—as far away as possible.

'No,' she said vehemently, and tried to move past him, but his reactions were fast and he instantly blocked her, his dominating body filling the doorway.

'I'm going to the airport.'

'Then I shall take you.' His tone was as overpowering as his body.

She looked from his face to the car behind him and noticed for the first time that the passenger door was open and the engine running. Her heart raced at the thought of being with him for just a little while longer, because despite everything that was where she wanted to be. But he would never want her as his wife now—not when he believed her capable of such deception. A deception she was innocent of.

'Why?' She couldn't help herself asking, as if in just a few seconds he would have changed his mind about her.

'You are my wife, and as such I will drive you to the airport.'

He left her in no doubt that there wouldn't be any further discussion on the subject and she dropped down into the low sports car, nerves taking flight in her stomach as he climbed into the driver's seat.

She glanced across at him as the air inside the car filled with his raw masculine scent—one that would haunt her for ever—only to find he was looking at her. Furiously she glared at him, then looked away. She wasn't going to be a victim of his charm this time. The sooner she got to the airport the better.

The drive along the busy roads was fast and painfully silent. Each time she looked at him his stern profile hinted at the anger he held in check. Each passing second became tenser than the last, the air more laden

and heavy, and she breathed a sigh of relief as the airport came into view.

He passed the entrance and she panicked. 'Where are
we going?'

'My plane is waiting on the Tarmac.'

'You don't need to do that. I'll book on the next flight.'
She tried hard to keep her desperation from him, but
it wasn't just him she was annoyed with. She'd almost
hoped he was coming to London too and that he did
want her.

'We shall be in London by midnight.'

'We?' She silently cursed that last thought—that last
futile wish.

'Did you really think you could walk out so easily?'
He turned to look at her briefly as he manoeuvred the car
into the airport and headed for the plane. Within seconds
of them stopping he was out of the car and at her door,
and once their passports were checked he took her hand
and led her up the steps of the plane.

The door closed and a strange stillness settled inside
the cabin. Santos sat in one of the white leather chairs,
his long legs stretched out before him, looking relaxed,
but she knew from the tension in his face he was anything but.

Georgina resigned herself to the situation and sat
down, fixing her attention on the darkening skyline rather
than look at the man who'd turned everything in her life
upside down, including her heart. She consoled herself
with the fact that at least she was going back to London.
Once there she could so much more easily walk away
from Santos. But that thought didn't make her feel as
she'd wanted it to. It made her heart ache. Pain lanced
through it, shattering it into pieces. But she couldn't let
him know.

* * *

If Santos had thought the flight to London was tense, then the drive through London's streets was worse. Georgina sat at his side, irresistibly close, yet undeniably far from him. He knew she was trapped in her deceit. The evidence was stacked against her. She'd deceived him, tricked him into marrying her so her sister and his brother could take all he'd worked so hard for over recent years. This time Georgina's gamble wasn't going to pay off.

'I can't stay here.'

Georgina's words drew him up sharp. She'd realised where they were. The storm, it seemed, raged on.

'Take me back to my own apartment, please.'

He didn't say anything, just shook his head once as she looked across at him, her face partially lit by street lamps.

'Santos, please, don't prolong the agony.'

The anguish in her voice was so acute it was almost physical. But what did she mean, agony? Had their time together been so awful?

'Agony? What agony?' he snapped at her recklessly, instantly furious with himself for allowing her to see even a moment's loss of control.

She looked taken aback, as if she hadn't meant to say those words. 'Just admit it's time we went our separate ways, Santos. Things haven't worked out.' She hesitated for a moment as the car pulled up outside his apartment. 'We've both been deceived—let's leave it at that.' She sounded tired, as if struggling with defeat.

'You are my wife, Georgina, and as such I want you with me when Carlo and Emma return. I want us to present a united front.' He couldn't admit it yet—not even to himself—but he seemed to be clutching at every possible reason for her to stay, as if he didn't want her to go.

The chauffeur opened the car door and he stepped out

into the cold autumn night. Light rain had fallen and the small amount of traffic that passed swished by on the wet road. He walked round to the other side of the car and opened Georgina's door, marvelling at how suddenly she seemed at ease. Was he even now falling into line with one of her devious plans?

She stepped out onto the pavement and looked at him. 'I don't see why we should keep up the pretence any longer.'

'No?' He walked towards the entrance doors, glancing back and hoping she would follow. He wasn't in the mood for any more in-depth discussions. 'Do you not want to continue until Emma comes back? It would be better if she thought you were happy, would it not?'

He watched as her expression changed from defiance to realisation that he spoke the truth. He certainly didn't want Carlo to think he'd married Georgina in a bid to secure the business; it was an ongoing issue between them. One that now threatened everything he'd ever cared about.

'You're right.' She sighed and smiled sweetly at him—a little too sweetly, convincing him that even now she played the game, using him as she had from the very beginning. 'It wouldn't do if they found out what we'd done—for reasons other than love, of course.'

Opening the door, he walked towards the lift, pressed the button and turned to her. Did she *have* to keep brandishing that word about? As if it was the very centre of everything that had happened?

Irritated, he looked above the lift doors, anxious to see if it was coming. 'It will be for the best,' he said tersely.

'That's debatable,' she tossed at him as the lift doors opened and she walked in. 'I've yet to decide just who it will be best for, but tonight, at least, I'm prepared to stay here.'

He didn't know what to say to that—his usual quick thinking had totally deserted him—so he remained silent as the lift took them up to his apartment, acutely aware of her so very close to him. He could smell her sweet floral scent and clenched his hands into fists in a bid to stamp out the threatening fire.

Santos unlocked the door and Georgina couldn't believe she was back at his apartment. Everything she'd planned had gone wrong and, worse, had been for nothing. She'd told Santos she could have just encouraged Emma and Carlo to run off and get married and now she wished she had. At least then she wouldn't have tasted something she could never have. She wouldn't have fallen in love with a man who openly admitted he wasn't capable of love in any form.

She sighed wearily. The last few days had been emotionally challenging for all the wrong reasons and she just wanted to be on her own.

'It's late,' she said softly as he flicked on the lights in the kitchen. 'I'm going straight to bed.'

She looked across at him, wanting to add that she was going alone, that she would spend the night in the same room she'd occupied before, but something in his expression held her back. Her heart began to race as the intensity of his gaze rested on her, as if he too couldn't bring himself to suggest she sleep alone.

He walked towards her, his footsteps echoing on the wooden floor, and like an animal caught in car headlights she just stood there and watched, mesmerised by him. Nerves made her bite gently on her bottom lip as he stopped in front of her, so close and yet so far.

'Where are you going to sleep, *mi esposa*? With your husband or alone?'

His accent had become more defined, sending shivers of awareness all over her. When his gaze rested on her lips she stopped biting them and smiled, almost tasting the saccharine of it.

'Alone.'

With you, her mind screamed as that one word left her lips. She wanted to sleep beside the man she loved, feel the warmth of his body next to her. But she reminded herself the man she loved didn't really exist. That man had been pretence and nothing more. This was the real Santos.

'Then I shall say *buenas noches, mi esposa.*'

He moved closer. Instinct told her he was going to kiss her, and heaven help her she wanted him to, but if he did...

She stepped back. 'Goodnight, Santos,' she said as firmly as possible, before retreating to the safety of the room she'd previously occupied.

Santos watched her go, confusion racing through him. Why was he trying to prevent her from leaving? Just what kind of power did she have over him? Perhaps it was better if they slept alone—although his body protested at the idea. He knew he needed time to think. He had to be sure of what to do next and at the moment he hadn't a clue.

With an exasperated sigh he tousled his hair and turned on his heel. Strong coffee was what he needed. And work. Going to an empty bed when Georgina slept in the next room was not going to be an option. Neither was going to her and trying to explain—to himself as well as her—why he didn't want her to go.

The aroma of fresh coffee lingered in the air, and

the taste of it invigorated his senses as he headed for his study. He had reports to catch up on and an aching need to deny.

A neatly stacked pile of post almost made him groan aloud. He wasn't in the mood. But as he sat at his desk the postmark on one letter caught his attention. A solicitor's name glared out at him from the large white envelope. Anxiously he tore it open, but was totally unprepared for what he saw.

So unprepared he had to read it again.

Carlo had renounced all claims to his father's estate in deference to him. Santos closed his eyes in relief, but that was short-lived as the implications of the letter hit home. What would this mean for him and Georgina?

He tried to get Carlo on his mobile, but it went straight to voicemail. Annoyed, he hung up. He wasn't about to leave a message. Instead he tried to focus on his work, but all sorts of jumbled thoughts raced through his mind. He'd never felt this disorientated or distracted before.

After several hours he gave up on trying to work or contacting Carlo. He picked up the letter again and headed for the kitchen, unable even to consider trying to sleep. More coffee was required. As it brewed he read the letter again, trying to understand why his brother had felt the need to do this when he'd offered to buy him out several times. What point was he making?

Exasperated, he tossed it on the kitchen table and walked over to the windows. The faint light of dawn crept across the sky, and with it he hoped would come answers and solutions.

It was still very early, but Georgina knew that Santos was likely to be up and about, so she quickly scanned the living room, relieved to see it empty, and headed for the kitchen. She flicked on the kettle and searched for a mug, needing as much caffeine as she could get after her sleepless night. She noticed the partly drunk cups of cold coffee—evidence that either Santos had been entertaining or he too had had a bad night.

The coffee's aroma revived her and she leant back against one of the kitchen units to sip her drink, wrapping her hands comfortingly around her mug. It was then that she noticed the letter. It looked official, and at first she turned the other way, but as she did so a name caught her attention.

She looked more closely and nearly gasped at what she saw. The letter very clearly stated that Carlo had renounced his claim on his father's estate.

Guilt rushed through her for even thinking of looking at Santos's mail, but that was hotly followed by anger and disappointment. This letter changed everything. Santos would inherit his father's business without the need for a wife—or an heir. He didn't need her any more. So why was he tormenting her like this? Insisting she stay with him? To punish her?

She should feel relieved. At least she could walk away from him and try and piece together her life. Emma had Carlo and didn't need her any more, so she could get that longed-for peaceful cottage in the country.

The coffee turned bitter in her mouth and she put the nearly full mug down on the side, turning her back on the letter and all it meant. She felt sick when she should be relieved that she could at last walk away from this sham of a marriage. She should be heading out of the door right now and not giving the man she'd married a second thought. But she couldn't.

She couldn't just walk away.

She loved him.

'They're back.'

Santos's voice broke through her rambling thoughts. His hair was still damp from the shower. The last time she'd seen his hair wet they had just shared the most amazing moment in the shower. Did he remember that? She looked at him, as immaculate as ever in his designer suit, and found it hard to believe he would.

'Are they all right?' She pushed aside her memories and worries as she watched him walk past her into the kitchen. She was mesmerised by him, by the powerful aura he exuded, and found all she could do was watch as he organised fresh coffee.

'Of course they are. We'll have dinner with them tonight. Sort everything out.'

He sounded cheerful, not at all weighed down by the problems of the last few days. That letter had obviously made everything right for *him*, but when was he going to tell *her*? Then it hit her. How long had he known?

'No.'

The word rang out in the kitchen and he stopped and looked at her, a frown creasing his brow.

'I can't.'

'Don't you want to see Emma? I thought it would be what you wanted?' He looked puzzled. He flicked the switch on the coffee machine and walked over to her. 'What's the matter, Georgina?'

The concern that should have been in such words was missing, replaced by suspicion.

She bit down hard on her tongue. She wanted to tell him she knew about the letter, wanted to demand to know when he'd known about it. But as she looked up into his face, searched his eyes, all she could do was shake her head.

He reached out to her, holding her arms loosely, and

looked at her. 'What's wrong?' And this time he did sound concerned—but not for her, surely?

Wrong? *Everything* was wrong. And suddenly she knew she couldn't walk away from him without telling him why.

'You wouldn't understand.' She dropped her gaze, not able to bear his scrutiny any longer. And if he turned on the charm she'd never resist, never be able to explain anything.

'I could try.' His voice wasn't as firm as usual, and a waver of doubt lingered in it.

'No, Santos, you couldn't. You don't do love. You don't know how it feels to love someone so much you'd do anything for them, only to find they've deceived you.' The floodgates had opened and the words tumbled out as she looked up at him again, her eyes begging him to understand.

He let go of her arms and stepped back a pace, his tall, athletic body dominating her, as big a hurdle for her to overcome as the shock of seeing the letter.

'Don't do this to yourself, Georgina.'

'What do you want me to do? Shut myself away from love just like you have?'

He stood, immovable and silent as she waited for him to say something. Finally he spoke. 'You're right. I don't understand.'

She closed her eyes for a second against the pain of his admission, then opened them and looked at him, injecting as much firmness into her voice as possible. 'There's no reason for us to be together any more, Santos.' She hesitated as she saw the firm set of his shoulders. 'I'm going home.'

'Leaving, you mean?'

She watched his jaw clench as he stood, all but blocking her way out of the room.

'Yes, leaving.' She walked past him into the living area, her arm brushing his as she did so. The shock of that contact made her take in a sharp breath.

Santos clenched his hands into tight fists and bit down hard. He wanted to tell her to stay, but he didn't know how to—let alone why. Was it because not only was she the first woman who hadn't succumbed to his charm immediately, but the first woman to walk out on him?

But she *wasn't* the first woman to walk out on him. His mother had done the same. He'd stood and watched her leave, not understanding why. He'd felt helpless then too.

'Georgina.'

Her name snapped from his lips and for a moment he wondered if he'd actually spoken, then he heard her footsteps stop. Ominous silence filled the apartment.

He took in a deep breath and left the kitchen. She stood by the front door. Last time she'd tried to walk out on him he'd gone with her, but this time he couldn't. This time all he could do was watch her go. He couldn't risk opening his heart to her.

She raised her brows at him in question. She wouldn't even speak to him. Should he ask her to stay? Tell her he wanted to understand? That somewhere deep inside he was beginning to understand that elusive emotion love?

But still he couldn't.

'My solicitor will contact you with regard to the divorce.'

CHAPTER TWELVE

GEORGINA HELD THE letter in shaking hands. Santos hadn't wasted any time. He must have instructed his solicitor to file for divorce the moment she'd left his apartment. But what had she expected? That he would miss her? Come after her and declare his undying love?

He'd admitted that he didn't understand. They'd been almost his last words to her that morning.

Well, if he thought she'd hide away and meekly sign the papers then he had another thought coming. She would show him she could be as strong as he was. She would go down fighting. Fighting for the love she couldn't deny herself but had to.

With that in mind she tapped in to the same fiery determination that had given her the courage to march into his office and suggest they marry in the first place.

She put on her charcoal suit, her high heels and applied make-up. Then she pulled out her rarely used briefcase, put the letter inside and left, slamming the front door behind her. The few persistent photographers waiting intently outside her flat almost fazed her—they'd been camping out since the details of their marriage had hit the headlines, desperate for a story—but she passed through them, refusing to answer their questions or make a comment, quickly hailing a taxi.

By the time the taxi pulled up outside the Ramirez International offices it had started to rain, but she refused to rush in, head down against the rain. With her head held high she walked determinedly in, hardly giving the rain a second thought. Alone inside the lift she had time to check her appearance. It was vital she looked as sleek and sophisticated as possible. He must never know how devastated she was by the last two weeks, how little sleep she'd had recently.

She smoothed her hands down her skirt, took a deep breath and walked proudly out of the lift as soon as the doors opened. His secretary looked up as she pushed open the heavy glass door, but Georgina wasn't about to stop and ask permission to see her husband. He was going to listen to what she had say whether he liked it or not.

'Excuse me, Miss…' the shocked woman said as she made her way straight towards Santos's office.

Georgina stopped and turned to face her. 'It's Mrs,' she said firmly. 'Mrs Ramirez. And I'm here to see my husband.'

With that she turned and walked down the wide corridor that led to his office. Nothing was going to stop her now.

She paused briefly outside the door, her hand poised above the handle. Last time she'd stood there full of nerves, hardly able to believe she was about to propose to a man she'd never met.

Not for one minute had she thought she would find him so devastatingly attractive. And if she'd known that from the very first moment their eyes met a sizzle of desire would weave a spell so strong about them she would have turned and run, regardless of her motives.

She'd never expected to fall in love with him so quickly and so completely.

It had taken the letter instigating their divorce this morning for her to realise what she had to do—that she couldn't run any more. She'd stood by and watched two men she'd loved in very different ways from the way she loved Santos leave her. This time she was determined it would be different. This time she wouldn't shrink from the pain. This time she'd face it head-on.

She took a deep breath, gathered all her nerve and opened the door.

He was sitting at his desk, looking cool and composed. Her heart lurched just at seeing him, but she couldn't let that get the better of her now.

'To what do I owe this pleasure?'

His words were as cool and clear as a mountain stream but she couldn't falter now.

She put her briefcase on his desk, looked him in the eye and flicked it open. The dark depths of his eyes glittered as he watched every slow, purposeful movement. Taking out the letter, she placed it on the desk and then closed her briefcase.

'Don't play games, Santos. You know why I'm here. To put an end to our marriage.'

But not until he knew how she felt—knew she loved him. But telling someone who hated even to hear the word, let alone acknowledge the emotion, wasn't going to be easy.

He stood up, his height as intimidating as the breadth of his shoulders, but she held his gaze, trying hard to ignore the lurching of her heart.

'A marriage *you* instigated, Georgina. Here, in this very room.'

Santos moved from behind his desk and came closer to her, even now unable to resist the challenge her eyes fired at him. The first time she'd stood in his office, with fire and determination burning in her eyes, he'd wanted her.

He still wanted her. The force of the attraction hadn't lessened after spending the night with her. It had increased.

'One you willingly went along with. You changed it to suit your needs simply to get a business. You didn't think I was worthy of an explanation about the heir you needed to inherit everything.'

Her angry accusation had found its mark but he wouldn't let her see that.

'You make it sound calculated when it wasn't.'

He leant against the edge of his desk, folded his arms across his chest, fighting the urge to tell her everything. Then he remembered the pain in her voice when she'd told him she couldn't have children.

'I had no idea then that you couldn't have children.' His voice sounded unsteady even to him, and she closed her eyes, her long lashes shutting him out. He reached out to her, his hand touching her arm in a gesture of concern. She jumped back from him, her eyes now blazing. 'I'm sorry.'

She remained silent, her steady gaze holding his, and he wished she'd let him close. He'd never meant to hurt her. She had made him feel things he'd never thought he would. He still found it hard to comprehend the aching void in his life, an ache born out of love. But now she hated him.

'It's not that I *can't* have children, Santos.'

She spoke in a harsh, raw tone, her words snagging his conscience.

'I just couldn't bring a child into the world for that reason. I would have thought you of all people would understand that.'

His mind roared as the pain of his childhood rushed back at him. He'd been a mistake. One that had forced his mother into marriage with a man she couldn't love. With dreadful clarity he realised Georgina was right. If he'd had to he would have resorted to fathering a child just to get the business—a child that he didn't want. But wasn't that why he'd never married? To avoid such a decision?

Guilt slashed at him, making his next words harsh and serrated.

'If I could have avoided that I would have done.'

'The same as you could have avoided all this.' She pointed fiercely at the letter which lay on her briefcase. 'If you'd just talked to Carlo he wouldn't have had to go to the extremes he did. You denied Emma her big day.' She paused for a moment, her dark eyes flecked with gold sparks of determination. 'You should still talk to Carlo.'

Again she was right, and he gritted his teeth angrily. Talking to Carlo hadn't been an option before, but he could put that right. With an exasperated sigh he thrust himself away from the desk and strode towards the windows. Raindrops ran down them, diluting the view of London.

'Don't hide from it, Santos. You used me to score points on your own brother.'

The accusation flew at him but he kept his back resolutely to her. She made him feel exposed, vulnerable. Damn it, she made him feel emotions he didn't want—emotions he didn't need.

He turned to face her, and despite the hardness of her expression he saw the pain on her face, felt it radiating out.

'I was caught up in battle started by my mother. On her deathbed she made me promise never to let go of what was rightfully mine. When you so calmly offered marriage I never meant it to go any further.'

She made a sound that was a mixture of a gasp and a whimper—a sound full of pain. 'So seducing me, getting me into your bed, was a mistake too?'

He watched the rapid rise and fall of her chest and realised she wasn't nearly as rational as she wanted him to believe. 'No, Georgina,' he said as he moved towards her, his tone lower and huskier just from his memories of that night. 'I wanted you then as much as you wanted me.'

She blushed, and it shocked him to realise how he'd missed that innocent blush.

'I hate you for that.'

She hated him.

The venom in her voice left him in no doubt that she meant it and something changed inside him—as if somewhere a key had turned, unlocking something, some sort of emotion he wasn't yet ready for.

'Don't play the wounded party with me when you already have one very convenient marriage behind you.' Anger was the best line of defence. It would supress whatever it was she'd unlocked, because right now was not the time to analyse it.

'Richard never forced me into his bed. He didn't seduce me and I love him for that.'

Her words rang loud and clear in his head, as if she were at the top of a bell tower.

Santos gritted his teeth against those words. She'd loved Richard. It was as if he'd stepped back a few decades—as if he was witnessing the love his father and stepmother had shared, a love that had excluded him. But that exclusion hadn't made him feel raw with the pain he now felt.

'So you openly admit you married him for money?' He maintained his angry defence—anything other than accept what the raging pain inside him might mean.

'Yes, I did!' She flung the words at him. 'He asked

me, he saw I needed help and offered it, but I had no idea then just how ill he was. That's why he insisted I marry him—because he knew it was the only way to be sure he could provide for me into the future.'

He didn't want to hear it, yet at the same time he did.

Her face softened. 'He loved me, and for the chance he gave me I loved him.'

Santos was consumed with jealousy. He couldn't hear anything else other than that she'd loved Richard.

Georgina watched as Santos's face hardened. He couldn't even stand to hear the word *love*—couldn't contemplate such an emotion existed. He'd been denied it as a child and now, as an adult, he was determined to continue to deny himself.

She knew she was taunting him, using that word again, but she pressed on, hoping he'd see how she felt. 'I loved him in a compassionate way. There wasn't even a flicker of a spark of passion. It was a comfortable love. A safe love. Not the way I love you.'

Silence stretched between them. She remained tall and straight, even though she wanted to crumple on the floor right in front of him. The silence lengthened.

She shouldn't have said anything—shouldn't have opened her heart to his ridicule. Not when she knew how he scorned love. A lump gathered in her throat, almost choking her. This was no different from watching her father walk away. No different from having to say goodbye to Richard. As if her love had made them leave. She knew it wasn't true, but the pain of it had made it feel that way.

Fear of going through that again was what drove her now. It was why she'd come here—why she was exposing herself so utterly to Santos's contempt. If she was yet again to lose a man she loved, she was going to make her feelings clear.

'Do you really expect me to believe that when these last weeks have been nothing but a big lie, an act for you?' His words were sharp, heightening the tension between them.

'It wasn't a lie. There were times...' She paused, feeling heat spread across her cheeks as she remembered their wedding night, the passion they'd shared. That night there hadn't been any pretence, any acting on her part. She swallowed hard and continued. 'There were times when it was real.'

'Would that be the moment you kissed me at the party, or the morning you all but seduced me into staying on the yacht? Or the times when all your acting skills were called upon so that you could cover for Emma and Carlo running off to get married?'

The cynicism in his voice lashed at her like hail, each word stinging. How could he still believe she had had any part in it?

'I had no part whatsoever in their marriage,' she fumed at him, frustration rising like a spring tide. 'They deceived me too, Santos.' She stood facing him across the office, the expanse of soft cream carpet seeming to grow bigger between them with every passing second. 'They were desperate.'

'Back to that again, are we?'

Each word was like a bullet in her heart, each one wounding her further.

'I can see that whatever I say won't make any difference to you, Santos. You're incapable of love.'

'I made that perfectly clear from our very first meeting.'

In exasperation she covered her face with her hands

briefly, dropped her head and took in a long, shuddering breath. She couldn't take it any more, and gave vent to her frustration. 'You're so cold, so proud, and so damned stubborn. It was a mistake coming here.'

She pulled her jacket tighter about her body, as if it would deflect the hurt. For a moment his gaze lowered, caught by the movement. He took a step closer to her, his eyes meeting hers once more. She stepped back instinctively, needing space to be able to think.

'So why *did* you come, *mi esposa*? Tell me. Why?'

His accent became heavy and to her dismay he moved closer still, rendering thought almost impossible.

She whirled round and grabbed the papers from his desk, knocking her briefcase to the floor in the process. 'To sign these.' She waved the papers at him furiously. 'To put an end to something that should never have been started.'

'You could have sent them via your solicitor.' His calm voice irritated her further.

'And I wish I had. But I was taking a chance—a gamble.' She watched as he frowned, his dark eyes narrowing. 'I had to know.'

He said nothing, as if he was trying to take in what she said, so she dropped the papers on the desk purposefully, picked up a pen and signed, tossing the pen back onto the polished surface next to the papers.

'And now I do.'

Santos watched her sign the papers, listened as the pen crashed to the table. Each breath was hard to take, as if he was being suffocated. He hurt. Pain raced through him.

Even as she walked across the office he couldn't say a word, couldn't move, as if he'd been frozen in time. What the hell was the matter with him?

Something snapped, as if chains had broken. He inhaled deeply. The noise caught her attention and she turned to look at him. Her face was pale.

'I know I was a fool.' She threw the words at him as if he was nothing more than dirt at the edge of the road. 'I gambled and I lost.'

He tried to make sense of her words. What was she trying to tell him?

Not the way I love you.

His mind replayed what she'd said moments before. Purposefully he moved towards her, and when she turned again panic tore through him. If she left now he'd never see her again. He couldn't let her go. Not yet. He loved her; he'd just refused to admit it.

'I gambled too.'

The words hurried out and he clenched his hands, trying to keep himself from reaching for her, from preventing her from leaving.

She spun round and faced him again, her eyes sparkling with molten gold. 'Not with emotions, you didn't.'

She moved towards the door so suddenly he was taken off guard.

'You gambled with your brother's happiness, your greed. You won, Santos, and I hope you're happy.'

Happy? He was the furthest thing from happy. He hadn't felt like this since the day his mother had calmly left, saying goodbye as if she was just going shopping.

'Georgina.'

He tried to form the words, tried to tell her he hadn't gambled with Carlo's happiness—at least not intentionally. He wanted to tell her he'd gambled his own—and hers. Something he hadn't even realised until just a few seconds ago.

'Don't, Santos. I don't want to hear how you're driven by power and the need to control everything.'

'That may have been true once.' The words rushed out and for the first time in his adult life he knew he was losing.

'And it still is.' Her words were softer now, as if she'd given up fighting.

Mutely he watched as she opened the office door and paused in the doorway.

'Goodbye, Santos.'

His reaction was so swift he didn't have time to think. All he wanted to do was stop her from leaving, from walking out of his life for good. A life that wouldn't be the same once she'd gone.

He reached out and took hold of her arm, propelling her back into the room, and kicked the door shut on the enquiring glances of passing staff. She looked up at him, her brown eyes wide, darkening rapidly, her breathing hard and fast. But it was the current of pure electricity between them that told him he was doing the right thing.

He didn't want her to go. It wasn't possession. It wasn't power. It was more than that.

It was love.

He loved her.

This passionate woman had unlocked his heart, healed his wounds and shown him how love could be. He'd just been too stubborn to realise.

Georgina stepped back as he let her go, watching the show of emotions cross his handsome face. His pain and confusion were palpable, and she wanted to reach out to him—but to do so would be her undoing. Again she stepped back, but he moved closer until she had nowhere to go, the wall against her back.

'This is what you do to me.' His voice was hoarse with emotion. 'I can't think around you. I can't sleep without you by my side. I can't let you go.'

Her heart fluttered wildly and she dragged in a ragged breath. 'Santos…?' His name was barely a whisper from her lips.

He placed his palm on the wall above her shoulder, his face coming closer to hers, bringing him irresistibly close. Too close.

'I want you, Georgina,' he said huskily as he lowered his head to kiss her.

She moved sideways, away from temptation, but instantly he placed his other hand above her shoulder. Trapping her.

'I want you with a passion so raw it almost hurts. In fact it does.'

She looked up into his dark eyes, so close now she could see how enlarged his pupils were, see the desire swirling there.

Say it, her mind urged him, but she refused to utter the words aloud. The blood rushed in her ears as her heart thumped and she bit her bottom lip hard. She would never beg anyone to say it. If he loved her he had to tell her.

'I've never known this before, Georgina.'

'What?' she asked in a timid whisper, hardly daring to hear the answer.

'Love.'

Her heart sang as he rubbed the pad of his thumb over her lips, easing the pain where she'd bitten into them hard.

'I've never met a woman like you. From the moment you walked in here my fate was sealed. I just didn't know it then. I couldn't admit it—not even to myself.'

'Can you now?' she said in a cracked whisper.

He took her in his arms, pulled her close against him. 'I love you, Georgina. My heart belongs to you and I never want it back.'

Her knees weakened and his arms tightened around her as he brushed his lips over hers. She pushed against his chest so she could look into his eyes. 'I love you, Santos.'

With that he claimed her lips in a kiss so passionate it took all her breath away, leaving her light-headed.

'Can we start again? Begin our marriage now, with honesty and love?'

As she looked up into the handsome face of the man she loved sunbeams lit up the office, casting a glow all around them. Once again the storm was over—and this time it was for good.

'Only if it means we get another wedding night,' she teased.

He laughed gently. 'Now, *that* I can promise you, *mi esposa.*'

EPILOGUE

THE LEAVES WERE turning all shades of gold and brown as Georgina looked around the country cottage garden. Autumn sun cast its last lazy glow as it slid slowly behind the hill.

'Happy anniversary,' Santos said softly as he came to stand behind her.

He wrapped his arms around her. She leant back against him, happier than she'd ever been.

'You've brought me to the country for our anniversary weekend?' She hadn't doubted he'd remember their first anniversary—she just hadn't expected him to help her realise one of her dreams, even if it was only for a weekend. It would be a wonderful place to give him her gift.

'I've done more than that, Georgie.' He nuzzled her hair and then kissed her head. 'I've bought you this piece of the English countryside. This place is yours.'

Georgina swivelled round in his arms and looked up at him, excitement almost exploding inside her. 'This place? You've bought it?'

'I most certainly have, and now is your chance to show me just what is so wonderful about living in the countryside.'

'Oh, Santos, it's perfect.'

She couldn't believe that this cottage, with roses rambling around the front door, was all hers. He opened the door and led her inside. It had been furnished and decorated to the highest standard, just as she would have expected from Santos, but it still maintained that country charm she'd always longed for.

'In fact it's more than perfect.'

'There's more, *mi esposa*.'

'What more could there be than this?'

'Emma and Carlo will be joining us.'

'They will?'

'It's their anniversary too, and I thought it would be nice to be together, but we still have a few hours before they arrive. Carlo has become a workaholic since he opened his own hotel, and he wouldn't leave until he'd sorted everything out for the weekend.'

Georgina laughed at the image of her brother-in-law putting the business before a weekend with Emma. 'Perhaps there is more of you in him than you realise?' she teased, and reached up to brush a kiss on his lips.

'Well, you should know what we Ramirez men are like by now.'

He kissed her and passion sparked to life, zipping between them.

She pulled back from him and looked into his eyes, which were darkening by the second. 'I have a gift for you too.'

He put her at arm's length and smiled. 'Can you beat this?' he asked as he took her into the living room, which looked cosy and inviting.

'You're going to be a father.'

'Are you serious?' He looked deep into her eyes, studying her reaction.

She nodded, unable say anything. After years of telling herself she'd be the worst mother a child could have, she was still apprehensive.

'When?' His words seemed choked and hard to come by.

'You're impatient, aren't you?' she teased gently.

'Not impatient. Overjoyed. And very much in love with you.' He kissed her softly and with so much love she fought back the tears of happiness that threatened.

'April,' she said as his lips left hers. 'Our baby will be born in April.'

'That,' he said huskily as he smiled down at her, 'is a cause for celebration.'

She laughed and snuggled against him, relishing the strength of his arms around her. 'I love you so much, Santos,' she said as she heard his heartbeat.

He swept her off her feet and, looking down at her, smiled. 'I'm the happiest man alive and it's all thanks to you. How did I ever manage to exist before you arrived in my life?'

He edged his way out of the living room towards the stairs, a stream of Spanish rushing from his lips as he looked at the narrow staircase.

Georgina laughed.

'Put me down.' She placed her hand on his cheek and kissed him briefly. 'This is one flight of stairs you *won't* be able to carry me up.'

* * * * *

Snow, sleigh bells and a hint of seduction

Find your perfect Christmas reads at
millsandboon.co.uk/Christmas

MILLS & BOON®

Why shop at millsandboon.co.uk?

Each year, thousands of romance readers find their perfect read at millsandboon.co.uk. That's because we're passionate about bringing you the very best romantic fiction. Here are some of the advantages of shopping at www.millsandboon.co.uk:

* **Get new books first**—you'll be able to buy your favourite books one month before they hit the shops

* **Get exclusive discounts**—you'll also be able to buy our specially created monthly collections, with up to 50% off the RRP

* **Find your favourite authors**—latest news, interviews and new releases for all your favourite authors and series on our website, plus ideas for what to try next

* **Join in**—once you've bought your favourite books, don't forget to register with us to rate, review and join in the discussions

Visit **www.millsandboon.co.uk**
for all this and more today!

MILLS_WEB